Piece o[...]

'Keeps the pages turning, a desi *Bridg[...]*

'A story of corporate one-upmanship with enough insights into the workings of a multinational firm (with marriage as a side accompaniment). The pace never drops... [Swati] is in control of her protagonist and her environment' – *Business Standard*

'A whiff of fresh air... What holds the attention is [Kaushal's] total lack of pretentious claims, her no-nonsense approach, the take-it-or-leave-it attitude, and the conversational ease with which the narrative simply whizzes by, sweeping the reader along with its irresistible, irrepressible joie de vivre' – *Tribune*

A Girl Like Me

'A touching story of the breathless exuberance of a young teenager's life' – *Deccan Herald*

'Young adults will find a lot that is like their lives in this book- from the single-handed bloody combat with trigonometry to the super-busy, always travelling parents. As for older people, hey it's a chance to understand their eternally mysterious sixteen-year-olds. With a wince and a smile.' – *Outlook*

'A deeply personal and nuanced story. *A Girl Like Me* has a lot in common with A Girl Like You.' – *Hindustan Times*

'Heartbreak and promise meet in this fun slice of teenage life' – *Times of India*

'A gripping and true to life account of a typical teen's life' – *The Hindu*

Drop Dead

'Filled with the drama of a good, gripping thriller' – *The Hindu*

'A master of the popular fiction category... Kaushal's writing is crisp and refreshing' – *Verve*

'The perfect holiday read' – *Mail Today*

ALSO BY THE SAME AUTHOR

Piece of Cake
A Girl Like Me
Drop Dead

Lethal Spice

SWATI KAUSHAL

hachette
INDIA

First published in 2014 by Hachette India
(Registered name: Hachette Book Publishing India Pvt. Ltd)
An Hachette UK company
www.hachetteindia.com

1

ISBN 978-93-5009-769-4

Hachette Book Publishing India Pvt. Ltd
4th/5th Floors, Corporate Centre,
Sector 44, Gurgaon 122003, India

Typeset in Minion Pro 10/13.2
by InoSoft Systems Noida

Printed and bound in India by
Manipal Technologies Ltd, Manipal

For Sanah, Anika and Diya…
Three lovely young ladies who make the world
a *much* better place.

part 1

All the world's a stage,
And all the men and women merely players…

William Shakespeare, *As You Like It*

1

SUNDAY, 14 OCTOBER 2012
ST. MARY'S CONVENT SCHOOL, SHIMLA

The assailant was six feet tall. He had an ugly scar on his square jaw and a thick moustache above thinned, leering lips. His eyes were narrowed, his attitude threatening, as he grabbed the young girl's wrist.

'Back off!'

'What was that?'

'*Baackk off!*'

He gripped her wrist tighter. She turned, helpless, to the slender woman who stood a few paces away.

'Allow me,' the woman said, stepping forward.

'BAACKK OFFFFFFFFF!'

The barked words boomed out, ricocheting off the walls and seats and ceiling. They drew gasps and stepped up heart rates all the way to the back of the auditorium. In the front row, the school principal, teachers and class monitors recoiled from the power and menace that was the Superintendent of Police, Shimla, as she stood there, body clenched, eyes narrowed, hand raised club-like in her would-be assailant's face.

The assailant let go of the girl's wrist and took several steps back.

'That's how you do it,' SP Niki Marwah said, turning to her audience. '*Loud* and *aggressive*. You want to draw the attention of others to your situation, so they can come to your aid and send your attacker the clear message that you are not an easy target.'

Her gaze swept over the young, impressionable faces ranging in age from eleven to eighteen; it lingered on those that seemed the most timid and vulnerable. She looked directly into the eyes of a short, skinny girl who sat, wide-eyed, in the second row.

'Remember,' she said, 'confidence is key – no matter how small you are or how big your attacker may be. If you repel him with confidence and fury, it will tell him that he's picked the wrong person to mess with. Chances are, he *will* back off.'

She looked gravely around the auditorium, her gaze alighting on another young girl who appeared to be hanging on to her every word.

'Almost every single assault starts with a seemingly vulnerable victim,' Niki said. 'Do not allow yourself to be weak. Never be a victim.'

She walked the length of the small stage, left to right and back again, her gaze engaging, nudging, exhorting. Be bold. Be confident. Be unafraid, she seemed to whisper in their ears.

'So let's try it once more,' she said. 'Loud, aggressive, as if your words are bullets that you're shooting into your attacker's face. One, two, three…'

'BAAACKK OFFFFF!' the whole auditorium thundered and this time the explosion of sound was loud enough to freeze an entire army of assailants in its tracks.

'That's more like it.'

The SP turned to the 'assailant' who was now standing back, listening to her words with an attentive and respectful air.

'Inspector Manoj Bhargava here is a black belt in karate and a trainer with the Punjab Police Academy. He will take you through some basic self-defence techniques that I want all of you to master before you leave this auditorium. Not because Shimla is not safe, but because it is important for everyone – male or female, strong or frail – to be able to look out for themselves, to feel secure and confident wherever they go.'

Her gaze swept over the rapt faces that filled the auditorium. 'So one last time, before I hand over to Inspector Bhargava, repeat after me: "I will never be a victim!"'

'I WILL NEVER BE A VICTIM!' the audience roared.

Niki smiled, handed the mike to Inspector Bhargava and walked briskly off the stage.

2

Five kilometres across the valley, backstage at the Gaiety Theatre, that famous Shimla landmark on the Ridge, slender, light-eyed, stunningly beautiful Pallavi Aanand also reminded herself to not be a victim. She was smart. She was talented. She was the granddaughter of the late and legendary Shri J.S. Aanand of the multi-crore Aanand Group of Resorts and Hotels. The world was hers for the taking.

And now here she was, one of the top six contestants on *Hot Chef*, India's hippest new reality show on television, about to begin its first ever shoot with a live audience, to be telecast prime time to an estimated ten million viewers.

Pallavi, born with a silver spoon in her mouth, educated at the finest schools the world had to offer, gifted with both beauty and brains, knew it was a contest she just had to win. She was destined to win. *Hot Chef*, and all it had to offer, was hers.

Which was why it rankled that now, in this, the most important contest, at this crucial stage, Leena Dixit would be going on first. Because Leena, not she, had won the previous round. Because Leena's father, a decrepit old geezer in a wheelchair, had put in an appearance in the previous episode and swayed the audience vote with nauseating stories of what a virtuous cow his daughter was.

'She gave up her seat in engineering college to look after me,' he'd blubbered into the camera. 'She's been holding two jobs to support the family and pay the school fees for her brother and her sister. She calls me every night to remind me to take my medicines...'

Some girls had all the luck, Pallavi thought, disgusted. If she tried calling *her* father every night it would be to find a different female companion answering the phone, every time.

Pallavi straightened her shoulders and shook off the momentary stab of self-pity. No, she was not going down *that* bitter road again. She'd left it behind; and if there was anything she had even less time for than other people's sob stories it was her own.

Little Leena from middle-class nowhere could go on first and enjoy

her two seconds in the limelight. It would be for the very last time – if
Pallavi had anything to do with it.

If looks could kill, Leena thought, as she caught the flash of hatred
in Pallavi's eyes, we'd all be long dead. She, Vicky, Shaq – even KK
and Mala and Rajat. Pallavi would have annihilated everything and
everyone that stood in her way – contestants, judges, directors,
producers – till she alone was left standing, crowned queen of the
entire universe. Or, at the very least, of *Hot Chef*.

But it took more than foreign degrees and deep pockets to win,
Leena knew. It took hunger and pain, the pain of wanting something
so desperately that it gnawed big, frantic chunks off you, as though a
wild beast were trapped inside, flailing and fighting to get out. And
Leena Dixit, star-crossed daughter of a disabled state government
employee, knew exactly what that pain felt like.

For Pallavi, winning *Hot Chef* would probably mean another
feather in her cap; a box ticked, a point proved, some play money to
throw away on her next shopping trip overseas. But for Leena it would
be nothing short of salvation. She felt the sudden flutter of butterflies
in her stomach as Rajat Tripathi, the show's charismatic host, took
his position centre stage and Jimmy Zariwala, the lanky, ponytailed,
openly gay creative director, mimed the countdown of the final few
seconds.

Focus, Leena told herself. *Cook. Cook your heart out. It's what you
love. What you live, breathe, want.*

After all, food was what Hot Chef was supposed to be about, what
she was all about. It was her thing, her special gift. It was what she'd
been doing to perfection for the past eight weeks as she served up
ker sangri in Jaisalmer and karimeen in Cochin, scooped aloo subzi
into hollowed-out kachoris in Chandni Chowk, and served up patthar
gosht at the Charminar and sarson da saag in Amritsar. It was what
had carried her through thus far – talent and passion, and that special
kind of killer instinct she'd been surprised to find lurking deep within
her, which was being sharpened and honed as, week by week, the
weakest links fell away. Sweet-natured Ramanna, with the crushing

bank loan and the unmarried sister, had been the first to go; Puneeta, with the nervous stammer and the butterfingers, next; Vidya, who could chop an onion in five seconds but couldn't tell her baking soda from her confectioner's sugar, in Week Five. And now they were in mid-season, with just six contestants left, and *she* was amongst them.

Tonight was the much-hyped 'Tokyo to Timbuktu' night and each contestant was about to give the performance of a lifetime. Leena told herself, as she did every week, that while one more contestant would be eliminated before the night was over, it would not be her. She fingered the small Ganpati pendant she wore around her neck and thanked him once again for watching over her, for guiding her hand when she'd picked her cuisine last week.

She'd been called to do so in random order after Vicky had chosen Mexican; Shaq, Japanese; and Pallavi, Lebanese. The twin minefields of French and German cuisine, named on strips of paper, had still been lying curled up in the customized *Hot Chef* fortune cookies along with the other non-starters, Irish and Russian and, god forbid, English. But she'd managed to evade them all; when she'd opened up her cookie and read the short word printed in purple, she'd almost fainted with relief.

Thai.

Where ginger and lemongrass and red chillies ruled. She could live with that. Better still, she could create magic with that.

She watched now as Jimmy, bustling in the wings in his tight black tee-shirt and harlequin pants, mimed the final countdown. Three... two...one...

The stately curtains with their rippling fabric started to ease apart and a long, subdued roar of applause filled the historic hall.

'Ladies and gentlemen, our first contestant. From Thane, Maharashtra, the immensely charming, amazingly talented heartthrob of millions – Miss Leena Dixit!' Rajat announced in his Bachchan baritone, his Kapoor grin in place.

Instantly, shrieks and catcalls and chants of 'Lee-na! Lee-na!' filled the air.

Leena felt a shock of adrenaline shoot through her. This crowd was cheering for her. This frenzy, this fever, those handmade signs that read, 'Leena, oh Leena, dil tu ne chheena!' were for her. For unknown Leena Dixit, who, till just a few weeks ago, had spent her mornings in a back kitchen packing tiffins for Thane office-goers and her nights in a call centre selling insurance plans to customers in Canada. For Leena, who knew all about insulin and bedpans and catheters and living wills but very little about lights, cameras and action. For Leena, whose moment had finally come and who was going to seize it with both hands.

She stepped out into the deafening applause, her hands folded in traditional Thai greeting, a determined smile on her round, chubby face. She knew in that moment that whatever else happened she was not going to let them down.

3

A few doors down from the Gaiety, up on the third floor of the historic Municipal Corporation Building, Niki sat alone in her office, wrapping up yet another marathon Sunday. Another Sunday that had fallen victim to the eternal backlog of files that sprouted like weeds no matter how often or how hard she hacked away at them. Another sunlit Sunday, when she could have gone trekking or biking or climbing instead…

Her gaze went, as it often did, to the tiny picture that sat on her desk. It had been taken just a couple of months ago in the snows at Rohtang Pass; it showed her and Ram, cheek to cheek. They had hats on their heads, scarves round their necks, devil-may-care masti in their smiles. What a trek it had been, Niki remembered, what a week, what an unforgettable experience! It had made her want to sprout wings and fly, to grow roots and stay forever in the high mountains. Instead, she had done neither. The week had come to an end in the tragic manner of all magical things. Ram had set out for a year-long Master's in Italian cuisine that would keep him in Florence until May, and she had come back to Shimla and a mountain of paper that made the peaks at Rohtang Pass look like mere road bumps.

The price one paid for a week of romance, she sighed, as she signed off on the last set of files that Pradeep, her PA, had left her with. It had been three months since she'd seen Mom or Dad or Dadi, even though they lived barely three hours away; weeks since she'd caught up with her best friend, Kam; and several days since she'd *spoken* with Ram. She glanced at the clock on her wall. It was almost six. Which meant it was around 2.30 p.m. in Florence. Which meant Ram would be at the tiny *ristorante* where he interned on weekends, serving up bowlfuls of steaming pasta to hungry hordes of inebriated tourists. Not a good time to call…

Long-distance relationships, Niki sighed, as she sat back to gaze a moment out her window at the darkening expanse of the Ridge, where the tourists were bustling in all their sweater-clad, camera-clicking, mid-October glory. Love and leisure and the cool breeze on one's cheeks – they were all casualties of her high-pressure job, falling by the wayside, along with other long-lost pursuits such as eating, sleeping and hanging out with friends.

Somehow, over the course of the past two years, her work had ballooned and blotted out everything else. It was all-consuming, isolating, exhausting. And, yet, she knew she would not trade it for anything in the world.

She was the Superintendent of Police, Shimla, she thought with a wry smile, as her eyes swept over the glittering, darkening, tree-covered valley outside. It was her jurisdiction, as far as the eye could see; her responsibility. She was its master and its servant; she was made way for, respected, wherever she went. But respect was a two-way street; and in order to maintain that respect, she had to make sure she did her job and did it well.

So did she, she wondered, as her gaze skimmed over the stack of files and folders in her out-tray, did she do it well?

There was much that she had accomplished in the two years she'd been in this post, much to be proud of. Crime had dropped to its lowest level in decades, the new traffic beat system they'd put in place had led to significant unclogging of bottlenecks along the busiest highways, and the new online public information and complaint system was hitting record resolution rates. The Special Women's Hotline that she had fought so long and hard for was now fully functional and staffed round the clock and she had managed to push through her request for an increase in the number of women constables to be recruited next year. And yet, there was so much more to be addressed and overcome. The perennial water shortage, the rising pollution levels, the inadequate roads that became dangerous and impassable in bad weather, the frequent traffic diversions on account of VIP visits, the scourge of unauthorized construction that flourished under protection from those in high office. – none of these problems were completely or even at all under her control; and yet, she felt an overwhelming responsibility to continue to try and solve them, to do more, so much more.

'Boss?'

Startled out of her reverie, Niki turned to see ASP Shankar Sahay, cool and casual in faded jeans and striped shirt, poke his head in her office door.

'You alive?' he asked, quirking an eyebrow.

'Is that a philosophical question?' she countered.

'No, just an existential one,' Shankar grinned, sauntering into her room. Measuring in at just over five feet five inches, clocking in at twenty-five years of existence, smart, savvy and terminally cool, ASP Shankar Sahay considered himself to be a tour de force of evolution, God's precious gift to humanity. A Bandra boy brought up on ocean views, foreign cars and gourmet wholegrain sandwiches, he had, nonetheless, managed to acquire a working man's appreciation for mountain air, Made-in-India Jeeps and Joginder's elaichi chai. Sharp, tough and secretly devoted to his boss, he had matured under her tutelage from a cocky young trainee to a fine young officer and was one of the 'accomplishments' Niki was proudest of, though she was damned if she'd ever admit it.

'What are you doing here anyway?' he asked now, giving the paperweight that sat on her desk a twirl that made the orange and gold flecks inside it spin round and round.

'It's *my* office,' Niki said.

'It's also Sunday.'

'Which begs the question: what are *you* doing here?'

'I'm taking a friend's friend out to dinner tonight,' he grinned. 'She's a personal trainer. Certified Hot.'

'So let me ask again,' Niki said, with the ghost of a smile, 'what are you doing *here*?'

'I just stopped by for some aftershave.'

'You keep aftershave in your office?'

'No, do you?'

Niki rolled her eyes. 'Go!' she said.

But Sahay lingered, eyeing the papers on her desk. 'Is that the Women Constables Training Centre proposal, Boss?'

'The Chief wants me to put the final touches on the presentation and email it to him for his meeting tomorrow.'

'But that's almost fifty pages! You'll be here all night!'

'Not *all* night, hopefully.'

Sahay sighed and pulled out his mobile. 'Sunaina?' he said. 'About tonight, something's come up at work… Yeah, *I* know it's a Sunday, but my *boss* doesn't. What can you do?' He held up a hand as Niki started to protest. 'How about I give you a call tomorrow evening? Will you be in town? You will? Excellent… I'll call you.'

'I didn't ask you to postpone your dinner,' Niki said as he put the phone back in his pocket.

'I know, but the PowerPoint presentation was crying out for mercy.'

'I am very good at PowerPoint,' Niki bristled. 'I am going to *kill* this presentation.'

'That's what I'm trying to prevent,' was the cool response.

4

Pallavi Aanand's smile didn't falter as she watched Leena walk onto the main stage at the Gaiety, but her mind was racing. She may have been born in London and raised in Singapore, she may have studied in New York and Paris, but she knew good old Indian competition when she smelled it. And for once, there was a strong whiff of it coming off Leena Dixit.

That Leena could cook was something Pallavi knew and disregarded, as one does the thousands of small-time cooks at the thousands of nameless restaurants across the country. More important for Pallavi tonight, Leena *looked* like competition. The new side-swept bangs elongated her baby face and framed those large, cocker spaniel eyes to advantage; the high-heeled shoes showed off surprisingly slim ankles; and the purple orchid outfit was actually flattering on her short frame, drawing attention to those plus-size curves in all the right places. Leena, Pallavi hated to admit, looked *hot* tonight.

Well, Pallavi thought, two could play that game. She tugged at the silver waistband of her belly dancer's skirt, pulling it lower down her slim hips, and adjusted the coins dangling off her halter-neck blouse to show more Wonderbra-induced cleavage. Then, as she heard Rajat call out her name and the rhythm of the dumbek and the oud filled the hall, she gyrated out onto the stage with the grace of a gymnast and the oomph of a stripper. The audience, as expected, went wild.

Vicky, the next contestant up, joined enthusiastically in the applause backstage, then adjusted his sombrero, hiked up his Mexican guitar and waited for his name to be called. Pallavi in her Chikni Chameli avatar would be a hard act to follow, he knew, and anyone else in his shoes would have despaired. But not Vicky. Boarding-school reprobate and medical-college dropout, self-taught guitarist and amateur chef, Vicky Gulati was the kind of guy who blazed his own trail, who could make broccoli sexy and beetroots rock. Permanently dishevelled and sweetly unkempt, with more devilish charm than was fair for any one person to possess, he was the kind of guy who could turn every rule on its head and still come out tops. If anyone could pull off a ham Mexican Mariachi costume and a ridiculous moustache and still charm the pants off every single member of the audience, it was Vicky. And the food he turned out would be daring and delicious. And he would coast right through to the next round. Because Vicky Gulati was a born star.

Shaqeel Khan, or 'Shaq' as he'd been dubbed on the show, smiled momentarily as he caught Vicky's eye. Pallavi, Leena, Vicky – they were all in their elements tonight. But Shaq was not the kind of guy to let that bother him. In fact, there was very little that fazed Shaq. He was a survivor; he'd worked his way up in the world, from waiting tables in Lucknow's dhabas to running the kitchens at the Gurgaon Taj. Big-city charm, public-school English, German precision knives, French classic sauces – by sheer force of will and against every expectation, Shaq had mastered them all. It was a hard-won victory, one that came with money and prestige, a brand new Honda City and a fourteenth-floor flat in a posh new colony. Yet, inexplicably and just six months into the job, Shaq had thrown it all away for the madness that was *Hot Chef.*

He stretched his long arms out in front of him now and noted with satisfaction that his hands were steady. He lowered them to his sides again. Looking at him, as he stood cool and relaxed, his chef's hat in place, the cuffs of his white shirt rolled back to reveal tanned, muscled arms, it was impossible to guess how much he had riding on this challenge.

Of all the cuisines in the challenge, he had picked the most difficult one: Japanese food, the bomb of bombs. Hiroshima and Nagasaki all rolled into one, as Leena had put it, not entirely unsympathetically. Sushi, sashimi, seaweed, miso soup... Wasabi or no wasabi, it was not the kind of cuisine an Indian audience had any kind of palate for. And so Shaq, who had the demeanour of a sage and the instincts of a gambler, had decided to go double or nothing and cook the food Teppanyaki style, over a live, dramatic flame to the accompaniment of a painstakingly rehearsed but highly risky juggling of knives.

He'd almost lost his left ear during the last rehearsal, the eight-inch Chinese cleaver missing him by millimetres, and he'd nicked his palm at the taping of the promos. But the two-second image in the montage, of Shaq with a blur of knives high in the air shot against a black backdrop and to the frenzied beat of Japanese taiko drums, had seared the screen and made it all worthwhile. Now, with the inevitable just moments away, Shaq felt a comforting calm. Success or failure, whatever the result, one thing he knew: it would be spectacular. If he pulled it off, it would guarantee his move to the next round.

And if he didn't?

Shaq was prepared for that eventuality, too...

A few feet behind him, Sharon Sen stood in her cleavage-spewing, hip-hugging dress, its layers of ruffles caressing tantalizing flashes of leg, busily inspecting rosebuds. She had picked Spanish cuisine – *madre mia!* – and she was going to dance the flamenco. *Olé!* And what was a flamenco dancer without the stem of a perfect rosebud between her teeth?

Saucy, sexy, avant-garde painter, Sharon was in her element tonight. This was the drama round, after all, and there was not one contestant who could hold a candle to the drama that was the dare-all, bare-all, controversial Ms Sen. From the very first episode, where she'd sashayed into the camera frame in her itsy-bitsy bikini and downed a frothy piña colada before tossing a live lobster into a steaming pot, she'd held her audience spellbound. Nobody ever knew what 'Ms In-Sane', as she'd been dubbed by the media, would do next; but they did know it would be *espectacular*. From trickling ice cubes down her neckline (I'm so hot, darlings!) to going green (lips, teeth and tongue included – for the planet, precious!) to sucking suggestively on Manu Patel's finger (the middle one they'd realized later, and edited it out), Sharon Sen had done it all. And, as Shaq would matter-of-factly say to the others, if only she could actually *cook,* the rest of them would be burnt biryani by now.

Dev Nair, the beefy, Brandoesque sixth and final contestant wondered, as he watched Sharon tuck a second rosebud between her magnificent breasts, whether she'd bite the celebrity judge this time around. After last week's episode, in which she'd made up for her bland saag by accidentally 'falling' into the judge's lap, he wouldn't put anything past her. Not that at this point he ought to care. He was doomed; he'd picked French cuisine, and the only French thing he knew about was the French kiss. Perhaps, if one asked Sarika, who'd dumped him just a few months ago, not even that.

He thought now of her parting words as she told him she was leaving him for her co-star in the new hit soap, *Boss Bhi, Bahu Bhi.* 'Face it, Dev,' she'd said, her mascara-caked eyes channelling fake pity as she walked out the door to that bastard Monish's Toyota waiting outside, 'you may be cute, but you just don't have what it takes.'

Well, screw Sarika and screw Monish and screw everyone else who'd ever told him he didn't have what it took! Screw his teachers, his school principal and those smug classmates who'd gone on to graduate top of their class. Screw his dad and his uncle and his brother who'd spend their entire lives selling chunky gold sets to obese matrons from that tiny mousetrap of a jewellery store his grandfather had opened more than fifty years ago. And screw all those judges at all those auditions who'd rejected him over and over and over again. From *KBC* to *Sach Ka Saamna*, from *Voice of India* to *Dance India Dance*, from *Roadies* to *Splitsvilla* – he'd auditioned for them all, and been rejected by them all. Over and over again, till he'd attained a certain notoriety on the reality-show circuit, become an inside joke. And still he'd kept trying. He'd danced and sung and done stand-up comic acts; he'd put on the attitude and poured on the charm and built up his body; he'd spent nights standing in audition lines and days delivering pizza. And through it all he'd clung to his dream.

Finally, after fifty-eight rejections, it had happened, like he'd known it would. He had got selected. For a cooking show. Even though he could barely boil an egg.

He *did* have what it took, he would have liked to tell Sarika now. And all it took, when all was said and done, was plain old determination. And a little bit of luck.

His gaze travelled across the stage to the front row, centre, in the auditorium, where the judges sat. They were rich and famous, all three of them; they graced magazine covers and TV ads and product launches. They were luck's random honourees too – KK, celebrity chef, who'd started out with a nondescript dhaba thirty years ago; Mala, the housewife-turned-surprise-winner of the show's previous season, and Ashika De, the upcoming Bollywood star. They might be good at what they did, but so were thousands of others. And the fact that they were sitting in the front row at the Gaiety tonight, with the whole world watching, their money multiplying quietly in their bank accounts, was because Lady Luck had chosen to shine on *their* heads. Now *they* would be the ones deciding with whom to share that light.

For a moment, Dev felt overcome by a surge of pure hatred. That someone should have such power over him. That any human being should have such power over any other…

Then he heard Rajat call out his name and he stepped out onto the stage, flashing his roguish Brando smile again.

5

Keep calm.

Mala Joseph, seated in the centre of the packed auditorium's front row, waiflike and ethereal under the keen gaze of an array of stage lights and multiple HD cameras, smiled brilliantly and joined in the applause as the curtains closed on Dev Nair's unimpressive French mime act, feeling much like a mime herself.

Buck up. You can do it, she told herself firmly as the contestants regrouped and took their positions on the stage for the next round and the cameras and lights dimmed for a few forgiving moments. *Breathe in, breathe out. Smile.*

All too quickly, the curtains swept open again to reveal the rearranged stage, now with the six contestants standing at attention at their respective workstations, each under their own spotlight, each throbbing with a tumult of barely contained emotions. The audience thundered with renewed applause, the orchestra started up again and the auditorium grew thick with anticipation.

It was going to be harder than she'd thought, Mala realized with a sinking feeling. The surroundings were too charged, the lights too bright, the music too strident. And she was tired. So very tired. She sat back in her velvet-upholstered front-row seat and allowed her mind to wander as the music ended with a final, ear-splitting drum roll and Rajat took over. His deep, resonant voice felt like a beloved friend, an old caress, as he addressed the contestants and went over the rules of the cooking round. 'You will each have thirty minutes to prepare one signature dish that best represents the cuisine you have chosen. The ingredients you will use have been placed in a tray to your right...'

Last year, she had been up there on stage, Mala mused. Amped up, fingers flying, heart thumping at three times its normal rate. Cooking as if her life depended on it. And it had. Because last year, *she* had been a contestant and each week had been terrifying, thrilling, a constant explosion of adrenaline. She'd found herself in the midst of genius and, with each challenge, she'd discovered something sexy and powerful and exciting within her. *Hot Chef* had electrified her, made her come alive. It had given her wings and fuel and the secret of flight. And she'd been flying ever since. Higher and higher...

But she had made the mistake of flying too high, too close to the sun. And now she was charred, her wings scorched; what surrounded her was not the heady scent of success, but the bitter stench of fear. Fear and, what was even more unbearable, a deep, all-encompassing, enduring *sadness*.

She glanced down at the pink silk dress she was wearing for the filming today, its scooped neck showing off a hint of cleavage and accentuating the glow of her sandalwood skin. Her frizzy curls had been schooled into soft locks that fell in lustrous waves around her shoulders and her slim ankles were perched on high-heeled designer sandals. How glamorous she looked; what a far cry from the homely housewife she used to be, with fresh flowers in her wet hair, its damp tendrils clinging to her forehead as she turned out appams and stew in her tiny kitchen, the radio playing Carnatic music as she worked! *Hot Chef* had picked her out from a sea of anonymity and planted her in front of the world. Gone were the days of riding pillion on Joseph's trusty Hero Honda, of heading to the cinema with stars in her eyes. These days, she flew business class. She was the cinema; she was the star; she was every man and woman's dream come true. And she was miserable and wondering how much longer she could live this lie.

Well, she thought. It wouldn't have to be that much longer now. She fingered the clasp of the small clutch purse she held in her lap. She knew what she had to do and she was going to do it. No matter how difficult the task, there would be no more procrastination.

She looked up, roused from her musings by the suddenly quieted auditorium. Someone had cut the music; a hush had descended on the packed theatre. Up on stage, Rajat was counting down the last five seconds of the cooking segment – four, three, two, one… '*Knives downnn!*'

Already, Mala wondered, as she sat up with a start.

The contestants were standing back, the cameras were closing in on the plates in front of them and all around her, people were on their feet, cheering and applauding. Mala rose to her feet with a bright, hasty smile and exuberantly joined in.

'Tasting in ten,' she heard Jimmy hiss into her earpiece as the curtains slid closed and the lights dimmed yet again.

Mala sank down in her chair, depleted. Just ten more minutes. Ten minutes in which the stage technicians would dismantle the stalls and rearrange the props and the make-up artists would touch up eyes, cheeks, lips, hair. Ten minutes for the contestants to refresh themselves and reassemble on the bench, now being moved to the left, and for the judges to claim their rightful positions at the linen-covered table in the middle of the stage. Then the curtains would part again and the lights would shine and Mala would smile that sweet Mona Lisa smile that had endeared her to the entire nation.

Tasting was the segment of the show where she earned her hefty contract; where the cameras would capture, in close-up, every loving detail, as she put delicate forkfuls of food into her tiny mouth and came up with insightful pronouncements on the falafels and the empanadas and Thai chicken curry. Mala closed her eyes and went over in her mind the phrases she'd prepared in advance. 'You look so beautiful in that dress!' That one always came in handy and Leena did look beautiful tonight. 'What a spectacular performance!' for Shaq, who had truly outdone himself with those knives; and 'Mmm… that smells goo-ood!' which almost always came in useful, though she could smell something that had been burnt badly tonight.

She felt a stab of pity for whichever one of them had done it. They were a roguish bunch, this year's contestants, but she knew, first-hand, that it was not easy to be in their shoes. To have so much hanging by a thread. To want, so badly, to win. She knew, too, what it was like to be judged. Not just by the audiences and the public, but by the trinity of judges who had the power to sway opinions, who held the contestants' futures in their hands. And to have as one of those judges the talented, terrifying Kemaal Kapoor, who was both super-chef and super-businessman, mentor and judge; who had single-handedly created not only the super-hit *Hot Chef* franchise, but also the juggernaut that was Kemaal's Kebabs, famous for serving no less than the most incredible kebabs in the world.

That KK was a living legend, there was no doubt. Just as there was no doubt that even though he was kinder and more generous than anyone she knew, he could also be wily and ruthless...

Well, Mala thought, glancing briefly his way as they took their positions up on stage in the darkness. One last time. One last night on the job, standing shoulder to shoulder underneath the spotlights. And then it would all be over.

She looked around her for a moment, at the cast and the crew in the wings, at Rajat, dear, sweet Rajat, as he took his place behind the mike, at the packed auditorium that ballooned out around her. She felt a heavy, crushing sadness descend upon her. She closed her eyes, her fingers tightened around the purse she held; she forced herself to think of Joseph, his eager face, his smooth jaw, the loving light in his eyes. More than ever, she wished she could see him now, hold him in her arms, smooth back his thick, unruly hair.

'Judges, take your seats,' she heard Jimmy's voice hiss in her earpiece.

She lowered herself into the chair on the stage, placed her purse in her lap and took a sip of water from the sealed bottle on the table after unscrewing its cap. She fingered the clasp of her purse and waited as Rajat primed the audience for the tasting round. No, she told herself firmly, no more second thoughts. No more indecision. Time to go for it – and to let go...

6

Up in her third-floor office, SP Marwah put the final touches to the Women Constables Training Centre proposal, saved it and turned her laptop over for ASP Sahay to add the expert flourishes that were his speciality. She watched him play with fonts and graphics for several minutes, transforming plain bullet points into works of art and headers and footers into animated weapons. The guy was a wizard with software, she had to admit, as he inserted yet another incredibly effective mnemonic in the final slides and rearranged a complex web of content into a simple, powerful three-step graph. She clapped him on the back as he finished up with the last slide and saved the changes. Then she walked to her window, wearily massaging her tired shoulders. What she saw outside froze the blood in her veins.

On the narrow street, three floors below, a mass of people was gathering like a swarm of bees, their arms flailing, their feet flying, their mouths wide open.

She threw open the window.

She heard someone scream.

'Gas attack! Help! There's a gas attack!'

'People are dying!'

'Help!'

Niki shut the window and spun around on her heel. 'Call the Fire Department, First Armed, Anti-Terror, Shimla Medical, Deepika,' she said, pushing her phone towards a startled Sahay. 'Tell them it's a Code Red.'

In one fluid motion, she grabbed her leather jacket off her chair and her pistol from her drawer. She sprinted out the door and down the hallway, hurtling down the steps and nearly colliding with the armed security guard who was running up towards her.

'What the hell...?'

'Ma'am, there's a stampede outside!'

Across the sprawling ground-floor hallway and outside the bolted doors, the crowd was growing thicker and darker like a cloud of smoke.

The doors and walls resounded and vibrated with their thundering footfalls.

'Open the doors!' Niki yelled.

'But ma'am – '

Niki raced down the final few steps, threw herself across the hallway and yanked open the doors.

An enormous mass of humanity swept in with the force of a tsunami. Niki had just enough time to dive to the floor on one side, as men, women and children all tumbled in, weeping, shrieking, hysterical. She snatched a little girl out of the crowd's path as she fell to the floor, shielding the child with her body. As she crouched over the girl, the crowd came tumbling in pushing, shoving, clawing, staggering, falling, dragging...

The guard, coming belatedly to his senses, fell to the ground beside the SP, shielding her from the pounding feet with his rifle.

'You're safe, you're safe!' Niki shouted, as the people continued to hurtle past her. 'Watch out, watch your step, *careful*!'

And then, after what felt like an eternity, it stopped. Niki jumped to her feet, ran to the door and slammed it shut. She drew a painful breath of air into her starving lungs and turned to face the terrified crowd.

'You are safe. I am the Superintendent of Police, Shimla, and I repeat – *you are safe.*'

Many in the crowd broke down and started sobbing uncontrollably.

'Can anyone tell me what is going on?' Niki asked.

A young man at the front of the group spoke up. 'There's been a poison-gas attack at the Gaiety, ma'am! The judges have collapsed... They made an announcement for everyone to evacuate the building.'

'Okay,' Niki said. 'Now I want you to know that we have alerted all emergency services. Police personnel, fire engines, ambulances, medical staff are on their way. Is there anyone here in need of immediate medical attention?'

The crowd murmured and glanced around.

'Anyone missing any family members?'

Again, people looked around nervously. No one spoke up.

'Anyone feeling ill?'

Many voices piped up. Niki held up both hands. 'Anyone who feels he or she needs to lie down, stay here. Constable Khetrapal,' she motioned to the guard, 'will help you with first aid and any other assistance you need. Everyone else...' She paused as the alarm of an approaching fire truck became audible in the distance and grew louder. 'Please head to the back of the building. The ambulances should be here shortly. Please remember, there is no need to panic. You are safe here.'

She nodded reassuringly to the crowd and, stopping only to grab a walkie-talkie and the ancient face mask that Khetrapal had hastily located in the first-aid kiosk, slipped out the door and into the dark, chilly night.

Outside, everything was eerily quiet. The bulb in the street lamp to her left flickered with a buzzing sound. A bird shrieked shrilly in the distance. From the west, as Niki ran out into the street, the sounds of the sirens grew louder, closer; and a fire truck pulled up towards her, followed closely by a large, dark truck. Niki clicked on her walkie-talkie and ran past the fire truck towards the other truck. She waved her arms, motioning for it to stop.

A stocky man, masked and in full combat gear, alighted from the truck, armed and alert. From his uniform, she recognized him to be an officer of the First Armed Police Battalion.

'I'm SP Niki Marwah,' she said, identifying herself.

'Deputy SP Dutt, ma'am,' the officer said, lowering his rifle and snapping to attention. 'I have ten men in full combat gear, another twelve on their way. We have a Code Red?'

'At the Gaiety. I want you to clear and cordon off the Ridge and the Mall – Scandal Point to Ladies Park. No one comes in besides the emergency vehicles.'

'Ma'am.'

'Have your men surround the Gaiety Theatre and await further instructions. Stay on high alert.'

Niki turned as another truck rolled in. In the passenger seat, she recognized Inspector Nagpal of the Anti-Terrorism Cell.

'SP Marwah,' he said, jumping out as the truck braked to a stop.

'Inspector Nagpal. We have a poison-gas attack and reported casualties at the Gaiety. Your team is ready?'

'I have arms, ammunition and air-testing equipment in the truck, ma'am.'

'Good. Make sure everyone has protective gear and then head inside. Exercise extreme caution. I want to know what you find as soon as you get in.'

Nagpal turned to execute the SP's orders, while Niki ran towards the first of the ambulances that was just coming up from the Mall Road.

'This area has not been cleared yet,' she said as soon as the driver, who had halted at her command, started rolling down his window. 'Stay inside and await further instructions.'

She turned to listen as the walkie-talkie in her hand crackled.

It was her assistant, Inspector Deepika Chauhan, telling her that they had two units poised and ready at Scandal Point and a third at Lakkar Bazaar.

'What's the situation like?' Niki asked.

'Under control, ma'am,' Inspector Chauhan said. 'We've started evacuating the surrounding areas. We're escorting people to safety at the fire station.'

'Any injuries or casualties?'

'None so far.'

'Okay. Find out if anyone was there at the Gaiety at the time of the attack. Take down their statements. Await further instructions.'

'Boss!'

SP Marwah turned as ASP Shankar Sahay came running out into the night, a muffler wrapped haphazardly round his face, covering all but his eyes.

'Where's your mask?' Niki thundered.

He took the mask she held out and hurriedly pulled it on.

'Did you call everyone?' Niki said.

'I did, boss.'

'And the Chief?'

'His PA is trying to reach him now. What's going on, Boss?'

'A Code Red.'

Sahay swallowed. They had never had a Code Red before in Shimla as far as he knew; they had probably never had one in the entire history of the Himachal Police. *And now poison gas. At the Gaiety, on a Sunday evening, with the Chief away in Delhi.* He tore his mind away from the impossibility of it and tried to recall all that he had been taught at the academy about Code Reds and poison gases.

'What do you want me to do?'

'Stay here, keep calm,' Niki said. 'The Anti-Terror team and the First Armed Battalion are entering the Gaiety now. Everyone else is on standby.'

'So we just stand here and wait?'

'Until they clear the area,' Niki nodded. 'We need to know what we're up against,' she said grimly. 'There's no knowing what we'll find – how many people are inside, how many alive, how many armed or dangerous...'

ASP Sahay looked around at the shadowy figures that were creeping up slowly towards the Gaiety; still others ranged around the Ridge, alert, waiting, weapons cocked. It was a chilling sight. He knew he would never forget it, regardless of the outcome. He could only pray for the best. And prepare for the worst.

DGP Kapoor, Head of Himachal Pradesh Police, in Delhi for a battery of policy meetings at the Home Ministry, was relaxing at the end of a busy weekend at the home of his school friend, the Commerce Secretary, his mobile phone, for once, switched off. Over chilled beer, masala peanuts and homemade pakoras, an intense discussion about the fluctuating tensions at the Wagah border and the economic implications of further easing travel restrictions was in progress, when Bharti, his friend's wife, came hurrying out, phone in hand, a worried frown across her forehead.

'It's your PA, Bhai Sahab,' she told the Chief. 'She's been trying to reach you. She sounds frantic.'

The Chief set down his glass of beer and took the phone. His eyes widened, then narrowed, as he listened to the urgent message from the other end.

'Put me through to Marwah right now!' he barked into the receiver.

Niki, waiting in tense silence on the Ridge for what felt like the longest 60 seconds of her life, jumped as the walkie-talkie in her hand finally crackled to life. She frowned as she tried to decipher the garbled, distorted words of Inspector Nagpal at the other end.

'Repeat that, please.'

'We are inside the main auditorium,' Inspector Nagpal's voice, suddenly crisp as the night air, crackled through the walkie-talkie. 'There are no detectable toxic gases in the area. I repeat, there are *no* toxic gases in the area.'

'And casualties?'

'We see two bodies down on the main stage. Female – '

'*Stay away!*'

Niki jumped as the Chief's voice – calm, steely, unmistakable – bellowed into the walkie-talkie.

'DGP Kapoor here,' he said, quite needlessly. 'Stay away from the stage, Inspector Nagpal! It could be a trap.'

'Sir.'

'Your first priority is to clear the area. Proceed slowly and with extreme caution through every part of that auditorium – hallways, bathrooms, storage. Check and secure every square inch of that theatre. I want to know if you find anyone else in there, dead or alive.'

'Sir.'

Niki bit her lip as the line went silent. 'The two women down, sir,' she said after a moment, 'shall we – '

'No, Marwah. Not before we have an all-clear.'

Niki thought of the women lying on stage, dead, and a battery of life-saving ambulances and medical gear standing helplessly by. She hoped it would not be too late...

'Boss?'

Niki turned as ASP Sahay's whispered voice broke into her thoughts.

'I have Inspector Chauhan on the line. She has some important information.'

Niki took the phone.

'Ma'am, I have a witness from the Gaiety who says it was something in the food,' Deepika said.

'The *food*?'

'Yes, ma'am. They were shooting an episode of a cooking show. He says the judges collapsed while tasting the food.'

'What about the poison gas?'

'There may be no gas.'

Niki hung up and looked around her. All of Shimla's emergency-service personnel were ranged up and down the Ridge, prepared for the worst. On her walkie-talkie, she had the Chief of Himachal Pradesh Police and the Home Ministry braced for the worst.

'There is no gas.'

Niki turned back to her walkie-talkie as Inspector Nagpal's voice came on again.

'We have tested and inspected all areas,' his voice confirmed, louder this time. 'There are no toxic gases. No weapons, no bombs, no imminent threat.'

There was a second's silence. Then, '*What?*' the Chief's voice thundered, before morphing into an ear-splitting disturbance.

Inspector Nagpal's voice calmly repeated the news.

Niki expelled her breath in disbelief.

'We have evacuated several persons who were hiding in one of the dressing rooms,' Inspector Nagpal continued. 'They appear to be disoriented and suffering from stress and mild trauma. One of the men is complaining of chest pains. First Armed is escorting them outside onto the Ridge now.'

'I'll have an ambulance meet them there,' Niki said.

'We have about twenty people, ma'am.'

'Three ambulances, then,' Niki said. 'And the two women on the main stage?'

'One of them is breathing, ma'am.'

Which meant the other wasn't... 'I'm coming in.'

'No!' the Chief's voice rang out. 'I want you to stay put, Marwah.'

'But sir – '

'I need you *outside* the Gaiety, *on* the phone and *on top of this mess*! Is that clear?'

Niki winced at the controlled rage in the Chief's voice. 'Sir,' she said.

'Okay. So since it appears that this is no longer a national security issue,' he said, addressing the IB team who was also in on the call, 'I'll take it from here. Thank you for your assistance. Goodbye.'

'Now,' the Chief said, after a moment. 'Marwah?'

'Sir?'

'Who called the Home Ministry?'

'I did, sir.'

'And who sounded the Code Red?'

'I did, sir. I'm sorry, sir.'

'Don't be.'

Niki was silent.

'You did the right thing. Never be sorry for doing the right thing.'

'Sir. Shall I start scaling things down now, sir?'

'That's your call; you're the one on the ground. Make sure you satisfy yourself completely before you start standing down.'

'And the two women down, sir?'

'Send in the medical personnel right away.'

7

'This way, ma'am.'

The 320-seat main auditorium at the Gaiety, with its emerald green walls, period balconies and magnificent arched ceiling, was brightly lit and markedly empty, save for the heavily armed and masked Anti-Terror police personnel and guards of the First Armed Police Battalion.

Niki followed Inspector Nagpal down the cascading rows of seats and up the steps at the side onto the main stage. Behind her, she heard ASP Sahay's sharp intake of breath at the sight that met their eyes.

The historic stage was a mess of overturned furniture, spilled food and drink, crumpled linens, scattered cutlery and shards of broken glass that glinted under the bright glare of the floodlights. A pungent smell, part bitter, part sharp, heavy with oil, spices, meats and herbs, and laced with something more ominous, hung in the air. From the wings came the echoing sounds of boots stamping, of wires swishing, of equipment being dragged and moved; above, the stagelights burned with dazzling intensity. But what caught and held the officers' gaze, to the exclusion of all else, as they stood at the top of the stage, was the body that lay sprawled amidst the mess.

Kneeling beside the inert figure, part hidden by the three upended chairs and the long table that now lay on its side, was a male nurse in hospital whites. He looked up as Niki and Shankar approached.

'We've rushed the other victim to Shimla Medical,' he said, correctly interpreting the SP's questioning look. He glanced at the figure on the floor and shook his head. 'We were too late for her, though.'

Niki nodded and knelt down beside the dead woman. She was small and slender; her thick, dark hair formed a lustrous halo around her tiny head. Her eyes were bulging; her hands gripped her throat; her face, twisted in an expression of sheer agony, was a bright magenta, as though dyed in a bizarre fashion.

'Is it the stage lighting or is she unusually pink?' the SP asked, with a glance up at the lights.

'It's not the lighting,' a voice spoke up from behind her.

Niki spun round to see a man standing at the edge of the stage. He was middle-aged and well dressed, with an urgent, anxious air about him.

'Ma'am, this gentleman says he has some information,' said the SI who stood barring his way.

Niki beckoned the man forward.

'That's Mala Joseph,' the man said, indicating the body. 'She was one of the judges on the show.'

'And you are… ?'

'Dr Gautam Bhandari,' the man said, introducing himself. 'I have a private practice in Chhota Shimla. I'm also on the Shimla Medical College panel of consultants.'

'Why aren't you at the hospital, then?' Sahay asked, frowning. 'We have many injured people there in need of urgent medical attention.'

'They'll be fine,' the man said, almost to himself. He saw the frowns on the officers' faces. 'I was here when it happened; I was in the audience,' he explained.

Niki's brows shot up. 'Are you okay?' she asked sharply.

'I'm fine, thank you.' He glanced at the body again. 'They called for a doctor as soon as she – Mala Joseph – collapsed. So I rushed up on stage.'

'Was she alive when you did?'

'Barely,' the doctor said. 'Cyanide works fast, too fast.'

'*Cyanide?*'

The doctor nodded. 'That smell of bitter almonds, the cherry red colour – they're classic textbook symptoms. Except that the poison was ingested, not inhaled, as I'd feared earlier. I should have realized that, but what with all the fainting and gagging and nausea…'

Niki glanced at ASP Sahay, who had hurriedly pulled out his notebook and pencil and was struggling to keep up.

'Dr Bhandari,' she said, 'slow down. This is extremely serious. Could you explain exactly what happened? From the beginning, please?'

'Certainly, ma'am.' The doctor took a breath and began again. 'They were filming the TV show, *Hot Chef*, at the Gaiety this evening,' he said. 'My wife, my daughter and I were sitting in the third row of the auditorium's centre section. Seats C10, C11 and C12 – right there.'

Niki glanced at the area he indicated.

'The contestants had finished the performance and cooking rounds,' Bhandari continued, 'and they were on the "tasting" round. The judges were seated at this table here and the contestants were over there.' He pointed to a bench at the back of the stage.

'It must have been around eight-thirty, I think. The judges had just finished tasting the dishes prepared by the first five contestants. Then right after Rajat called the final contestant's name, they dimmed the lights and announced a break.'

'Rajat?' Sahay asked.

'Rajat Tripathi, the host of the show. You must have seen him; he's everywhere on TV these days… Anyway, he announced that there was a technical problem and requested everyone to stay in their seats while they fixed it. Then they started to play a video of the previous episode on the backdrop. I'm not sure what it was exactly, because just then I felt my phone vibrate. I was on call this evening, you see. So I took my phone out to answer the call and that's when it happened.

'I heard a thud, followed by a shriek. I looked up from my phone; there seemed to be some kind of commotion up on stage. Then someone called out, "Lights! Lights!" and, "Doctor! We need a doctor on stage!" So I jumped up from my seat and rushed forward.'

The doctor paused, remembering. 'It was very dark. I couldn't even see the steps; I almost fell over them in my hurry. Then just as I was fumbling my way up, the lights came on. And I saw everyone was gathered around the judges' table, bending over a figure lying on the floor.

'I pushed through the crowd,' he continued, 'and found Rajat and KK – that's the other judge – on their knees beside Mala. She appeared to be unconscious. Her face had turned this unnatural colour and there was a distinct smell of bitter almonds in the air. And that's when the bulb went off in my head. Cyanide.'

'So let me get this straight,' Niki said, frowning. 'At this time, there was only one victim?'

'Yes, ma'am.'

'And the other woman who was sent to the hospital?'

'Ashika De, the third judge,' the doctor replied. 'She fainted later.'

'But what about the stampede? Why did everyone run out, screaming about poison gas?'

The doctor looked sheepish. 'I'm afraid that's my fault,' he said. 'Cyanide is highly poisonous, especially if it is inhaled. So I panicked and sounded the alarm.'

'You told them it was poison gas?'

'I advised everyone to cover their faces and evacuate the theatre without delay. At first, people were slow to respond, but then Ashika collapsed and that led to complete chaos. People started screaming and running all over the place. Luckily, Rajat had the presence of mind to grab the mike and direct the audience to go to the emergency exit doors at the back.'

'And what about the people who were on stage?'

'We all rushed backstage and into the green rooms on the second floor. And that's where we waited till those guys,' he indicated the Anti-Terror officers, 'arrived.'

'So everyone got out safely?'

'I think so,' Dr Bhandari replied. 'Everyone, except...' He stood looking down helplessly at the dead woman on the floor.

Niki was silent for a moment. Then, abruptly she said, 'Thank you. Thanks for coming forward and speaking with us.'

'I'm sorry to have created all this trouble.'

'You did what you thought was best in a tough situation.'

Niki nodded to the SI who was waiting respectfully for her to finish. 'SI Rajnath will show you to a vehicle,' she told Dr Bhandari. 'I think you should head on to the hospital. I'm sure there will be many there who could use your help. And give us a call if you remember any other details that you think might be important.'

'Unbelievable!' Sahay muttered, watching the SI escort the doctor out of the auditorium. 'To think that this guy single-handedly created a Code Red!'

'Better safe than sorry,' Niki said, recalling the Chief's words.

'We should be grateful it turned out to be nothing.'

'Not nothing,' Niki said gravely, with a glance at the body of the young woman lying a few feet away.

'Mala Joseph,' Sahay sighed. 'What a horrible way to go.'

'Shall we take her away now?' the paramedic asked.

Niki nodded. So tiny, she thought, as he placed a white sheet over the body, as moments later, it was carried out on a stretcher. So young.

8

The report on Niki's laptop, marked 'Extremely urgent' and sent at
1.30 a.m. from the email address of the Head of Emergency Services,
Shimla Medical College, was chillingly succinct.

```
Gender:           Female
Age:              28 yrs
Height:           152 cm
Weight:           48 kg
Hair:             Black
Eyes:             Black
Complexion:       Cherry red
DOA:              Sunday, 14 October 2012
TOA:              9.38 p.m.
```

Mala Joseph, Niki thought, remembering the body sprawled on the
main stage at the Gaiety last night. So young, so tragically altered from
the images on her computer – starry, sparkling images from magazine
covers, news articles, interviews, press releases, blogs, chats… In all
of them, the eyes were bright, the hair silken, the complexion most
definitely *not* 'cherry red'.

So how did one go from being the glowing face of a young generation
to a cold corpse on a table? How did a dazzling smile disappear in the
twinkling of an eye?

Niki took a deep swig of Joginder's extra-strong early morning
elaichi chai and skimmed her way down the rest of the report.

```
Probable cause of death pending post-mortem examination
is Potassium Cyanide ingestion. Blood levels indicate the
presence of 2,154 mg of the substance in the victim's
system. Potassium Cyanide is considered fatal to humans
in doses of 200 mg or more.
```

So, Niki thought. Cyanide – and enough of it to kill ten people.

'The victim would have shown symptoms of severe cyanide poisoning almost immediately upon ingestion,' Dr Kaul had added separately, in a side note. 'Typical signs of cyanide poisoning are inability to breathe, progressing to cardiac arrest, followed by coma. Loss of consciousness would almost certainly have ensued within 2–5 minutes after consumption.'

Niki put down the sheet and pondered that last, critical fact. *Loss of consciousness within two to five minutes of ingestion.*

Which meant that Dr Bhandari's estimate was accurate – and it almost always was – Mala had consumed the poison on stage under the very eyes of the cast, the crew and a 300-strong audience.

She looked up as there was a knock and her door swung open. Never a morning person even under the best of circumstances, it was with an unusually heavy sigh and deeply shadowed eyes that ASP Sahay walked in and sank down in her visitor's chair.

'Sorry I'm late, boss,' he said, even though it was still early. 'I had to swim through a river of press outside. They've all been whipped into a fine frenzy. You'd think we were on the verge of a nuclear war. All because of one trigger-happy Dr Bhandari.'

'Who was only doing his job,' Niki said. 'And the media is doing theirs. Did you get any sleep last night?'

'Define "sleep".'

Niki poured some chai from her flask into the plastic cup and passed it across the table. Shankar tossed half the thick, syrupy liquid down his throat and gave the paperweight on his boss's desk a lacklustre twirl.

'So Mala Joseph has a husband and a mother,' he said presently, watching the shiny flakes swirl about in the glass casing. 'I called the husband. Woke him up in the middle of the night to tell him his wife had collapsed.'

Niki grimaced. 'How did he take it?'

'He didn't really seem to register what I said. Said he'd get to Delhi first thing; get on the morning flight to Jubbarhatti. I told him I'd meet him at the airport. I'm worried he may get mobbed by the media once word gets out.'

'I'll come with you.'

Niki turned her head as there was the slightest of knocks on the door and Inspector Deepika Chauhan, her assistant, stepped in.

Petite and slim, with a small, round face framed by black hair that was permanently pulled back into a tight ponytail, Inspector Deepika Chauhan somehow always managed to look at once much younger and much older than her 26 years. Sent over four months ago to replace the redoubtable Inspector Gupta – who'd been promoted and transferred to Sirmaur against his best efforts – Inspector Chauhan had proved herself a worthy successor. In her first two months on the job, she had assisted in two major arrests; in her third, she had taken down a local mafia operative with a well-placed bullet to the leg. Well trained, firmly grounded, discreet and thorough, Deepika had managed to win both Niki's heart and approval with the breathtaking efficiency and near fanatic dedication she brought to the job.

'SP Marwah,' she said now, snapping to attention, touching her inspector's cap, 'ASP Sahay.'

'Come in,' Niki said, returning the greeting with a smile. 'What's it like out there?'

'Getting back to normal, ma'am. We've dismantled most of the roadblocks and lifted the bulk of the traffic restrictions. Schools and colleges will open on time, as will all government offices and heritage sites. All teams have orders to be vigilant, but to allow normal movement of traffic and people.'

'And the Gaiety?'

'Closed, ma'am. We've blocked off all access from the Ridge and the Mall.'

'The Scene of Crime team was working at the Gaiety through the night,' Sahay added. 'I talked to Inspector Pande before coming here. I've asked him to join us for the morning meeting.'

'Good. Any updates from the hospital?' Niki asked.

'Almost everyone has been discharged, ma'am,' Inspector Chauhan said.

'*Almost* everyone?'

'They kept Ms Ashika De overnight for observation and also Mr Agrawal, the kitchen manager, who had complained of chest pain and was found to have an erratic EKG. They were hopeful of discharging them both this morning.'

'Meanwhile,' Sahay said, 'I've started piecing together the facts based on the few statements we were able to take last night.'

'And I have all the department heads gathered in the Briefing Room, just as you asked,' Deepika added.

Niki glanced at the clock on the wall; it was still a few minutes shy of eight. 'They're all there?' she asked.

'SP Kumar from Crime, SP Baruah from Communications, SP Prakash from the Lab and SP Chandra from the Anti-Terror Cell,' Chauhan confirmed. 'I've settled them all in with some tea and biscuits.'

'What about Manoj?'

Manoj Gehlot was Shimla Police's newly appointed Public Relations Officer and Niki was glad to finally have someone to handle that side of affairs, especially in a situation like this one.

'He arrived at the same time as I did,' Sahay said. 'Wanted me to let you know he's scheduled the press conference for nine.'

Niki drained her cup and stood up. 'Then let's go,' she said.

9

The Briefing Room at the offices of the Superintendent of Police, Shimla, was a large rectangular room on the north side of the Municipal Corporation Building, with whitewashed walls, stone floors and an ancient fireplace that had fallen into disuse. Stumbling upon the abandoned room in a draughty corner of the building when she'd first joined, Inspector Deepika Chauhan had immediately commandeered it and, with breathtaking efficiency, had had it cleaned, restored and commissioned for her boss's frequent team meetings. Going a step further, she'd furnished it with a large white marker board, a pull-down projection screen, modern AV equipment and some cheerful canvases painted by local schoolchildren. A large Himachali rug brightened up the cold stone floor and an enormous teak conference table, discovered lying deep in the bowels of the building's cobwebbed storeroom, had been brought up to anchor it, along with a dozen slightly used chairs donated by the Chief's wife who'd been looking for an opportunity to renovate her dining room in a more modern theme.

If further proof were required of Inspector Chauhan's resourcefulness, it could be found in the cosy fire that burned in the fireplace, in the aroma of elaichi and ginger chai that wafted in the air and in the fact that even though it was not quite 8 a.m. on a Monday morning, the room was bustling with half a dozen senior officers standing around with steaming cups of tea in hand, chatting in animated tones about the events of the previous night. They straightened as the door swung open and the Superintendent of Police, Shimla, strode in.

Two years ago, it had been a challenge for many in the room, when Niki Marwah, newly promoted and transferred from Kullu, had taken charge of the district. There had been more than a few ruffled feathers and many eyebrows raised in incredulity or, at the very least, in doubt. Their new colleague and, in some cases, their superior, turned out to be young, beautiful and single – qualities one did *not* expect to find in a senior law-enforcement officer. And the fact that when she smiled she often unwittingly derailed their train of thought didn't help matters either.

But they'd learned in the course of the past two years that SP Marwah, contrary to appearances, was no pushover. That she could be sweet as roses and stubborn as stone. That she knew the law like the back of her hand and wasn't afraid to enforce it. That she alone amongst them had once faced down an angry mob, armed with nothing but a baton and the exceptional ability to connect with people and get inside their heads.

She now strode into the room in her low-slung office Oxfords, her short, peach-scented hair swaying gently about her shoulders, her grey pants and blue shirt discreet, yet flattering. She took her place, not at the head of the table, but a few chairs down. And yet there was no doubt in that room as to who was in charge.

'Thank you, all, for coming in so early,' she said, with a quick nod round the room. 'You're aware of the incident at the Gaiety last night. I've been in touch with DGP Kapoor. He will be returning to Shimla tomorrow afternoon, as scheduled. He has instructed me to proceed with the investigation into last night's incident on a priority basis.

'It is now clear that the terror scare was unfounded,' Niki continued, 'and the poisoning was limited to one victim – Ms Mala Joseph. Consequently, the Code Red issued last night has been called off; all educational institutions and government offices are open and traffic restrictions and blockades that were set up around the city removed. Shimla City is open for business as usual.'

There were murmurs of appreciation and subdued wonder as those who remembered how things used to be before SP Marwah took over marvelled at the speed and efficiency with which she worked.

'I'd like to start this meeting by personally thanking everyone who responded with such promptness and dedication to duty last night,' Niki said. 'Inspector Nagpal of the Anti-Terror Cell and his team; the entire First Armed Police Battalion, various divisions of Shimla Police, Fire and Ambulance divisions. Last night proved beyond a doubt that, whatever the challenge, Himachal Police is ready.'

'Hear, hear,' SP Chandra said and everyone thumped the table.

'There was one casualty last night. My department will be investigating the circumstances of her death under my direct supervision,' Niki said. 'However, in the light of the larger threat to the city, the sensational nature of the incident, the high profile of the deceased and the security implications for the Gaiety and other heritage sites, I thought it best to convene a joint briefing session.'

'High profile?' SP Kumar asked.

'She was a popular TV celebrity. Her Facebook page alone has over one lakh "likes",' Sahay confirmed.

'It's going to be the lead story in all the national news media,' Manoj added.

'Which means we need to handle this with both speed and sensitivity,' Niki said. She glanced across the table at Sahay. 'ASP Sahay, could you please take us through what we know so far?'

'Certainly.' Sahay walked up to the whiteboard at the front of the room, wrote the name, 'Mala Joseph', in thick blue marker and circled it.

'Mala Joseph, twenty-eight years old, married, no children,' he said. 'TV star, celebrity chef, collapsed last night on the main stage of the Gaiety Theatre at 8.45 p.m. during a live taping of the show, *Hot Chef*, of which she was a judge. She was taken to Shimla Medical College and pronounced dead on arrival. The preliminary medical report indicates a lethal level of potassium cyanide in her blood.'

He glanced across the table at Manoj, who was scribbling away furiously, trying to get everything down.

'I've forwarded the reports to you,' he mouthed, indicating his laptop.

Manoj nodded and put down his pen.

'So she died of cyanide poisoning,' SP Kumar mused.

'That is the preliminary finding, yes.'

SP Chandra sat forward in his chair, looking grim. 'Potassium cyanide is a highly dangerous, highly regulated chemical. I'm thankful that the gas threat turned out to be a false alarm, but it disturbs me that a dangerous substance like that could find its way into Shimla and into a heritage site like the Gaiety, on top of that!'

'We should review security measures at all heritage sites and VIP locations,' Niki agreed. 'Although the amount of poison consumed – about two grams – which is roughly the size of a small tablet or capsule, could have been brought in, undetected, in virtually any small container or purse or even pocket.'

'And would not have been captured by any metal detector or discovered during a visual check,' SP Kumar added.

'But it's a valid safety issue and I'd appreciate any assistance or inputs you could provide,' Niki went on.

'We'll get that security review started on a priority basis,' SP Chandra said. 'And I'll see what the Centre's guidelines are on toxic chemicals screening.'

'You'll need to check each and every person who was at the Gaiety last night,' SP Kumar mused.

'Which is close to five hundred people,' Sahay agreed.

'I'll have my teams assist you with intelligence and any other inputs you need.'

'Mine too,' SP Chandra added.

'In the meantime, I could put out a press statement to quell fears, reiterating the enhanced safety measures we are taking,' Manoj suggested.

SP Baruah, who'd been peering at the whiteboard through his glasses, frowned at Sahay. 'What exactly is this "hot chef"?' he asked.

'It's the latest hit TV show,' Sahay answered, surprised that the SP hadn't heard of it. 'It's a reality cooking show, telecast every Friday and Saturday night on YTV, which is currently India's leading youth channel.'

'A food show on YTV? Does it have many viewers?'

'It is the most watched reality show on YTV.'

'Today's youth is into *cooking*?'

'Cooking is just one aspect of it,' Sahay said. 'The other usually involves some kind of thrill-based challenge or other. So far, this season, they've had the contestants dance on top of a moving train and drive Formula One cars; they've even had them jump through rings of fire. Last night was the "Tokyo to Timbuktu" challenge, highlighting cuisines from all around the world. Each contestant had to present a song-and-dance performance and cook a dish from a different country.'

'The contestants must be very talented,' SP Kumar remarked.

'And highly motivated,' Sahay added. 'The first prize is five crore rupees in cash, a flat in Versova and a year-long contract with YTV. And that's not counting all the publicity, endorsements and other opportunities that open up for the winner.'

'I should have become a chef,' SP Baruah murmured. 'And how do they choose the winner?'

'By elimination,' Sahay said. 'Every week, one contestant is voted off, based on a combination of "hot" points that are awarded by the

TV audience which votes in and "chef" points awarded by the judges who taste the dishes prepared.'

'And last night?' SP Kumar asked.

'The victim collapsed before the judges could finish the tasting round. Consequently, nobody was voted off last night.'

ASP Sahay clicked on his laptop and projected a page on the screen.

'I've managed to construct an initial timeline,' he said, 'based on some of the testimonies we got last night. Now according to one of the executives of the show, a core team of seventy-five crew members flew in last Thursday morning from Mumbai to start setting up for the show.'

'Seventy-five?' SP Baruah marvelled.

'It's a big show; it has a big budget. They have their own event team, production team, stage team, technical team, stylists and a food team that travels everywhere.'

'Where did they put all these people up?'

'The Wood Pines Hotel. They checked in shortly after noon on Thursday and spent Thursday and Friday customizing the Gaiety to suit their requirements, arranging for supplies and hiring temporary staff for the shoot.'

'And what about the contestants and judges?' SP Kumar asked.

'The producers, director, judges, contestants all flew in from Mumbai on Saturday afternoon,' Sahay said. 'Everyone besides the contestants checked into the Cecil. The contestants, who are kept in seclusion and isolated from the rest of the show, were put up at the Madison.'

'Madison?' SP Chandra frowned.

'It's a tiny boutique hotel ten kilometres up NH22, just before Wildflower Hall. There are just seven standalone cottages up on a hill overlooking the valley, all completely secluded. It's become quite a hot favourite with the Bollywood set.'

'They're the ones with the money,' SP Chandra said with a roll of his eyes.

Niki cleared her throat.

'Right, so everyone arrived Saturday afternoon,' Sahay continued.

'There was a dress rehearsal at the Gaiety on Saturday evening from 4 p.m. to 10 p.m., following which the theatre was vacated by the show's crew. The custodian, a theatre employee, testified that he locked up the theatre at 11.45 p.m.'

Sahay clicked to the next slide. 'Sunday morning,' he continued, 'the food, stage, technical and production teams returned to the Gaiety shortly after 10 a.m. The stylists, executives and cast arrived at three and went straight to make-up. The doors were opened to the audience at 5.25 p.m. and everyone was seated by 5.55 p.m.

'The taping of the show began at 6 p.m. The host, Rajat Tripathi, started off by introducing the three judges, who took their seats in the centre of the auditorium in the front row. Then the six contestants – Leena Dixit, Pallavi Aanand, Vicky Gulati, Shaqeel Khan, Dev Nair and Sharon Sen – came in one by one as their names were called out and performed their song-and-dance routines on stage.

'The performance round ended at 6.45 p.m. and was followed by a fifteen-minute interval. Then, at 7 p.m., all the contestants came back on stage for the cooking round.'

'They cooked *on* the stage?' SP Kumar asked.

'Yes, sir. Six custom-built cooking stations had been set up for them on the stage, each pre-equipped with burners and appliances and all the ingredients they needed to prepare their food.'

'And where did these ingredients come from?' Niki asked.

'The *Hot Chef* pantry, which had been installed in the open space just behind the stage. It's basically a set of two ten-by-six modular kitchenettes that arrived by road from Mumbai on Thursday, along with the food crew. They're fitted out with an industrial-grade deep freezer and multiple refrigerators, microwaves, food processors, ovens and a temperature-controlled walk-through pantry. The crew installed the kitchenettes at the Gaiety on Friday and had them equipped with fresh food items on Saturday.'

'So all the food that was on stage last night came through this back kitchen?'

'And they were under the charge of the Pantry Manager, Mr Agrawal,' Sahay nodded.

'The one who's still in hospital? Let's talk to him as soon as he's discharged,' Niki said, catching Deepika's eye.

'The cooking round started at 7.15 p.m., shortly after Rajat finished explaining all the rules,' Sahay continued. 'The contestants cooked one dish each at their individual workstations. The segment ended at 7.45 p.m., after which the contestants left the stage and the curtains closed. This was followed by another break, during which the technicians dismantled the stalls and set up the judges' table for the tasting round.'

'And the dishes that the contestants had prepared?' SP Prakash asked.

'Were placed on a special cart by the contestants before they left the stage,' Sahay said. 'This cart stayed on stage throughout the break. The curtains came up again at 8 p.m. The three judges, who'd been sitting in the front row of the audience while the cooking segment was in progress, now came up on stage and took their places at the tasting table.' He drew a rectangular stage on the whiteboard with his marker and within it an elongated tabletop with three ovals behind it. 'Sitting left to right, facing the audience were Mala Joseph, Kemaal Kapoor and Ashika De,' he said, filling in their initials in the three ovals.

'Kemaal Kapoor? As in Kemaal's Kebabs?' SP Baruah asked, frowning.

'Also known as the Kebab King of India,' Sahay confirmed. 'Probably one of the biggest names in the industry. He's the owner of the Kemaal's Kebabs franchise; they have restaurants in Lucknow, Delhi, Kolkata, Agra, Jaipur and Bangalore. KK, as he's widely known, is also the author of the bestselling *Kemaal Ka Khana* cookbook series, co-founder of Kemaal's Institute of Culinary Excellence in Hyderabad and co-creator of *Hot Chef*.

'I ate at the Kemaal's Kebabs in Delhi once,' SP Baruah said in a voice that was almost wistful. 'Best kebabs I ever had in my life.'

'Mala Joseph, the deceased,' Sahay said, pointing to the leftmost oval on the whiteboard and nudging the conversation back to the case, 'was the other celebrity judge on the show. Not as big a name as KK, but she exploded on the culinary scene when she won the previous season of *Hot Chef*. Since then she's appeared in all the media lists as one of India's most promising young stars.'

'And Ashika De? Isn't she an actress?' SP Baruah asked.

Sahay nodded. 'She was a guest judge only for last night's episode,' he said. 'The show has different celebrity guest judges every week.'

'And she also collapsed?' SP Kumar asked.

'She did,' Inspector Chauhan replied, speaking up. 'But the hospital confirmed that she had no cyanide in her system. She apparently fainted due to low blood-sugar levels. They put her on an IV last night; she will most likely be released this morning.'

'So let me get this straight,' SP Chandra said, sitting forward in his chair. 'There were two other judges on stage, but Mala Joseph was the only one who consumed the cyanide?'

'As far as we know,' Sahay replied.

'And this was during the time they were tasting the dishes?'

'According to the three crew members we have interviewed, the incident occurred towards the end of the tasting segment.'

'So the cyanide must have been in something she tasted!'

'Or not,' Niki reminded him. 'Can you elaborate on this tasting segment, ASP Sahay?'

'Certainly.' Sahay opened a document called 'Hot Chef Format' on his laptop. 'I grilled Pankaj Mathur, the assistant production manager, about the tasting last night,' he said. 'According to him, the tasting segment is the one element of the show that basically stays the same in every episode, irrespective of location or type of challenge. They have a standardized "*Hot Chef* Tasting Table" format, with a preset arrangement of plates, glasses, cutlery and napkins. That's for consistency and fairness of scoring, which KK takes very seriously, apparently. There are also score sheets, pens, notepads and sheets of paper for each judge. Also, a sealed bottle of water each and the trademark "Hot Chef Tea Tray".'

'Tea tray?'

'KK's a big tea buff, apparently,' Sahay said. 'He has one dedicated guy on the show called Abbas, whose job it is to brew fresh tea and coffee for the judges. He makes it in the pantry and brings it out on this elaborate silver filigree tray right before tasting.'

'Before tasting?'

'That's when he brings it out. Then he leaves it there on the table for the judges to refill if they want.'

'And what did Mala drink? Tea or coffee?'

'Mathur didn't know. We can check with Abbas; we have yet to talk to him.'

Niki nodded thoughtfully. She remembered seeing a large silver tea service amidst the debris on the stage the previous night…

'Let's talk to this Abbas guy as soon as possible,' she told Deepika.

'The tasting segment got under way a little after 8 p.m.,' Sahay continued. 'Once the judges were seated, the contestants were called back on stage. They took their seats on a bench that was placed on the right-hand side of the stage.' He drew a double row of lines inclined away from the judges' table to indicate the bench. 'Then, one by one, they were called by Rajat to pick their individual dishes from the tasting cart, take them to the judges' table and serve them there.

'Leena Dixit's prawns in green curry with jasmine rice was the first dish to be tasted, followed by Pallavi Aanand's mint falafels on a bed of tabouleh,' Sahay read from his notes. 'Both dishes earned high praise from the judges. Vicky Gulati's white bean enchiladas with apple and goat cheese topping came next.'

Niki felt her stomach rumble, even though it was rather early in the morning. She had to get Ram to make those enchiladas when he got back from Italy. If he ever got back from Italy…

She turned her mind resolutely away from Ram and enchiladas and back to the case.

'Shaq served his dish of teriyaki lamb after Vicky,' Sahay continued. 'All three judges tasted the lamb and then Dev Nair presented his coq au vin. There was a problem with this last dish, apparently. Mala said it was burnt; KK pronounced it inedible; and Ashika complained that it had an unpleasant smell. All three judges took a small bite and all three spat it out.'

'Mala too?'

'Mathur distinctly remembers Mala spitting it out into a napkin.'

'Okay, then?'

'Then Dev Nair returned to his spot,' Sahay continued, 'and they called the last contestant, Sharon Sen, who started shrieking as soon as she got up and rushed backstage, clutching her dress. At this point,' Sahay said, turning to face his audience, 'the director called, "Cut," the lights were dimmed and the host requested everyone to stay in their seats while they took a short break. Two minutes later, at approximately 8.41 p.m., Mala Joseph collapsed.'

'Two minutes after the lights were dimmed?' SP Chandra, who'd been leaning forward with his elbows on the table, sat back with a deeply furrowed brow. 'It says in the prelim report that death occurred within two to five minutes of ingesting the poison. Which means it must have been something she ate during the break.'

'Or right before it,' Niki agreed.

'The coq au vin?' SP Baruah said.

'Could be, except that the other judges had the coq au vin too.'

'We'll have it tested all the same,' SP Prakash said, 'once it comes to the lab.'

'I'll have my team take a look at the camera footage,' SP Baruah said. 'They were recording the show, weren't they? They had cameras trained on the judges and the tasting table?'

'Yes,' Sahay said. 'However, they stopped the cameras when the director called, "Cut."'

'You mean when the last contestant rushed backstage?' Baruah frowned. 'So the last two minutes before Mala collapsed… ?'

'We have no recording of them. Not a single camera was rolling.'

'And we have no evidence either,' a deeply displeased voice rumbled from the back of the room as the officers digested the news.

Niki turned to see Inspector Pande, the head of the Scene of Crime team, standing just inside the door, cleaning his glasses.

Niki waited. Big, heavy, severely myopic and yet sharply observant, there was little that escaped Inspector Pande and Niki was grateful for the thoroughness and attention to detail that he brought to the job. But she'd learned, long ago, that Inspector Pande moved at his own pace and to his own internal rhythm. Trying to hurry Pande was like trying to hurry a mountain. It just couldn't be done. And so she waited, patiently and with considerable bemusement, while Pande finished with his glasses. Finally, apparently satisfied, Pande replaced his spectacles on his bulbous nose, cleared his throat and shuffled ponderously to the front of the room.

'I am just coming from the Gaiety,' he announced in sombre tones. 'We've finished processing the main stage.'

'And?' Sahay asked.

'We found many things that had been spilled and crushed and trodden on. Food, glass, stationery, utensils, tissues, napkins, tea, coffee and multiple shoe marks all over the stage.'

'There was a panic situation,' Niki sighed, remembering the mess.

'Which explains why the evidence is completely compromised. And as there was a significant time lapse between the time of death and the time we got there, not to mention the Anti-Terror Cell and the First Armed trampling all over, it is very likely that any trace of cyanide would have been either removed or destroyed.'

'So there's no evidence,' SP Prakash said flatly.

'And no camera recording either,' Baruah added bitterly. 'Wonderful.' He threw down his pencil in a hopeless gesture.

'But there is a casualty,' Niki reminded everyone in the dejected silence of the room. 'Mala Joseph. Age twenty-eight. Survived by a mother and a husband. And evidence or not, we *will* find out what happened to her.'

The mood amongst those gathered and waiting since the early morning on the tightly controlled, restricted-access Ridge, was tense. The terror scare of the previous night was unprecedented and even though it had turned out to be a false alarm it had come as a stark reminder of the ever-present threat to daily life, shattering the idyllic peace and serenity of the sleepy hill station. It had jolted everyone – residents, tourists, city officials and the media – and it was pushing them all to take a closer look at the things they had always taken for granted.

It would take a while for the jitters to fully subside, Niki knew. But it was important to reassure the public that they were taking things seriously and to spell out the measures her department would be taking to enhance security. And so she spoke at length into the waiting cameras and microphones, taking pains to highlight the speed and efficiency with which the police had responded to the situation and reiterate their preparedness and organization in the face of danger. She detailed the enhanced security arrangements that had already been put in place across the city and mentioned the comprehensive evaluation and review of the city's safety and emergency systems that the Crime Division would be undertaking. Only after she'd exhaustively addressed the issue of public safety did she turn her attention to the question of Mala Joseph's death.

'There was one casualty last night,' she confirmed. 'But we have ascertained that the death was not in any way connected to a larger conspiracy or threat. Consequently, my department will be investigating the incident in the normal course as a suspicious death.'

There was a clamour of voices as journalists jostled for attention.

'Can you confirm the identity of the person who died? Was it Mala Joseph, the celebrity chef?'

'Or Ashika De, the Bollywood star?'

'We heard there was more than one person in critical condition?'

'Ms Mala Joseph was pronounced dead at Shimla Medical last night,' Niki confirmed. 'Ms Ashika De, who was also rushed to the hospital and treated for nausea and weakness, is fine and will be discharged this morning.'

'Was cyanide involved?'

'Do you suspect foul play?'

'Was it suicide?'

Niki held up a hand. 'Ms Joseph was a talented young woman,' she said, her tone grave. 'An icon, a role model, a friend, a colleague, a wife, a daughter. Any speculation at this point would be disrespectful to her family and to her memory. Let me assure you that we will be vigorously investigating the circumstances leading to her death.

Mr Manoj Gehlot will keep you informed as and when we have more details. Thank you.'

She motioned for Manoj to take over as the clamour of voices started up again, and walked resolutely to her waiting Jeep.

'The Cecil,' she told her driver as she climbed in.

10

Niki was silent on the short drive down the 'authorized vehicles only' Mall Road. The road was deserted, save for a few school-bound children and locals in colourful sweaters who looked back curiously as the police Jeep, its red light flashing, zipped by. It was a fine, bright morning, with the sunlight filtering through the trees and cottony white fluffs of cloud in the sky, but for Niki, the events of the previous night and its lone, tragic victim cast a dark shadow across it all.

Mala Joseph, dead of cyanide poisoning, in *her* city, on *her* watch and under the most sensational, baffling circumstances imaginable. It was a bad situation on several counts, not least of which was all the publicity and speculation that she knew would follow. She could already see cyberspace abuzz with tweets, posts, pictures, sound bites, competing theories... Suicide or foul play? Tragically inevitable or somehow avoidable? Police inaction or overreaction? They would be all over the internet and television and newsprint by the evening; the hysterical headlines and artful articles gleefully mining the minutest details of the Code Red and its aftermath, the people involved and, worst of all, the life and death of the poor woman at its epicentre. Why Mala? Why cyanide? Why Shimla? Why now?

The scrutiny was unavoidable, Niki knew. They were difficult questions, but ones that needed to be asked and that demanded answers all the same.

She roused herself as the white and green façade of the Oberoi Cecil glided into view and Ramesh, her driver, slowed down to a halt. Without any clear evidence, it was not going to be easy figuring out what exactly had happened last night. But one way or another, she had to get to the bottom of it. She owed herself and the dead woman at least that much…

The *Hot Chef* guests had been given exclusive use of the entire third floor in the new wing at the Cecil, she was informed moments later by the pleasant young woman at the hotel's front desk. Ms Joseph had been given Room 337 on the north side. 'The search teams arrived half an hour back,' she added. 'Shall I take you there, ma'am?'

'I'll find my way, thanks.'

She took the elevator up to the third floor and walked down the plush carpeting to the end of the hallway to her left, where a constable stood guard outside Room 337. He jumped to attention as he saw the SP and pushed open the door.

The room was spacious and elegant, Niki saw, as she stepped inside. It was decorated in the classic style in keeping with the hotel's hundred-year-old heritage, with a gleaming hardwood floor, period furniture, luxuriously upholstered sofas and richly patterned rugs. A partially open door to Niki's left led to a marble-floored bathroom; to her right, above a burnished wood console, hung a gilt-edged mirror. A tasteful arrangement of fresh flowers and a bowl of fruit adorned the black granite top, along with a couple of silver candlesticks. Further inside the room, across the brocade-covered four-poster bed and the generous expanse of the room, a balcony opened out onto a view of the Shimla hills.

The room was furnished for comfort and relaxation, quite clearly; for lazy mornings, over steaming mugs of chai and cozy evenings tucked in bed. Ordinarily, the mood in the room would have been uplifting. This morning, however, it was tense and teeming with crime-scene technicians as they bustled about with their gloves and cameras and flashlights and kits.

Niki made her way over to the far side of the room, past the bed and the sofa, to where ASP Sahay was crouching beside Inspector Pande inside a wood-panelled walk-in closet, sifting through drawers and shelves with gloved hands.

'Find anything?' she asked.

'Nothing that looks like cyanide,' Pande grunted, as he continued to grope inside a pillow cover. 'There was some jewellery and an Omega watch inside the room safe, though.'

'How about a suicide note?'

Pande shook his head.

'Didn't think there would be one,' Niki murmured.

Sahay glanced up. 'Why not?' he asked curiously.

'Come with me.'

Niki led the way out to the balcony and pointed down. 'What do you see down there?'

Sahay looked down at the concrete path three floors below. 'A sheer drop?'

'And what would be your chances of surviving if you were to jump?'

'None, I imagine.' Sahay stepped back. 'I see your point, boss. Why go through the trouble of cyanide when you could just jump instead?'

'Exactly.'

'So you're saying it wasn't suicide?'

'I'm thinking, why *cyanide*?'

'Unusual choice,' Sahay agreed. 'But it gets the job done.'

'But why do it in public?'

'I don't know… To make a statement of some kind?'

Niki shook her head. 'There has to be a better explanation…' She turned to watch the technicians working inside the room. They were a well-trained team; she was confident she could count on them to do a thorough job. 'Did you notice anything out of the ordinary when you got here?' she asked, turning back to Sahay. He had a good eye for detail, she knew.

'Not really,' Sahay said. 'It was reasonably tidy; the bed was made. There was a camera and an iPad on the writing desk; Pande's already tagged them to be sent to Communications. '

'What about her mobile phone?'

'Haven't found one so far.'

Niki frowned. There hadn't been one at the Gaiety Theatre either, as far as she knew. And yet, who travelled anywhere without a phone these days? She looked up as Inspector Pande pushed open the door and stepped out onto the balcony, followed by one of the technicians.

'We found this in the suitcase, ma'am,' the technician said, holding out a mid-sized teddy bear with a pink ribbon around its neck.

Niki regarded the fluffy toy with its button eyes.

'She bought it yesterday on the Mall,' Inspector Pande said. 'Here's the receipt.'

He smoothed a crumpled piece of paper in his thick-gloved hands and held it out. It was a receipt from the Supreme Gift Store on Mall Road, dated from the day before. It listed three transactions: the first for a PLSH toy for Rs 2,000, the second for Zandu Balm for Rs 70 and the third for Masala Kurkure for Rs 60.

'The balm was on the bedside table,' the technician said.

'And we found this in the waste basket,' Pande added, holding up a bag of Kurkure. 'It's been opened, but barely touched. There was also a banana that was peeled, but not eaten, two empty water bottles and a used coffee filter with dregs.'

'Did you find any pills or medicine?' Niki asked. 'Capsules, tablets?'

'Just vitamins and some herbal cough drops,' Pande said. 'I'm sending all consumables to the lab.'

'Do that,' Niki nodded, 'and keep looking, Inspector. Also, talk to the hotel staff. Find out if anyone visited her in her room, if she made any calls, if there was anything out of the ordinary in her behaviour.'

Niki pulled off her gloves, walked back into the room and moved thoughtfully towards the door. *Zandu Balm. Kurkure. Cough drops. Teddy bear. Cyanide.*

How did those dots connect, she wondered.

A trim young man in a grey suit and vivid blue paisley silk tie was waiting just outside the door texting on his phone, as Niki stepped out. He straightened hurriedly and held out his hand. 'Madam, sir, I'm Lalit Bansal, Guest Relations Manager here,' he said by way of introduction. 'On behalf of the management, I'd like to say how deeply shocked and saddened we are by the death of Ms Joseph. Also, that we are anxious to do everything we can to assist you in your investigation.'

Sahay pulled himself up to his full five feet five inches and regarded Lalit Bansal with the withering disdain he reserved for men who wore paisley ties. 'For starters, we'll need you to ensure the privacy of the deceased and the confidentiality of the investigation,' he said, with a pointed look at Bansal's mobile.

The young manager hastily shoved his phone in his pocket. 'Yes sir, absolutely sir! We always – '

'And make sure you keep the media out and Ms Joseph's room out of bounds.'

'Yes, sir. Absolutely, sir.'

Niki's lips twitched. Shankar Sahay in full IPS glory was always an impressive sight to behold. 'Inspector Pande will be taking statements from all the staff members who came in contact with Ms Joseph,' she said. 'He'll also need the phone log for calls made to and from her room.'

'Yes, ma'am. Not a problem, ma'am.'

'And is there a quiet place where we can interview the *Hot Chef* guests?'

'Yes, ma'am. Follow me, ma'am.'

Lalit led them back down the hallway and into a tiny room tucked away behind the elevator bank. It was a small but functional space, furnished with a plush red leather sofa and matching chairs arranged around a low, rectangular coffee table.

'This lounge is for the exclusive use of the third-floor guests,' Lalit explained. 'It has cable and internet access and I can put a "Do Not Disturb" sign out in front.' He looked anxiously at Sahay who was eyeing the room with apparent disfavour.

'That should work, thank you,' Niki told the manager. She turned at the sounds of a commotion coming from the open doorway. The constable who'd been posted outside the elevators appeared to be struggling to restrain a distraught yet determined woman.

'Ma'am,' the constable said apologetically to the SP, 'this lady says she needs to speak with you urgently.'

'I do!'

The woman, galvanized by the SP's questioning gaze, pushed the guard aside and came bounding forward. She appeared to be in her mid-thirties. She was tall and exceedingly skinny – the effect being amplified by the black tunic she wore over leopard-print leggings and her four-inch heels. Her eyes, heavily lined with kohl, were wide and pleading; her slim fingers, tipped with saffron nail polish and adorned with several large gemstones, scoured through her mane of thick, highlighted hair. 'Everything's a complete mess and I have no idea what to do!' she wailed.

Niki motioned for the guard to close the door. 'I'm SP Niki Marwah and this is my colleague, ASP Sahay,' she said. 'What is the matter?'

'SP! Wonderful! I'm Ruby. Ruby Talwar. The executive producer of *Hot Chef*. Soon to be the ex-producer of *Hot Chef*. Though, thankfully, not the *late* producer of *Hot Chef*. At least, not yet. Although, who knows? God, this is such a nightmare!'

'Please, won't you have a seat?' Sahay suggested.

'And could you please arrange for some water and refreshments?' Niki requested, glancing at Lalit Bansal, who stood hovering by the sofa.

'Yes, ma'am. Certainly, ma'am.'

Ruby sank distractedly down in an armchair as the door closed on the manager. She threw her head forward and raked her fingers through her dishevelled hair again. 'Oh, I thought we were all going to die last night!' she cried, tossing it back.

Niki took a seat on the sofa beside her. 'Ms Talwar, rest assured that there is no threat to anyone's life,' she said. 'Last night's terror threat turned out to be a false alarm, as you must know by now, and as a precautionary measure, we have enhanced security here at the Cecil as well as at the other venues where the members of your show are staying. Your safety is our first concern.'

'Yes, it's just all so terrifying…!'

'I understand. And I am very sorry about your colleague.'

'Mala!' the woman wailed, ready tears springing to her eyes. 'Poor, poor girl! I still can't believe she's gone! How completely, insanely dreadful! How did it happen? How *could* it happen?'

'We'll have to wait for the post-mortem report before we know the full details,' Niki said. 'What we do know is that there was a lethal amount of potassium cyanide in her bloodstream.'

'Potassium *cyanide*?' Ruby shrieked. 'Oh my God! So that doctor was right! Oh, this show is totally jinxed! We've had one disaster after another ever since the first shoot! I knew we were doomed at that mahurat, when the damn coconut refused to crack!'

She caught the look that passed between the officers. 'This might sound crazy to you, but everyone knows that a coconut that doesn't crack is like the kiss of death. Means your show is totally screwed! I begged KK and Jimmy to let me redo the mahurat, but they said I was being absurd. And now look…!'

'What other disasters have been happening?' Sahay asked, pulling out his notepad. 'Besides the coconut?'

'You mean when have disasters *not* been happening! There's been some accident or the other during almost every episode.'

'Such as?'

'Such as that short circuit right before we started filming the second episode. The whole set caught fire.'

'The whole set?' Niki frowned. 'Did anyone get hurt?'

'No, luckily only the production staff and the judges were there when it happened; the contestants were still backstage. But we had to redo the set and a section of the stage, and we had to postpone the shoot by two whole days!'

'And did you find out how the short circuit occurred?'

'No, how? The electricians are subcontracted studio employees and the studios are all falling apart… Rusted wires and faulty circuit boards everywhere…'

'Can you give us the name of the studio where this happened and the names of the contractors and the electricians?'

'I suppose my assistant in Mumbai could dig them up.'

'Please. And what can you tell us about the other accidents?'

'Well, in the fourth episode,' Ruby said, 'the whole two-storey set came crashing down! Right in the middle of the dress rehearsal! And I'm not talking about some flimsy plywood-and-foam thing either.

This was a huge twelve-foot contraption, with steel rods and scaffolding and bridges and pulleys and bolts and planks and whatnot; and the whole thing just collapsed! And I was standing right there, discussing something with Jimmy and Mala and I heard a clattering sound and a big whoosh and...Mala!' she exclaimed, blanching suddenly. 'Oh. My. God! I was standing right there with *Mala*! And that baking soda incident...that was Mala too!'

Sahay cocked his head. 'Baking soda incident?'

Ruby slumped down in her chair and covered her face with her hands. A gigantic sapphire twinkled on the middle finger of her left hand, competing with an equally large pukhraj on the index finger of her right hand and a red coral the size of a plum on the ring finger. 'Oh God! It was Mala all along!' she groaned.

'Ms Talwar,' Niki said, 'please, could you tell us what exactly happened?'

Ruby uncovered her face. 'Yes, of course. My God, I can't believe how blind I've been... I mean, even though it didn't seem worth freaking out over back then, since no one actually got hurt, thank God, how could I have not seen it?'

'Not seen *what*?' Sahay asked, unable to keep the exasperation out of his voice.

'That the accidents all involved Mala! The short circuit, the set collapse and then, two weeks ago, during a rehearsal for the seventh episode, the baking soda snafu! And even though it was KK who was giving a demonstration of the recipe and God knows who knocked over the jar of baking soda, it was Mala who opened the *new* jar!'

'Of baking soda?' Niki persisted, trying to make sense of the garbled account.

'Well, that's what the jar's label *said*. Except that when Mala unscrewed the cap, she recoiled from the smell; and when she tasted it, she immediately rushed to the bathroom and spat it out. She said there was something wrong with it; just the merest taste of it had made her feel nauseous.'

'So it wasn't baking soda?'

'Who knows what it was? Mala said it tasted like naphthalene or phenyl or something. I thought maybe the pest-control guys had left something behind.'

'In a jar of baking soda?' Sahay asked, incredulous.

'Not likely, right?' Ruby turned to Niki, the alarm and dismay apparent in her tear-streaked face. 'Oh, I'm toast! Oh, this is all my fault! And KK and Jimmy's! If only they'd let me redo the mahurat!'

'*She* was shook up,' Sahay remarked once Ruby had left the room.

'I don't blame her,' Niki said, 'Short circuits, set collapses, pesticides mixed with food...'

'Someone needs to be fired for negligence.'

'Or something very shady is going on.' Niki pulled out her mobile phone and dialled her assistant. 'Inspector Chauhan,' she said as soon as the Inspector came on the line. 'Where are we with the witness statements?'

'I'm at the Wood Pines Hotel, ma'am. We've started recording statements. Right now, I'm with the stage and productions teams.'

'Good. Take down all the information you can about last night and also find out about the accidents that occurred during the second and fourth episodes and the dress rehearsal for Episode Seven.' She gave Deepika a quick account of the incidents Ruby had described. 'And talk to Mike Mistry,' Niki said, glancing at the information Ruby had given her. 'He's the Director of Photography at *Hot Chef*. Have him hand over all the tapes from last night's recording, especially the ones from the cameras that were covering the judges.'

'I'll have them sent over to the AV department, ma'am.'

'Also, ask Mistry to get us camera footage for the previous incidents.'

'Yes, ma'am.'

'And have Crime Division start pulling together background checks on the *Hot Chef* crew. That includes all the people who were at the Gaiety yesterday and also those who weren't there, but are associated with the show in any way – suppliers, contractors, cleaners, technicians.'

'It might take them a while, ma'am.'

'I know. But I want to make sure we get to the bottom of all these so-called "incidents".'

'Yes, ma'am. Also, ma'am, I noticed that the *Hot Chef* studios are in Chembur East. I have a contact in the police station there; shall I ask him to inspect the show's sets?'

'Absolutely,' Niki said. 'Any updates on the status of the kitchen manager, Agrawal?'

'He was discharged from the hospital an hour ago, ma'am. He's back in his hotel room and resting. I'll be speaking to him later. And also Abbas, the tea-coffee guy.'

'Call me as soon as you find something,' Niki murmured before putting her phone away.

11

'Mala Joseph was a jewel! A star! The Madonna of the Indian kitchen! Julia Child and Julia Roberts all rolled into one!'

Jimmy Zariwala, the long-haired, bright-eyed creative director of *Hot Chef*, dubiously dressed in a black Grateful Dead tee-shirt and cobalt blue jeans, gazed out the window of the third floor lounge. He sighed elaborately and pressed manicured fingers to his temples. 'And to think we almost didn't include her in Season One, because KK thought she wouldn't appeal to the audience. Surreal! But I could see she had charisma. And that fish curry she made for the auditions… Man! My grandmother would have sold my grandfather for that recipe!'

He crossed one lanky leg over the other knee and fiddled with the shoelaces on his red Converse sneaker. 'Anyway,' he said, 'we took her on. Best decision we ever made. She went on to win the damn thing. And the audiences loved her. We offered to make her a judge this season, because we couldn't risk losing her. And now we've lost her anyway. To cyanide. Man!'

'Did you see how it happened?' ASP Sahay asked.

'No, how man…? I was too busy having hysterics over Sharon's dress! I'd been telling her it was too tight, but does she ever listen? Mary in wardrobe had such a nightmare trying to stitch it back together!'

'We were speaking with your Executive Producer, Ms Talwar, earlier,' Niki said, attempting to bring his attention back to Mala.

'Ruby? She's a doll.'

'She also mentioned some accidents that had happened in the previous episodes.'

'Accidents?'

'A short circuit, a set collapse; also, something to do with baking soda?' Sahay added, noticing Jimmy's frown of incomprehension.

'Oh, those.' The frown disappeared; the slim shoulders lifted in an expressive shrug. 'Yeah, we've had our share of snafus. But then this is Bollywood, not Hollywood, what can you do? And when you're shooting a show on the scale of *Hot Chef*, accidents are bound to happen.'

'Ms Talwar seemed to think you had more than your fair share of accidents this season.'

'She told you about the coconut that refused to crack?' Jimmy smiled and shook his head 'Ruby… She's the best in the industry, but she's the one who's a bit cracked, you know?'

'I wouldn't describe caution as being "cracked",' Niki said. 'Not after what happened last night.'

'No, of course, you're right.' Jimmy rubbed his stubbly chin with a sad, thoughtful look. 'Cyanide… Imagine! I wonder what it tastes like…' He noticed the officers frowning at him and caught himself up with a shake of his head. 'Anyhow, those incidents Ruby told you about; those were completely random. That fire, that set collapse – well, sets get put up and taken apart so fast these days, it's almost inevitable. You know what it's like – flimsy materials, careless labour, everyone bustling about… And that jar that people mistook for baking soda – that's the kind of idiotic thing that drives me crazy, I swear! You have these pest-control guys coming and nuking the place, leaving all kinds of things lying about, reusing bottles and jars without removing the labels, storing phenyl in milk bottles and country liquor in vegetable-oil cans! Completely bizarre. I saw this bugger carrying kerosene in a water bottle once, would you believe? Told him it was dangerous, someone could get killed, but do you think he learned?' Jimmy sighed and shook his head. 'But what happened last night, cyanide, *that's* serious. I can't think of any way *that* stuff could have got onto my sets.'

'And yet it did.'

'But who would bring cyanide to a live taping? And why?'

That was the five-crore question, Niki agreed silently. 'Do you know if anyone had a grudge against Mala?' she asked.

'Mala? No way! Man! She was the best. Everyone loved her. Me, Ruby, Rajat, the contestants, set boys, make-up girls, food, wardrobe – everyone!'

'Do you know of anyone who *didn't* love her?' Sahay asked, rephrasing the question. He looked up as there was a tap on the door and the guard stationed outside popped his head in. 'Sorry, ma'am, sir, but I have Mr Kemaal Kapoor with me. You wanted me to let you know when I found him?'

'Thanks,' Niki nodded. 'Please show him in.'

The first thing Niki noticed about Kemaal Kapoor, the so-called Kebab King of India, was that he was big. Bigger, taller, significantly rounder and quite a bit older than in the glowing pictures she'd seen of him in the show's promos online. The white kurta he wore stretched tight across his substantial belly; its crystal buttons flashed in the fluorescent overhead lights; a strong scent of musky after-shave preceded him as he walked into the room. There was a red cut above his lip where he had nicked himself while shaving, apparently; it gave him a slightly sinister air as he stood a moment just inside the doorway, regarding the officers with a watchful, measured look in his heavy-lidded eyes.

'I was told the police wanted to speak with me right this instant,' he said, looking from Niki to Sahay. His tone, while polite, managed to imply that he was not used to being thus summoned.

Niki indicated a vacant chair. 'Please have a seat,' she invited. 'I'm

Niki Marwah, Superintendent of Police, Shimla. This is my colleague, ASP Sahay. And you know Jimmy.'

'Haven't seen you all morning, man,' Jimmy said, turning to look up at KK. 'How are you doing?'

'Coping.' KK pulled out the armchair Niki had indicated and sank down heavily. He glanced at Niki and grimaced. 'I've been on the phone with the lawyers and sponsors and the network all morning. This thing is a complete disaster. Plus, we have no idea what we're going to telecast next weekend.'

'I'm thinking a tribute to Mala,' Jimmy said. 'Something simple, heartfelt and quick?'

'Good idea,' KK said. 'I'll have Ruby set it up and clear it with the network. Shall we tell them an hour next Saturday?'

'It'll be a scramble...'

'But you'll manage.'

'It's the least we can do,' Jimmy sighed and sat forward in his chair. 'I was just telling SP Marwah how much Mala meant to all of us. Don't know how we'll carry on without her!'

'Her death is a crushing blow,' KK agreed. He crossed his arms over his chest and a square diamond, larger than his fingernail, flashed on his ring finger. 'In my forty years in the industry,' he continued, 'I have seen hundreds, maybe thousands of promising young chefs, but no one with as much talent as Mala Joseph.'

'And her career was just taking off,' Jimmy added. 'She had all these brand endorsements lined up, her agent was negotiating a solo show on Star next season and she had movie offers flying at her, fast and furious. She could have been the next big Bollywood discovery, man!'

'And yet her heart was always in the food.'

'Yeah... She was so excited about that new restaurant franchise you were starting up together!'

KK's lips tightened momentarily. 'Oh, that was just an idea, nothing concrete,' he murmured.

'What kind of idea?' Niki asked.

KK shrugged, clearly loath to share it. 'Oh nothing; I've been toying with the idea of north-south fusion food for a long time. I'd mentioned to Mala that we might work on it together....'

'Mala told me it was going to be the next big thing in the world of food!' Jimmy enthused.

KK's lips creased in an indulgent smile. 'Mala was always excited about everything,' he said. 'It was one of her most endearing qualities.'

He looked round as the door behind him swung open with a slight knock and a waiter stepped into the room bearing a large tray.

'Ah, tea,' KK said. 'I hope you don't mind, I ordered some for everyone.' He motioned for the waiter to set the tray down on the coffee table.

'Thank you,' Niki murmured, bemused, as the waiter glided away.

'My pleasure,' KK said, smiling briefly at the officers. 'I love tea. It doesn't solve life's problems, but it certainly helps you get through them... May I pour you some, SP Marwah? And you, ASP Sahay? And Jimmy, of course.'

Niki watched as he poured the tea expertly into the four porcelain cups, added milk and sugar and handed them out. Despite the man's bulk, there was a fluid grace to the way he moved, an easy expertise that spoke of years of practice. He tore open a sugar sachet and poured the contents into his own cup, then did the same with another and another.

'Mala Joseph,' he said again, putting his spoon down finally and taking a small sip. 'I still can't believe she's gone. She was like a daughter to me...'

'You always said she reminded you of Shraddha,' Jimmy said.

'She did. Shraddha's my daughter,' KK explained to the officers. 'She's just a few years younger than Mala.'

'And just as talented,' Jimmy added. He turned to Niki. 'I tried to sign her on the show for the next season, but KK wouldn't let me.'

'She's my daughter; it's against the rules. Besides, she's getting married in January.'

'She is? That's awesome,' Jimmy said, clapping him on the shoulder.

'We just finalized the date last week,' KK said.

'Congratulations,' Niki and Shankar murmured.

'Thank you.' KK shook his head. 'Time, it just flies. Seems like just yesterday when I was swinging her around on my shoulders...' He took another sip of his tea . 'She's a good girl, my Shraddha; I'm proud of her. And I was proud of Mala, too. It was so gratifying to see her bloom...' He turned to Jimmy. 'Remember how timid she was when she started last year?'

'Like a little lost puppy,' Jimmy agreed. 'I was just telling them how we almost didn't take her on.'

'And now she's gone. What a waste. What a senseless disaster.' KK put his cup down on the table and looked up at Niki with a keen, questioning gaze. 'That doctor last night said it was cyanide...?'

'It was.'

'Unbelievable. And I was sitting right next to her. Less than a foot away!'

'Which is why your testimony is crucial.'

Sahay set down his empty cup on the coffee table and picked up his notepad. 'Tell us about the last few minutes before Mala collapsed,' he said. 'We're specifically interested in the last five minutes. Did you see her eat or drink anything in that time?'

'In the last five minutes?' KK shook his head. 'There was that coq au vin that we all tasted. Dev Nair's dish. He'd burnt the chicken, the idiot; it tasted foul. We all spat it out. Mala, too, I'm quite sure, and one of the stage guys removed the plates. And then Rajat called Sharon's name. And Jimmy called, "Cut".'

'She ripped her dress, man,' Jimmy said.

'I heard,' KK said. 'Anyway, the lights went out; it was pitch dark for a moment. And then a few seconds later the video montage started to play on the backdrop behind us and there was a little light, not much.'

He sat back in his chair, his brows slightly knitted together in his wide forehead as he remembered. 'It was actually very dark,' he said. 'I can't remember seeing Mala at all after that. And I had my back to her, too. Ashika had just asked me a question about weighted scoring on the aroma index and it was while I was explaining it to her that I noticed Mala. Rather, I felt something brushing the back of my chair. And when I turned I saw Mala falling to the ground. She was clutching her throat and gasping…

'I jumped out of my chair and knelt down beside her. I thought maybe she was choking on something and Rajat rushed over and joined me; he had already called for a doctor… And then the lights came on and that's when I saw her face, her eyes…' His voice broke off abruptly and he closed his eyes.

'You tried, man, you tried…' Jimmy said, patting his shoulder.

'We did,' KK nodded. He opened his eyes after a moment, brushed an invisible tear off his face. 'Rajat and I. But that doctor pushed us away. So we just stood there… I have never felt more useless in my life.' A spasm of pain, mixed with anger, flashed across his face.

'I wonder where she got hold of the cyanide…' Jimmy mused.

'You can get hold of anything if you really want to,' KK bit out.

Niki glanced curiously from one to the other. 'So you think Mala committed suicide?'

'What else could it be?' Jimmy shrugged.

'And how about you?' she asked KK.

'I have no idea,' he sighed, shaking his head. 'But I know that not everyone is cut out for fame and fortune. And Mala was a shy, sweet girl, thrust suddenly into the national spotlight. It's possible she buckled under the weight of it all…'

'She had been moody the past couple of days,' Jimmy agreed.

'Moody?' Niki asked.

Jimmy grimaced. 'Nothing really, she'd just been a bit off, you know? A bit wooden at rehearsal the night before, forgetting her lines, looking distracted – that kind of stuff. She stayed in her room almost the entire time we were here; didn't even join us for dinner in the hotel restaurant on Saturday night. She told Rajat she wasn't feeling well, that she was planning to turn in early.'

'Do you know what was bothering her?' Niki asked.

'Not really.'

'Try asking Rajat,' KK said.

'Rajat Tripathi?'

KK nodded and Niki thought she detected a flash of derision in his eyes. 'He and Mala were close,' he said.

12

The solitude and stillness of the Madison Hotel, with its tall pine trees and sweeping vistas, felt like a sanctuary after the trauma of the previous night. Seated on one of the benches that overlooked the valley, behind the red-roofed cottages and white-fenced garden, her feet perched on the stone balustrade in front of her, Leena Dixit felt momentarily calm as she looked out over the sun-dappled hills. 'It's beautiful out here, isn't it?' she whispered.

'I'm cold,' Vicky, seated beside her, whispered back.

Leena smiled, despite everything. 'You're never serious, are you?'

'Not if I can help it.'

'So…what do you think is going to happen now?' she asked after a moment.

'Let's see…' Vicky looked at his watch. 'It'll be ten-thirty,' he said, 'in about ten seconds.'

'I was talking about us, silly. The show. Mala.'

'There's not much that can happen to Mala, that's for sure.'

'No…' Leena said, blinking back tears.

Vicky draped an arm round her hunched shoulders. 'Hey, buck up, Leena Ballerina!'

The endearment, so silly, so precious, brought a fleeting smile to her lips. 'I wish we were back in Mumbai,' she sighed.

'You know what *I* wish?' Vicky said. 'I wish we were back in "last night". I wish I could turn the clock back; stop it right before Dev served that damn coq au vin of his.'

'You think it was the coq au vin?'

'Hi, you two.'

Leena turned to see Shaq strolling down the path towards them, his hands in his pockets, his steps unhurried. 'What's going on?' he asked.

'We're trying to find a way to turn the clock back,' Leena sighed.

'I know what you mean...'

He joined them on the bench and propped his feet up on the balustrade rail beside them. They sat lined up and silent for a moment, the three of them, a pair of pink chappals flanked by scruffy sneakers on the left and leather loafers on the right, watching a cloud overhead drift leisurely by. Strip away the contest, the calamity of the night before and the transience of it all and this could be paradise, Leena thought.

'So...any news?' Vicky asked, without turning his head.

'They're scrapping last night's episode,' Shaq replied.

'All of it?' Leena thought of all the effort and inspiration she had put into her Thai curry and felt tears of anger and frustration prick her eyes. 'Are you sure?'

'It was on the B&B network.'

The B&B network; it was a term they'd coined for Barkha and Binod, their 'contestant managers'. Although 'Bhalu and the Beast', 'Blah and Blech', 'Barker and Binchod' were some of the other creative titles that Vicky had come up with. For Barkha and Binod came from that special class of people who earned their keep by doing the kind of miserable jobs no one else wanted to do and, somehow, miraculously, delivered. Whether it was hitting the Sassoon Docks at three in the morning in the middle of a downpour or arranging for last-minute air travel in the middle of a pilot strike or magically conjuring up a setful of stray cats and dogs and even rabbits for filler shots, they performed each task with consistent detachment, automation and efficiency.

Which is how they had come to be, for the duration of the show, at least, the contestants' lords and masters. For, by the terms of participation on the show, the contestants were to have no contact with the outside world, except under the watchful eyes and with the express approval of Barkha Patel and Binod Bose. There were to be no phone calls that were not screened, no correspondence that was not intercepted, no TV shows that were not pre-approved, no internet, no mobiles, no connection whatsoever. Rich or poor, talented or otherwise, the contestants were, for the duration of the show, at the complete and crushing mercy of Barkha and Binod.

'Dev must be break dancing,' Vicky said. 'I thought he was a sure-shot elimination this time, with that "coq au *sin*" of his.'

'The boy has a charmed life,' Shaq said.

'He should never have been allowed on the contest in the first place!' Leena exclaimed. 'He can barely make tea. Sharon, too.'

'But they're both good-looking and sexy and that's what the audience likes,' Shaq shrugged.

'Why couldn't they have just made this show about food?' Leena said. 'For once?'

'Because then there would have been no contest,' Shaq said with an amused smile. '*You* would have won hands down.'

Leena felt that breathless surge of pleasure that always overwhelmed her when someone complimented her. As if she were momentarily weightless. 'You don't mean that,' she said, pink-cheeked.

'Of course I do. Why else do you think I was juggling knives?'

'And what do you think my manly moustache was all about?' Vicky added with a twinkle.

'I honestly don't know. Mala said your enchiladas were *sublime*.'

'She was actually talking about my "moochhaladas".'

Leena felt a snort of laughter burst from her. Then her expression turned sombre. 'Poor Mala,' she sighed. 'Of all the horrid things to happen…'

Shaq, who'd been staring up at the sky, closed his eyes. 'Bad things happen all the time,' he said and his voice had a bitter edge to it, borne of years of harsh experience, Leena knew. She pressed his hand as it rested on the bench beside her. He might be undemonstrative, but she knew how fond he had been of Mala.

'It's a fundamental law of nature.' Vicky spoke up on her left. 'Good things happen to bad people; bad things happen to good people. Moral of the story: be bad.'

'Be very bad,' Shaq agreed.

'Stop it, you two,' Leena said. 'You know that's not true. Mala was the sweetest person ever.'

'And she killed herself in the nastiest way imaginable.'

'How do you know that?' Leena demanded, rounding on Vicky.

'Well, I've never tried it, but I've heard cyanide's not exactly sugar frosting.'

'No, I meant, how do you know she killed herself?'

Vicky was silent for a moment. Then, 'I can't think of anyone else she killed,' he said. 'Can you?'

Ashika De, Bengali bombshell, seasoned model and soon-to-be Bollywood sensation, lay propped up in bed against several fluffy white pillows, her lustrous hair tied in a loose braid, her classically beautiful face pale and drawn. As her assistant opened the door, she put down the steaming mug she'd been sipping from and looked up with a wan smile. 'Thank you for coming to my room, Ms Marwah, Mr Sahay,' she said, as the assistant arranged a couple of armchairs near her bed for the officers. 'I'm so sorry, but I'm completely exhausted; the doctors have told me to rest...'

'I understand,' Niki said, taking the proffered seat.

Sahay, who'd resolved in advance to not allow himself to be distracted by the actress's beauty (although he secretly was), ignored the chair, walked over instead to the far side of the room and propped himself up against the wall. 'Do you feel well enough to tell us about last night, Ms De?' he asked, briskly pulling out his notepad.

'I can try,' Ashika said winningly. 'Would you care for some tea first?'

'We just had some, thanks.'

Ashika turned to her assistant. 'Neha, can you ask someone to send up another cup of green tea for me? And please make sure no one disturbs us.'

She waited for the young girl to step outside, then turned to the officers with anxiety writ large in her expressive eyes. 'I'm trying to keep up a brave front, but the fact is I am a complete mess after last night,' she whispered. 'One moment everything was fine, the next, Mala was on the floor...'

She closed her eyes with a shudder, then opened them again. 'It was horrifying,' she continued. 'She was lying there with that scary expression on her face, her body convulsing, her eyes and mouth wide open; and then that doctor started yelling, "Cyanide! Cyanide!" and it was like there was a giant hand gripping my throat. I couldn't breathe! Then my knees went wobbly and everything became dark…'

She sighed and lay her head back against the pillows. 'They told me at the hospital that I'd fainted from low blood sugar. But Mala… Well, she's *dead,* right?'

'She died of cyanide poisoning,' Niki confirmed. 'But she was the only one. No one else tested positive for it.'

'So she's the *only* one who inhaled it?'

'Actually, she ingested it. She *ate* the cyanide.'

'In the last few minutes before she died,' Sahay added.

'Then *that's* what she must have been texting about! She must have planned to do it all along! Oh, how horrible!'

Niki started forward in her chair. 'Are you saying you saw Ms Joseph texting on her phone?'

'Yes, one of those smart phones. She had it in her purse.'

'She had a purse?'

'A small black clutch,' Ashika nodded. 'She had it on her lap.'

'Are you sure?' Sahay frowned.

'Oh yes. It was one of those classy satin things. Very chic. Went rather well with her outfit, I thought.'

Sahay looked dubiously at the actress. 'So you saw Mala take her phone out of her purse and text on it?'

'Yes, during the break,' Ashika said.

'The *last* break?'

'The one after we tasted Dev Nair's coq au vin,' Ashika confirmed. 'God, *that* was nasty! Anyway, they stopped filming right after we tasted that dish and someone cut the lights and then they were playing that video on the backdrop. And I remember I asked KK how I was supposed to score the coq au vin's aroma, given that it had been completely burnt, and he was telling me something about an aroma index and I was distracted by Mala – I could see her, even though KK was sitting between us, because he was leaning forward and she was leaning back. And I saw her take her phone out of her purse and start texting. And I remember thinking: what is she texting in the middle of the show?'

'And then?' Niki asked, her eyes intent on Ashika's face.

'Well, after a minute, she leaned forward,' Ashika said. 'I couldn't see what she did; she was hidden behind KK. And then, I'm not sure, but I think she reached in her purse again… And she put her hand to her mouth. Like this.' She cupped a hand over her mouth and raised her chin a fraction. 'And then, ten, maybe twenty seconds later, she fell…'

Niki pulled out her phone and dialled Inspector Pande's number as she and ASP Sahay walked briskly back to the elevator bank. 'We have a witness who saw the victim text on her phone and eat something from a small black purse that she had on her lap,' she said without preamble.

'There was no black purse at the Gaiety,' Pande said, equally succinct. 'And no phone either.'

'Any chance they could have been sent to the hospital, along with the victim's belongings?'

'I'll check right away.'

'Please.'

'Who could she have been texting?' Niki wondered out loud as she hung up. 'And what about?'

'Could have just been something trivial, boss,' ASP Sahay said. 'People are always texting or tweeting or posting status updates. Do you know how many "Whatsup, I'm bored" texts and tweets and chats I've been subjected to?'

Niki shook her head. 'People do send trivial messages all the time, Shankar, but not moments before they die.'

'And certainly not if they're about to kill themselves,' Sahay agreed.

13

'Rajat Tripathi?'

The young man who sat hunched over and brooding on a barstool in the darkened hotel bar looked up with a start. He was of medium height and lean build, with a boyishly handsome face that Niki knew she had seen before, somewhere on TV. The twinkle in the thick-lashed eyes and the dimples that usually creased his cheeks were nowhere in sight today as he glowered at the officers.

'The bar is closed,' he said.

'We're not here for drinks.'

Niki leaned an elbow on the counter next to his half-empty glass. 'I'm SP Niki Marwah and this is ASP Shankar Sahay of the Shimla Police. We're here to talk to you about what happened at the Gaiety last night.'

'Hell.'

A pungent smell of whisky emanated from Rajat as he raked his hands through his hair. His chin was dark with stubble; the black shirt he wore over distressed jeans was crumpled and creased, as though he had spent a restless night in it. Yet, despite his unkempt, drunken appearance, there was something sweetly appealing in the apologetic smile he mustered up as he invited the officers to join him.

'I'm so sorry, I didn't mean to be rude,' he sighed. 'It's just that I'm really not at my best today...'

'I understand.' Niki indicated a nook in the far corner of the bar, where four high-backed leather chairs were grouped around a square cocktail table. 'Shall we talk over there?'

'Sure, why not?'

Rajat walked over with unsteady steps and pulled back a chair. He waited for the officers to be seated. 'Would you like a drink or something? I can go find the bartender...?'

'No, thanks, we're fine,' Niki said.

Rajat lowered himself carefully in the chair beside her. He sat forward, resting his forearms on his knees, his fingers gripped tight between them. 'I'm sorry, I don't normally drink. Certainly never before noon. But today...'

He pushed his hair back with his hands, then sat back in the chair, sagging against its stretched leather frame. 'How can I help you?' he asked.

'How about starting with the events on stage last night?'

'Yes. Last night. It started out like any other episode, I suppose...
I mean, the stage was smaller than we'd anticipated and so the stage
team had to make some last-minute adjustments...'

Niki watched his profile as he recounted clearly, though with some
effort, the events of the previous night. The teething troubles with the
microphones, the minor missteps during the cooking round as Dev
misplaced his apron, the desperate hunt for green tea for Ashika, the
last-minute relocation of the bench where the contestants sat during
tasting – all minor, inconsequential occurrences that went unremarked
by everyone except him and Jimmy. He spoke in a deep baritone that
was both slurry and mellifluous, and Niki recalled reading that he had
been compering shows since his schooldays and that even though he
was still in his twenties he was one of the most seasoned, sought-after
faces in the industry.

His voice turned husky as he recalled the final moments before Mala
collapsed. 'I was frantic. I called for a doctor, an ambulance, I tried to
get her to breathe, to say something,' he said. 'But it all happened so
fast! And then I just stood back and watched her die. Right there on
the floor, right before my eyes. She was gasping, suffering, and I just
stood there and watched. I let her lie there, dying. And now she's gone.
Just like that.' He caught his breath and laughed shakily. The ragged,
brittle sound echoed in the empty bar. '*Gone.*'

'She was gone the moment the cyanide entered her mouth,' Niki
murmured.

Rajat sniffed loudly; he swiped at the water that was streaming
from his nose with the back of his hand and reached for a cocktail
napkin that lay on the table to finish the job. 'I'm sorry,' he said after a
moment. 'So you've confirmed that it was cyanide?'

'Consumed minutes before she collapsed,' Sahay confirmed,
watching him closely.

'You were on stage,' Niki said. 'Did you see her? Did you see Mala
eat or drink anything unusual before she collapsed?'

Rajat shook his head. His knuckles were white as he gripped his
hands tightly in his lap. 'She seemed fine right through the tasting.

She spoke naturally, she tasted all the dishes… Maybe, if you checked the camera footage?'

'We will,' Niki said. 'Except there is no footage of the final break.'

'Yes, we'd cut the cameras because of Sharon's dress…' He frowned. 'You think that's when – ?'

'It's possible,' Niki said. 'Tell me, Mr Tripathi, do you know if Mala had a purse or a phone with her on stage?'

'Yes, she always kept her phone with her. In case "Dear Joseph" were to call. Joseph is her husband. They were always texting each other.'

'Do you know if she texted him during the break?'

'No. I went backstage during the break to check on Sharon and costumes. Though why Mala would need to text Joseph or anyone else in the middle of the show…'

Sahay, who'd been regarding Rajat quietly, leaned forward in his chair and fixed him with a shrewd, searching gaze. 'Do you know if there was something that was troubling her?' he asked.

'Troubling her? No.'

'I understand that you and Mala were close?'

'Yes,' Rajat said, looking up, his tone almost defiant. 'We were. So?'

'Jimmy Zariwala mentioned that Mala didn't join the others for dinner on Saturday night; that you told them she wasn't feeling well?'

'Oh, that. Yes, she bailed on us for dinner. Said she wasn't feeling good.'

'Did she say what was wrong with her?'

Again the hesitation, Niki noticed, before he shook his head.

'May I remind you that you are currently testifying to the police?'

Rajat closed his eyes and a muscle convulsed in his throat. 'Look, she didn't tell me and I didn't ask what exactly was wrong with her. I mean, not my place to pry, right?'

'Did she look unwell?'

'She was tired; we all were. Besides that…' Rajat shook his head.

'Did she mention anything else? Anything that was on her mind?'

'Look, if you really want to know, this is how it went: Saturday night after rehearsals, we got back to the hotel and as we were waiting for the lift, she said she was going to skip dinner and go straight to bed because she wasn't feeling too well. I asked her if she was trying to give Ruby a heart attack by falling ill right before the show. And she said, no, she was saving that bit for when she would tell Ruby she was quitting the show. I said, what a great idea, I'd quit too; we could both quit together and sail off to the Bahamas for a week of sordid adultery. And she said sure, but we should ask Ruby and Jimmy to join us so we could make an orgy of it...'

He shook his head, blinked back tears. 'That's what I loved about her,' he said. 'That crazy sense of humour. She looked the Sati Savitri type, but she'd say the most wicked Savita Bhabi things. And with such a straight face, too. God, I'm going to miss her...!'

'I wonder what was really ailing her...' Niki mused, as she stepped out into the hotel lounge, moments later, with ASP Sahay.

'There was something going on, for sure,' Sahay agreed.

'I find it interesting that she talked about quitting the show.'

'You don't think it was just banter, boss?'

'Banter usually has its basis in something real, Shankar. It's possible she'd been thinking about quitting; that's why she mentioned it.'

'Or she could have just been flirting with Rajat. Think there was a little workplace romance going on between them?'

'Not last Saturday night,' Niki said. 'Mala went up to her room alone after rehearsals, by all accounts.'

'And yet I picked up a definite vibe back there. Especially when Rajat mentioned she was always texting "Dear Joseph". Reeked of jealousy.'

'Speaking of "dear Joseph",' Niki looked at her watch.

'His flight should be getting in soon,' Sahay concluded.

The constable posted at the hotel's main entrance straightened as he saw the officers striding towards him. 'Ma'am, sir,' he saluted, holding the door open for them. 'The media...' he warned.

The restless crowd gathered outside, being kept at bay by a couple of baton-wielding, vigilant constables, sprang to life as Niki and Shankar stepped out.

'Ma'am, sir, one moment please,' a voice called out.

'What did you find?' another asked.

'Why aren't we being allowed to speak with the *Hot Chef* people?' a third complained.

'Oh, for heaven's sake!' Sahay exclaimed.

Niki shot a cautionary look at him. 'This is an ongoing investigation,' she said, turning to face the crowd. 'Please give us time; we'll let you know as soon as we have any leads. Thank you.'

'Media!' Sahay said, as moments later Ramesh drove the Jeep down the Mall road towards Jubberhatti Airport.

'It's a big story, Shankar; they're all hungry for information.'

'And they'd have it – if they just let us do our jobs in peace!'

'Their job is to make sure we do ours well,' Niki reminded him gently. 'Not necessarily "in peace".'

14

A quiet, air-conditioned hush marked the newly commissioned forensics lab in Shimla. Behind the glass-paned walls, white-coated technicians worked quietly, peering into microscopes, labelling tubes, computing and tabulating results on hi-tech computers.

Inspector Pande stood a moment soaking in the monochromatic environs, the sterile air, and felt a deep sense of bliss. The forensics lab was his temple, his meditation centre; it had the same effect on him that scented candles and body massages had on other people.

'We received a package from the hospital containing the personal effects of the victim just a little while ago,' the lab manager said, stepping into the room behind him. 'I've asked my deputy to bring it out.'

He handed Pande a mask, a lab gown that didn't quite fit around the inspector's substantial belly and plastic covers for his hair and shoes. Then, all geared up, the two men pushed their way through a heavy steel door into a secluded area of the room marked, 'Restricted Entry, Hazardous Materials', where a lab technician was awaiting them, similarly clad. Beside him on a table was a small brown carton labelled: 'Personal effects of deceased MALA JOSEPH.' At the manager's signal, the technician broke the seal on the carton and stepped back.

Inspector Pande reached into the carton and carefully lifted out a pink silk dress. It was faintly creased, bearing the traces of an evening's wear. He went over the garment, top to bottom, front to back, while the technician took pictures, then put it down in the sterile tray next to the carton. No food stains, no visible trace, Pande noted. He reached into the carton once more and pulled out the next item – a pair of pink high-heeled sandals that still bore the faintest impression of Mala's small, dainty feet. Size four, he observed. Almost new.

In a small plastic bag covered in bubble wrap, he discovered a chunky bracelet in exactly the same shade as the dress, pink earrings, a necklace and a slim gold wedding band. 'M.J. Forever', the engraving read.

He put the items back in the plastic bag and turned his attention to the next object in the carton – a small black purse.

His eyes gleamed with anticipation as he lifted it out. It was light and fit easily in his hand; it had a tiny metal clasp that gave way under the slight pressure of his fingers to reveal a pink satin lining. Inside were three 1,000-rupee notes, four 500-rupee notes, two hundreds, a Visa and an Amex credit card, a nail file, a tiny cross, a Band-Aid and a pink lip balm.

Pande unscrewed the cap of the lip balm and sniffed it cautiously. It smelled faintly of raspberries. He replaced the cap, unzipped the tiny zipper compartment of the purse. Inside lay a single strip of pills, seven intact, one missing.

Very carefully, cauliflower nose quivering, Pande removed the strip of pills. The silver foil at the back of the missing pill was partly ripped, but the name of the drug was clearly visible. 'Fluoxetine Hydrochloride,' he read.

He put the strip back in the purse and the purse in the tray, then turned to the lab manager and the technician. 'Photograph everything,' he instructed, 'and then expedite a toxicology screen and fingerprints on all these items.'

'All of them? It might take a while,' the lab manager said.

'Well, then you'd better get started,' Pande grunted. 'Wasn't there also a mobile phone?'

The technician shook his head. 'This is all that the hospital sent us.'

'The victim had a smart phone with her at the time she died. Check again.'

Pande stepped back through the doorway and pulled off his gloves and gown. He waited for the bars to spring up on his mobile, then dialled his boss's number.

'We found the purse,' he said. 'There was a strip of pills inside. Prozac. One of the pills was missing.'

'Prozac?' Niki glanced at Sahay who sat beside her in the Jeep. 'Isn't that prescribed to treat depression?'

'Amongst other things,' Sahay murmured.

'What about her phone?' Niki asked Pande.

'No phone at the lab. We'll check again at the Gaiety,' Pande said. 'It's possible that it got misplaced in all the confusion.'

Or stolen, Niki thought, hearing the unspoken words loud and clear. 'Let me know as soon as you find it,' she said.

She hung up and sat back, a deep frown between her brows. Outside, the flat green expanse surrounding the Shimla airport swung into view.

'Problems, boss?'

'There's still no sign of the phone. It should have been there on stage or with her things. It could be a vital piece of evidence.'

'It could have her final words, even a suicide message,' Sahay mused. 'But boss, if she'd really texted someone, wouldn't the recipient have got it?'

'Let's hope so,' Niki said as the driver slowed to a halt.

The young man who stepped out from the airport terminal in dark pants and a navy sweater over a plain white shirt was smart and well turned out, even though he was not exactly Bollywood material. He had a bulging leather overnighter and laptop case in one hand, a mobile phone in the other. He stowed the phone away in his pants' pocket as he walked uncertainly out into the midday sun, turning his head this way and that. His dark sunglasses flashed in the sunlight as he scanned the crowd of relatives, taxi drivers, chauffeurs and hangers-on.

'Joseph! Joseph Albert!'

A flashbulb went off as he looked up in the direction of the voice. A young man stepped forward with a mike. 'What is your reaction to the news of your wife's death?'

'Did you know if she was carrying cyanide?' another called out.

'Look this way, profile please!' a man with a camera directed, as another flashbulb went off.

'Step away!' A voice bellowed from behind them.

The man looked up gratefully at the officer who pushed through the crowd, glaring at the journalists and cameramen. He turned as he felt a gentle tap on his arm and looked up to meet a pair of dark, sympathetic eyes.

'Mr Albert? I'm SP Marwah of the Shimla Police,' the woman murmured. 'Please come with me.'

Sahay was still glowering as Niki led Joseph towards the parking lot. 'Shameless, just shameless!' he muttered under his breath. He noticed Joseph glance nervously at him. 'Oh, hello,' he said and held out a hand. 'I'm ASP Sahay. We spoke last night. Sorry about that back there. It's hard to keep those guys at bay. Freedom of the press and all.'

Joseph clasped the ASP's outstretched hand and grimaced as a cringingly cheery ringtone resounded from inside his pants' pocket. 'Excuse me,' he said. He took out his phone and put it to his ear with a harassed air. 'Yes, yes, Mom, I'm here. Yes, I'm fine. I'll call you when I've seen her. Yes, I promise. Don't cry, don't cry, please! It'll be fine, you'll see. No, don't answer the phone or the door; just lie down and try to get some sleep, okay?'

He hung up and turned to the officers. 'That was Mala's mother,' he sighed. 'She's been in bad shape ever since I told her Mala had collapsed... You're sure it's Mala, right? Maybe there's some mistake?'

'Her colleagues on the show confirmed it was her,' Niki said, her voice filled with regret. 'But I know you'll like to see for yourself.'

She led the way to the waiting Jeep.

'Shall we go?' she prompted, as he gazed uncertainly at her. 'To the hospital?'

'Oh yes! Of course! That's best, maybe, in case there's been some mistake…'

He sank into the seat beside her with a weary sigh and took off his sunglasses. His eyes, Niki noticed, were tragically hopeful.

Half an hour later, those same eyes were dull, reddened and constricted with pain as Joseph stepped out of the morgue at Shimla Medical.

Niki felt her heart go out to him. He took a few unsteady steps towards her, reaching out to the wall to support himself, his face distorted in grief. 'My God,' he whispered, sagging against a nearby pillar. 'My God…'

A loved one gone, never to return, and the prospect of carrying on without her… It was the most difficult thing a human being could be called upon to contend with, Niki knew. She waited for the first, heavy tide of his grief to abate; then, when his chest had stopped heaving and his body had ceased to shudder, she led him to a quiet corner in the waiting lounge. He sank down on the plastic chair and took a tentative sip from the cup of coffee that the constable, under Sahay's instructions, had brought over.

'Vending-machine coffee,' Joseph murmured. 'How Mala hated the stuff!' He caught himself as Sahay frowned. 'I'm sorry! I didn't mean – I mean, this coffee is fine; it's just that Mala hated it. I mean, she loved coffee, but only black – no milk, no sugar – and God forbid we ever ran out.' He took another sip from the cup and drew a sighing, ragged breath. 'She was so easy-going about the big things in life and so particular about the small things! Where I bought the fish, where I parked my scooter, how I made her morning cup of coffee… Oh she gave me such a hard time if I got her coffee wrong!' He shook his head, gazing down with unseeing eyes at the pattern in the hospital's tiled stone floor. 'To think that yesterday was the fifth anniversary of the day I proposed to her…

'I was supposed to be here, you know. I was going to fly in and surprise her. Take her out for dinner, sightseeing… But then this last-minute business trip to Dubai came up.' He shook his head, fresh tears starting in his eyes. 'I was on the flight back home last night. We'd barely touched down when you called. How could this happen?'

'That's what we're trying to understand,' Niki said. 'Did your wife mention any problems, anything that was troubling her?'

Joseph shook his head.

'Was she suffering from depression?' Sahay asked.

'We found some Prozac in her purse,' Niki added.

'Yes, she's been on Prozac for a while,' Joseph said. 'Dr Dastur said she'd taken to it really well.'

'Dr Dastur?'

'At Breach Candy. Everyone says he's one of the best mental-health specialists in Mumbai. He started her on Prozac two months ago and she'd been so cheerful and energetic ever since; just like her old self all over again…'

Joseph rubbed his temples wearily with the palms of his hands. A slim gold wedding band on his ring finger flashed momentarily in the overhead lights. 'She'd been under so much stress lately,' he sighed. 'Of course, *Hot Chef* was the most wonderful thing that could have happened to her, but it came at such a price! Long hours, exhausting schedules, constant media scrutiny – they took their toll on her. She wasn't eating, wasn't sleeping; she was tired and anxious all the time. Dr Dastur said it was not uncommon amongst people with high-profile careers, that a few months on Prozac would put her right back on track.'

'And was she taking her medicine regularly?' Niki asked.

'Yes, as far as I know.'

'Did she happen to mention feeling unwell lately?' Sahay asked. 'Did she mention being unhappy at *Hot Chef*? Did she ever talk about quitting the show?'

'Quitting?' Joseph shook his head. 'No, she loved *Hot Chef*. Why do you ask?'

'Apparently, she told Rajat Tripathi that she might quit.'

'They must have been joking around,' Joseph said, a flash of annoyance passing momentarily across his face. 'They were always talking nonsense when they got together, she and Rajat. He's quite a loose screw. But Mala was fond of him for some reason.' It was clear from his voice that he couldn't fathom why. 'But no, she was very happy at *Hot Chef*. And she'd have told me if she wanted to quit. She told me everything. What was going on at work, what she was thinking, even what she had to eat for breakfast. We were always in touch, wherever we happened to be. And even though we both travelled a lot, we made time for each other. We Skyped, we called, we texted… See.' He reached in his pocket, fished out his phone and pressed a couple of buttons. His gaze grew teary as he glanced at the phone's screen.

'May I?' Niki asked.

Joseph turned his phone around and held it out. Niki looked down at the conversation thread on the screen.

'Happy anniversary, sweetheart!'
'You too!! Wish you were here.'
'How's shimla?'
'Beautiful. Just walked past scandal point. Nothing scandalous about it.'
'Like otter's club, where there are no otters!'
'☺ we'll start shooting soon. Have to run'
'Me too. They just announced boarding.'
'Call when you get there.'
'Good luck with the show. Xoxo.'
'Xoxou2'

Niki looked at the time stamp for the last message. It had been sent at 5.15 p.m.

15

The late afternoon clouds were gathering; the steep hill roads bustling with pedestrians, cyclists, tourists and shoppers, all soaking in the remaining hours of sunlight, before the evening chill set in. Niki felt her stomach grumble; she glanced at the clock on the wall as she strode into her office. Two-twenty p.m.! No wonder she was starving. She hadn't had anything to eat since that bowl of cold cereal she'd gulped down at six in the morning. She should have stopped by Joginder's. But then, where was the time?

'Hungry?' she asked Sahay.

'I could eat this thing whole,' Sahay said, picking up her paperweight and giving it an appraising look. He reached for her thermos of tea. A few stale drops trickled down the spout into the plastic cup he held under it.

Niki picked up her phone. 'Pradeep? Can you get me a fresh thermos of chai and a pack of biscuits, please?'

'I can do a little better, ma'am.'

Moments later, one of the peons tapped on the door and walked in, a large tray in hand. Niki gaped as he set it down on her desk. On it, in addition to the fresh thermos of chai and pack of biscuits she had asked for, were plates, spoons, napkins, a platter stacked high with steaming parathas, a large bowl of thick, creamy yoghurt and three smaller ones with mango pickle, green chillies, butter.

'Pradeep?' Niki said, blinking at her PA as he followed the peon in with the day's mail and a file marked 'Immediate Attention'.

'Inspector Chauhan had called, ma'am. She asked me to order parathas from Joginder's for you.'

'Where is Inspector Chauhan?'

'Still at the Wood Pines, ma'am.'

'Have her come to my office as soon as she returns.'

Niki pulled forward the pile of papers, rolled up her shirtsleeves and sank down in her chair. She reached for a paratha, broke off a bite and popped it into her mouth, chewing hungrily, while Sahay folded his own into a neat roll and took a discreet bite. She was on her second paratha and third file when there was a tap on the door.

'Deepika,' Niki said, as Inspector Chauhan stepped in. 'God bless you. Sit down, grab a plate.'

'Thank you, ma'am, but I ate earlier.' She looked at ASP Sahay. 'There are also some gulab jamuns in the pantry, sir.'

'Boss, Inspector Chauhan needs a commendation. Right now.'

Niki grinned and polished off the last of her paratha. 'Deepika,' she said, 'what have I done to deserve you?'

Inspector Chauhan looked down at her hands, her face pink with pleasure. She could have mentioned a hundred things and more that her boss had done, but knew that she would never be able to bring herself to say them. So she coughed discreetly and recounted, matter-of-factly, the testimonies she had spent all morning collecting. 'We've been making good progress,' she said. 'The *Hot Chef* crew is quite shaken, but they've been cooperating.. We should be done with all the statements by the evening.'

'Anything worth a second look?'

'Well, ma'am, one of the make-up girls, Tina Sethi, mentioned that Mala looked a bit pale before the shoot. But when she questioned her about it, Mala just brushed it off, saying it was just a touch of altitude sickness; that she never did well in the mountains. Tina said she wished she'd probed further, since she got the feeling something more was going on.'

'Did she have any idea what it could be?'

'No, ma'am. She said whatever it was must have been personal. Mala got along extremely well with every one on the show. In fact, according to Tina, Mala was quite a favourite amongst the crew.'

Niki nodded thoughtfully. It was a consistent picture of a personable young woman, a popular co-worker, with no apparent problems other than a touch of altitude sickness. And yet there was something about it that didn't ring true...

'Did you talk to Mistry about the camera tapes from last night's show?' she asked.

'Yes, ma'am. I had the tapes sent over to the AV Department, but the supervisor there, Inspector Ganguly, told me that they would need special equipment to play back the footage. He'll only be able to set it up by the evening. He did say he'd try and have a couple of technicians go through it overnight.'

'So, hopefully, we'll have something by tomorrow... Did Mistry or any of the other technicians or crew have anything to say about what happened last night?'

'No one noticed anything amiss, ma'am. I talked to each of the cameramen, especially the two who were covering the judges' table. They couldn't recall seeing anything that looked suspicious either on the table or in Mala's vicinity. We'll know more when we go over the tapes.'

'What about Agrawal, the kitchen manager? Did you talk to him?'

'Yes, ma'am. He was in bad shape, though.'

'How so?'

'He was very upset. Kept saying that it was his fault. That he was manhoos and Yamraj was following him everywhere. That none of this would have happened if he hadn't joined the show; that Ruby Madam would fire him now for sure.'

'Great,' Sahay said. He finished his last bite of paratha and wiped his fingers carefully with a napkin. 'So all we have to do now is arrest him, wrap up the case and go home and get some sleep.'

'If only,' Niki sighed. 'What exactly did he mean when he said Yamraj was following him?'

'Well, before joining *Hot Chef*, he was working as an assistant chef at a hotel in Haridwar, ma'am. He moved there after a year at a hotel in Varanasi. Before that, he was working at a hotel in Vrindavan.'

'So his speciality is religious destinations,' Sahay said. 'Not my career of choice, but I can't see anything "manhoos" about it.'

'Apparently, it was Haridwar that got to him, sir. He said he could handle the constant stream of the bereaved, but when the management asked him to develop a "cremation special" menu he started to see Yamraj in his dreams. That's when he decided he'd had enough. He quit the hotel and headed straight to Mumbai. He claims he joined *Hot Chef* because he was sure nothing could be further from Yamraj than working with energetic youngsters.'

'Except, Mala has died.'

'Yes, sir. Agrawal said Yamraj had followed him from Haridwar and taken Mala to punish him.'

'Wonder if we can put Yamraj behind bars...'

'The man is obviously still shaken up by last night's events,' Niki said.

'That's what I think, ma'am.'

'Did he mention anything about the previous incidents?'

'No, ma'am, he didn't know much about the short circuit or the set collapse. But he did seem to have an ongoing grouse against the pest-control company. Said they were careless and always in a hurry; that's why he always watched over them like a hawk and checked carefully after they were done. He said that there was no way they could have "accidentally" left a jar of poison in his pantry.'

'What about the cyanide last night?'

'Ma'am, he was very emphatic about that too. Said there was no way the cyanide could have come from his pantry. In fact, I grilled him for a long time about procedures and safety last night. He maintained that he always followed best practices, whether in Mumbai or in Shimla. He showed me his logbook, where he has been recording all purchases with invoices, dates and times, as well as a daily record of all items that are taken out of the pantry. He also said that he always did a stock check at the end of each episode, as well as a thorough cleaning of the pantry, but last night he couldn't – because of what happened.'

'And who else besides Agrawal had access to the pantry yesterday?'

'The kitchen staff, the theatre-cleaning staff and the food-prep crew. Also, the show's producer, director and host and the six contestants.'

'That's a lot of people.'

'Yes, ma'am. But the only people with keys to the pantry were Ruby Talwar and Agrawal.'

'And he kept the store locked?'

'Except when there was a rehearsal or a shoot on. He said there was too much coming and going during a shoot to lock the door.'

'So last night…?'

'The pantry was locked until 4 p.m. It was open access after that.'

'So anyone could have tampered with the ingredients during this time.'

'Yes, but Agrawal maintains that he was there the entire time.'

'And what about that guy who makes the tea?' Niki asked. 'Abbas? Did you speak with him?'

'Yes, ma'am. A.R. Abbas. He's a long-time studio employee; said he'd been serving tea and coffee since the days of Ramanand Sagar's *Ramayan*. He claims to know the particular likes and dislikes of every single person on television; in fact, he maintains that once he's served tea or coffee to someone, he remembers their drink forever.'

'And did he remember what he served and to whom last night?'

'Yes, ma'am. He said he'd brewed fresh coffee for Mala, who always had it black and strong, no milk or sugar, and he made green tea for Ashika, no sugar or milk either. And KK always has orange pekoe steeped for four minutes with a little milk and three sachets of sugar. Abbas said he prepared the beverages fresh during the break, before the tasting segment, poured them into the cups, placed them on the tea tray, along with a pot of hot milk and a bowl of sugar for KK, and then brought the tray out and placed it in the centre of the tasting table right before tasting started.'

Niki turned to Sahay. 'Refresh my memory,' she said. 'What was on that table when Mala collapsed?'

'Plates, knives, forks, napkins, bottles of water,' Sahay said. 'Tea tray, cup of black coffee, cup of green tea, cup of orange pekoe, milk pot, bowl full of sugar sachets.'

'All it took was two grams,' Niki said, chewing on the tip of her pen. 'That's the problem, isn't it? Anyone could have slipped two grams of cyanide in any of the items.'

'Or she could have brought it with her in her purse.'

'But the question I keep coming back to is: why? Why would Mala kill herself? Why would anyone else want to kill her?'

She turned to Deepika. 'Inspector Chauhan, we need to work on background information on Ms Joseph. Let's start checking out her friends and family, agent, neighbours... See if you can find anyone who had reason to wish her ill, anyone who benefits from her death. Also, give Dr Dastur at Breach Candy a call. Ask him about Mala's mental health and if she'd mentioned anything that had been troubling her lately.'

'Yes, ma'am.'

'And pull together all the information you can find on *Hot Chef*.

The judges, the producers and directors, the contestants. I want to know what goes on behind the scenes and off camera. Who are the big personalities, the main stakeholders; what are the politics and who, if anyone at all, could have wished Mala harm. Also, follow up with the Crime Division and see if they've found any red flags on any member of the show's cast and crew.'

'I'll have a team start working on it right away.'

'Thank you.' Niki got up, shrugged on her blazer and picked up the folders and papers she'd been initialling.

'Going somewhere, boss?' Sahay asked.

'The Madison,' Niki said. She walked out of her office, stopping by Pradeep's desk to hand him the papers. 'I'll be back by six,' she told him. 'Get all the teams together for a meeting in the Briefing Room, please.'

'So we're meeting the stars of the show,' Sahay mused, joining her. 'The future "Hot Chefs". Think one of *them* might have had a hand in it?'

'They were the ones who prepared the food,' Niki said, as she skipped down the steps. 'And it's their futures that are at stake.'

16

The Madison, the latest in a spate of ultra-premium Shimla hotels, was set high on a hill amidst a thick cluster of pine trees, giving the property a feel of tranquillity and timelessness. It had a discreet entryway off the road to Kufri and from there a long, wooded driveway wound up the hillside for a good half-kilometre before it ended in a small reception area outside a sprawling brick bungalow. A nervous-looking young man, who introduced himself as Rohit Sharma, the Hospitality Manager, stood waiting outside to greet them. 'The *Hot Chef* guests' bungalows are farther up,' he said, pointing to what looked like the summit of the hill. 'It would be best if we drove up there.'

He climbed into the Jeep and Ramesh revved the protesting vehicle up the narrow, winding driveway past picturesque vistas and spacious cottages. Sahay read off the names of the cottages as they passed them:

Jankinivas, Ramnivas, Chitrakoot, Gokul, Krishnalok, Radhagram…

'You can stop right here,' Sharma instructed Ramesh, as two brick cottages, set far back along the crest of the hill, appeared on the horizon. He alighted from the Jeep and led the officers down the cobblestone path towards them. 'We've been asked to ensure complete privacy for the *Hot Chef* contestants,' he explained, as Sahay glanced at the tall trees on the grassy slopes that seemed to enclose them. 'In fact, we were asked to disconnect all phone lines, internet and cable TV connections and hold back all newspapers and magazines, too, until Ms Patel had vetted them.'

'Barkha Patel? The Contestant Manager?' Sahay asked.

'Very tough lady,' Sharma said. 'Of course, it's not easy shielding the contestants from the public, especially in light of last night's tragedy. The media have been calling all morning. Luckily, here at Madison we have lots of experience holding off the media and guaranteeing our guests complete privacy.'

He paused as they reached the first of the two bungalows. 'Lakshminivas,' Sahay read on the brass plate in the brick wall. The manager lifted the knocker on the door and let it fall with a sharp, heavy rap. Inside, a melodious chime rang out once, twice… Five times.

The manager shaded his eyes from the sun and shifted his weight from one foot to the other. 'Perhaps they are resting?' he said. He lifted the knocker once again and let it fall, then peered uncertainly through one of the frosted-glass windows that flanked the door.

'I'm not sure if I should disturb them.'

'Then allow me,' Sahay said, holding his hand out for the master card key.

'Oh no, of course, just that Ms Patel does not like to be disturbed…' The manager reluctantly slid the card in the lock and watched the light turn from red to green. He withdrew the card and pushed the heavy door gingerly back on its hinges.

'Hello?' he called, as he stepped in hesitantly. 'Ms Patel?'

The hallway was deserted, Niki observed, as she and ASP Sahay stepped into it, behind Sharma. It was done up in a rugged, log-cabin style, with dark wood floorboards, wood panelling on the walls and a barrel-vaulted ceiling with exposed beams. There were tall windows at the far end through which the afternoon sunlight slanted in, painting elongated rectangles on the floor.

'Ms Patel?' The manager called again, his voice echoing in the empty space. He walked to a set of French doors at the back of the hallway to the right and looked out. 'She's outside,' he said in a relieved voice. 'I think she's sleeping.'

'Then let's wake her up,' Sahay said. He slid the door open and stepped out onto a large brick patio. The stout woman who lay asleep on the cane sofa under a bright green umbrella, magazine in lap, opened an eye.

'Ms Patel?' the manager said, stepping forward hastily. 'Sorry to disturb you, ma'am. The police are here, ma'am.'

'Ms Patel, I'm ASP Sahay of the Shimla Police,' Sahay said shortly. 'And this is the Superintendent of Police, Ms Marwah. We have some questions for you.'

The woman lowered her feet reluctantly to the ground. 'I'll go round up the contestants,' she said, suppressing a yawn.

'If we may have a word with you first?' Niki said.

'Me? I wasn't even there!'

'I have a few questions about the contestants,' Niki said. 'I understand you're the best person to ask.'

'I could write a full Mahabharata about them.' Barkha sighed and sank back in her chair. 'Care for some tea?'

'No, thanks.'

'*I'll* need tea,' Barkha said, turning to the manager. 'And maybe this time you could try to send it before it freezes?'

'Yes, ma'am, sorry, ma'am, right away, ma'am,' Sharma fawned, before hurrying away.

'I wasn't even there last night, like I said,' Barkha said, once she was alone with the officers. 'Rehearsals and tapings are the only times when the contestants are *not* my responsibility. So yesterday evening was my precious time off. Binod was supposed to be at the Gaiety to escort the contestants back after the taping.'

'And where were you?' Sahay asked.

Barkha stuck out her large feet in their chunky brown sandals for his inspection. 'The spa,' she said, wiggling her shiny red toenails in his startled face. 'Manicure *and* pedicure. And then I came back here. There is nothing like having the whole place to yourself, you know. I'd forgotten what it was like. No drama, no showdowns, no petty arguments. Just silence...' She sighed wistfully. 'I was planning to fall asleep watching *Golmaal* in my room, when Binod called and told me to rush to the hospital. It was 3 a.m. before I saw my bed again!'

'You escorted the contestants back here?'

'Had to. And calm them down, sort them out, pander to their nonstop nakhras!' She shook her head sorrowfully. 'It's tragic, what happened to Mala, I agree, but I was really looking forward to a break, you know. It's a thankless enough job, as it is, minding these villains. Nothing but trouble, the lot of them.'

'Why do you say that?'

'Well, they're all young and ambitious and they all want to win. The money, the fame, the fans – they want it all. That's why they're here. That's why they've put their lives on hold, left their friends and families, done just about everything to get here. I suppose you can't blame them for trying every trick they can in order to win.'

'What kind of tricks have they been trying?' Sahay asked.

'Every kind that I know of!' Barkha snorted. 'And I know of many; I have a Master's degree in psychology. They think I'm just a fat fool and that I have no idea what they're up to, but I can see right through them. I know they'd all happily slit each other's throats if they had to. Even that sweet, saintly Leena... The sly look she gets in her eyes when she thinks no one is watching! Oh, there are years of pent-up frustration behind those wide, innocent eyes of hers...'

'I understand she's one of the most talented contestants on the show?' Sahay asked.

'Yes, but you need more than talent to win in the real world and Leena knows it. And Pallavi, who's got both talent *and* pedigree, knows it too. For all her London and Paris training, she's basically got the instincts of a street cat. And she needs them, now that she's on the streets herself.'

She leaned forward with a confidential air. 'Her uncle, B.S. Aanand, the group Chairman and CEO, has cut her off from the family fortunes,' she said. 'Because of the father. Complete loser type! Drink, drugs, women, gambling – you name it, he's done it. And after the embezzlement scandal last year, the family cut him off entirely. He stole crores, apparently. God knows where the money went. I heard Pallavi was waiting tables in New York to pay off her debts and buy a plane ticket back home...'

Barkha sat back with a spiteful smile on her face. 'She likes to pretend that she's still Miss High and Mighty, but unless she wins *Hot Chef*, she's just a nobody like everyone else. Or, actually, a nobody who *used* to be somebody, which is even worse.'

She looked up as the patio doors slid open and a waiter appeared, oversized tea tray in hand. He set down a cup of thick, steaming tea, along with a plate of chocolate wafers, a bowl of cashews and a large platter of pakoras. Barkha tested one of the pakoras with a frown. 'They're cold,' she told the waiter.

'Sorry, ma'am, I'll get some more – '

'Yes, but you can leave these!' Barkha snapped and the waiter hastily let go of the platter.

'Idiot!' Barkha muttered, as the man scurried away. She selected a pakora and bit into it. 'So where was I?' she asked Niki, chewing absently.

'Pallavi Aanand.'

'Oh yes. Spiteful little brat. But she's got talent, that's for sure. Unlike Sharon Sen. They call her Ms InSen, you know. And with good reason...' Barkha took a long, noisy sip of her tea, frowned and reached for a sachet of sugar.

'We heard she ripped her dress last night,' Sahay said.

'We should be grateful she didn't rip someone else's dress,' Barkha tittered. 'That girl is certifiably mad. Sad story, actually. Mother was unstable; they say she died of complications from drug addiction. And father, unknown. There was a stepfather, but he died when Sharon was thirteen. Sharon and her sister were both shipped off to live with some relatives after that.' She stirred the sugar into her tea and took another sip. 'Sharon's a fighter, though. The kind of person who'll do anything and everything to survive...'

Barkha reached for another pakora, popped it whole between her slightly protruding teeth. 'And then we have the boys,' she said, munching steadily. 'Charming devils, one and all. I wouldn't turn my back to any of them, even for a minute.'

'And why is that?' Niki asked.

'Because they're capable of anything, given half a chance. Take Dev Nair. Handsome boy, but so far luck's not been with him. He was auditioning for three years, before he got this break on TV. Can you imagine? Three years of grovelling and rejection and ridicule, before he gets in front of an audience. And now that he has this chance, I'm sure he'll do whatever it takes to stay in the game long enough to get that golden Bollywood film offer. I would, if I were him. Especially if I were as lousy a cook as he is. I heard that the dish he made last night was complete garbage.'

'And Shaqeel,' Barkha continued. 'They call him "Shaq" on the show. And rightly so. One never knows what's going on behind that smooth façade of his. He grew up working in dhabas, you know; his parents died when he was young. God knows when and where he went to school. But look at him now, speaking English and standing shoulder-to-shoulder with all these public school types, even beating them all, week after week.'

She harrumphed, but there was a grudging admiration in her voice all the same. 'He's destined for great things, that boy,' she said. 'But he scares me. He might smile and laugh with the rest of them, but he's seen a dark life. And for all his "cool" ways and easy-going manner, I know that that darkness is still there in him.

'And then you have Vicky Gulati.'

'Isn't he the youngest contestant?' Sahay asked.

'And probably the most dangerous one of the whole lot.'

'How so?'

'Well, he's brilliant, he's charming and he's completely unpredictable.

He comes from a very good family, actually; both parents are doctors, gold medallists. Vicky's very intelligent, but he's a troublemaker. He got expelled from boarding school in Class X, topped the CBSE Board exams in Class XII. All-India rank 9.' She shook her head in disbelief. 'He joined medical college after that, but then, just four months later, he was rusticated. Then he was hanging out in Mumbai for a while, working as a waiter at one of these new-age restaurants and playing in a rock band at night. And then six months ago, for some inexplicable reason, he auditioned for *Hot Chef*...'

'Why inexplicable?'

'I don't think he really cares about winning,' Barkha said. 'I think he's in it for something else.'

'Such as?'

'I have no idea, which is what worries me.'

'Why, has he been behaving erratically?' Niki asked.

'Oh no, he's been an angel! But I have a feeling it's just a matter of time before something blows up...'

Barkha set down her cup and polished off the last of the pakoras. 'It's not like I'm saying any of the contestants had anything to do with what happened to Mala last night,' she said. 'Why would they? They all liked her, as far as I can tell. Now if KK had been poisoned, it would be a different matter...'

'They don't like him?' Niki asked.

'Like?' Barkha snorted. 'No one likes KK. But they're all terrified of him. Every single one of them.'

'So we're amidst delinquents and assassins, if that woman is to be believed,' Sahay remarked drily once they were alone on the patio.

'Think she was exaggerating?'

'Seemed a bit paranoid, certainly. I feel sorry for those poor contestants.'

'One of them stands to win five crores,' Niki reminded him. 'A sum, to put things in perspective, you probably wouldn't have earned on your current salary even by your hundredth birthday.'

'When you put it that way...'

'Money is a powerful motivator,' Niki nodded. 'Especially for those in dire need of it.'

But was it a strong enough motivator for murder, she wondered.

'SP Marwah?'

Niki looked up to see Barkha stepping out onto the patio, slightly out of breath. Behind her were two young men, one as dishevelled as the other was neat, and a short, slightly plump girl who followed them out with an apprehensive look in her large, rounded eyes.

'I have Vicky, Shaqeel and Leena here for you,' Barkha said, indicating the trio with a peremptory sweep of her chubby arm. 'The other three have gone out with Binod. I'll have him bring them to you as soon as they return.'

'Thank you.'

'Enjoy,' Barkha told the three contestants with a sarcastic grin, before shuffling back into the cottage.

Niki turned to the youngsters with a smile. 'I'm SP Marwah and this is ASP Sahay of the Himachal Police,' she said by way of introduction. 'We know last night's been an ordeal for you, so don't worry, we'll keep it short. Please have a seat.'

So it's happening, Leena thought, as she took a seat on the sofa beside the SP. I'm being questioned by the police. She felt the perspiration start up in her armpits and forced herself to relax. She knew what she was going to tell them; she'd already gone over it in her head several times. And yet... She glanced sideways at Vicky, who was lounging easily in his chair. He had picked up one of the sugar packets that lay on the tea tray that the waiter had left behind and now he tore it open and poured its contents into his mouth.

'Are you okay?'

Leena realized with a shock that the SP's gaze was fixed on her face, on her fingers that were mauling the Ganpati pendant round her neck. She lowered her hand to her lap and balled it into a tight fist.

'Yes, I'm fine.' She forced a smile. 'I mean, considering last night...' She bit her lip and stared down at the patio floor. 'Is it true that Mala died of cyanide poisoning?'

'Yes.'

'But how? Where could it have – oh!' Leena recoiled as a wasp flew up from a nearby bush and settled on the tiny mound of sugar that Vicky had spilled on the table. Like lightning, Vicky's hand shot out and squashed it inside the paper packet he'd been playing with. He picked up the bruised insect, its legs still quivering, and crushed it slowly and surely between his fingers. He looked up to meet the SP's gaze on him.

'It's a trick Shaq taught me,' he said with the hint of a smile. 'Apparently, they get so delirious about the sugar, they forget to defend themselves.'

'I also told you not to *squash* them, because then it attracts more of them,' Shaq said.

'Which is why this little guy is going in my pocket.' Vicky slipped the sachet with the wasp into his pocket and held out his hands. 'See? No evidence, no crime.' He glanced at Leena who was staring at him, aghast. 'Arre, don't be such a darpok, yaar! It's just a wasp.'

Niki, who'd been silently watching the exchange, wondered how much of this was staged for her benefit and why. The guy liked to flirt with danger, he seemed to declare, and he didn't care who knew. In fact, it was almost as if he wanted her to know. Why?

'So about last night,' Sahay said, turning back to Leena. 'We believe that Mala consumed the cyanide very shortly before she collapsed. Right after she tasted the dishes that you all had prepared, in fact.'

'But there was nothing in any of our dishes!' Leena said. 'I tasted my Thai curry myself. It was fine.'

'Actually, it was more than fine,' Vicky said. 'Mala said it was "delightfully succulent", KK said it had the "perfect degree of spiciness", and Ashika said she loved the lemongrass shoots, that she could eat a bowlful of them alone.'

'Leena was a big hit last night,' Shaq told the officers with a smile. 'Vicky too.'

'I made enchiladas,' Vicky shrugged. 'Not my best creation, but not my worst either. Definitely not poisoned.'

'Mala said they were sublime,' Leena said.

'She didn't think my teriyaki lamb was either succulent or sublime,'

Shaq said. He turned to the officers with a rueful smile. 'But I knew that before I even tasted it. The flame had been too hot while I was cooking it and there was nothing I could do about it. The meat dried out.'

'That was just bad luck,' Leena said.

'I've had worse things happen to me.'

'Shaq here is the King of Cool,' Vicky said playfully. 'He tried to slit his throat last night with three spinning knives. Too bad he didn't succeed with even one of them.'

'*My* knives the world can see, my friend,' Shaq said. 'Whereas you keep yours hidden.' He looked at Niki. 'I can assure you that there was no cyanide in my teriyaki lamb, ma'am.'

'What about any of the other items on the tasting table?' Sahay asked. 'Did you notice anything unusual when you went up to the judges' table and served your dishes?'

Leena shook her head. 'I went first,' she said. 'The table was clean.'

'And I went on after Leena and Pallavi,' Vicky said. 'The used plates had been cleared; the judges had new plates. There was nothing on the table besides water and the tea tray.'

'And did you notice anything out of the ordinary or out of place?' Sahay asked Shaq.

'I didn't see anything that looked like cyanide,' Shaq said, considering the question. 'There were clean plates and cutlery. Mala's bottle of water had been uncapped; the cap lay next to it; a third of the water had been drunk. Her cup of coffee was half-empty; it had a smudge of lipstick near the rim. KK had drunk most of his chai, too; the sugar packets he had used were in a small bowl. The milk pot was half-full. Ashika's cup of green tea had barely been touched, though; the tea bag was still inside. Also,' he added, 'there was a smudge of enchilada sauce on the edge of the tablecloth that was away from the cameras and a piece of coriander on Ashika's side of the table.'

'How do you know all this?' Leena marvelled.

'A good chef always knows where everything is.'

'A useful skill,' Niki observed. 'Do you know what was on the table during the final break? When Sharon had to leave the stage?'

'After Dev's coq au vin?' Shaq shook his head. 'The stage assistant cleared the judges' plates, but after that...' He shrugged. 'The lights went off.'

Vicky crossed one leg over the other and shook his head. 'It was very dark and we were seated at an angle behind the judges, about twenty feet away,' he said.

'I had my eyes closed all through that break, anyway,' Leena said. 'Just praying for it all to be over.'

'My eyes were open,' Shaq said.

Niki raised a brow.

'And what did you see?' Sahay asked.

'Well, I was seated at the end of the bench, closest to the judges' table, to Mala,' Shaq said. 'It was dark, but there was a little light reflecting off the video playing on the backdrop.' He looked into the distance with a faraway gaze, remembering. 'KK and Ashika were talking. KK was drawing something on a sheet of paper and Ashika was nodding as he said something to her. They were speaking too softly for me to hear them.'

'And Mala?'

Shaq sighed, his forehead creased with fine lines. 'She seemed a bit restless,' he said. 'She kept looking round, at the wings, at the others, at the audience. Then she took out her phone and bent over it; she seemed to be tapping on it. Then she just went still for a long moment. Her head was bent, her hands were clasped, like she was praying. I remember thinking, why is *she* praying? Then suddenly, she lifted her head, clapped her hand over her mouth and took a sip of her water. She was very still after that. And then, a few seconds later, she clutched her throat, half-rose in her seat and fell to the floor.'

'You *saw* all this happen?' Leena said, her voice a horrified whisper.

'Yes, even though I didn't understand what was going on at the time,' Shaq said.

His face was pale, Niki saw.

'Oh my God!' Leena said.

'That's rough, man,' Vicky said. He sat forward, cupped his hands below his chin. 'So you're saying she took out the poison and consumed it right there in front of you.'

'But why?' Leena cried. 'She was a winner of *Hot Chef*! And such an amazing cook! She had everything! And she always seemed so happy...'

'Not always,' Vicky said quietly. 'I saw her crying on Saturday.'

'When?' Niki asked.

'At rehearsals. Must have been four-thirty or so... I'd stepped outside for some fresh air and I saw Mala standing by the stone wall across the road from me.'

'And she was crying?'

'She had her back to me; she was leaning over the wall. And when she turned, I noticed she had tears coming down her cheeks. So I went up to ask if she was okay.'

'You *talked* to her?' Leena gasped.

'You spoke with a judge behind our backs?' Shaq said.

'Please, let him finish,' Niki said, holding up a hand for silence. She turned back to Vicky. 'What did she say?'

'Nothing. She just wiped her tears and told me to get back inside before Binod saw us and reported me for fraternizing with a judge.'

'Man, *I* should report you,' Shaq muttered.

'Hey, I saw someone I knew who seemed upset; I reacted spontaneously,' Vicky shot back. 'What would you have done in my place?'

'How does it matter?' Leena said sadly. 'She died anyway, didn't she?'

17

Niki sat back in the falling dusk and chewed thoughtfully on her pencil. Beside her, ASP Sahay updated his notes on his smart phone and checked his messages.

'So now we have two witnesses who saw her eat something from her purse,' Sahay murmured, putting his phone away. 'Seconds before she collapsed.'

'It could have been the Prozac,' Niki said.

'Or cyanide.'

Niki shook her head. 'It still doesn't add up,' she said, almost to herself. 'I know the testimonies seem to suggest that she had the cyanide in her purse, but I still find it hard to believe. Why would she?'

'She definitely had something on her mind,' Sahay said. 'Jimmy mentioned it, Tina noticed something was amiss, Vicky saw her crying. And she did tell Rajat that she wasn't feeling well...'

'But she didn't tell her husband. In fact, she didn't tell him anything. She merely said Shimla was beautiful. She went for a walk. She even bought a teddy bear!'

'Maybe something changed between then and Sunday night, boss? Maybe that's what she was texting about?'

'But to whom?' Niki got up and paced the brick patio, her brow furrowed. 'And where is this so-called text message? We're missing something, ASP Sahay. Something simple, yet critical.'

'Are you the police?'

Niki looked up at the owner of the penetrating, authoritative voice. The girl who'd spoken was tall, slim, beautiful. She stood in the doorway that led out onto the patio, subjecting the officers to a disdainful stare.

'Pallavi Aanand?' Niki guessed.

'And Dev Nair.' The girl let go of the French door and stepped out, dragging a handsome, hesitant young man along with her. 'Barkha said we had to talk to you.' She scowled to emphasize her displeasure at the task.

'SP Marwah and ASP Sahay!'

A short, beady-eyed man tumbled out onto the patio behind the two youngsters, hand outstretched, an ingratiating smile on his face.

'I'm Binod Bose, Assistant Contestant Manager,' he said. 'Barkha asked me to meet you here. Sharon went to freshen up; she'll join us shortly. But I have Pallavi and Dev here.' He turned to the two contestants. 'Now listen up,' he said, his voice high and officious, 'these two police officers want to ask you about what happened last night. Make sure you answer all their questions.'

Pallavi held her middle finger up in his face.

Dev smiled embarrassedly. 'How can we help you, ma'am, sir?' he said, turning to the officers.

'Have a seat,' Sahay said, indicating a nearby chair. He looked at Binod, who was making himself comfortable on the sofa. 'Mr Bose, could you wait inside, please? We'll take your statement later.'

'Oh,' Binod said, looking rather crestfallen. 'Okay, I guess I'll go check on Sharon, then.'

Sahay waited for him to leave, then turned to the two contestants. 'So, as Mr Bose explained, we have a few questions for you.'

'And we have a few questions for *you*,' Pallavi shot back.

'Certainly,' Niki said, unruffled. 'What would you like to know?'

'Well, you're supposed to be the "police", right? Here to *protect* and *serve*? So how come there was this whole "gas attack" tamasha? We were locked up like sardines in that green room forever, terrified for our lives. Not to mention the complete chaos at the hospital! Such a commotion, over *nothing*!'

'We had to take those steps to ensure your safety, in case there actually *had* been a gas attack,' Sahay bristled. 'You should be thankful there wasn't. And I wouldn't call Mala Joseph's death "nothing".'

'Yes, and how did she die? How come you couldn't protect Mala? How could a normal, healthy person like her drop dead in the middle of a show, just like that?'

'You tell us; you were there.'

'I know. I *was* there. Which means, it could just as easily have been *me* who died! Someone has to take responsibility for what happened!'

'But if someone decides to kill herself, Pallavi, what can the police do?' Dev reasoned.

'How do you know she decided to kill herself?' Pallavi said.

'What else could it be?'

'Carelessness? Murder? Conspiracy? A hundred different things!'

'You're right,' Niki said. 'It could. And that's what we're here to try and find out. Do you have any specific reason to believe it was any of those things you mentioned?'

'I don't know,' Pallavi muttered. 'I just know that cyanide has no place in a food show. And that someone has to be held accountable. I mean, there is no security to speak of on this show! Anyone can walk on and off the sets – no IDs, no accountability. It's a bloody joke! And that pantry is like a railway platform; you're just a half-step away from typhoid and cholera. That Agrawal needs to be fired, like, yesterday.'

'Now that's not true, Pallavi,' Dev protested. 'The pantry's always been tidy. Agrawal does a very good job.'

'Then what was that "poison in the baking soda" all about? And what do you call last night?'

'Whatever happened,' Dev said, slightly flabbergasted, 'I'm sure it had nothing to do with Agrawal!'

'But how do you *know* that?' Pallavi insisted.

'Do you think the pantry manager tampered with the food last night?' Niki asked her.

'I'm just saying he *could* have.'

'But why would he?' Dev said.

'Money, what else? How much do you think he makes? Or those kitchen assistants who work for him? Prop boys? Cleaning crew? If the price were right, who knows what they'd be willing to do.'

'But who would bribe them?' Dev asked, perplexed. 'And why?'

'How would I know? *I* didn't kill her!'

'Let's go back to what we *do* know,' Niki said. 'Tell me about last night. Did you notice anything odd about the pantry or about any of the items that came from it?'

'No, how could I? I was focussed on my cooking,' Pallavi said sullenly.

'What about you, Dev?'

Dev shook his head.

'What about your coq au vin?' Pallavi said, turning to him. 'That was more than odd, I can tell you!'

'Now wait a minute,' Dev said, sitting up indignantly. 'Okay, so I burnt the chicken – we all know that – but it wasn't poisoned!'

'How can you be sure?' Pallavi said.

'Hey! Come on, this is not one of your high-society jokes, yaar!

It's a police investigation. Don't make me out to be some kind of a murderer in front of the police!'

'I'm not *making* you out to be anything,' Pallavi said. 'I'm just saying your chicken was the last thing Mala ate.'

Dev looked imploringly at Niki. 'Ma'am, please ignore what she's saying. I swear my chicken dish was – '

'Daarrlings! Did I miss something?'

The lilting voice that sailed out across the patio had Pallavi wincing, while Dev stopped mid-sentence. Niki turned round to see a voluptuous woman step out onto the patio and stroll leisurely towards them. She had shining almond-shaped eyes, a pointed chin and a heart-shaped face framed by a mane of lustrous hair that cascaded down to her hips. She wore black velvet sweatpants, a magenta ganji that seemed barely equal to the task of containing her sizeable breasts and a partially zipped-up black velvet hoodie. She was not classically beautiful, like Pallavi or Ashika, but Niki could guess that once she got in front of the camera she pretty much eclipsed everything and everybody else.

'We're being grilled by the police,' Pallavi drawled.

'Lovely!' The woman beamed down at the officers. 'Sorry I'm late. I'm Sharon In-Sen.'

'SP Marwah and ASP Sahay,' Niki said, bemused, introducing herself and her deputy. 'Is that how you always introduce yourself?'

'No, but that's how people always refer to me. Not that I mind. Better insane than a royal pain,' she added, with a mocking look at Pallavi.

Sahay, who'd been gaping, shook his head, as if to clear it. 'So, Miss Sharon,' he said firmly, 'what can you tell us about last night?'

'I believe it was quite something,' was the wistful reply.

'Excuse me?'

'Mala's suicide. That's what you're talking about, right? I only wish I'd been there to see it.'

Sahay stared at her, nonplussed.

'Sharon, these people are the police,' Dev hissed. 'Be serious!'

'I *am* serious, caro mio. Suicide: it's the ultimate statement, the grand finale, the primal scream; it's the most complete act of empowerment, of total emancipation from society, from all established norms. Sort of like sticking your finger up life's ass, you know?'

Sahay wrinkled his nose in distaste at the image.

'What makes you think it was suicide?' Niki asked.

Sharon lifted her shoulders in an eloquent shrug. 'What else could it be? Murder?' She shook her head in disdain. 'No one on this show has enough brilliance to come up with that. Besides me, of course, but I didn't do it. How could I? I wasn't even there. I had a situation with my dress; it was a tad tight. Cheap made-in-China fabric. And then, as soon as I got up, the whole thing just ripped down the front. Next thing I knew, my boobies were hanging out. So I had to rush off the stage. They have a strict policy – no nips or pubes on YTV.'

She shook her head sadly, a dainty finger playing with a tendril of hair. 'To think I missed Mala's ultimate performance! I wish she'd waited till I came back. And she never even got to taste my dish! It was…mwaah!' She kissed her fingers. 'Imagine going out on Dev's coq au vin when she could have gone out on my paella instead!'

18

The sky was dark; the officers from the various divisions that had been working on the Mala Joseph case, some of them since the previous night, were gathered and waiting in the Briefing Room when Niki finally got back to the office. Present, in addition to Inspectors Pande and Chauhan, were Inspector Nagpal from the Anti-Terror Cell, ASP Mishra from Crime Division and ASP Bali from the lab. They got to their feet as SP Marwah swept in through the door, ASP Sahay in tow.

'Please take your seats,' Niki said. 'We've all had a very long day and Manoj wants me to speak with the Press again at seven. So let's just quickly look through the day's reports, take stock of where we are and plan to meet again tomorrow morning, shall we?'

She turned to Inspector Pande who sat across the table from her amidst a pile of photographs, peering at one, then the next, through a magnifying glass. 'Where are we on evidence collection, Inspector Pande?'

The Inspector put the photographs away reluctantly. 'The SOC teams have photographed and processed all the main areas of the Gaiety,' he said. 'The two auditoriums, halls, storage rooms, bathrooms, dressing rooms, back kitchen. Did you know there are secret passages and dungeons at the lower level? And a chamber where soldiers were held and tortured?'

'Did you find any evidence of it?' Inspector Nagpal asked.

'Didn't have time. But maybe one of these days, when one has some time off…' Pande pulled off his glasses and started to rub them absent-mindedly.

Sahay shifted in his chair and coughed.

Unmoved, Pande cleaned his glasses, put them back on his bulbous nose and peered down at his notes. 'We've processed the Gaiety,' he repeated, 'and we'll be wrapping up the area outside it by tomorrow afternoon. We've also searched the victim's hotel room and personal possessions and sent all relevant items to the lab.

'The victim's iPad and camera were sent to the Communications Division,' he continued. 'It had pictures and videos taken at various locations with family, friends and some of the show's cast. There were also emails to various parties. SP Baruah's team will be compiling a list of all emails sent and received in the past six months, as well as a list of associates.'

'Any useful leads?' Niki asked.

'Nothing at first glance. The Communications team will start going through it in more detail tomorrow.'

'What about her phone?'

Pande shook his head. 'We searched the entire theatre again,' he said. 'In the fifth row, we found a wallet stuck inside a seat, with four thousand rupees in it. Also, a pair of broken Prada sunglasses in the seventh row from the back, that looked like several people had stepped on it. And there was a diamond earring on the stage that was claimed by Ms Ashika De.'

'But no phone?'

'No phone.'

'It must have been there,' Niki said. 'We have two witnesses who saw Mala texting on it.'

'Looks like someone stole it,' ASP Mishra said.

'I have my men making enquiries in the grey market,' Pande said. 'We'll find out in case it shows up anywhere in Shimla.'

Unlikely, Niki thought with a rueful sigh.

'We sent one hundred and thirty-seven food items to the lab for testing,' Pande continued. He glanced at ASP Bali. 'I'm told it will be days, maybe weeks, before they can test them.'

'We're processing the personal effects and items collected from the main stage on a priority basis,' ASP Bali said. 'That alone will take till the end of this week.'

'Do we have any results yet?' Niki asked.

'We've examined the victim's purse and its contents,' ASP Bali nodded. 'The pills in the foil were fluoxetine hydrochloride, as labelled. Everything else tested negative for cyanide.'

'Does this mean there was no cyanide in the purse?' Sahay asked.

'No, it just means that if it was in the purse, it was well packaged.'

'It would have been well packaged,' Niki said. 'Whether it was in her purse or in someone else's.' She turned to Inspector Nagpal. 'Tell me, Inspector, how does someone get their hands on two grams of cyanide?'

'Well, ma'am, cyanide is mostly used for industrial purposes,' Nagpal said. 'In mining, electroplating and gold and silver plating. There are about thirty to forty bulk suppliers across the country – most of them in Maharashtra or Gujarat, a handful in Delhi, Bangalore and Hyderabad, two in Punjab. They sell the chemical in solid or liquid form, in denominations ranging from a hundred grams to a hundred kilos.'

'But we're talking about two grams.'

'A quarter teaspoon or a small pellet the size of a Crocin tablet,' Nagpal said with a nod, 'which could be found at any of the thousands of chemical-testing and research labs across the country, unfortunately, or in any of the scores of unregulated shops that supply them. Also at hospitals, and in school and college labs. Not to mention at any one of the thousands of jewellery manufacturers.'

Which meant it was next to impossible to track where the cyanide had come from, Niki knew. Unless they had a concrete lead. She turned to ASP Mishra. 'How are we doing on background information on the show's cast and crew?' she asked.

'We've been focussing on the local hires today, ma'am. No red flags so far. The information on the Mumbai people will take some time.'

Niki sighed. Background checks involved painstaking work, she knew. Excruciatingly slow, but they might get lucky if anyone popped up with a criminal record or dubious employment history...

'Also, look into the show's suppliers and studio contractors,' she said. 'Check if anyone has previously worked in research labs or has any connections with the jewellery industry.'

'Yes, ma'am.'

'I spoke with my contact in the Chembur Police, ma'am,' Inspector Chauhan spoke up. 'He said he'd check on the contractor and the electrician involved in the short circuit and set collapse and send a team to conduct a search of the sets as soon as possible. As early as Saturday, maybe.'

Niki tried not to despair. Saturday was five days away. But the Chembur Police had their own work to do.

'I also spoke with the owner of the pest-control company that services the *Hot Chef* sets,' Deepika continued. 'He insisted that their licences and papers were in order and all of his employees were certified and trained.'

'Which doesn't mean one of them wasn't negligent,' Sahay said.

'Just that we have no means of proving it,' Niki said. 'Any progress with the show's tapes?'

'The AV department has started going through them, ma'am.'

'Good. I'd like to see the segment of tape that captures the moments right before the final break.'

'I'll have them set that up for you as soon as possible, ma'am.'

'Thank you. And where are we on the post-mortem?'

'Dr Kaul will be performing the post-mortem tomorrow at noon, ma'am. He should be able to send us the results by the evening.'

Niki nodded, then looked at her watch. It was almost seven. Time to wrap up the meeting. 'So, to summarize,' she said, 'we've collected all the physical evidence from the crime scene, initiated cyanide tests and recorded all the witness statements. We've started going through the information and we've started running background checks on the witnesses.'

And come up empty-handed, Sahay thought glumly.

'Nice work, everybody.'

Shankar squinted up at his boss. She was smiling encouragingly at the tired, gloomy faces around her.

'This is not an easy case,' she said. 'But we knew that at the outset. What's important is that we're moving forward. That's what an investigation is all about – diligence, patience, tenacity. You keep checking off the leads; you keep narrowing down the possibilities; and you eventually get there. We've made a lot of progress today,' Niki continued, 'and we have plenty on our plate for tomorrow. So I'd suggest you all get a good night's sleep and I'll see you back here tomorrow morning at nine.'

She paused as Deepika's cell phone, which lay on the table in front of her, lit up and vibrated.

'Sorry, ma'am,' Deepika said, glancing down at it. 'It's from Dr Dastur's office in Mumbai. He was out of the office when I'd called earlier.'

'Answer it, please.'

Deepika lifted the phone to her ear and spoke quietly into it. Her eyes narrowed as she listened, then widened. 'Are you sure?' she said into the phone. She listened, frowning, for another minute. 'Yes, thank you; this is most helpful,' she said finally. 'Yes, I'll be in touch if I have any further questions.'

She hung up and turned to Niki.

'That was Dr Dastur, Mala Joseph's physician, ma'am. He just told me that Mala had tried to kill herself six months ago.'

'What!'

'She was admitted to the Emergency Room at Breach Candy Hospital after consuming a fatal dose of sleeping pills. She spent two days in the ICU and was put under Dr Dastur's psychiatric care after she was discharged.'

The room was silent for a long, loaded moment.

Then ASP Sahay's voice thundered, 'And Joseph Albert didn't so much as *mention* any of this?'

In a quiet room overlooking a grove of pine trees at the Regal Hotel in Shimla, Joseph Albert sat alone with his glass of Scotch and stared at the screen saver on his phone. It was a close-up of Mala, taken on their honeymoon. Her hair curled in damp tendrils along her scalp and her small forehead gleamed with perspiration. Her chin was tilted up; her nose shone in the sun; her eyes were half-shut against the glare; her smile...

Joseph took a sip of his drink and allowed that smile to settle inside him. It was a smile like no other, a crown jewel, a priceless diamond.

Tomorrow, they'd rip into that smile and destroy her forever.

He felt the sob catch in his throat. He focussed with fierce determination on the picture on his phone. He was not going to fall apart. *He was not.* He filled his glass again, to the rim this time, and tossed back a large gulp. He felt the fire rise to his eyes. His mind drifted to a hazier, happier time, to the day he'd proposed to her, with his knee on the cold church floor, a tiny ring in his pocket, his heart in his mouth. He'd been sure she'd say no. That it was too soon, that they were too unsuited, that he was too boring, that there was someone else... For how could it be any other way, with her so lovely and him so unworthy?

But he'd proposed anyway and she'd smiled – that lovely, heartbreaking, sphinx-like smile...

He jumped as the phone in his hands suddenly trembled and sprang to life. He felt his heart leap. *Could it be...?*

But the person calling him was not Mala, he saw. How could it be Mala? How could she call him when she was dead? SHE. WAS. DEAD. That smile on the screen saver he'd been staring at, the text messages he'd been reading over and over again, the voice messages he'd been listening to all day – they were just a mirage, a memory, a reality that had been snuffed out. Mala was *dead*; and his phone was just a tease.

It lit up and vibrated again; and Joseph gritted his teeth. It was evil, it was salt in his wounds, this phone. He wanted it to stop torturing him; he wanted it to go away, for it all to go away. He took another sip of his drink, and another until he had drained his glass.

The phone vibrated yet again.

He got to his feet and, with an anguished roar, flung the phone into the great emptiness that surrounded him.

He collapsed, sobbing, to the floor.

When the hotel manager opened the room door with the master key on the Shimla SP's express orders, he found the occupant lying curled up on the floor, tears pouring down his cheeks, alcohol on his breath, the remnants of a broken glass in his hand. He had a glazed look in his eyes when the manager turned him over. Then he curled up, buried his head in his knees and started to shake with sobs again.

The SP told the manager over the phone to make him comfortable and let him be.

19

It was past nine by the time Niki finally wound up and left the office. The hallways were empty, her footsteps echoed in the silence as she walked down the steps to the main entrance. She nodded wearily to the guard as he pulled the door open for her and braced herself as she stepped out, exhausted, into the chilled night air.

The wide sweep of the Ridge was deserted for the second night in a row, the lamp across the street still flickering in the expanse of inky darkness. The clouds that had been gathering since the late afternoon had thickened as the evening progressed to night; there was not a single star in sight at this late hour. Niki signalled to Ramesh, who pulled up her Thar from its parking spot and held the door open for her. Niki walked around to the driver's side, wished Ramesh a pleasant evening and slipped in behind the steering wheel with a grateful sigh.

She drove slowly down the familiar roads, past the little landmarks that marked her way home. It had been a gruelling twenty-four hours and she had been running on little else besides pure adrenaline. Now, finally alone at the end of the day, she felt a deep fatigue invade her limbs and cloud her thoughts. She straightened her shoulders resolutely and sat up, erect, behind the wheel. Another few minutes and she'd be home...

A nice, warm bath to wash away the tiredness, followed by a quick call to Kam who'd called twice earlier, and then to bed to black out or dream of Ram...

She sighed. It was past two in the morning in Italy now; too late to call him. Again. Perhaps it was just as well. She was too wound up from the day's events anyway. Hopefully Chitra, her goddess of a maid, would have kept a cosy fire going in the fireplace and Brij, her long-time cook, would have kept a simple dinner of her favourite peas pulao and chicken curry ready on the table. That was the upside of a well-run household, Niki reflected gratefully. Nothing for her to do once she got home but relax...

An hour later, fed, showered and changed into a pair of flannel pyjamas, feeling much more human with her favourite pashmina shawl wrapped around her shoulders, her fuzzy slippers on her feet, Niki padded into the lounge with a bowl of kheer and a mug of ginger-elaichi chai. She curled down on the settee in front of the TV, settled back against the oversized cushions and noticed the arrangement of fresh flowers that Chitra had placed on the end table. There was a note nestling amidst the curled rosebuds. 'Miss you. Ram,' it said.

Now, more than ever, she wished he were here, instead of thousands of miles away...

She put the note back amongst the flowers and lit the vanilla-scented candles that were afloat in the silver bowl on the table. She inhaled deeply as their soft aroma floated through the air, and reached for the TV remote, surfing channels before finally stopping at *Bollywood Buzz*. Nothing like the glitterati and their shenanigans, as Kam had just advised, to chase away the end-of-day blues.

She watched absently as the chirpy young reporter speculated on rumours of a rift between Ranbir and Katrina. Really? She'd had no idea they were even dating! And Akshay Kumar was the highest grossing actor last year... Well, good for him. Was Karan Johar going to sign Bong bombshell, Ashika De, for his next film? 'Rumours are rife that Ashika is one of the favourites in consideration for the lead role in KJo's next,' the reporter gushed. 'The movie will be based on the life of troubled film star Parveen Babi who, after attaining dizzying heights of stardom, died alone in her flat under mysterious circumstances – '

Niki frowned as one of the candles in the bowl flared up and then fizzled out and smoke rose from the blackened wick. She clicked off the TV and sat a moment, gazing at the blank screen in the sudden quietness of her empty bungalow. A pervasive sadness, one she had so determinedly kept at bay all day, rose up and engulfed her.

Mala Joseph, she thought with a heavy sigh. Meteoric, brilliant, full of promise. Now extinguished. She leaned her head back against the cushions and recalled, as she'd done countless times over the years, another tragic day, another inexplicable death...

Priti Grewal.

Bright-eyed, thick-haired, a year older than Niki and, in spite of her tiny frame, infinitely wiser. They'd been neighbours and inseparable; tiny, soft-spoken Priti and big, hearty-voiced Niki. Together, they'd tried out outrageous hairstyles and dubious face creams; together, they'd dressed up their dolls and beat up the neighbourhood bullies. Together, they'd climbed rickety trees and whispered about their fragile dreams – of becoming a movie star, a Nobel Prize winner, a discoverer of life on another planet...

Priti Grewal, Niki thought, with a pang that had not lost its intensity with the years. She'd been clever and funny and absurdly shy. She'd been all of fifteen years old when she'd jumped off her third-floor rooftop and broken her neck.

They never did find out why she had done it. They'd assumed she'd slipped, that she'd climbed onto the low railing trying to reach for a wayward kite, a runaway dupatta, a butterfly – she was always in such a hurry, so careless, the poor, blighted thing…

An open-and-shut case, the police inspector who'd come for a cursory visit had said. He'd advised them to raise the height of the railings on the balconies and gone away to file his report and leave the family to mourn in peace.

But Niki knew it was no butterfly or daydream that Priti had been chasing. She'd noticed the funny way her friend had been walking that morning, the redness around her eyes, the dark red patches on her neck and shoulders and under her bra straps that she had tried to pass off as an allergic reaction. No, Priti hadn't slipped that evening when no one was home except her uncle; she'd not been trying to reach for any kite.

Even at fourteen, Niki had known that. And even if it was suicide or an accident, someone else was responsible, almost as surely as if they'd pushed her over with their own two hands. Even if they had left no evidence; even though they had got away with it.

She'd been filled with an impotent rage back then, the rage of a powerless fourteen-year-old in a world where inconvenient realities were swept away with the morning dust and no one was allowed to ask awkward questions.

But she wasn't powerless now. It was her job to ask awkward questions. And uncover the truth. And make sure no one got away with it.

She got up from the settee and knelt over the extinguished candle. Inside the pool of molten wax, the wick was drowning. Niki stuck her finger into the hot pool and propped the wick up. She trimmed back its burnt tip. Then holding it up, she relit it, watching its small flame struggle and kick into life once again.

Mala Joseph, she vowed quietly. There's no way I'm going to rest without getting all the answers.

20

The next morning dawned dark and gloomy, with a thick fog that lay over the valley like a woollen blanket, enveloping peaks, engulfing trees and dissolving the silhouettes of the buildings, old and new, that sprouted all over the rolling hillsides. Nothing appeared to be moving outside; there were no people or shadows or even sounds; nothing but a white cottony mist that filled the air and floated all around.

Up on the third floor of the stately red building that presided over the Ridge and the Mall, the Superintendent of Police, Shimla, sat in her high-backed office chair, staring out her window. She watched the smoky puffs of down billow past, only to be chased by more smoky puffs of down, and wondered if the weather was in some way emblematic of the Mala Joseph case.

The truth was out there, obscured but undeniable, like the valley. There were several wisps and strands of evidence, fragments of information scattered about like pieces of a jigsaw puzzle. All she had to do was find the appropriate pieces, put them together the right way and the true story would emerge. Who? What? How? Why? The answers to all these questions were lying amongst these very fragments, hiding in plain sight – if only one knew where to look.

Mala had consumed two grams of cyanide on Sunday night, on stage, at the Gaiety. For now, these were the only facts Niki had to work with. Everything else was work in progress, unfortunately.

The sleeping-medicine overdose, the moodiness, the crying, the talk about quitting the show – they were all pointing in one direction.

The previous mishaps on the show, the lack of security and accountability suggested a different story.

And then there were the critical missing pieces, including any conceivable motive, any clear beneficiary…

Mala Joseph, who were you? What was really going on with you?

Niki poured a steaming cup from the thermos of chai that she'd had the foresight to bring with her, and started reading through the profile that the Crime Team had emailed over late last night.

Mala Mary Joseph, only child of Mary Elizabeth and Thomas Anthony Joseph. Born 28 February 1984, Kottayam, Kerala. Currently residing in Versova, along with her husband and mother. Father died of heart attack in March 2009.

She attended St. Joseph's Convent Girls' School in Kottayam, then MG University, where she got a BA in Home Economics and a Master's in Nutrition. She worked as a nursery school teacher in October 2008, then left in April 2009 after her father's death. On 15 July 2009, she married Joseph Albert and moved to Bangalore.

Niki sat back and pictured it. An only child, born and brought up in an all-girls school in a quiet, sleepy town. Life humming along on an even keel, till the father's demise. Then suddenly, three months later, married and swept off to live in a big, bursting metropolis. Bereavement, marriage, relocation – three huge, momentous changes in three short months. How would that have felt? Like a shot in the arm or a punch between the eyes?

It was telling that Mala had not taken up a job in Bangalore, opting to stay home instead. Had she been sad or happy in her small suburban flat, as she settled into her new life?

A neighbour in Bangalore described her as 'sweet, lively, helpful'. 'She was always cooking something, sending all kinds of delicious food over,' this neighbour was quoted as saying. 'I still remember that karimeen she made. I had never tasted anything like it!'

Mala auditioned for *Hot Chef* in June 2011; was declared the winner in December. She won ₹5 crore in cash and a contract for her appearance as a judge on the next season's *Hot Chef*. She and her family moved into the Versova flat in March 2012.

And that was just the beginning. Niki's gaze skimmed down the list of other projects that had fallen into Mala's lap, subsequent to her winning *Hot Chef*. It was a long, lucrative list: a ₹55 lakh three-year endorsement deal with the Holiday Hotels and Resorts Chain; a ₹30 lakh deal with Kitchen Kraft Appliances; a ₹20 lakh deal with Chatpat Masalas; a ₹12 lakh deal with Gangadin Sweets and Namkeens; a ₹10 lakh deal with Menon Jewellers; a ₹8 lakh advance for a book titled, *Mala's Mouth-Watering Recipes*.

And those were just the ones that she'd signed off on. There were also projects that had been in the works when she died: a contract to star as a recurring guest in a popular sitcom; her own TV cooking show; conversations with UTV and Red Chillies Entertainment for movie roles. Also, confirmed by her agent, some very hush-hush negotiations to appear on *Hot Chef UK* as a judge.

'Mala was the next big thing,' the agent was quoted as having told the investigators. 'She had the Midas touch. Everything she touched turned to gold.'

Except cyanide, Niki reflected.

She took another sip of her chai and turned to the other document on her desk, a one-page write-up that Inspector Chauhan had meticulously prepared for her. A section with seemingly inconsequential and irrelevant details, except that Deepika knew that her boss would find them neither irrelevant nor inconsequential. That her boss maintained that it was often in the seemingly irrelevant details that the true clues lay hidden.

Amongst the lesser-known details about Mala Mary Joseph were the following: she was a devout Catholic, who went to Mass at St. Mary's every Sunday, while she was in Bangalore. She shared a distant but cordial relationship with her in-laws in Kochi, who mentioned that she was a 'respectful, quiet girl'. She used to ride a moped in Kottayam; she had a valid driver's licence. She'd been a regular blood donor at the local Red Cross. She was a registered eye donor and organ donor. She used to tutor her maid's daughters, ages twelve and ten, in Bangalore. She had a regular fishmonger with whom she always drove a hard bargain. She always bought extra meat and fish for the neighbourhood's stray cats and dogs. She drank coffee, always black, unsweetened, piping hot, several times a day; she always prepared dinner when she was home. She liked to read *Femina* and *Good Housekeeping* and *India Today*, according to the magazinewalla, and sometimes *Cosmopolitan*, *Society* and *Vogue*. She liked her driver to drive slow; she kept packets of biscuits in the car for beggars at traffic lights; she liked to listen to Radio Mirchi. She was partial to sleeveless blouses and the colour pink. According to her hairdresser, she had been thinking about cutting her hair short. She did not possess any teddy bears.

Niki sat back and chewed on her pen. It was an intriguing portrait of a bustling life; a lively young woman who appeared to have stayed grounded in her personal life, even as her professional life took off. And yet, this same young woman, seemingly anchored in her personal life, soaring in her profession, had taken a lethal dose of sleeping pills six months ago and died of cyanide poisoning thirty-six hours ago...

'Morning, boss.'

Niki looked up as Shankar Sahay, his hair damp and curling with moisture, pushed open the door and walked in.

'Can you believe the fog?' he said. 'I had to crawl my way over on all fours. And look at you, fresh as sunshine! And chai to boot!'

He poured himself a cup from the thermos and took his place in the visitor's chair, his gaze skimming over the report on Mala. 'She was an organ donor?' he asked, picking out the telling fact, just as Niki had known he would. 'They can't use her organs now, can they?'

'No.'

'I guess when you've got suicide on your mind, you're really not thinking about your organs.'

'And when someone sets out to kill you, neither is your killer.'

Sahay twirled the paperweight on his boss's desk absently. Suicide was a delicate matter with his boss, he was well aware. And yet, with the doctor's damning testimony from the previous evening and the witness testimonies about Mala's troubled state of mind...

'I have Joseph Albert cooling his heels in my office, by the way,' he told Niki.

'He's recovered from last night?'

'Has a hangover from hell, but he's here. I picked him up from his hotel myself.'

'Then let's go see what he has to say.'

ASP Sahay's office, one floor down from Niki's and on the other side of the building, was freshly painted, brightly lit and impossibly cluttered, even though he hardly ever spent any time in it. Ubiquitous crates and cartons littered the floor; the desk was covered with files, papers and an assortment of personalized items, all deemed 'indispensable', including a miniature Sachin Tendulkar-autographed cricket bat, a model handcrafted Concorde, an indecipherable logarithmic clock, a Darth Vader bobblehead and a jar filled with what Sahay claimed was the essence of Bandra Bandstand, but was actually more like a medley of smelly rocks, dirt and sand.

On most days, Niki shook her head in exasperation when she walked into Sahay's office. Today, however, she had no time to reflect on his disorderly work environment; her gaze settling immediately on the young man who sat slumped in the visitor's chair under the guard's watchful eye, his shoulders drooping, his chest sagging.

He looked up as she walked into the room and Niki wondered if he'd consumed anything besides alcohol since she'd last seen him. His eyes were puffy, his face blotchy; his skin was tinged grey. He looked like he might pass out any minute. Niki pushed the glass of water that sat untouched on Sahay's desk towards him and pulled out the chair beside him.

'Drink up,' she ordered.

Joseph's chest rose and fell in a deep sigh. He took a sip of water and forced himself to swallow. 'I'm sorry,' he said and a silent stream of tears started down his cheeks. 'I don't know how I forgot to mention the sleeping pills...'

'Why did she take them?'

'It was an accident.'

'Accident?' Sahay, who stood leaning against his desk, arms crossed over his chest, frowned.

'She swore that's all it was,' Joseph cried. 'She'd had a really bad cold all week and then, that night, she came back from Delhi and went straight to the medicine box to get some of that biochemical medicine she always keeps handy. She said she must have accidentally taken her mother's sleeping pills instead.'

'A whole fistful of them?'

'She said she was tired and half-asleep and dazed from the inflamed sinuses. She didn't know what she was doing.'

'And you believed her?'

'What else could I do?' He spread out his hands helplessly. 'I was on tour when it happened. I came back from Madurai to find out she was in the hospital. I rushed there straight from the airport and she was lying in the ICU, so small and helpless, attached to all those tubes...' Tears sprang to his eyes again. 'She opened her eyes when I called out her name. And I was so thankful...'

'And she never mentioned if anything was bothering her? Besides the inflamed sinuses?'

'No.' He shook his head. 'But I insisted we visit Dr Dastur for a follow-up all the same, even though she didn't want to. And I encouraged her to start taking the medicine he prescribed. I used to make sure she had it every night before bedtime...'

He bit his lip, blinking back fresh tears. 'I know what you think of me,' he said. 'That I must be some kind of blind idiot who had no idea that his wife was in trouble, who couldn't care less. But that's not true. I cared about her. I loved her, more than life itself...

'The first time I met her,' he said, his voice full of memories, 'was at her father's funeral. She was kneeling in front of the altar in a white dress, her face lit by the altar candles... I'd had a bad day,' he said, shifting his gaze to Niki. 'A client of mine had just refused to renew their contract, and the taxi I'd hired to Kottayam broke down midway. I remember taking a bus the rest of the way, thinking I'd quickly pay my respects at my uncle's friend's funeral and be on my way. And then I saw Mala... I'll never forget the way she looked that day. The way she turned her head and smiled at me... Her smile lit up that whole cathedral...

'She told me later that she'd been praying for strength and solace, for a saviour. And when she saw me, she knew God had answered her prayers. But I was no saviour.' In Joseph's voice, there was regret; in his face, despair. 'Just an ordinary guy who'd fallen hopelessly in love with her...who just wanted to make her happy...'

'And yet, she was on antidepressants,' Sahay said, unmoved.

'That was because of the show!' Joseph turned imploringly to Niki. 'I tried so hard, with every drop of energy, to make her happy. To give her everything she wanted. I rented a new flat in Bangalore – with two bedrooms and a balcony and a large open kitchen – and Mala filled it with flowers and music and her cooking. If you'd ever tasted her cooking…' he drew a ragged breath and closed his eyes.

'How did you feel when she won *Hot Chef*?' Sahay asked.

'I was so proud!'

'Weren't you envious?'

'Envious? No, why would I be envious?'

'Your wife became an overnight sensation, a national celebrity. She won a huge sum of money. Most men in your position would be envious,' Sahay said.

Joseph gave the matter a moment's thought, then shook his head emphatically. 'No, I could never be envious of Mala. I remember I was in Coimbatore when she won the final. I treated the whole sales team to dinner. I was dancing in the streets!'

'But what about after? Once the initial euphoria died down? Once you realized she was a star and you were just her husband?'

'Not *just* her husband! I loved her. And I wanted to support her in her career. That's why I told her we should move to Mumbai. So that she could focus on *her* career!'

'And what about your job in Bangalore?'

'I was a sales executive at a paints company,' he shrugged. 'I knew I could get a similar job in Mumbai. And I did. Two weeks after moving to Mumbai, I had an offer for Manager, Sales, at Five Star Sports. Two months after that I landed them a huge account in Dubai and they promoted me to AVP and put me in charge of the entire Middle East. Which meant I had to start working longer hours, travel, be away…' He sighed. 'That was the hard part. I had quit my old job and moved to Mumbai so I could be with Mala, but my new job ended up taking me away from her anyway. I barely saw her in these past six months. And she was working like a maniac, too. Her agent told her that was how it was in showbiz; you were either working in overdrive or not working at all. So I encouraged her to give it all she had.'

His voice grew bitter. 'I should have seen what it was doing to her. I should have seen what a toll it was taking on her, on us.' He glanced up, his eyes filled with self-loathing. 'Do you know how many days I spent on the road in the last six months? Ninety-six. That's ninety-six days that I could have been with Mala instead…'

Niki looked up as there was a tap on the door and Inspector Chauhan poked her head in. 'Ma'am, may I have a word?'

Niki stepped out into the corridor and closed the door behind her. She looked down at the sheet Deepika held out.

'Joseph James Albert, born 20 Jan 1987, Cochin,' she read. 'Joseph completed school in Cochin, then did his Engineering from Bangalore University and his MBA from Symbiosis. He started out as a sales executive at Orion Paints Inc., Bangalore.'

'Orion Paints,' Deepika said, 'has a sister company called Carnatic Chemicals.' She held out a product brochure she'd downloaded from the Internet and pointed to Item 57, which she'd highlighted in yellow.

'Potassium cyanide,' Niki read.

Joseph was sitting in the same spot, murmuring lackadaisically in response to a question Sahay had asked him, when Niki stepped back into the room.

'You worked for Orion Paints in Bangalore?' she asked without preamble.

'Yes, I was with them for two years.'

'And they have a sister company, Carnatic Chemicals?'

'Yes. It's a smaller company, under a different management, but part of the same group.'

'And it manufactures potassium cyanide.'

Joseph frowned. 'Well, I suppose they must… It's a solvent used in jewellery making.'

'And perhaps also in poisoning?'

Joseph reared back sharply in his chair; his mouth fell open.

'Tell me,' Niki said, 'and this time, without any histrionics: did you at any time have possession of or access to that potassium cyanide?'

'No, how could I?'

'You were never in close proximity of the chemical?'

'No! Well… I mean, technically speaking, there was a shared godown, but completely separate sections, clearly demarcated. I never even saw the chemicals side! I swear!'

'And what about Mala?'

He shook his head vigorously. 'The only time she visited me was at the office.'

'So she never came to the godown?'

He started to shake his head, then stopped abruptly. 'Well, just once, last year,' he said. 'I was at a production meeting at the godown. Mala and I were supposed to go for a dinner afterwards. So I told her to meet me there. She got there early and I told the peon to make her comfortable in the manager's room while I wrapped up my meeting.'

'So she was in the manager's room the entire time?'

'I think so. When I finished with my meeting, I found her waiting right outside. She said she'd just been looking around. You don't think – you can't think – oh my God!'

'It's possible…' Deepika mused, as a few minutes later, the three officers stood in the hallway outside ASP Sahay's office. 'If it was just two grams, it wouldn't have been that difficult.'

'There was a security guard at the warehouse, supposedly,' Niki said.

'Mala was the wife of an employee,' Deepika said. 'The guard probably wasn't very vigilant.'

'Then again,' Sahay said, 'what was she doing wandering around a chemicals warehouse? And I'm not sure I believe Joseph either, boss. He could just be making everything up. Maybe he's the one who stole the cyanide? Maybe he's the one who put it in her purse?'

'But why? Somehow, he doesn't strike me as a killer.'

'And even if he did put the poison in her purse, it would be hard to make the case that he put it in her mouth,' Sahay conceded.

'Especially since he was on a plane from Dubai at the time she ingested the poison,' Deepika agreed.

'All right,' Niki said, 'so here's what I want you to do. First, Inspector Chauhan, get the exact date of Mala's visit to the Carnatic Chemicals warehouse. She must have signed some sort of logbook. Also, get the names of the security guards and the peon who was on duty that day and grill them.'

'Yes, ma'am.'

'And coordinate with the Bangalore Police to send someone to Carnatic Chemicals. Have them do a thorough inspection of their warehouse, stock check, review of safety and inventory procedures. I want to know if it's possible to just wander in and make off with two grams of cyanide, just like that.'

'SP Ma'am!'

Niki turned as Pradeep, her PA, came hurrying down the corridor towards them. 'Ma'am, there's a Dr Bhandari here to see you.'

'The doctor from the crime scene?'

'He said he had something important for you,' Pradeep nodded.

'Where is he?'

'Downstairs, in the waiting room. Shall I bring him to your office?'

'Please.'

Dr Bhandari wore a sheepish expression as Pradeep showed him into Niki's room. He walked forward, hand outstretched and a shamefaced apology on his lips. 'SP Marwah, I'm so sorry,' he said. 'I don't know how this happened, but I found this in my pocket this morning.'

Sahay, who had followed Niki into her office, froze as Bhandari reached into his coat pocket and fished out a phone.

'I realized just this morning that it isn't mine,' Bhandari said. 'Problem is, I have exactly the same model. I must have picked up the wrong one in all the confusion at the Gaiety that night and slipped it into my pocket, thinking mine had fallen out. And then I forgot about it.

'It was switched off,' he added. 'I only noticed it when I took my suit out to wear again today.'

Sahay took the phone from Bhandari's outstretched hand and turned it on; he looked at Niki as a screen saver with a picture of Joseph Albert sprang to life.

'It's hers,' he said. He pressed a few buttons, then his brows shot up. 'Boss, you have to look at this.'

Sahay had pulled up the text-message screen on the phone, Niki saw, leaning forward. On it was a text message, typed, but not sent.

'Joe, I'm so, so, sorry,' she read. 'I've made a mess of everything. And I can't fix it. So I'm quitting. Everything. The show. The ads. This whole, unbearable life. I hope you'll underst'

21

DGP Kapoor, Head of the Himachal Pradesh Police, was not pleased.

He had arrived late from New Delhi after battling through a traffic-clogged highway and fog-related delays; his morning appointments had had to be cancelled; and on his desk, in addition to the weekly crime, traffic, missing persons and online complaints reports, were half a dozen newspapers, each and every one of them featuring a detailed account of Sunday's gas-attack scare, the sensational death at the Gaiety and blown-up, ominous-looking pictures of a deserted Ridge.

'Poison Valley', 'Queen of the Kill?', 'Goodbye, Gaiety?' and 'Death Theatre' were some of the headlines that especially made him cringe. And although the police department had mercifully not had to face the usual flak for its handling of the issue – the two leading dailies even going so far as to laud the rapid response orchestrated by the Shimla Police – there was far too much media scrutiny, speculation and chatter for his liking.

And the situation was still far from normal. The Ridge wore a desolate, after-party look; the shopkeepers on the Mall complained of a sharp drop in business; restaurants were empty. Several hoteliers had called his office complaining of en masse cancellations by nervous tourists; a scheduled visit by a delegation of Chinese dignitaries had been summarily cancelled; the future of the Gaiety was in limbo. And in Delhi, North Block was asking uncomfortable questions, needlessly flexing its muscles and preaching on about the need for greater oversight by the Centre. It was not a situation he could allow to continue.

Except that the Superintendent of Police, Shimla, seated across from him in his visitor's chair, seemed to feel differently.

'Sir, it's important that we solve this case, no matter how long it takes,' she argued vigorously. 'It's important for the city as well as for the deceased and her bereaved family.'

'Turn it over to Chandra, then. Crime can handle it.'

'Yes, sir, but my teams are already working on several leads. They've made a lot of progress – '

'Crime Division can take over your leads. The physical evidence and testimonies have been collected, I understand?'

'Yes, sir, but – '

'Hand it over, Marwah. You have many other things on your plate.'

Niki was silent. She knew that technically, once the initial phase of the investigation had been completed, she was expected to hand most cases over to the Crime Division. But once she did that, she knew all the momentum she'd managed to build up would dissipate; the teams she'd mobilized would move on.

'Anyway,' the Chief said, leaning back in his chair and surveying the case-file summary from under his knitted brows, 'it looks like a clear-cut case of suicide. You have *two* witnesses who saw the victim eat something from her purse, *four* who testify to her having been upset and behaving oddly. You have a prior history of suicidal behaviour as confirmed by a reputed physician, you have probable access to the poison and you also have what appears to be a suicide message on the victim's phone, typed right before she died. Every single piece of evidence points to suicide.'

'Not every single piece of evidence, sir.'

The Chief took a sip of the strong black coffee his PA always kept handy at his elbow. There was something about SP Marwah that made every situation seem needlessly complicated. Yet, he always found it impossible to win any argument against her, much less stop her once she got going.

'Let's go over it again,' he said wearily, rolling his chair forward. 'It says in the doctor's report, doesn't it, that Mala Joseph almost killed herself less than six months ago?'

'With an overdose of sleeping pills, sir, not cyanide. And she insisted it was an accident.'

'And we believe her, of course,' he said with a biting sarcasm that was completely wasted on Niki. 'But she *was* mentally ill.'

'She was on depression medication, yes, sir. As are millions of others.'

'She wrote about wanting to end her life.'

'No, sir,' Niki said, oblivious to the Chief's eyebrows knitting together in a line of displeasure above his nose. 'Why would she want to end her life?'

'Maybe because she wrote in her text message that she was – and I quote – "quitting…this whole, unbearable life",' the Chief said, enunciating every word for optimum impact. 'We have it in *her* words, Marwah. Her *last* words. Her *dying* words.'

'Yes, sir, but we don't have her *last* word.'

'I beg your pardon?'

'She didn't complete the last word, sir,' Niki said. 'She only typed "Underst –"'

'I may not be a linguistic genius, Marwah, but I'd be willing to say she was typing the word "understand".'

'Maybe, sir, but she didn't *complete* the word.'

'But what else could she have been meaning to say?'

'That's not the important part, sir. What's important is that she *didn't* complete it. If she had planned to kill herself, she would have completed that word. Think about it, sir: who kills herself in the middle of a word?'

The Chief blinked for several seconds. 'The poor woman was disturbed,' he finally said, dismissing the moment of doubt Marwah's words had created.

'But sir – '

'She was behaving erratically all day long! She peeled a banana and didn't eat it. She opened a pack of Kurkure and threw it away. She started a word and didn't complete it. It's not that big a leap.'

'Sir, I know it's important to close the case, but we shouldn't be hasty.'

'Which is why I'm saying, send it to Crime.'

'Maybe I can send it to them at the end of the week?'

The Chief shook his head; an obstinate look came into his eyes. 'Marwah,' he said, 'I appreciate your enthusiasm and dedication. But you can't afford to spend the entire week on this one case, dammit!'

'Yes, sir, but – '

She broke off as the landline phone at the corner of his desk rang. DGP Kapoor picked it up irritably and put the receiver to his ear. 'What is it Bharti?' he snapped at his PA. 'The governor's office?' he frowned. 'Well, connect me then… ah, good morning, ma'am.'

So Her Excellency, the governor, was calling, Niki surmised.

'Yes, ma'am,' the Chief continued, 'Yes, I just got back from Delhi. Yes, the meeting went well; we have high-level clearances on the Women Constables Training Centre proposal; I'm hopeful about getting the official confirmation before the year-end. Thank you for your support on that, ma'am.'

A smile rose to Niki's lips. So it looked like they might be getting the training centre off the ground, after all…

'The Gaiety case?' the Chief continued. 'Yes, ma'am, very unfortunate. But we've made considerable progress. In fact, we're quite close to wrapping it up. Yes, it's looking like suicide…'

Niki opened her mouth to protest and, anticipating her response, DGP Kapoor promptly swivelled around in his chair so that he had his back to her.

'Yes, ma'am, SP Marwah is the officer handling the case, ma'am.'

Niki stiffened at the mention of her name.

'Undoubtedly, ma'am,' the Chief said again. 'An outstanding officer. One of the best we have.'

They were discussing her. Why?

'You have?' the Chief turned round in his chair suddenly and beamed at Niki. 'That's wonderful news! She's the perfect choice!'

For what?

'Yes, it's a great opportunity,' he said into the phone. 'Yes, absolutely. I'll send her right over, ma'am. No problem.'

The Chief put down the phone and regarded Niki with a mixture of affection, delight and unbridled pride. 'Congratulations, Marwah,' he said. 'You are the governor's nominee for the National Women's Security Task Force's chief liaison officer.'

'Sir?'

'Strictly confidential, of course, but pending their approval and confirmation, you will be working directly with the home minister and the task force responsible for making recommendations on the setting up of the National Women's Security Force.'

'They're setting up a National Women's Security Force?' Niki felt her head swim.

'And the governor is on the Task Force Selection Committee. She believes they need someone young and dynamic, who understands what the young women of today need, to cut through the bureaucracy and shepherd the proposals through the channels. Someone like you.'

'But sir – '

'It's a great honour, Marwah.' He held out his hand across the table. 'Congratulations.'

Niki swallowed and shook her boss's proffered hand. 'Thank you, sir. I'll certainly try and do my best. *If* I'm selected.'

'Well, between you and me, I'd say it's more a question of *when* than *if*. They could look all around the country and not find a better candidate.'

'Thank you, sir,' Niki said. She felt light-headed and dazed, not just by the opportunity, but also by the absolute trust the Chief had in her. 'Um, coming back to the case, sir – '

'Let it go.'

'But sir?'

'There are meetings scheduled in the capital on Thursday and Friday to discuss the setting up of the task force. They'll be meeting some prospective nominees. The governor wants you to make it there.'

'Certainly, sir, but – '

'And she has asked you to attend a briefing session later this afternoon at her office. In,' he glanced at his watch, 'less than an hour.'

'I'll be there, sir. But the case – '

'Is as good as closed. As soon as you have the post-mortem report, you can start wrapping up and then hand over the remaining paperwork to the Crime Division. They'll take it from there.'

22

Niki was silent on the drive back from the governor's office, but her mind was abuzz, still tingling from the briefing session and the discussions around a job that, if it materialized, would change the trajectory of her career forever. Chief liaison officer to the home minister…

'We need real and lasting change,' the governor, a tiny lady, soft-spoken in manner but steely in resolve, had said to her just moments ago. 'Change in attitudes, in behaviours, change that enables and empowers young women to lead this country forward. It won't be easy.'

Niki had no trouble agreeing with that.

'There will be resistance at all levels,' the governor had warned her. 'New Delhi is a hard place; there are powerful people with vested interests at each and every level. Small-minded people, wrong-minded people, people with their own selfish agendas, people even within the administration, who feel threatened by the idea of women participating more openly in society and in the workplace, who are unable to reconcile their long-held beliefs with the changing reality. We need someone who can bulldoze her way through all that.'

The governor had regarded her solemnly through her horn-rimmed glasses and Niki had tried not to feel overwhelmed.

'We need a youthful presence,' the governor had said, 'but a strong one. Someone who is energetic and fearless. Someone who knows how to get what she wants. I have a feeling that you are that person.'

Niki had tried, but failed to speak.

The silver-haired lady had smiled softly. 'There are some who will doubt your readiness for such a critical job; who'll see your youthfulness as a liability, not an asset. They have other names in mind – officers with more experience, more backing. Which is why I want you to go to Delhi and meet them. I think you are the best person for the job. And by Friday afternoon I want to make sure everyone else on that selection committee feels the same way. Do you think you can change their minds, SP Marwah?'

'I'll certainly try my best, ma'am.'

'Remember, this is bigger than you or me or Shimla or anything else you have done before,' had been the governor's parting words. 'This will have the power to impact women of this country for generations to come. This can change women's lives forever...'

The words had stayed with Niki as she left the governor's office; they echoed in her mind as her Jeep pulled up outside her own office.

This can change women's lives forever...

The office was quiet when Niki got back, even though it was just past six. The adrenaline, the energy, the sense of urgency that had kept the hallways buzzing and the phones ringing had died down in the few short hours she'd been away, she couldn't help but notice. The teams that had been working on the Mala Joseph case had apparently moved on already, propelled, inexorably, by the powers above.

Niki turned on the lights in her room and sank into her chair, trying not to feel dejected. Move on, the Chief had said unequivocally, and she had no choice but to obey. And yet...

She pulled her laptop open, quickly scanned the several emails that had accumulated over the course of the afternoon. She paused at the one she'd been waiting for, the one from Dr Kaul. She clicked on the attachment named 'POST-MORTEM RESULTS OF MALA JOSEPH'.

'The cause of death, to the best of my knowledge and belief: potassium cyanide poisoning,' the words on the last page, filled out in ink in a spidery hand, read. Signed: Dr Suharsh Kaul, Department of Forensic Medicine.

Niki picked up the phone on her desk and dialled Dr Kaul. 'So it's official?' she asked. 'Cyanide?'

'And a very pleasant evening to you too, Niki.' Dr Kaul's voice was gently reproving.

'Sorry, Suharsh. I just – '

'I know. You have a case to solve. Yes, it's cyanide; I just emailed you a copy of the report.'

'Thanks; that's why I called. Did you happen to find anything besides cyanide in her system?'

'I got the note you had sent across last night,' Dr Kaul said. 'So I ran a toxicology for fluoxetine in her system. There was none. In fact, she tested negative for all drugs.'

Which meant that whatever she may have eaten from her purse, it hadn't been the Prozac.

'I did find something rather unexpected, though,' Dr Kaul added, with an odd inflection in his voice. 'Don't know if it has a bearing on your case…'

'What was it?'

'The victim was pregnant.'

'What!'

'In fact, she was ten weeks along.'

Niki hung up the phone and stared down at the picture of Mala on the front page of the newspaper that lay on her desk. She looked the picture of health and happiness; her cheeks were smooth and round, her hair lustrous; her lips parted in a brilliant smile. Her eyes, beautiful, long-lashed, were alive with energy and laughter.

She'd been pregnant?

Niki expelled the breath she'd been holding in and rubbed her eyes. She'd been blind. Totally blind. How could she have not seen it? This was the critical missing link, the piece that explained everything!

Mala was pregnant. That's why she'd been moody and listless, pale and erratic. That's why she'd talked about quitting the show...

Niki glanced at the picture again, tried to imagine what it must have felt like. Exciting? Terrifying? To get pregnant at a time when her career was just taking off... It couldn't have been easy contemplating the choices ahead of her. Is that why she'd been crying that evening when Vicky spoke with her? But she'd gone for a walk on the Ridge that afternoon. She'd bought a teddy bear. A fluffy white one, with brown eyes and a pink ribbon round its neck. She'd bought it for her baby. Her very first gift for the child growing inside her...

Niki jumped out of her chair and shrugged on her blazer. There it was, the proof that she'd been looking for, that showed beyond all doubt that Mala had not killed herself. Why would she buy a teddy bear for her future child in the afternoon and then kill herself in the evening? It was unthinkable...

She had to tell the Chief, she thought, as she stepped out of the office and headed for her Jeep. She had to tell him that they were about to make a huge mistake...

But first, she had to tell Joseph. He was the father; he had a right to know. She thought of him with a renewed pang of sorrow and regret that his grief would now be doubled...

She found Joseph Albert sitting alone in the deserted business centre of his hotel, a laptop perched on his knees, a pile of papers spread on the sofa beside him. He seemed to be staring with unseeing eyes at his screen. He looked up blankly as Niki walked up to him.

'SP Marwah.' He set his laptop aside and got quickly to his feet. 'Were you trying to reach me? I must have forgotten to turn on my phone. I'm so sorry – '

'That's okay,' Niki said.

He swallowed and looked sheepishly down at the carpet. 'I'm sorry about earlier,' he said. 'In your office. I was so distraught. I couldn't think straight. In fact, I've been behaving irresponsibly all this while, I know, falling apart like this. But I'm determined to be strong now. I have to be. For Mala's sake and her mother's sake. I finally decided to come down here to the business centre to return the phone calls, respond to the emails. It's overwhelming how many people have reached out, asking how they can help...'

He blinked rapidly, as if holding back tears.

'I've made arrangements with her family church in Kochi for a quiet funeral,' he continued, his voice wobbly but resolute. 'It's a small church on a sleepy lane... But it was where she grew up; I know she'd like it to be her final resting place. I'll take her back there as soon as the hospital gives me the go-ahead... When do you think that will be?'

Niki felt a lump in her throat. 'Shall we sit?' she suggested.

'Oh, of course, please, where are my manners!' Joseph cleared his papers from the sofa and waited for her to be seated, then sat down himself. 'Can I order some tea for you? Coffee?'

'No, thank you.' Niki braced herself, then turned to him, a grave look in her eyes. 'I came down here to share the results of the post-mortem with you.'

Joseph nodded; his face stiffened as he struggled to control his emotions. 'So they're done.' He closed his eyes. 'What did they find?' he asked in a low voice.

'We've confirmed cyanide as the cause of death.'

He sighed deeply and dabbed at the trickle of moisture that escaped one eye.

'The doctors found something else in the autopsy that I wanted to tell you about in person.'

He opened his eyes. 'You mean besides the cyanide?'

'I'm afraid so.'

'There was something else going on with her? What was it? A tumour?' He sat forward, a mixture of dread and horror and hope in his face.

Niki wished the answer were as comforting as that. A tumour, untreatable, fatal – a simple explanation; Mala had killed herself to escape the pain and indignity of the inevitable. It would have brought some solace and a sense of closure to the young man sitting beside her.

'No,' she said, 'not a tumour. I'm very sorry, but your wife was pregnant, Mr Albert.'

'*What!? No!*'

'I'm afraid the doctor confirmed she was ten weeks –'

'That's impossible!'

'I know this must be very distur –'

'No!' Joseph said, jumping up. 'You *don't* know. You *can't* know. You have no idea!' He took a few unsteady steps away from the sofa, then came back and stopped in front of her. 'We had all the tests done,' she heard him say, his hands balled into tight fists as he stared down at her furiously. 'They confirmed it. I'm infertile. I can't father children. Never could; never will.'

He sank down into the sofa, gripped his head in his hands. 'So tell me this, Ms Marwah,' he sobbed, 'if *I'm* infertile, how could my *wife* have been pregnant?'

23

In the absence of any physical evidence establishing criminal intent and based on the deceased's previous history of hospitalization due to an overdose of benzodiazepine, the office of the Superintendent of Police, Shimla, has inferred that the death of Ms Mala Joseph at the Gaiety Theatre, Mall Road, The Mall, Shimla, Himachal Pradesh 171006, at 9.38 p.m., Sunday, 12 October 2012, is likely a case of suicide by ingestion of Potassium Cyanide. From the available forensic evidence and interrogation of eyewitnesses, it has been determined that the Gaiety Theatre's management and personnel and other individuals present on the scene bear no liability whatsoever for the incident. No charges have been filed and the case is hereby referred to the Himachal Pradesh Crime Division.

It was with a heavy heart that Niki signed off on the final files of the Mala Joseph case and placed them in her out-tray.

By the following morning, they would be gone from her desk and with that, her connection with the victim, as unsettling as it was short-lived, would be irrevocably severed. It was just as well, she thought, as she wrapped her muffler around her neck and slipped her laptop into her briefcase, that she was heading to Delhi, that she would be gone until the following Monday.

She nodded tiredly to the night guard at the main entrance and stepped out onto the darkened street, bracing herself for the cold. Night had descended swiftly, the temperature having dropped by several degrees since the evening, a sombre reminder that winter was on its way. A sharp gust of wind blew off the mountaintops and tugged at her collar, sending a shiver down her spine. She huddled tighter in her blazer, pulling its lapels close about her, making a mental note to pick up her winter jacket from the dry cleaner's once she returned from Delhi.

She walked slowly towards her Thar, parked across the road, and watched her breath rise through the frosty night, drifting eastwards in the direction of the Gaiety Theatre. Just forty-eight hours, she thought. Forty-eight hours, since it had all happened…

She reached her Thar, took the key from Ramesh, thanked him and dismissed him for the day. She stood a minute, watching Ramesh disappear down the Ridge on his bicycle, then opened the door of her vehicle and stepped inside. The next minute, she had stepped back out and was briskly retracing her steps.

She strode past her office and the respectful, yet curious gaze of the guard; she continued, shivering slightly, up the Ridge and towards the forlorn silhouette of the darkened theatre building that bordered it.

She nodded to the guard who stood on duty outside and waited a moment in darkness while he unlocked the doors and fumbled with the light switches. Then the lights came on and the fairy-tale-like theatre sprang into view, ethereal, symmetrical, beautifully restored. Above her head, the ceiling glowed in the light from the chandeliers; around her, the pillars and balconies and handsome green walls gleamed with a timeless splendour. After the dreariness of the wide expanse outside, the beauty of the interiors came as a shock.

Niki turned her gaze away from the opulence of the seating area and towards the shrouded gloom that was the stage up ahead. It was dark, dark as it would have been two nights ago. Then the guard turned on the stage lights and the historic theatre came alive.

A theatre, Niki reflected, that had been the scene of countless dramas – of comedies, intrigues and tragedies; a stage that had been danced and trodden and wept upon; that had changed with every act; that had refreshed itself after every performance.

Except the last one.

Unlike all the others, the last performance, the last tragedy, had been real. And it had left its mark, a blemish that was not visible to the naked eye, but was there, nevertheless. And while the auditorium would be handed over to the management tomorrow, the stage made ready again, that blemish would remain.

Niki made her way slowly up the steps at the side of the stage; she paused at the top and looked out across the empty wooden floor. It had been cleaned and disinfected; the props, the sets, the tables, the chairs – they had all been removed; but Niki could still picture it as it had been two nights ago…

The anticipation, the excitement amongst the audience, the energy and adrenaline amongst the contestants, the spotlights shining on the heads of the judges, the cameras capturing, from multiple angles, their reactions, as one by one, they tasted the dishes…

Then Rajat calling the final contestant, the applause cut short by the ripping sound as the dress tore, the director calling, 'Cut!'; the confused looks as the lights and cameras were turned off. Then as the audience started to murmur, Rajat's reassuring voice on the mike and the video montage coming on the backdrop.

In the foreground, as Rajat receded into the wings, KK turning to converse with Ashika.

And Mala all alone…

Mala, sitting quietly, glancing furtively around her. What had she been thinking? Was there any hesitation as she pulled out her phone?

Did her fingers tremble as she typed out that final message to her husband, to the man who loved her so dearly and whom she had betrayed? Was the guilt really so crushing that she couldn't bear to even complete the message, to press 'Send'?

Apparently. But not so crushing that it had prevented her from reaching in her purse and pulling out the poison.

Niki recalled the look on Joseph's face when she had told him about the baby. It had been a look of disbelief, of betrayal...

She felt a wave of anger wash over her. Mala, she thought, how could you? How could you screw up your life in such a sordid fashion? And then the sheer senselessness, the inhumanity of the final act...

Niki remembered the tortured, lifeless figure she'd seen in the morgue and felt her eyes sting. She walked slowly across the wooden stage, stopped at a spot just left of centre and peered down. It was old, the floor scratched and scuffed, but clean. It had been swept, dabbed, mopped, polished; it shone with a soft glow under the bright lights of the stage. This is where she had fallen, Niki thought, where she had taken her final breath.

Very slowly, she crouched down and brushed the floor lightly with her fingertips. Then she straightened, and with a quick nod to the guard who stood waiting walked briskly back down the stage and out the auditorium.

Behind her, as she strode down the Ridge and to her waiting Jeep, the grand theatre plunged into darkness again.

24

It was late Tuesday night in Nizamuddin, New Delhi.

The ancient neighbourhood was relatively quiet; the bustle and excitement of the evening's prayers had dissipated; the throng of visitors and shoppers in the crowded bazaars and narrow gullies had thinned out and disappeared long ago. Here and there, the last of the residents and shopkeepers were wrapping up the night's final tasks before returning home, some to the families that lived in the crumbling quarters directly above, others to newer, more upscale establishments nearby. Nizamuddin West, home to the 700–year-old dargah of Hazrat Nizamuddin Auliya, with its labyrinth of gullies, lawns, chaurahas and bazaars, flanked by mosque and temple, police station and slum, railway tracks and congested buildings as well as highways and massive, ultra-modern bungalows, was both a testament to a grander time and a symbol of a vibrant new one.

As the clock ticked on past 11.30, a large, silver-haired man rode a rickshaw into the main gully, empty now, given the late hour. He paid off the rickshaw-walla, alighted and stood a moment in the narrow lane, looking up at the thirty-year-old sign above the century-old door.

Kemaal's, it read, in three different languages, the letters glittering under artfully placed lights.

KK felt the magnificence of it permeate him, reorient him, as it always did. Kemaal's, where it had all begun over thirty years ago – with six aluminium tables, a kitchen the size of a closet and a vision that was larger than anything the world had ever seen…

It had been a huge gamble, requiring luck, lucre and a certain type of lunacy, but KK had managed, somehow, to be blessed with all three.

It had not been an easy journey from obscurity to fame. He had worked harder and longer than he himself had thought possible; he had laboured and hustled and connived and bludgeoned; and he had kept at it until, against every odd, Kemaal's had flourished, swallowing up the barber shop to its left and the leather-goods shop to its right, the meat shop and tikka stalls two doors down, along with the modest dhaba in the gully behind. Kemaal's in Nizamuddin now covered half the gully, stretching from end to end like an express train with interconnected cars; and while its exterior was modest, the glittering sign over the ancient door left no doubt as to its rightful place in the world.

KK stepped under the sign now and nodded to Altaf, the burly, moustachioed guard who had stood outside for the past fifteen years and who now respectfully held open the heavy, panelled door.

From inside the restaurant, the sweet fragrance of rose water and cardamom wafted out.

KK stood a moment, breathing it in. Then he stepped onto the lavish Persian rug that adorned the main hallway, passed beneath the antique chandelier that used to belong to the Nawab of Pathari and looked with quiet pride round the tasteful front dining hall, its floors covered in plush carpeting, the faux-plaster ceiling sculpted with a perfectly symmetrical Mughal motif. It was rich and refined, quietly luxurious; it was the perfect setting for a restaurant that offered the finest kebabs in the country.

The dining room was relatively empty at this hour; a large group seated at a round table in the left corner was being served seviyaan kheer by Suleman, one of his trusted waiters, while closer to the door, on his right, a family was leaving, their plates wiped clean. KK moved towards them, his hand extended for a hearty handshake, disclaiming with a self-effacing smile as they complimented him on the food, the décor, the service... Then, with a gracious nod to the people at the table still eating their kheer and an invitation to linger over their meal as long as they wished to, he continued into the next room, where there were more tables and where, behind a small counter in a corner, he knew he would find Vishal, his trusted manager, bent over the night's accounts.

The bespectacled young man stepped forward as soon as he saw his boss. 'Sir! Welcome! We heard about the terrible tragedy, so sorry...!'

'Yes,' Kemaal acknowledged. 'It is a terrible tragedy.'

'And how are *you*, sir?'

'I'm alive, my friend.'

'I can't tell you how happy we all are about that, sir.'

'It's good to be back here,' KK said. He clasped Vishal's fingers briefly, then indicated the accounts. 'Things been okay while I've been out?'

'For the most part, sir. There was just a minor mishap involving that new helper we hired last month...'

'Mishap?'

'Sir, he broke one of the china bowls while washing it. From the Heritage collection.'

KK winced. It was one of the more expensive collections and hard to replace. 'Deduct the cost from the fellow's wages and then kick him out,' he said. 'There is no room for mishaps at Kemaal's.'

'Yes, sir. If you could also take a look at the new menu cards...'

Half an hour later, matters of immediate business attended to, including the hiring of two additional waiters and the approval of proofs of the newly printed menu cards, KK bade a tired Vishal good night.

'I can stay if you'd like me to,' the young man offered.

'No, you can go, Vishal.'

'I hate to leave you alone tonight, sir.'

KK smiled. 'Go,' he said, 'your wife will be waiting.'

'But sir – '

'Don't worry, I'll be careful to lock up before I leave. And in any case, what harm could I possibly come to with Altaf Bhai outside?'

He waved the young man out into the night, then closed the door and stepped back inside, savouring the silence, now that he was finally alone. He ran a loving hand over the tiny brass statuettes on the console; his gaze went, as it always did, to the picture above them. It had been taken just a few years back at their silver-jubilee celebration, marking the completion of a quarter-century of success; it showed him shaking the hand of the chief minister. Below it was framed an award for excellence in the field of dining.

His gaze went again to the handsome wooden console, to the vase full of roses, the shallow bowl of after-dinner mints. He picked a pack from the bowl, tore it open and placed it in his mouth. The familiar taste of cardamoms and cinnamon, sunflower seeds and saunf, gulab and chandan, filled his mouth.

He chewed slowly, enjoying the taste, and moved on past the four interconnected dining halls and through the swing doors to his state-of-the-art kitchen, where, to his left was his walk-in freezer, stocked with the finest cuts of lamb, chicken and other more exotic meats, and to his right were the refrigerators packed with trays of marinated, minced, ground and skewered meats, awaiting their turn in the giant tandoors. Before him, as he stepped onto the freshly mopped floor, everything was spotless, while around him, the rich aroma of spices, ground fresh twice every day, hung in the air. He breathed it in appraisingly; it was his special blend of over a hundred different herbs and spices, put to daily use in his kitchen, engraved in his mind.

It smelled sublime.

He stepped towards the third refrigerator, pulled out a tray of kebabs at random and pressed one between his thumb and forefinger. Like makhmal, he thought with satisfaction, feeling the full, yielding texture. In the days of the nawabs, it was said, the leg of the lamb was minced and ground thirteen times to a buttery, melt-in-your-mouth consistency so that even a toothless baby could eat it. KK didn't grind his meat thirteen times. But his kebabs were the best to be had anywhere in the world.

He continued his inspection of the stores, the supplies, the gadgets, the tandoors, the coals, the freshly hung homemade curds, the juicy heads of garlic, the small, firm onions, gingers bursting with flavours that bled the moment one scratched them with one's thumbnail... And the mint, the bright green mint that he grew in-house and guarded jealously...

It was fresh, the mint, and rich with flavour. He snipped a tiny head off the stem and put it in his mouth. Then, his senses sated with the sights and scents that defined him and his life's work, he headed towards the innermost door. He entered the six-digit code on the recently installed keypad, pushed the door open and stepped inside.

It was a small space, sparsely furnished, with a table, a swivel chair and a wall full of photos, awards, certificates and distinguished tokens of recognition. In pride of place above the chair was the framed recipe for the original Kama Kebab. Passed down the generations, written in a curling, calligraphic, slightly shaky hand, by the man whose picture hung above it.

KK gazed up at the picture and felt a lump grow in his throat. That the man whose genius his restaurant enshrined should have been so talented; that his talents should have remained so unappreciated...

Well, he had worked hard to change all that. It had taken decades of toil, but he'd done it. He'd built a testament that would endure, a culinary empire that was growing. He'd done the old man proud, even if he was no longer around to see it...

He felt tears start in his eyes. Damn his soft heart, he thought; he was a sentimental old fool. Or maybe he was still reeling from all that he'd been through.

Mala, he thought. Sweet, darling Mala; she was gone, bless her, and there was not a thing anyone could do to bring her back...

KK sighed heavily and sat down in his chair. He took a key from its hiding place in the special compartment below his desk and inserted it in the locked drawer. From it, he pulled out a plain yellow envelope and emptied out a sheaf of papers.

KK, we need to include a pinch of marjoram in the Konkani stew recipe; it really rounds out the flavour...

KK, here's my amended recipe for fish moilee with some added garam masala at the end. Try it; it makes a world of difference!

Dearest KK, have you tried switching the quantities of ginger and garlic in your khatti khumbi? I served it to some visitors from the BBC last night and they couldn't stop praising the results. Of course, I told them it was entirely your recipe...

KK, I've been putting the finishing touches to the recipes for our joint venture; I'll send you the final documents by the 12th, I promise, once we get back from Shimla. So excited!

He gazed down at the last note, dated 7 October 2012. It was quaint, he thought, how she always dated her notes so precisely; even if they were just scraps of paper, even if the neat, rounded words had a breathless, school-girlish exuberance. He thought of her again, of her twinkling eyes, her radiant smile...

She never did make it back from Shimla, poor girl, he thought; they never did get to discuss the final recipes. He blinked away unwarranted tears; he put away the handwritten notes. No, he thought, there was no room for sentimentality in business. And what was done was done. Now all that remained was to make sure her recipes lived on.

Kemaal's Malabar... It would be a colossal culinary triumph.

He heard the soft buzz of his mobile in his pocket and answered it. 'Yes, Shobha,' he said.

'Sorry to disturb, ji.'

Shobha, her voice hesitant, solicitous, apologetic; as familiar and constant as the deepening lines of his face. 'You reached?' she asked.

'Yes, Shobha.'

'Busy?'

He paused. 'Nahin, bolo?'

'You'll have dinner, na?'

It was their little ritual, their intimate dance. No matter which day of the week or what time of night. *You'll have dinner, na?*

'Yes, Shobha,' he replied, like he always did. Even though it would be two in the morning, possibly later, before he got home. She'd wait up, he knew. Just like she always did.

'What shall I make?' she asked, just like she always did.

'Chapattis.'

'And ghiya?'

'Yes.' Simple, fresh, a cleansing of the palate. Like a dip in the Ganga.

'I'll be here a little while longer, Shobha.'

'I'll be waiting, ji.'

Westwards across town, past Safdarjung and IIT and JNU and the forested Cantonment, beyond the high-rises and flyovers that studded the city, the world-class New Delhi Indira Gandhi International Airport was winding down after another hectic day filled with hundreds of flights, tens of thousands of passengers.

Two a.m. It was the leanest part of the non-stop, twenty-four-hour day, a small window of time after the last flight had departed and before the earliest one landed, free of passengers, baggage, even airline personnel. In the central Domestic Departures lounge, the shutters were down in the luxury retail brand stores; others were lit, but empty.

A couple of sweepers in airport uniforms went methodically about their work, their arms rotating long mop handles with the ease and ennui of a motion repeated countless times.

'Sir, side.'

The dishevelled young man who'd been sitting with dark glasses still on, motionless as a statue, staring sightlessly into some nameless void, looked up at the sound of the sweeper's voice.

'You can sit there.' The sweeper indicated with a wave of his mop's handle the rows of empty seats on the other side.

Wordlessly, the young man collected his things.

'Sir, you are on TV, na?' the sweeper asked, peering closely at him.

The young man's lips tightened; he shook his head.

'That cooking show, sir? On YTV? *Hot Chef*? Sir, you are Rajat Tripathi!'

'No.'

'But you look just like him! Carbon copy!' The man promptly pulled out a mobile phone from his shirt pocket. 'Sir, please, photo?'

Rajat removed his glasses and sighed. The man leaned close and, with one arm holding the phone and the other around the 'carbon copy', clicked a picture.

'My wife will be so happy,' he chuckled, tucking the phone gleefully back in his pocket.

Rajat glanced at his watch.

'You missed your flight, sir?' The man looked at Rajat's overnight bag and duffel. 'Want to get some rest? There is a sleeping lounge upstairs.'

'No, thanks.'

'Sir, it is very comfortable…'

But Rajat had already grabbed his belongings and was running, two steps at a time, up the stalled 'up' escalator.

Once out of the sweeper's sight, he selected one of the several café seats on the top level overlooking the central atrium and sat down again. The man was a pest. Pushing him to get some sleep. Why should he sleep? He had not come here to sleep. He had come here to remember.

He looked down at the deserted Departures lounge, at the rows of empty seats and shuttered shops and wondered, once again, why he'd done it. Why stay, when he could easily have got on that last flight back to Mumbai? But he'd stood there in the middle of the lounge, rooted to the floor like a zombie, watching them bustle by – the crew and contestants, tired, spent, anxious to get home, get some rest, get back to their normal lives.

All, except him.

'Carry on,' he'd told an incredulous Ruby, who'd come looking for him after repeated boarding announcements. 'I have some work to do.'

'Here? In the middle of the night?'

'Here. In the middle of the night.'

'And what about the show?'

'I'll be there tomorrow morning.'

Ruby had cursed and harangued and cajoled, but he'd stood his ground. She'd left, finally, with dire but empty threats; she had had too many other problems to solve without worrying overmuch about Rajat. 'At the studios at ten sharp – or else!' she'd said by way of farewell, making a dash for the boarding gate.

And now here he was, finally alone, at the deserted New Delhi airport in the wee hours of the morning, accomplishing what exactly?

His gaze wandered once again over the seating area below, finding the two seats that he'd stayed behind for, the two seats where they had sat, he and Mala, just two days ago, on their way to Shimla. She had been quiet; he had teased her about avoiding him.

'Why would I avoid you?' she had sighed and rested her head on his shoulder.

He had felt that familiar charge of electricity course through his body at her touch; he had looked quickly round the lounge to see if anyone was watching, before taking her hand and lacing his fingers through hers.

He held up his hand now and spread his fingers, remembered hers laced between his own. His vision blurred as tears, held back for the past two days, filled his eyes.

She was gone and there was nothing left of her, besides the indelible mark she had left on his life. Those text messages, those emails, those saucy Post-It notes; those cocktail glasses smeared with lipstick, that single wavy strand of hair on his shirt where she had leaned her head and which he had found still stuck there as he had packed to leave.

It had brought him to his knees – that single strand of dark, thick, long hair, curling stubbornly at the bottom. It had reminded him of her, of the playfulness and stubbornness and brilliance that had been her...

He'd loved her. So, so much...

But not enough, he thought bitterly, reaching for his hip flask. Not nearly enough.

25

The *Hot Chef* house was quiet, finally. A large farmhouse built on two acres of farmland in Panvel, away from the noise and hustle of the metropolis and the expressway, tucked away at the end of a never-used lane, it had been rented and refurbished by the producers of the show for the express purpose of housing the contestants in comfort and seclusion. There were six large bedrooms on the upper level, with separate wings for the boys and the girls; the main level had a living room, a dining room, a lounge and a bar area, and a 600 sq. ft kitchen equipped with all the gadgets and utilities the contestants' hearts could desire.

KK was a man with both vision and means. 'You are the chefs of the future,' he had proclaimed as he'd ushered the contestants in that first day after the final selections. 'This is where you are going to create the greatest dishes of the century.'

They'd stood, wide-eyed, looking around, and they had believed him. This white-tiled kitchen, with its granite counters and maple cabinets, its marble floor and temperature-controlled shelves, its deep freezers and infrared grills – it had been enough to inspire even the most challenged amongst them to dream that this could be the place where they achieved greatness.

Tonight, the kitchen was empty, its chrome surfaces and white floor glowing in the moonlight that shone in through the spotless windows. Outside, a short burst of wind briefly stirred the leaves of the trees that surrounded the property and shielded it from prying eyes. Inside, the digital clocks on the multiple gadgets switched their red displays from 2.59 a.m. to 3.00 a.m. in one precise, perfectly coordinated instant. In the doorway, Leena Dixit stood in her Hawaii chappals and nightie, taking in the marvel and mystery of it all.

She removed her chappals and touched the threshold reverentially with her fingertips before entering, then touched her fingers to her forehead. For Leena, there was no place more sacred, nothing that made her feel alive in quite the same way. She'd been tossing and turning restlessly in her bed for the last hour; now, as she stood in the kitchen, she felt all the tension and anxiety slip away. The traumatic events of the past two days, the long journey back, the relentless tick-tock of the clock on the wall, the new blister on her foot – all seemed soothed and bearable, now that she was here…

She headed for the large refrigerator at the far end of the kitchen, picking her way in the semi-darkness with ease. A glass of warm milk, a plate of biscuits, a handful of pistachios – that should help her sleep.

She pulled open the fridge door, popped open the seal of a Tetra Pak of milk and poured out a glass. She set it to warm in the microwave, then pushed through the swing door into the walk-in pantry. A medley of aromas assailed her nostrils.

She stood a moment, staring at the rows of cans, containers, condiments, preservatives, sauces, leavening agents, colouring agents, flavourings, spices; solid, everyday ingredients, neatly labelled and arranged in matching jars so that one never ran out, never had to worry.

Behind her, the microwave pinged. The milk was ready, but she stood rooted to the spot, her gaze travelling slowly, methodically, over the jars; the big white ones – wheat flour, rice flour, corn flour, refined flour, semolina, sabudana, poha, coconut powder, salt, sugar; and the smaller ones – arrowroot, cornstarch, baking soda, tartaric acid, sodium benzoate, caster sugar, rock sugar…

Her gaze paused at the small jar next to the rock sugar, the one that said 'confectioner's sugar'. Next to it, on the light maple wood of the shelf, was a tiny dusting of white powder.

She reached out to the powder, hesitated, then very gingerly, touched a few specks of the powder with her forefinger and brought them to the tip of her tongue.

She did not collapse. She exhaled the great wall of breath she'd been holding in. Confectioner's sugar, just like it was supposed to be, just like it said on the jar.

She was being paranoid. She turned resolutely away from them, the jars of white powder, the ground ginger, garlic, white pepper, rock salt, fish seasonings, Italian seasonings, Mexican essence… tiny jars filled with white powders; that's all they were.

Or were they?

Her thoughts drifted back to that other time in the kitchen, five weeks ago. They'd been alone, just the three of them: Vicky, Shaq and her. They had gravitated towards each other right from the start, the three contenders with the greatest talents and the toughest odds. Or maybe she and Shaq fit that last bill better; Vicky had just joined them, because, as he said, they were the 'smart and sexy ones'.

How gratified she'd been! It was the first time in her life she'd ever been called 'sexy' by anyone, let alone by the kind of guy who defined the very word. It had made her heart beat faster, the casual compliment accompanied by the careless flick of cool fingers against her bangs; it had made her face glow with pleasure.

They had become a team that morning, the three of them, by some unspoken agreement. They'd meet in the kitchen early in the morning, while the others slept, for their first cups of chai; they'd make their own and sample each other's and try and guess what special ingredient had gone into each. And how just a small change, an ingredient missing or an extra one added, could trigger a seismic shift, a complete disaster.

Like Girdhar, whom they'd been talking about that morning, five weeks ago, who'd been eliminated the night before; who'd managed to infuse his chicken curry with caster sugar instead of salt.

'What kind of cook can't tell salt from sugar?' Leena had marvelled.

'They do look alike,' Shaq had reasoned.

'As a chef, you've got to be able to tell them apart,' Vicky had said. He'd brought out four jars of white powder from the storeroom, their labels covered, to demonstrate. He'd lined them up on the counter, poured small samples out onto tasting plates. 'Go ahead,' he'd prompted.

She'd tasted the first sample gingerly. 'Sour,' she'd said, puckering her lips slightly. 'But salty too… citric acid?'

'Close. It's calcium citrate. What about the next one?'

'Tartaric acid,' she'd said right away.

'You have a bright future,' he'd pronounced.

Shaq, who'd been watching quietly, had held up a small packet filled with yet another white powder. 'So what's this?' he'd asked.

Vicky had blinked at it a moment, then patted his jeans pockets with a frown. 'That's mine,' he'd said.

'I know. But what is it?'

'Nothing you need to know.'

'Why? Is it something illegal? Inflammable? Poisonous?'

An odd, challenging look had shot across Vicky's face. 'Maybe yes, maybe no, maybe all of the above,' he'd drawled.

Shaq's eyes had widened a fraction. 'Cocaine? Anthrax? Nuclear waste?'

'Even *I* would have a hard time laying my hands on nuclear waste.'

Shaq had opened the packet, despite all Vicky's protests and warnings. 'So then let's see…' he'd said, pouring some out onto his palm. He had taken a pinch, transferred it to his mouth. Leena had felt her heart start to pound, even though she'd known they were just messing around.

'Flour.' Shaq had spat it out in the sink and rinsed his mouth with water.

Leena had exhaled the breath she'd been holding in. 'Why would you carry flour around in a plastic tube?' she'd asked, turning on Vicky.

'Why not?'

'You are seriously mental.'

She'd thought that had been the last of it. But a week later, she'd noticed the outline of another packet against the fabric of his jeans pocket. This time, it had been filled with tiny white pellets.

'What are those?' she'd asked.

'Watch and learn.' He'd opened a bottle of vinegar and poured the pellets in. Bubbles had come fizzing up and the vinegar turned a brilliant blue.

'Baking soda,' Leena had announced. 'But the colour?'

'Cabbage juice.'

'No way!'

'Way. I add vinegar, it turns pink; I add more baking soda, it turns blue. Neat, huh?'

She'd frowned as he unscrewed the lid on the salt jar and scooped a small quantity into a small white paper sachet. 'We're not supposed to take that,' she'd said. 'It's against the rules.'

'You follow rules?'

He'd made it sound so square and unsexy that she'd shaken her head promptly in denial. He'd grinned, then handed her another empty packet and she'd filled it with the first thing that had been at hand – sodium benzoate.

'So what are you going to do with your salt?' she'd asked.

'I don't know yet. Maybe I'll add it to Barkha's face cream.'

She'd giggled at the thought.

She'd not been giggling when, during that evening's challenge, Vidya's cake had not risen. It had gone in and sat there like a pudding and come out like a brick. Vidya had looked confused, horrified. They'd talked about it at the dinner table after she was eliminated.

'What an idiot!' Pallavi had said. 'Imagine confusing sodium benzoate with baking soda!'

'Imagine,' Vicky had agreed.

'How could that have happened?' Leena had whispered, when she'd found him alone in the kitchen.

'She should have checked her ingredients.'

'But sodium benzoate?'

'Don't worry, my lips are sealed.'

'But Vicky, I swear I never – '

'Shh…'

Vicky had placed his finger to her lips; she'd jumped at the intimate contact. He'd brought his face close to hers; his eyes had been alight with mischief. 'Who cares about Vidya,' he'd whispered.

'Yes, but…' Leena had heard her heart thudding in her chest. 'But what if they find out about – '

'About what?'

She'd looked away. Her eyes had fallen on the small, telltale packet inside his pocket. 'What's that?' she asked.

'You don't want to know.'

'Seriously, Vicky. This isn't a game any more.'

'Sweetheart,' he'd said, flicking her bangs with a careless finger, 'it never was.'

part 2

These are the four that are never content:
that have never been filled since the Dews began –
Jacala's mouth, and the glut of the kite,
and the hands of the ape, and the eyes of Man.

Rudyard Kipling, *The Jungle Book*

1

It was a warm afternoon in New Delhi, a bright sun setting the cream and red sandstone of the Secretariat Building aglow, but the atmosphere inside the spacious, carpeted room was decidedly chilly. Five men and two women sat along one side of an imposing oval table; none seemed particularly enamoured of the SP, Shimla, who sat alone on the other side.

Hands clasped tightly in her lap, Niki smiled, trying very hard not to reach for the pencil that lay on the table in front of her and chew on it. She had made a special effort for the interview – a carefully selected handloom sari with a discreet blouse, low-heeled sandals and hair in a tight chignon at the nape of her neck. The effect was smart, confident, professional, she hoped. Yet, nothing could make up for her youth, her gender or her lack of experience, judging by the scepticism on the faces of those who sat across from her.

'So how long have you been SP Shimla?' the Joint Secretary from the Police Division asked, though he was well aware of the answer she'd give.

'Two years,' she said.

'And before that?'

'I was SP, Kullu.'

'Lovely place,' one of the others commented.

'Very relaxing,' another agreed,

'Hardly any crime.'

'Of course, maintaining a low crime rate in a small hill station and policing a large metro are completely different matters,' the Additional Secretary, Urban Development, reflected.

'I would imagine the same principles apply, sir,' Niki said.

'Do refresh my memory, will you? What is the population of Shimla?'

'One and a half lakhs, although it swells past five lakhs during peak tourist season.'

The Joint Secretary of Policy Planning and the Additional Secretary of Urban Development exchanged indulgent smiles.

'The National Capital Region alone has a population of two crores,' the latter remarked. 'The pressure on resources, the law-enforcement nightmare,' he sighed. 'You have no idea!'

'Actually, sir, I think I have a very good idea. Shimla's problems are the same as Delhi's or Mumbai's or those of any other metropolitan area. Congestion, overcrowding, pollution, indiscriminate land development... And yet, despite the tremendous pressure on resources, in the past two years we've managed to maintain one of the lowest crime rates of all state capitals. We've been a leader in introducing SMS-based registration of complaints. We have a fully staffed women's safety hotline. We have one of the fastest turnaround times for grievance redressal. We have a thoroughly modernized, net-based consumer interface. And we have equipped every single police station with internet and web-based services.'

The Joint Secretary, Police, fidgeted in his chair with visible impatience.

'We are talking about women's security on a *national* scale,' he said, 'a women's security force serving *sixty crore* women. Four hundred times as many people as in Shimla. Your track record may be impressive, Ms Marwah, but what would you know about that?'

'Because I *am* one of those sixty crore women, sir,' Niki said, 'perhaps a bit more than you?'

The Joint Secretary reared back sharply. The others, who'd been murmuring something to each other, grew silent. She knew she had their attention now.

'It's my belief that women's security is not rocket science,' she said, looking each of them in the eye. 'It's not a "special" issue, like border security or internal security or counter-terrorism. If you ask me, we shouldn't be talking about setting up a special women's security force at all. Instead, we should be talking about what we can do to improve women's security *within* the existing infrastructure. We need stronger laws, better law enforcement. Not another segregated women's-only department.'

Niki ploughed on, despite the scowls that were deepening on the faces of her audience. 'All-girls schools, women's special buses, women-only lines – these are all comfortably arrived at solutions, but they only serve to segregate women,' she said. 'They send the wrong message. That women need special treatment, as though they were minors or disabled or otherwise unable to lead normal, adult lives. Whereas the reality is that women don't need special treatment; in fact, they need to be treated exactly the same as men – by employers, lawmakers, law-enforcement agencies, the justice system, the average man on the streets… No lakshman rekhas, no curfews, no restrictions. We should be able to travel anywhere, by day or by night, alone or in groups, for work or for leisure, wearing whatever we like, answerable to no one – just the same as men. For this, we don't need a special force; we need sensitization amongst the existing personnel at all levels; we need tougher laws, tougher enforcement of the laws. We need more women in the existing police force, not a separate one.'

Niki knew what the outcome of the meeting would be as she walked out of the meeting room. The outraged comments poured out through the open door and followed her as she strode down the hallway. Well, she thought, shaking her hair free of the annoying chignon, that was that. No need to pack her bags or say her goodbyes back in Shimla; Delhi wouldn't be needing her any time soon.

She paused a moment as she emerged into the bright sunshine of the afternoon, onto the rousing, historic grounds that marked the seat of power in the country. She could have played it safe, she supposed. But to what end? To secure a plum posting, climb a prestigious ladder, join the bandwagon of those who occupied seats of immense power and accomplished precious little?

No, she thought, it was better this way. She had spoken her mind, given voice to what she believed.

The selection committee had a right to know what her beliefs were and what they would get if they chose her. And if it was merely a yes-man or a yes-woman they were looking for she knew they'd have no difficulty finding one.

2

The *Hot Chef* studios in Chembur had been swathed in tasteful white for the shoot of the special episode: 'Mala Joseph, a Tribute'. The multilevel backdrop was hung with white chiffon and silk; the ceiling was festooned with white paper lanterns. Strands of pearls hung in loops from the crystal chandeliers and, in the centre of the gigantic set, a single long table was draped in elegant white satin and topped with ivory candlesticks and white roses in exquisite porcelain vases.

The six remaining contestants sat at this table, dressed in white salwar kameezes and kurta–pyjamas, their expressions smoothed into appropriate solemnity, while in the background, a lyrical score played soft, soothing music...

It was picture-perfect as tributes go, carefully designed and well rehearsed. And yet, for one reason or another, what should have been wrapped up in a couple of hours was now in its sixth fruitless hour, with no end in sight.

Jimmy straightened from the monitor, where he'd been reviewing the previous take, and rubbed his aching back muscles. 'Let's try it one more time,' he said, sweeping his long hair off his face.

The contestants groaned as one.

'We can do it, guys. Okay, cameras ready?'

The clapboard boy held the clapboard up in front of the main camera, ready to snap.

Up at the table, Sharon tossed her hair and undid another button on her white kurta.

'I can't believe you just undid your button!' Pallavi hissed.

'Quiet, please!' Ruby called from her seat off-camera.

'I'm hot,' Sharon shrugged, pulling the neckline apart to reveal a considerable expanse of creamy skin.

'This is a tribute, for God's sake!'

'But not to dehydration, darling.'

'Shut up, you two, or we'll never get done!' Dev said through gritted teeth, as he concentrated on holding his earnest expression.

'Come on, man, be serious!' Jimmy called out. 'And three, two...'

Up on stage, there was a loud, protesting, belching sound.

'Are you kidding me?' Jimmy exploded.

'I'm sorry, but I'm starving,' Dev explained with a rueful shrug. 'It's almost four.'

'We'll eat as soon as we have this shot.'

'I'm exhausted,' Sharon said, slumping at the table. 'This is taking too long.'

'Shut *up*!' Ruby, who'd been watching with growing exasperation, yelled. 'Or I'll personally toss the next person who opens his or her mouth out of the show!'

'You can't throw us out of the show!' Pallavi shot back. 'It says so in my contract.'

'Come on, sweethearts, we can do this. Let's just try this one more time,' Jimmy cajoled. 'And here's a little sugar pick-me-up, huh?' he said, handing out chocolate bars to Sharon and Dev.

Fifteen minutes later, fed, refreshed and focussed for a change, Dev finally read the words of tribute flawlessly off the prompter and smiled with just the right mix of bittersweet regret and fond nostalgia, before the cameras panned off him and moved on to Leena.

We're almost there. Don't bungle it, Ruby screamed inside her head, as she watched from her chair. Please.

Leena raised her head and looked straight into the cameras. Her throat convulsed; then slowly, touchingly, a single tear that had been welling in her left eye overflowed the rim of her dark, curling lashes and made its way down her smooth, made-up cheek. The camera followed it lovingly, pausing only at the gently quivering lip, as Leena smiled tremulously at the unseen audience. 'Mala Didi,' she said on a husky half-sob, 'you will be missed.'

'And cut!' Jimmy's voice cut through the silence.

The floodlights dimmed, the cameramen relaxed, the studio crew unfroze, Ruby sagged. Up on stage, Leena dabbed at the perspiration on her face with a tissue and took a sip from the bottle of water she'd placed on the floor.

'Good job,' Jimmy said, reviewing the camera footage on the side monitor. 'Nice touch with the tear, Leena.'

'If only we could all cry on demand,' Pallavi muttered beside her.

'We each have our talents,' Sharon shrugged. 'You, darling, can mouth off on demand.'

'And you, sweetie, can stick it – '

'How come everyone always – '

Ruby plugged her ears with her fingers. 'Jimmy, how much longer?'

Jimmy straightened from behind the monitor on which he was reviewing the shot. 'We have a keeper,' he announced grinning, with the triumphant air of a delivery-room nurse announcing a birth following a long and painful labour.

'So we're done? Oh Jimmy, I love you, love you, love you!' Ruby exclaimed, flinging her arms around his neck.

'Hey! Yuck! Let me go, man!'

'Ruby Madam?'

Ruby turned to see the guard, who usually stood outside the building, shifting uneasily behind her. His grim expression suggested that something was amiss, yet again.

'What is it, Narinder?' Ruby asked.

'Madam, the Chembur Police are here. They want everyone to step outside immediately. They say they have orders to search the building.'

3

MONDAY, 22 OCTOBER

It was a gusty afternoon in Shimla, a northerly wind lashing the last leaves off the deciduous trees and sweeping up whirlwinds of dust in the streets. The Superintendent of Police, back from her short trip to New Delhi, was firmly ensconced behind her desk, resolutely making her way through the several files that had piled up while she was gone, a task considerably aided by the tall thermos of chai Pradeep had procured for her. She initialled the weekly report on challans, took an invigorating sip and glanced up absently as Inspector Chauhan knocked lightly on her door and stood hesitating in the doorway.

'Yes, Deepika, what is it?' Niki pulled the next file towards her from her in-tray.

'Ma'am, about the Mala Joseph case...'

'It's with Crime now, Inspector.'

'Yes, ma'am. Just wanted to tell you that the Chembur Police conducted a search of the *Hot Chef* studios over the weekend.'

Niki's pen paused in mid-signature. 'Did they find anything?'

'Yes, ma'am. They sent across this package,' Deepika took a step in and Niki saw she was carrying a small brown carton in her hand. 'The courier just brought it in.'

Niki frowned at the heavily taped carton. 'What is it?'

'It's labelled "Hazardous Materials", ma'am. Shall I send it to Crime?'

Niki hesitated. 'No, let's open it first.'

Deepika set the package down on the far corner of the desk and carefully removed the various layers of packaging, tape and foil. Inside the small cardboard box was a sealed plastic bag with a tiny fragment of a dark green paper sachet inside it. The letters 'CEL' and half of what looked like a 'P' were printed in bold red across the top of the sachet.

'What's this?' Niki frowned.

'The attached note says it might be a wrapper from a ten-gram pack of Celphos, ma'am.'

'*Celphos?*'

'It's used in wheat and grain storage godowns, ma'am. To kill pests.'

'It's also the number one cause of death by poisoning in India,' Niki said, her voice grim. She typed the word 'CELPHOS' in the search window on her laptop and pulled up some images of the poison. The colours and fonts were identical to those printed on the fragment of paper on her desk.

'They found this at the *Hot Chef* studios?' Niki asked.

'In the pantry, ma'am, underneath the storage cabinets.'

Niki regarded the green paper fragment and thoughtfully placed her pencil between her teeth. 'You know what this means, Deepika?'

'I should send this to the lab for testing, ma'am?'

'And I should call the Chief.'

DGP Kapoor, stuck in the middle of a marathon conference call with Delhi and key states to discuss the Centre's new policy on drug-trafficking control and enforcement, picked up his mobile with a bored, distracted air. His preoccupied 'Hello?' was followed by a frown as he listened to the caller at the other end.

'You *what*?' he hissed into the receiver.

'I just received a package from the Chembur Police, sir,' SP Marwah repeated.

'Chembur, as in Mumbai, Maharashtra?'

'Yes, sir. They searched the *Hot Chef* studios on Saturday.'

'*Hot Chef*?' DGP Kapoor said. The Gaiety fiasco, he recalled, all of a sudden. His frown deepened. 'And they sent *you* a package?'

'Well, sir, we had asked for their help on the Mala Joseph case – '

'Which we closed last Tuesday.'

'Yes, sir. But the Chembur Police searched the studios last Saturday – '

'But why? It was an open-and-shut suicide case, as far as I remember.'

'As you say, sir. But they searched the studios in response to – '

'Dammit, Marwah, we ruled it a suicide!'

'I believe we did, sir.'

'It *was* a suicide!'

On the speakerphone, the DGP Karnataka was still vociferously elaborating on his comments on the Centre's proposals.

'Marwah,' the Chief said, turning his back on the loud, stentorian voice in the background, 'the woman almost killed herself with an overdose of sleeping pills six months ago.'

'Yes, sir.'

'She was married to one man, but pregnant by another.'

'Apparently, sir.'

'And she typed a suicide note on her phone right before she died. And don't you dare say she didn't finish the word "understand"!'

Niki was silent.

'So give me one good reason why it was not a suicide.'

'She bought a teddy bear, sir.'

'Did you say *teddy bear*?'

'A white one, sir. With a pink bow. I think she bought it for the baby.'

'A teddy bear,' the Chief repeated, his voice clearly conveying incredulity. 'And *that's* our reason for reopening the case? A teddy bear with a pink bow?'

'I'm not saying we should reopen the case, sir. Just that – '

'Well, that's what the damn husband is saying!'

'Husband, sir? You mean Mala's husband, sir?'

'Yes, that wretched man – what's his name… Joseph someone…'

'Joseph Albert.'

'Fellow's a pest! He's been calling me night and day. On my private mobile number, too! I have half a mind to arrest him on harassment charges!'

'He's grieving, sir.'

'Guy keeps pestering me to reopen the case,' the Chief continued, almost as if he hadn't heard what she'd said. 'Says there's no way his wife could have killed her unborn child. One in a million chance she'd kill herself, maybe, but not a chance in hell she'd kill her baby.'

'He did mention that Mala had really wanted a baby. They'd been looking into fertility options.'

'She found a damn effective one, I must say!'

Niki was silent.

'The case is closed, Marwah,' the Chief said with an air of finality.

'Yes, sir.'

'I don't want to reopen it.'

'I understand, sir.'

'God knows we have enough on our hands already.'

'It is a busy time of year, sir.'

'Right, then.'

'Right, sir.'

'And since you're on the line, you might as well send me the updated YTD numbers on drug seizures. You can coordinate with Mathur and Joshi for the latest numbers.'

'Right away, sir.'

Niki hung up. She turned in her chair and gazed out the window, fighting down the tumult of feelings.

She jumped as the phone on her desk rang again.

'Marwah,' she heard the Chief say without preamble.

'Sir?'

'What did you say was in the package the Chembur Police sent you?'

'Well, sir, I didn't say.'

The Chief took a calming breath. 'And what were you *going to* say?'

'That it was a fragment of a Celphos pack.'

'Celphos? You mean that agri-poison?'

'Yes, sir.'

'And they found a packet in the studio, you said?'

'A fragment of a sachet, sir. It had evidently been opened.'

There was a moment's silence at the other end of the line. 'This Mala Joseph woman,' the Chief said again, his voice weary, 'she bought a teddy bear on the day she died?'

'Yes, sir. From a gift store on the Mall.'

'Maybe she collected teddy bears?'

'No, sir. She did not have any teddy bears.'

'You checked?'

'We did, sir.'

'But she bought a teddy bear the day she died.'

'A white one with a – '

' – pink bow, you told me,' the Chief said. 'Could be for a niece or a nephew.'

'She didn't have any, sir. Also, she was a registered organ donor.' Niki held her breath. 'Anything else, sir?'

'No.'

'Right then, sir. I'll send you that drug-seizure data shortly.'

'Oh. Right. And Marwah?'

'Sir?'

'Talk to the Chembur Police. Ask them to forward us the report on their godown search.'

'Yes, sir.'

'And give those damn *Hot Chef* people a call. Ask them what the hell they mean by having all kinds of poisonous substances just lying around in their pantry.'

'Sure, sir.'

'And check if – ' the Chief stopped short and Niki held her breath. 'Dammit, Marwah,' he finally bit out, 'sort this out.'

'Sir?'

'I don't want my dreams to be haunted by teddy bears for the rest of my life, okay? So talk to whoever you need to, go down there or whatever, shake the damn truth out of this thing. Do whatever the hell you have to, understand?'

'Absolutely, sir.'

ASP Sahay walked into his boss's office an hour later to find her presiding over a table piled with folders and files, all marked 'MJ'.

'I take it those are not the Michael Jackson case files?'

'No, ASP Sahay, they're not.'

Sahay watched as the guard came in with yet another armful of files and placed them next to the existing stacks of files and folders on Niki's desk. 'So the reason you're decorating your desk with all these files is...?'

'The Chief asked me to review some of the information from the Mala Joseph case.'

'The *Chief* asked you? Wow, boss, how on earth did you manage that?'

'I didn't "manage" anything. The Chembur Police had searched the *Hot Chef* studios over the weekend. They found a packet of Celphos there.'

'Celphos! Are you sure?'

'I've sent the packet to the lab; we should know for sure by the evening.'

'There is something seriously wrong with that show,' Sahay said. 'But boss, hadn't you called off that search?'

'I guess I forgot to call it off.'

No one on the boss's team, least of all the boss herself, ever 'forgot' to do something, Sahay knew. He eyed Niki as she flipped open one of the files. 'I bet the phone calls didn't hurt either,' he teased.

'What phone calls?'

So they were not to talk about those either. But the boss had told him that Joseph had been calling her and that she had advised him to speak directly with the Chief, had even given him the Chief's private mobile number.

He looked down at the wealth of binders and folders on the boss's desk. There were more than a dozen. 'Um, what part of the case are you reviewing exactly?'

'All of it. We need to look at the case afresh, from start to finish; see what we've been missing.'

'Did you say "we"?'

'You, me, Deepika. We can divide these files up between us, go over them in detail, see if anything stands out. Shall we meet in my office at eight to discuss them?'

'Eight *p.m.*? You mean *today*?'

'We could meet at nine…'

Sahay sighed and reached for a pile of folders.

4

Evening fell early in the hills, especially in the colder, shorter days of October. By 8.30 p.m., most of the tourists were long back in their hotels, lingering over a drink, wrapping up dinner or relaxing in their rooms. All across Shimla, cosy fires burned in fireplaces, while old-time residents curled up on sofas and armchairs, knitting, reading, watching TV, surfing the web. Mall Road was silent, the Ridge deserted.

The imposing Municipal Building that straddled them both and housed the offices of the Superintendent of Police was also quiet, with most of the staff having left for the day. The long corridors were devoid of life, the row of offices up on the third floor of the building dark, but a soft glow of light leaked out from under the door of one large rectangular room at the very end, where SP Marwah and her two colleagues sat gazing at the video recording of the camera and audio footage from the Gaiety Theatre that played on the pull-down screen.

ASP Sahay reached for a slice of pizza from the carton that sat in the middle of the table, while on the screen Mala Joseph tasted and commented, watched and listened, laughed and flirted with the camera. Jimmy had been right, he thought; she *had* been a natural. She came across as wholesome, lovable, happy; it was almost surreal to think that this person, complimenting Pallavi on her falafels with such enthusiasm and generosity, would, just minutes later, drop dead on the floor. Sahay frowned as he sat chewing on his pizza, while his boss, seated beside him, chewed on her pencil, remote in hand. She froze the tape as Rajat called out Vicky's name and Mala reached out for her cup of coffee.

'Fourth sip of coffee,' she murmured.

'And the third time she's looked at her watch,' observed Inspector Chauhan, who sat upright in her chair, notepad and pencil in hand.

Niki played the tape again. Mala tasted Vicky's dish and complimented him profusely, as did the other judges, and then it was Shaq's turn. Mala was less fulsome in her praise this time, appreciating the effort, but pointing out that the end result was not up to the mark. She took another sip of coffee and then a sip of water as the plates were cleared; her fingers played with the pencil she held in her hand. Her gaze shifted from the audience to Rajat and then KK, the wings, down to her lap.

'She's definitely nervous about something,' Sahay said.

'She's nervous because she's decided to tell Joseph she's pregnant.'

The realization hit Niki with the force of lightning even as she said the words. She froze the tape and picked up the transcript that lay on the table in front of her.

'Joe, I'm so sorry,' she read aloud. 'I've made a mess of everything. And I can't fix it. So I'm quitting. Everything. The show. The ads. This whole, unbearable life. I hope you'll underst'

'*That's* what this text message was about,' Niki said, putting the transcript down. 'It wasn't a farewell message; it was a confession.'

'Which got interrupted, before she could complete it,' Sahay said.

'Because someone killed her,' Niki added.

She glanced at the case files that lay spread open between them, covering the large table. On top of the pile before her was a single document, several pages long, that was the official post-mortem report, open to the page titled: 'Toxicology Findings'. Under it, a single item was listed as 'positive'. Potassium cyanide.

'Boss,' Sahay said, following Niki's gaze, 'do you think someone killed her because she was pregnant?'

'Well, then, of all the people, her husband was the one who had the motive to kill her,' Deepika said. 'Considering she cheated on him.'

'Except that he had no idea she was pregnant,' Niki said.

'And he wasn't there,' Sahay reminded. 'So who?'

'Someone who *was* there,' Niki said. She pointed the remote and started the tape again. The movements of the judges on the screen unfroze, Rajat's voice came on to introduce the next contestant, with a short commentary on the history, origins and rarefied status of French food and its influence on cuisines worldwide. 'And today we will sample the best of that tradition with Dev Nair and his coq au vin!' Rajat announced. 'Come on up, Dev!'

The three officers sat forward in their chairs as they watched Dev walk up to the judges' table and serve his dish. They watched closely as Mala lifted a spoonful to her mouth. Her face puckered instantly into an expression of distaste, her hand reached for a napkin; she appeared to spit out the mouthful. She reached for the bottle of water nearest her and took a sip, swirling it around in her cheeks. 'It's burnt,' she said to Dev, who looked crestfallen.

'She spat the entire thing out,' Sahay murmured.

'So did the others,' Deepika noted, as KK and Ashika followed suit, tasting and spitting out their spoonfuls.

'It couldn't have been the coq au vin.'

'Unlikely.'

On screen, KK finished delivering what sounded like a biting tirade to a sheepish Dev, who turned back, dejected, and walked out of the camera frame towards the contestants' bench. Rajat's voice picked up once again, this time to describe the rich colours, flavours and traditions of Spanish cuisine.

Niki slowed the tape. All three officers held their breath as Rajat walked into the frame, calling out the name of the final contestant. 'The stunning, sexy, completely insane… *Sharon Sen!*' he announced, smiling wide, and turned to look towards the contestants' bench. A ripping sound, a muffled shriek; an audible gasp was heard off camera.

On camera, Rajat's smile faded, his brows came together, his outstretched arm fell. The last frame before the screen went blank showed the judges' table with all three judges turning their heads to see what was going on and a blurry image of Rajat's back as he crossed the stage floor.

'I don't see anything new, boss,' Sahay said, after a moment. He wiped his fingers with a napkin, took a sip of water and rolled his chair forward.

'The table is clear,' Deepika agreed.

Niki cupped her chin, her brow furrowed in concentration. Deepika was right. The used plates had been removed from the judges' table by the stage assistant and the space before Mala was clean.

'Which means the poison appeared after the cameras stopped recording,' she said, almost to herself. 'Which narrows it down to Ashika, KK and Rajat. They were the only ones there at the time.'

'I think we can rule out Ashika,' Inspector Chauhan said. 'She was barely acquainted with Mala, besides being seated across from her.'

'Not to mention her sheer terror at the thought of a poison-gas attack,' Sahay agreed. 'My money's on Rajat.'

'Why Rajat?' Niki asked.

'Because it's obvious he's the one who Mala was having an affair with. He and Mala were very "close"; half the show's crew thought there was something going on between them; even Joseph seemed jealous. And just look at all the texts she sent him!'

Niki glanced down at the file that contained the long list of text messages exchanged between Mala's phone and Rajat's. There were over fifty that had been exchanged, across multiple conversation threads, in just the last three days before her death; some of them, highlighted by Sahay, decidedly flirty in tone. And yet there was an openness, a lack of self-consciousness in the banter that made Niki wonder. How could Mala have been joking about Rajat's '80s Jeetendra-style haircut and his 'reduced chances of pataoing Ashika' if she'd been pregnant with his child? Wouldn't their conversations have had a darker, more serious tone?

'And,' Sahay added, 'he passed *right* by the table as the cameras went off; in fact, his hand probably brushed the tabletop as he passed by. He could easily have slipped her something, like a toffee or cough drop laced with cyanide.'

'But why?' Deepika asked. 'Even if they were having an affair, why would he poison her?'

'Because she got pregnant and he panicked,' Sahay said. 'Or because he wanted her to leave Joseph when she told him about the baby, but she didn't agree. Maybe that's what pushed him over the edge. He couldn't handle the rejection.'

'The jilted lover?' Deepika mused.

Sahay glanced at Niki, who was gazing thoughtfully at the last frame, still frozen with the three judges' heads in profile. 'What do *you* think, boss?' he asked.

'I think Rajat may have had the opportunity to slip her the cyanide. But so did KK.'

'He was sitting right next to her,' Sahay agreed. 'But why would he do it? Professional rivalry?'

'Or not. They were working on something together, I'm pretty sure,' Niki said. She picked up the thick file containing the transcripts of emails sent from Mala's iPad that the Communications Division had printed out, that she'd flipped through a couple of hours ago. 'There's a flurry of emails back and forth about various recipes that she appeared to have been developing. "Chatpat Stew", "Kochi Karhi", "Jhinga Chhole Masala", "Makhni Maachh".'

'They sound fairly innovative,' Sahay said.

'And they reminded me of that north-south fusion food joint venture Jimmy had mentioned.'

'The one he said Mala was very excited about,' Sahay nodded.

'And KK was extremely cagey about. He said it was at a very preliminary stage. But these emails from Mala seem to suggest otherwise.'

'You think the joint venture may have some connection with Mala's death?' Sahay asked.

'I don't know.' Niki turned to the last email that Mala had sent KK. 'Listen to this: *"I'll need more time to complete the final recipes, KK. Something's come up. I'll explain when we meet."* This was sent two days before she died.'

'And yet KK didn't mention it when we interviewed him,' Sahay frowned. 'Why?'

'Exactly.' Niki gazed at the screen again. KK's face, turned away from the camera, revealed nothing. 'Inspector Chauhan,' she asked. 'Where can I find KK? In Mumbai?'

Deepika shook her head. 'I spoke with Ruby Talwar this evening, ma'am,' she said. 'She told me that after the Chembur Police found that Celphos packet, they shut down the studio. They're doing a complete fumigation and restocking of the pantry and they've decided to temporarily vacate the studios until they can have a purification ceremony.'

'Purification ceremony?'

'A havan, I believe, ma'am. In the meantime, they'll be shooting the next episode at an off-site location in Madhya Pradesh. They are supposed to be on their way there tonight.'

5

The luxury tour bus, with the words 'Five Star Travels' emblazoned across its sides, sped westwards on Highway 75 dwarfing the tempos and two-wheelers it overtook and left in its wake. Its triple-reinforced rubber tyres spun soundlessly, making quick work of the two-lane highway. The distance markers zipped by, informing the passengers inside that the town of Panna was seven, six, five kilometres away.

Inside the bus, seated alone in the third row from the front, Pallavi Aanand went over the contents of the letter in her hands once more.

Madam,
    This is to bring to your attention the following:
    As of 20 October 2012, the settlement of arrears to the tune of Rs 20,56,000 (Rupees twenty lakh fifty-six thousand only), as detailed in our previous notices to you, dated 17 July 2012, 23 August 2012 and 19 September 2012 respectively, for billed and unbilled legal fees and billed and unbilled expenses incurred and disbursements made on behalf of our client, Mr Kedar Nath Aanand and family, residing at 17C Carter Road, Pali Hill, Mumbai 400050, is 195 days overdue and thereby delinquent.
    Given the failure of the aforesaid Mr Kedar Nath Aanand and family to honour the terms of our agreement, we hereby inform you that we are left with no alternative but to declare the said agreement null and void, terminate our longstanding client-attorney relationship and withdraw herewith the legal services we had been providing our client for many years. In addition, please be informed that in accordance with Clause No. 15 (a), Section IV...

Pallavi crumpled the letter between her fingers. Bastards, she thought. And now they were threatening to start legal proceedings for the appropriation and sale of their family home in Bandra, their one remaining home, which had belonged to her *mother's* great-grandfather...

She glanced out the window and gazed, as the bus made a sweeping turn, at the wide expanse of water that had sailed into view. Its glassy green surface, dappled with white lilies and framed by red earth and green vegetation, stretched out to meet the horizon. In the distance, a stately bird sat motionless on a tiny outcrop in the water. Beyond it, the shadowy outline of a hill on the far bank completed the picture of untouched natural beauty and created a fleeting impression of timelessness.

Pallavi felt her spirits lift as she gazed out across the water. The exhaustion of the past several weeks, the scorching heat of an afternoon excursion to Khajuraho, the implications of the legal notice she held in her hands, all faded for a moment as she watched the bird spread its wings and soar off. She followed its flight till it became a speck, suspended above the world and its strife; she tore the letter in her hands into tiny shreds. Then she slid open her window and let the fragments of paper sail away in the breeze.

So Dad was likely to cool his heels in prison, she thought. So *she* had to cough up ₹20 lakhs or see her mother's home attached and auctioned off to the highest bidder. So they had frozen all her bank accounts and seized all her 'assets'. Well, they could not seize this moment...or the moments that lay ahead.

The bus sped across the bridge and turned right off the highway. It plunged down a deserted dirt path, flanked by an undulating, unending line of tall trees and scrub, with not a single structure or soul in sight. As they drove deeper and deeper into the vegetation, Leena, seated across the aisle from Pallavi in the sixth row, looked out her window at the thick foliage that seemed to envelop them and felt her trepidation grow. She glanced over at Vicky, sitting beside her and scribbling busily on a sheet of paper.

'Looks like we're going into some kind of dense jungle,' she said.

'Maybe they just want to release Binod into his natural habitat,' Vicky quipped, without raising his head from the scrap of paper.

'What's that?' Leena asked, as he wrote, in the margin beside a set of calculations, LD: 26.16%.

'Your current chances of winning.'

'What?'

'I've been working out probabilities for each of us, based on past voting data.'

'Basically, you're just doing timepass.'

'Actually, it's very scientific. I have a fairly robust model into which I've factored in all kinds of variables. So far, you're in the lead. But Pallavi's close at 24.67 per cent.'

'That's utter nonsense. According to your model, you and Shaq are tied at just 18 per cent each.'

'As of now. Doesn't mean something can't happen any time to change that.'

'How about me offing Vicky?' Shaq volunteered from the seat behind. 'What would it do to my chances of winning?'

'Improve them by 45 per cent,' Vicky said.

'I'd say it's a chance worth taking. What do you say, Leena?'

'I say you guys are both mental.'

'Of course, our odds improve the most if we off Leena...' Vicky grinned.

The tour bus followed the path deeper and deeper through the thickening foliage until, finally, a kilometre or so in, it took a sharp right and jolted to a halt in a large clearing. Leena looked out at the row of dark green Jeeps that stood parked under a smart brick structure in the distance. Next to them were parked the Innova that had ferried the judges over and the other two buses that had brought the show's crew by road from Mumbai.

Barkha, seated in the front of the bus and busy on her mobile, got to her feet as the driver cut the engine. 'All right,' she said, turning to face the contestants, 'wake up. We're here.'

Leena peered at the array of cameras positioned all around the bus in the clearing. 'Where exactly is "here"?' she asked.

'They're still readying the cameras for the "arrival" shot,' Barkha continued, ignoring the question. 'Everyone stay in their seats.'

'But what about – '

Leena turned as the door at the front of the bus flew open and Jimmy, dashing in tight black jeans and a cheetah-print tee shirt, poked his head in.

'Made it here in one piece? Awesome. Welcome to the Jungle Book Resort at the Panna Tiger Reserve!'

'Ooh, I love tigers!' Sharon trilled.

'Is this another sightseeing tour?' Pallavi asked.

'No, this is the site of your next challenge,' Jimmy said. 'Five hundred unspoiled square kilometres of tall grass and dense jungle; antelope, deer, sambar, nilgai, chinkara, peacocks, eagles, vultures, jackal, gharial and, of course, the majestic tiger!'

The next challenge? Leena supressed a shiver of apprehension. 'What will we have to do?' she asked.

'For now, you just have to get ready for the arrival shot,' Jimmy said. 'Nothing too fancy; just everyone getting down from the bus and checking out the new venue. I want enthusiasm, determination, wonder, energy. A hint of something wild would be nice, but don't get too carried away. Take a moment to freshen up; put on some bright smiles; and then get down from the front door, single file, one at a time. Give the person in front of you fifteen seconds before you alight. I want Leena to go first, Pallavi second, then Sharon, Vicky, Shaq, Dev. And remember, no pushing or crowding or scowls or squints, or we'll be stuck here doing retakes all afternoon!'

6

It could have been worse, Leena consoled herself as she collected her things and waited at the top of the steps. After days of uncertainty and inaction, of mourning and tributes, of chewing on nails and not knowing, at least they were in another challenge. Even if it was in a creepy jungle; it was still better than hanging about the Hot Chef House, playing 'friendly' games of ludo and cards and snakes and ladders, all the time looking nervously over your shoulder and wondering what the others were plotting. At least, here, she could focus and cook and win again…

At the far edge of the clearing, obscured from view by the branches of a teak tree, Rajat Tripathi stood alone, a cup of black coffee in hand, readying himself for the arrival shot. He knew he needed to focus, to empty his mind of everything else and think only of his opening lines. A short mention of Mala and her 'constant presence', a reminder of the ephemeral yet blessed gift of life and then a smart, snappy segue to the 'call of the wild'. Ninety seconds and out. Easy as ABC. At least, in theory and according to Jimmy, who'd set it up, written the words, even helped him rehearse them. All Rajat needed to do now was to remember them and spout them with the right degree of emotion and animation, his voice rising from tender reminiscence through uplifting thought to a burst of fresh energy: ready-set-go-go-go!

Except that, try as he might, the words refused to come. Mala was a constant presence on the show, Jimmy had told him to say, and truer, more ironic words Rajat could not think of. She was a constant presence in his thoughts, in his dreams, right before his eyes. She was present everywhere – on the plane to Khajuraho, in the temples they had visited, in the hot jungle air, in the cup of black coffee in his hand that they had once shared and that tasted like ashes now…

He drained the last of the ashes with a furious impatience and almost flung the cup to the ground. No, he thought. He would not allow himself to fall apart. Not now; not ever. Mala was dead, but he had his entire life ahead of him.

'Rajat, ready?' he heard Jimmy call.

'Like hell,' he said and strode briskly over.

The main lounge of the Jungle Book Resort, a 20-acre facility of forty independent cottages that stretched along the west bank of the sparkling Ken River, was fronted by a large, veranda-like structure built high off the ground and reminiscent of an earlier, more peaceful time. Its hardened clay floor was decorated with colourful motifs and its sloping terracotta tile roof rested on sturdy columns and a bamboo frame. Beneath it, cane sofas and chairs were arranged in comfortable groups under bamboo ceiling fans; an antique chessboard with carved wood pieces was set out on a table between two high-backed chairs in a quiet corner. Nearer the front steps, a 78-rpm record was playing 'Aaj Phir Jeene Ki Tamanna Hai' from the film *Guide* on an ancient gramophone. Outside, terracotta jugs and vases were gathered round a hand pump. A charpoy sat under the shade of a leafy tree.

'The simple, bare necessities of life,' Vijendra Pratap Singh, the grizzled, gentlemanly owner-manager of the resort told Ruby, with a fond glance round the veranda. 'All of the comforts; none of the frills. At night, what you hear are the sounds of nature, not the air conditioner. You are going to love it here.'

'Yes, it's very beautiful, but is it safe?'

'Perfectly safe,' Vijendra assured her. 'The jungle and the river are natural barriers and the animals rarely venture near the inhabited areas.'

'It's not the animals I'm worried about!'

'I know what you mean,' Vijendra nodded with understanding. 'Luckily, in this part of MP, we don't have to worry about dacoits. But we do advise our guests to keep their valuables in the safety deposit boxes and to secure all doors and windows at night. And we have guards at the gates – two in the day and two at night. All four are well trained and very experienced. No need to worry about a thing.'

And yet Ruby was worried. 'What about the food arrangements?' she asked.

'I have had the storeroom cleaned and thoroughly checked, just as you requested,' Vijendra assured her. 'Your kitchen manager can check all the items himself, stock it with whatever supplies he needs and then keep the lock with him. The rest of the meals will be prepared in our kitchen by our chef, Gopal. He has been with us for many years; I know you will be impressed. And you are most welcome to tell him about any special concerns you may have.'

Ruby pondered over the most diplomatic way to ask Chef Gopal whether he had any poison in his kitchen…

Vijendra, meanwhile, had pulled out a heavy bunch of old-fashioned brass keys from a drawer in the console, along with a folded map. It was a sprawling sketch of the resort, Ruby saw, as Vijendra unfolded it and spread it on the table, with variously shaded green areas denoting the thick vegetation and, amidst them, clusters of thatch-roofed cottages that stood at the river's edge.

'I've placed your contestants in villas on the south side of the resort, which is our most secluded private area,' Vijendra said, pointing. 'The rest of your group will be on the north side.' He circled a small cluster of smaller cottages with his finger. 'I have reserved these six single-occupancy luxury cottages on the north side for your executive team,' he said. 'Cottages Eleven to Sixteen. Each is furnished with a king-size bed, brick fireplace, sun porch, courtyard, rose garden, minibar and Jacuzzi tub.'

Ruby did a double take. 'Did you say *Jacuzzi*?'

'Newly installed,' Vijendra beamed, 'and furnished with our exclusive range of complimentary aromatherapy oils and candles. At night, you can lie back and see the stars through the skylights. And did I mention our in-room champagne-and-chocolates service?'

The simple, bare necessities, Ruby thought with a happy smile.

Out by the resort's main entrance, the welcome shot was over, the cameras dismantled, the crew dispersed, everyone, besides the contestants, having been shown to their rooms for some much-anticipated rest after the hustle and heat of the long morning and afternoon. Tired, her nerves strained, her head pounding from the unaccustomed exertion, Barkha regarded Raghavendra Pratap Singh, the animated nineteen-year-old Assistant Resort Manager and only son of Vijendra Pratap Singh, with growing exasperation. His tight red tee-shirt was rolled up at the sleeves to flaunt burgeoning biceps; his camouflage cargo pants were held up at the waist by a studded metal belt; and his aviator sunglasses glinted in the late afternoon sun as he stood gushing over the girls.

'Pallavi, Leena… Wow! I'm, like, a huge fan! Please, call me Raghu. Or Rags. Sharon, ma'am, you're even hotter in person! Sizzling!'

'You're not half bad yourself, darling,' Sharon drawled.

'Oh, for heaven's sake!' Pallavi groaned. 'Can we go? It's like a hundred degrees out here.'

'I'm tired,' Leena agreed.

'Can we get a move on?' Barkha demanded.

'Sure! So sorry, Auntyji,' Raghu smiled, temporarily depriving Barkha of her power of speech.

He led the group to the two Jeeps parked in the shade of a sturdy teak and called out to the wiry old man who was dozing behind the wheel in one of them.

'Jaspal,' he said, shaking the old man gently by the shoulder, 'Chal, ustad. Mehmaan logo ko south side le chal.'

He turned to Barkha who stood holding her head, her face scrunched up against the sun's glare. 'The guys can go with Jaspal, Auntyji; the ladies can come with me. Do you need some help getting in?'

Barkha swatted his hand away and hoisted herself into the passenger seat with a muffled curse. Rags, oblivious of the murderous looks she shot at him, gallantly assisted the girls into the back of the Jeep, whistling happily as he stowed their luggage.

'Why are we going in the Jeep?' Leena asked, as he popped round again once the luggage was secured. 'Everyone else went that way.' She pointed to the path that led out of the clearing and towards the main resort building.

'That's because their cottages are here, on the north side.' Rags hoisted himself over the door of the Jeep and behind the wheel with practised flair and put the key in the ignition. 'You'll be in the cottages on the south side.'

'Segregation,' Pallavi muttered.

'The south-side villas are actually our best-kept secret,' Rags told her with a grin. 'You'll have complete privacy, a spectacular view of the jungle and, best of all, you'll be right at the water's edge! You'll see...'

Barkha held on to the sides of the Jeep as it jolted and bumped down one twisting path after another, as Raghu gunned the engine and held forth on the various particulars of his life, his college, his musical obsessions, his rock band, his hopes to land a gig soon.

'I'm actually just helping Dad out for the weekend,' he confided above the roar of the engine. 'Had to, when he told me who the guests would be!' He grinned at Sharon in the rear-view mirror. 'Next month, though, I'll be off to Mumbai with my buddies to play in the college festivals. Dad's not totally on board, but he'll come round...'

'I'm sure you'll be all the rage, darling,' Sharon assured him.

'Is that a kingfisher?' Leena asked as a bird lifted off from a tree in the distance.

'What? Oh, no, that's a babbler.'

'One in the car and one in the bush,' Pallavi remarked with a sarcasm that was entirely lost on her audience.

'The Ken River is actually home to over three hundred species of birds,' Rags said, belatedly remembering his role as guide and host. He slowed down the Jeep, so his guests could get a better look. 'It is one of the most beautiful, pristine rivers in the country and it cuts right through the heart of the jungle. It flows through two of India's largest states: MP and UP. And it is over 400 kilometres long!'

'Wow,' Pallavi said with exaggerated wonder. 'And exactly how many of those kilometres will we have to traverse till we get to our cottages?'

'Let's find out!'

Rags pressed down on the accelerator and the Jeep bounced forward once more. Barkha felt her teeth rattle in her head as he turned down yet another dirt path and emerged onto the highway.

'What are you doing, you maniac? We're back on the main road!'

'I know,' Rags grinned. 'Actually, the south side is just a ten-minute walk from the north side if you take the walking path through the resort. But I'm taking the long route because of the luggage. It's not far now...' He plunged the Jeep off the highway and onto another dirt path, which twisted and turned between thickly packed trees for several minutes, then slowed to a halt as they emerged into daylight again. 'And here we are...' he said in his best Rajat Tripathi imitation trill, 'the south-side villas, also known at the Jungle Book Resort as Bagheera's Den.'

The contestants gazed at the pair of picturesque villas that sat sparkling in the sunshine against a backdrop of oak trees. Each villa was made of mud, glazed a deep golden yellow, and had a vivid red terracotta tile roof, wooden doors and a wrap-around wooden deck.

Between the two villas was a clearing of baked earth, with deck chairs, hammocks and a fire pit. Behind the clearing, the wide expanse of the river sparkled golden in the late afternoon sun. It was as lovely as it was untouched; it seemed as miraculous as an oasis at the end of the long, gruelling day.

'Oh. My. God,' Sharon breathed. 'I could just dump my bags and jump straight in that river.'

'You *could*!' Rags enthused. 'There is a path at the back that leads to a secluded part of the riverbank. Complete privacy.'

'Is it safe?' Leena frowned.

'Oh yeah. The water is quite shallow at this point, just maybe knee-high. And we almost never get any gharial this close to the shore. Just some river snakes, but those are harmless. Not to worry.'

Leena shuddered involuntarily, while Barkha muttered something about how her real worry was not for the contestants but for the poor river snakes. 'No jumping in the river,' she growled, with a pointed glare at Rags.

Rags grinned and jumped out of the Jeep. 'As you can see, we have two separate villas, each with three bedrooms, attached baths, living room and kitchenette,' he said, leading the way down the path towards the villas. 'There's twenty-four-hour hot and cold running water, a phone that connects through the switchboard in each unit and also a mini fridge with some complimentary beverages.' He turned as he heard the sound of an approaching Jeep and smiled. 'Ah, there comes Jaspal. He'll settle the guys in that villa,' he pointed to the one on the left, 'and here are the keys to this one.' He handed Barkha a set of large brass keys on a ring and closed her stubby fingers over it. 'Don't tell anyone, but yours is just a tiny bit bigger,' he whispered.

He straightened and beamed round at the three contestants. 'All right, ladies. I'll let you all settle in and freshen up. And then I'll be back at five to escort you to the main lounge. Have fun!'

'I'm taking this room,' Pallavi announced, making a beeline for the largest room in the villa as soon as they were inside. 'And I'm calling first dibs on taking a shower.'

'Whatever,' Barkha said. She headed to the sofa by the bay window in the living room and eased herself down. 'As long as you don't disturb me.'

'I guess I'll take that room, then,' Leena said, picking the room that was closest to the door. It had a window, she noticed, that looked out onto the clearing and, past it, to the boys' villa, where Jaspal was just showing Vicky and the others in.

'And I'll take the river,' Sharon grinned, pulling off her tee-shirt.

In the boys' villa, in one of the smaller rooms, Shaq unpacked his bags, stowed his toiletries away in the bathroom and headed towards the kitchenette. He pulled out a bottle of soda from the mini fridge and snapped the cap open with his teeth. He took a long, thirsty drag and then sauntered outside to the clearing, where Vicky was lying on the hammock, watching the river flow gently by. Across the water, the tops of the trees glowed a golden orange in the sun.

'Nice,' Shaq said, easing himself into a deck chair beside Vicky.

'Like the gods set the jungle on fire.'

'You have a vivid imagination.'

'So where's lover boy? Lost him?'

'Sadly, no. He's singing songs in the shower. I was tempted to "misplace" his clothes.'

Vicky grinned. 'And Binchod?'

'Misplaced altogether, hopefully.'

'If only we were so lucky.' Vicky held out a hand for the bottle Shaq had brought with him and took a swig.

Shaq sat back in his deck chair and lifted his face to catch a momentary breeze. He smiled as he caught sight of the lone figure in the distance. 'Speaking of setting the jungle on fire...' he said.

Vicky followed his gaze to where, at the river's edge, Sharon Sen was walking across the stones in a bright orange bikini. She waded a few metres into the water, squealing in delight, and stood a moment, arms outstretched, ostensibly embracing the setting sun.

'Hey, Sharon!' Vicky called out. 'Planning to go skinny-dipping?'

'Only if you join me, sugar,' Sharon called back.

'I said no swimming in the river!' they heard Barkha roar from somewhere inside the girls' villa. 'Sharon, get back inside this minute! Binod, where the hell are you?!'

Binod, who'd been ogling Sharon from his window, leaned out reluctantly. 'No swimming and no loitering!' he called out in a stern voice.

'Hey, Binchod!' Vicky called.

'What?' Binod scowled down at him.

'Chashma laga le saale!'

An hour later, with the last remnants of daylight winking between the trees, Rags led the contestants jauntily down the walking path from the south-side villas to the main resort buildings on the north side. The evening sun twinkled through the sieve-like cover of branches and leaves as they followed him, single file, down the heavily wooded trail, and Rags, in no visible hurry, stopped now and then to point out the whimsically named points of interest along the way, such as Akela's Rock, Baloo's Back and a tiny stream gurgling under a footbridge that he called Kaa's Hiss. 'It might look like a piddly thing right now,' he said, picking up a pebble and tossing it into the water with a smooth flex of his biceps, 'but this little trickle was a ten-foot-deep torrent three monsoons ago. The water rose up to the tops of those trees.' He pointed to the row of trees in the distance that towered above a cluster of mud huts. 'See those lines on the trunks? They're water marks,' he said. 'The flood took out this whole area, including the bridge we're standing on.'

He continued down the path along the raised banks of Kaa's Hiss for a short stretch, then turned past a cluster of cottages that he pointed out as 'VIP digs, twenty grand a pop'.

'That's where Dad's put up your judges and top brass,' he said. 'But don't worry, your south-side villas are, hands down, cooler. All the Swedes and Aussies like to go there. To sunbathe and skinny-dip.'

They passed through a long stretch of tall grasses and brush to finally emerge onto a pebbled path that meandered through a wide, grassy expanse. In the distance, framed by the evening sky and the river flowing behind, the main reception lounge of the Jungle Book Resort looked serene and inviting.

Rags led the contestants through the deserted veranda and up a short flight of wide stairs. 'Wanna see our Jungle Book kitchen?' he said, pushing open a narrow door off the landing.

Leena followed the others into the small room and looked around with interest. The space was small, but functional. New chrome gadgets with a wood finish blended into freshly painted cabinetry without detracting from the rustic look of the place, and rows of gleaming copper-bottomed pots and pans and utensils hung from hooks and nails above the smooth stone counters. Above, industrial-grade lighting illuminated a spotless steel cooktop and, off to one end, an enormous wooden bench opened up to reveal a commercial-grade deep freezer. Dev pulled open a door hidden in the wall to reveal a newly stocked pantry and whistled. Vicky stepped closer to check out the array of spices, while Shaq stood admiring the plenitude of knives gleaming in the bright lights.

'Is this where we're going to cook?' Leena asked.

'I hope not!' Pallavi said. 'It's grotesquely cramped.'

'I've worked with twice as many people in kitchens half this size,' Shaq remarked.

'To turn out unremarkable meals for an ignorant audience.'

'We all start somewhere,' Shaq smiled, refusing to be baited. 'Anyway, relax, we won't be cooking in here.'

'How do you know that?'

'Because they didn't bring us all the way into the jungle to have us cook in a fancy kitchen,' Shaq said. 'Am I right, Rags?'

'I don't know, dude; I'm just the tour guide,' Rags grinned. He opened the door and led the contestants back out onto the wooden landing and up yet another flight of steps which seemed to lead right into the treetops above.

'Where are we going now?' Dev asked. 'Jack's Beanstalk?'

'You mean Vultures' Wannado, dummy,' Vicky corrected.

'Try Treetop Restaurant,' Rags beamed. 'World-famous restaurant and open-air bar.'

'Now you're speaking my language, darling,' Sharon called out, speeding up to join them.

The rickety steps wound around a massive tree trunk and ended in a platform that appeared to have been lifted straight out of a fairy tale and set down amidst the trees. The contestants mounted the last step one by one and emerged onto the platform to gape at the multiple tables set under glowing lanterns, the canopy of leaves that filtered the evening light, the trays of wildflowers that filled the air with a heady fragrance, the river that flowed directly below.

'Hi, you all!'

They turned to see, half-hidden behind the trunk of yet another enormous, gnarled tree, Jimmy, KK, Ruby, Rajat and a couple of new faces gathered around what appeared to be the bar.

Jimmy, who had changed into a midnight blue silk shirt and a pair of grey suede jeans, waved them over.

'Surprised, darlings?' he grinned, enjoying the bemused look on the contestants' faces as they walked hesitantly over.

'More like thirsty,' Sharon said, eyeing the bar.

'What's going on?' Vicky asked. 'How come we're in the same room at the same time? I thought we were the untouchables?'

'You are,' Jimmy said fondly. 'In the coolest possible way.'

'And just for tonight,' Ruby added, swooping down on them with Jacuzzi-inspired calm and goodwill, 'we thought it would be nice for us all to get together, to start afresh, on a new note.'

'So we're supposed to…socialize?' Leena asked.

'Is this part of the challenge?' Pallavi asked suspiciously.

'No, the challenge begins tomorrow,' Ruby said. 'Tonight, we're just getting together like good friends and colleagues.'

'But what's the catch?' Pallavi persisted.

'There is no catch.'

KK, seated at the other end of the bar with the two strangers, got up and lumbered towards them. 'This get-together was my idea,' he said, smiling down at them.

'Thanks, darling,' Sharon whispered to the bartender as he handed her a glass.

'It's been a tough week and a half for all of us,' KK continued. 'I know how much Mala meant to each and every one of us. And even though she will always be in our hearts, it is time to move on.'

'Bugger,' Rajat seemed to murmur as he gulped down his glass of Scotch.

'I don't need to tell you that it is impossible to fill Mala's shoes,' KK said to the contestants, ignoring him, 'because you all know that. But Ruby has managed to accomplish the next best thing to impossible.' He waved a hand towards the two strangers who had left their seats and were now standing behind him. 'Let me introduce you to our wonderful new judges...'

The new judges! Leena felt her heart flutter. She fingered her Ganpati pendant and smiled shyly at the strangers, praying that they'd take to her.

'Puru, Mansi,' she heard KK continue, 'may I present to you the very talented, amazingly poised cast of *Hot Chef* – Leena Dixit, Pallavi Aanand, Sharon Sen, Vicky Gulati, Dev Nair and Shaqeel Khan.

'And contestants,' he continued, 'it is my great pleasure to introduce you to Chef Purshottam Prasad, Dean of Kemaal's Culinary Institute, Hyderabad, who has kindly consented to step in as judge for the remainder of the episodes, and Miss Mansi Malhotra, winner of last year's YTV Fashion Designer of the Year award, who will be our guest judge for this very special "Jungle Mein Mangal" episode.'

Chef Prasad, a quiet, balding man in his mid-fifties, who, with his horn-rimmed glasses looked more like a professor than a chef, shook hands with each of the contestants in turn and looked them over speculatively.

Mansi Malhotra, meanwhile, clapped her hands together, smiling broadly, as her heavily kohled eyes swept over them. 'Oh my God!' she said. 'This is surreal. You guys are like fab! My favourites ever. But KK, what is "Jungle Mein Mangal"?'

'Yes, you've been very mysterious, I must say. What exactly are you planning?' Chef Prasad asked.

'Now, now,' KK smiled. 'I don't want to ruin the surprise. Let's just say it's going to be an episode to remember.'

7

SATURDAY, 27 OCTOBER, 4 A.M.

The vast, timeless expanse of the jungle that lay across the heart of the country seemed still and slumbering in the predawn hours. The sky was inky black, the wind chilly, as the six bleary-eyed contestants made their way down the narrow, wooded path to the main reception area on the north side of the Jungle Book Resort, where they were handed over by a barely awake Raghu to a lean man of indeterminate age who stood waiting in the small lounge off the veranda. He sized them up with a measuring glance and introduced himself as Mr Ganpath, their trainer.

Mr Ganpath waited for Raghu to leave, walked over and locked the door of the lounge, then turned to address the contestants who stood squinting in the room's bright lights, rubbing the sleep from their eyes. 'You'd best wake up as soon as possible,' he said with absolutely no expression on his face. 'Today is going to be a very long day.'

Dev, who was in the middle of a lusty yawn, felt the rest of it disappear down his throat.

'Today will be the day that tests your mettle and your ability to survive, truly survive,' the trainer continued in his deadpan voice. 'Without any extraneous help. No maps, no tools, no clues, no guides. Nothing – apart from your wits and guts. Now, has everybody brought along their wits and guts?'

'Everyone, besides Dev,' Vicky grinned. 'The poor guy has neither.'

'Huh?' Dev blinked, caught in the throes of suppressing yet another yawn. He noticed the amused smiles on Shaq's and Pallavi's faces and scowled. 'We'll see who's smiling at the end of the day,' he said. 'I'm a brown-belt karate champ.'

'Won't help much in the jungle,' Mr Ganpath said, unimpressed. 'Find your wits. And guts. And if you don't have them, then beg, borrow, steal, bite, cut, scrape, hack, collect, find…whatever. This is the jungle. Where everything goes. Except failure.'

He moved over to the wall behind him and pulled down a large screen on which was projected a map of the area.

'All right now, move in closer and listen carefully. We will spend the next hour going over the layout of the jungle. Then we will proceed outside and I will give you a crash course in nature, tracking, wildlife, the local flora and fauna of the place, what to eat to stay alive and what will most certainly kill you. Pay close attention; this will be your only orientation before your challenge begins. Any questions?'

'Can I get a cup of coffee?' Dev asked.

'Breakfast will be served at 8 a.m.,' Ganpath said briskly. 'After the morning session. Anything else?'

'Yeah, um…what's the challenge?'

'To get through the day without asking stupid questions?' Pallavi suggested.

'Okay, so dress appropriately,' Ganpath continued. 'Mornings in the jungle are chilly, which is why I asked you to bring your jackets. The afternoon will get hot; so you will change into loose, light clothing for the challenge. A cap or hat is essential; the sun can be merciless. Reflective sunglasses are not allowed; they distract the animals. Now, food. My advice is, eat a light breakfast and drink plenty of water. You will all be given a two-litre bottle of drinking water at the start of the challenge. After that, you'll be on your own. Keep in mind, there are no bathrooms in the jungle. If you need to go, squat behind any convenient bush or tree. But before you squat, remember to check for snakes; there are several varieties in the reserve and some of them *are* poisonous. Remember, this is a jungle, not a zoo.'

Leena resolved with a shudder to not drink any water. That way, hopefully, she would not have to 'squat'.

By 11.30 a.m., she had changed her mind.

The mid-morning sun burned directly overhead, the air was heavy with the scents and sounds of the jungle – the rustling of leaves, the crackling of dried grasses, the snapping of twigs; the humming, buzzing, clicking, chirping, singing sounds of countless insects busy amidst the tracks and droppings and decomposing carrion. Leena, flagging, parched, picked her way gingerly through the uneven path, several paces behind the others, her nostrils wrinkled in distaste, her feet weighed down by fatigue, her face shiny and clammy with sweat.

How much longer, she wondered, stopping momentarily to catch her breath. They had been tramping behind Mr Ganpath through the dry, baked wilderness for hours, it seemed. They had picked countless herbs, leaves, roots, shoots; they had stooped low over animal droppings and skirted round animal spoor; they had crouched and crawled and observed and noted. And now, with the sun a fiery circle of blinding light high in the cloudless sky, they were somewhere in the middle of the jungle, with no end in sight. And, she thought, the challenge hadn't even begun.

'Leena?' she heard Vicky call from beyond a turn up ahead.

She wiped the sweat dripping into her eyes and licked her dried lips; her throat felt like parchment.

'Come on, come on, no time to sleep now, pick up the pace!' she heard Mr Ganpath's voice bark as he sped over the last stretch of the overgrown pathway several paces ahead. 'This way, everyone...'

They all quickened their pace and hurried to follow him – Shaq and Dev with strong, lithe strides, Sharon and Pallavi with laboured yet determined ones; even Vicky, light and limber and, for once, devoid of his usual sarcasm.

Leena took a brittle, aching breath and hastened to catch up with him.

Ahead in the distance, under the shade of several makeshift tents in a clearing, the *Hot Chef* crew was busy preparing for the day's shoot. They had arrived an hour earlier, well rested and refreshed by a hearty breakfast in the resort's rooftop restaurant and had finished setting up the equipment that they had brought with them in the sturdy, dirt-encrusted Jeeps. Jimmy stood under the shade of an imposing tree in his orange WWF tee-shirt and moss green cargo shorts, discussing angles and lighting with a bunch of technicians, while all around a seasoned team of half a dozen cameramen – togged out in caps, sneakers and sunglasses and bearing shoulder-mounted equipment – waited, their cameras trained on the trees to the south. They grew attentive as Ganpath appeared through the cluster of thick trees.

'And action,' Jimmy called.

The cameras followed Dev, Shaq, Sharon, Pallavi and Vicky in turn, as each emerged from the cluster of trees. Bringing up the rear, grazed, bruised, streaked with sweat and stumbling forward, Leena barely registered what was going on. She kept walking even after the others had stopped, her gaze fixed on the large blue ice cooler that sat on the ground under one of the tents. She picked her way towards it, only to be brought up short by Rajat backing up in her direction and motioning her away.

'Get back!' he hissed in an undertone. 'You're in my shot.'

Leena blinked as he raised his mike and launched into a cheery, rehearsed introduction.

'So ladies and gentlemen,' he said, addressing the cameras, 'we are back! Back to the basics; back where it all began, long before civilization or farming or stoves or fridges or pots or pans were known to man; back to the jungle, where the real fight is fought, where our six contestants will rough it out and survive and, if they're lucky, scrape together a meal, just like their ancestors did, hundreds of thousands of years ago!'

Ancestors, Leena wondered, as she squinted through the blinding glare. Hundreds of thousands of years ago?

'All right, chefs,' Rajat said, wheeling round to address the contestants, while still managing to present his profile to the cameras, 'down that way is the trail that you'll follow.'

Leena looked at the overgrown path he was pointing towards. The trees that surrounded it were packed close together, their roots rising above the soil like varicose veins on elderly limbs. Flies and gnats flitted amongst the undergrowth. She thought she saw something slither for a fleeting moment before it was gone.

'You'll spend the first hour in the grasslands at the start of the trail,' Rajat continued, 'where you'll find many varieties of fruits and nuts and edible roots, leaves and herbs. You'll work independently, gathering up anything and everything you find.'

Leena looked into the cameras ranged all around her, focussed on her, and made an attempt at a faltering smile.

'You will make your way south and east, as you go along,' Rajat continued. 'Then at one p.m., you will rejoin the trail and make your way down to the riverbank. Go past the bend in the river, past the rocks, and you'll see a group of fishermen who will take you out on the river to catch your fish.'

'*We'll* catch the fish?' Leena asked, her voice faint.

'If the fish don't catch you first!'

Rajat grinned charmingly into the camera. 'Don't worry,' he said, 'there is plenty of fish in the streams at this time of year. Hilsa, bhekti, mahaseer, rohu… And there's also gharial. You might want to stay away from the gharials.

'At two o'clock, the boats will ferry you to the other side of the river, where there's a five-square-kilometre stretch of teak forest. You will forage for the rest of your ingredients there. You'll have until three to collect all that you can. Then when you hear the whistle, you will stop wherever you are and wait for the Jeeps to come and fetch you.

'You'll be driven to our special jungle campsite deep in the forest at three, where you will find all the things you'll need to prepare the food you gather. Namely, wood, water and fresh air.'

'So we're going to cook the food we collect?' Pallavi asked.

'Over a fire of your own making.'

'But there's hardly anything in the jungle that one can cook!'

'On the contrary, there are hundreds of varieties of edible plants,' Rajat said. 'Not to mention birds, rodents, insects…'

'Are we allowed to hunt?' Dev asked.

'No, but if you come across an unclaimed carcass, feel free to help yourselves!'

'Seriously, though,' Rajat said, turning back to the cameras, 'this is cool, guys, the way it was always meant to be! The jungle is a boon, a bounty, Annapurna. The local tribal population has been living off this jungle for centuries. Ram, Sita and Lakshman lived off this jungle in Chitrakoot, not fifty kilometres away. The Pandavas lived off it at Pandav Falls, just twenty kilometres away.'

'Do we look like the Pandavas to you?' Pallavi said.

'No, but you do look like survivors to me!'

'And cut!' Jimmy called.

'Nice, smooth opening shot,' he said, enthusiastically clapping Rajat on the shoulder. 'Well done, man.'

'Then that's it for me, I guess,' Rajat shrugged, his smile fading. He made his way back to the waiting Jeep, got in and pulled a chilled bottle of beer out of the cooler.

'All right, crew, next shot – "the challenge begins"!' Jimmy called, and everyone besides the cameramen got busy packing up.

Leena shaded her eyes and watched as the oasis, or rather, its mirage in the jungle, started to fade away. Umbrellas, hampers, wires and equipment were rolled, stowed and secured, the tents dismantled, the Jeeps loaded. The make-up girls flitted amongst the contestants, wiping brows, brushing hair, touching up faces, while an assistant passed round backpacks and fresh bottles of water.

'Don't we even get to sit?' Leena asked, wincing as Tina cleansed her face with a wet astringent that stung her cheeks.

'You start in ten minutes,' Tina said and dabbed on a wholesome smear of sunscreen.

Leena squinted past her to where every other member of the crew was waiting in the Jeep.

'Where are you all going?'

'To Raneh Falls.'

'But what about us? You can't leave us like this!'

'Don't worry, we'll meet you at the cooking site at three-thirty. The camera crew will be following you; you just won't see them. And Rajat and Jimmy will be out here somewhere – I think.'

'What if we run into problems?'

Tina stepped back to admire her handiwork and yanked down the corner of Leena's visor.

'Let's hope you don't,' she said with a sympathetic smile.

Back in the main area of the Jungle Book Resort, there was a humming efficiency in the climbing heat of the day. In and around the cottages, the housekeeping staff was busy, sweeping, swabbing, making beds; outside, the ground staff was trimming bushes, watering shrubs, mowing grass. In the reception lounge, Vijendra was checking accounts to the soulful strains of 'Gaata Rahe Mera Dil' on the gramophone, while in the cosy kitchen of the rooftop restaurant Chef Gopal was busy issuing instructions for the preparation of the afternoon meal.

'We're expecting only twenty-odd guests for lunch,' he said to Chanda, his assistant. 'Most of the others are either at the shoot or have gone to Raneh Falls for a sightseeing trip.'

Chanda heaved a sigh of relief. After the pressure of a four-course dinner for a hundred-plus people last night, lunch for twenty seemed like a breeze.

'KK was all praises for your Mughlai gobhi pasanda last night,' Gopal told her. 'He specifically asked me to compliment the chef.'

'That would be you, sir.'

'No, it's your recipe, your execution,' Gopal insisted. 'Who knows, Chanda, next year, you might be the one out in the jungle trying to win *Hot Chef* and I'll be the one cooking lunch for you?'

Chanda, her face flushed with self-conscious pleasure, disclaimed loudly. But deep down in her heart, she couldn't help wondering...

'Let's make sure our next meal impresses just as much,' she heard Chef Gopal say, as he moved on to study the rows of masalas neatly stacked in the newly installed cabinets and racks. 'Even though it's an informal one.'

'How about something fresh from the garden, sir?'

'That's a great idea, Chanda. The potato patch is ready for picking and we have tomatoes coming off by the bushel.'

'I also saw some carrots and cauliflowers we can use for a simple stew. Something hearty, perhaps, with fresh ground spices and herbs?'

Gopal smiled. It was just the thing. Plain basmati rice, sweet homemade yogurt, a hearty curry of carrots, potatoes and cauliflower, picked straight from the earth, and Bhopali gosht korma, for which the meat and masala paste, carefully prepared and stored the night before, was already waiting and ready. He pulled the large trays of marinated meat out now, sniffed the rich aromas appreciatively. He might not be a celebrity chef himself, but he could put together a decent meal, he knew. He frowned as the phone in his pocket buzzed with a text message, then groaned and glanced at his watch.

'It's Agrawal, the pantry manager,' he told Chanda with an exasperated roll of his eyes. 'Says he needs to consult with me on the safest way to transport the utensils and cutlery to the cooking site. And after I've set him up with everything already!'

'He seems like the nervous type,' Chanda said, smiling sympathetically.

'Why they have to cook outside when we have a fully functional kitchen here, I'll never know! These TV types!' Gopal sighed and removed his apron. 'Still, as Vijendra Sir likes to say, "Atithi Devobhava, the guest is God." I'll go and see what he needs. Shouldn't take too long, I expect.'

'I'll go and pick the vegetables in the meantime.'

Chanda watched as Chef Gopal hurried down the path to the waiting truck; she waved as he got in and took off. Then, with a happy sigh, she hung up her chef's apron, wrapped the pallu of her sari about her small waist, traded her kitchen clogs for her beloved Hawaii chappals and skipped down the steps to the kitchen garden, where row upon row of seasonal vegetables and herbs were carefully cultivated and coaxed under Gopal's eagle eye to yield their flavourful best. Cauliflower, cabbage, onions, potatoes; peas, beans, tomatoes, beets; spinach, coriander, mint, parsley...

Chef Gopal had the greenest thumb she'd ever known.

She made for the potato patch at the far end of the garden, shielding her eyes from the hot blaze of sunlight. It was uncomfortably warm for this time of year, but a whiff of cool breeze lifted off the river and soothed her heated cheeks. She released her thick mane of hair from its prison of pins; she ran her fingers through the silken strands before twisting them into a loose knot. She was alone in this secluded patch at this time of day, she knew; she pulled her sari up around her thighs and, tying it in a knot around her waist, kicked off her chappals and plunged her bare toes into the cool, moist earth.

The midday sun was hot, but the air was still cool, KK noticed, as he stepped out of his luxury cottage. After the shaded comfort of the cottage and the backlog of paperwork he'd spent all morning clearing, it was nice to be outside, to feel the heat of the sun on his head and along his arms. A brisk walk round the resort was just what he needed to work up an appetite and clear his head for the tasting and shoot in the evening. He wondered, as he walked past trees and bushes and fields of grain, how the contestants were faring. He hoped they were being creative; that they would have some real surprises in store.

A butterfly flitted past his nose and landed in a red hibiscus bloom growing on a bush at the side of the road. It hovered above it a moment, stopped to drink its fill of nectar, then lifted off in search of new treats. KK watched until it disappeared behind a clump of trees.

On impulse, he stepped towards the hibiscus and held the flower to his nose. He closed his eyes and inhaled deeply, catching the slightest whiff of a mild fragrance. He plucked the bloom, with its tiny circlet of leaves still attached to its stem, and walked on, enjoying the aroma that was more a suggestion than reality, an enticement rather than fact.

What a wonderful flower it was, the hibiscus, he thought. Luscious, beautiful, delicate, edible. A splendid topping for a summer salad, a sensuous garnish in a glass of iced tea, a playful addition in cake batter or homemade phirni. And maybe he could experiment with it in his kebabs, see what subtle, wonderful things it did to minced meat?

He turned right at a fork in the path and carried on under the dense cover of trees, not quite sure any more where he was heading and not quite caring very much either. He followed the path around the resort in a leisurely fashion, breaking off little herbs and shrubs as he went along and pocketing them, and found that he had circled back to the resort's main lounge.

The veranda was deserted, but he thought he heard the faint sounds of singing coming from somewhere behind it. He followed the melodious notes to the kitchen garden at the back of the building and traced their source to a small figure kneeling in the middle of the rich, black soil. It was a young woman, he saw, her back curved like the slender neck of a long jug, her breasts, straining against the thin fabric of her blouse, pert and full. As if sensing a presence other than her own, she abruptly fell silent and looked around.

KK moved towards her with an apologetic smile. 'Sorry, I didn't mean to disturb you!'

The girl sprang to her feet and let the hem of her sari fall back around her ankles. 'I was just picking some vegetables,' she said.

'Let me help.' KK walked across the potato patch to join her before she could protest and squatted down heavily beside her. 'Amazing,' he said, picking a clump of golden, perfectly rounded potatoes from the soil. He brushed off the mud and tossed them in her half-full basket. 'Your doing?'

'Chef Gopal Sir's, actually,' was the shy reply. 'I just help him.'

'You're a chef too?'

'Assistant chef, sir.'

'My favourite kind of person,' KK beamed.

The jungle grasses were sharp, overgrown, teeming with insects. Centipedes, ants and beetles scurried across the uneven paths from stalk to stalk; gnats and flies buzzed overhead; the sharp tips of the thinner, meaner stalks scratched arms and neck.

Pallavi muffled a shriek as something large and furry rustled across her ankles before vanishing behind a stump of tree. She cursed as she stepped on something soft and gooey. She lifted her shoe and viewed with distaste the mess of crushed fruit that clung to the sole, something that looked like those edible ber that Mr Ganpath had shown them earlier. She knelt down in the dirt and located another one and another. She dusted them off and tossed them into her basket; she regarded her booty and held back the tears.

Two bers. Forty minutes of labouring under the blazing hot sun, of being bitten and scratched and driven to the verge of nausea, and she had two bers the size of grapes to show for it. She wasn't even sure they were edible. She put one in her mouth and felt her taste buds recoil from the bitter, pungent taste. She spat it out and fell to her knees, holding her head in her hands. This was insane. There was no way she was going to survive this challenge.

And why should she have to? She was an heiress raised to run a multi-crore business, a chef trained in the best, most prestigious cooking institute in the world. And now, for no apparent reason, here she was, on her knees and about to lose it all, lose her final chance to win it all back, because she could not for the life of her find one edible thing in this rotten, rodent-infested forest. This whole challenge was a joke. The whole show was a joke.

She was going to take it up with the authorities as soon as she got back, she vowed. It wasn't fair to put her through this. Nowhere in her contract did it say she'd have to forage around in the wilderness, exposing herself to all kinds of risks. This was not what she'd signed up –

She came to an abrupt halt. Ten feet from where she knelt on the ground, nestling under a shady bush in the undergrowth and nearly obscured from view by the lush foliage around it, was an enormous cluster of beautiful, fan-shaped mushrooms growing from the trunk of a fallen tree. Hundreds of ripe, deliciously meaty, vividly pink oyster mushrooms, just like the ones she used to buy at the farmers' markets in Provence. She rubbed her eyes in disbelief; the mushrooms were still there. She sprang to her feet and fell upon them, wrenching them from the hard, dry tree trunk, crooning to them as if they were newborn babies sunning themselves in the afternoon heat.

Back at the resort, KK was pulling juicy red carrots from the earth, chatting amicably with his companion as they worked together under the hot sun. She was quite talkative, once she got over her initial awe, he found. She confided how her cousin, a cook in Khajuraho, had helped her train to become a chef; how he'd introduced her to Chef Gopal; how she'd only started working here a few months ago; how becoming assistant chef at the Jungle Book Resort was a dream come true.

'Is it?' KK asked with an indulgent smile. 'But hard work, I'm sure. Not to mention the long hours and the loneliness.'

'Not at all, sir,' she said, 'it is usually very lively here in season and I get to meet so many great people. Like you,' she added shyly.

'Me?'

'Sir, you are my idol,' she exclaimed, then blushed furiously. 'You are every chef's idol.'

She got up and dusted off her hands, looking down at the basket of vegetables that was now full. Carrots, potatoes, cauliflower, tomatoes – she had everything she needed. 'I'd better get these inside,' she said.

'What are you going to do with them, if I may ask?'

'Just a simple stew,' she said. 'With fresh ground spices and some sage and thyme.'

'Sounds delicious. Let me help.'

'Oh no, sir, I – '

'I insist. I'd love to see how you use that thyme.'

Chanda's silver anklets tinkled round her slim ankles as she skipped up the steps to the kitchen and in through the swing door. In a trice, she'd traded her chappals for the spotless black clogs in the corner and donned her chef's hat and apron, quickly tying its strings behind her back. She waved an arm self-consciously around the small, well-appointed space and studied KK's face for approval.

'It's perfect,' he smiled. 'Shall I put these down over there?' He walked over and set the basket down on the counter next to the sink, turned on the tap and started rinsing the vegetables.

'Oh, sir, you should let me do that!'

'I know how to wash vegetables, trust me.'

'No, sir, it's not – '

'Of course, if I'm in your way, I'll leave.'

'Not at all, sir, please stay,' she said, colouring. 'It's an honour...'

'The pleasure is all mine. Fresh ripe veggies and a sweet young colleague – what could be better? And maybe I can show you an old chef's trick or two?'

He pulled out his pocketful of herbs and set them down on the counter, then turned to pick up a chopping board and knife. 'So you live here?' he asked, working quickly and efficiently, his expert hands making short work of the carrots and potatoes.

She nodded and started to pluck the tiny thyme leaves off their stems. 'Yes, sir. I have a cottage just outside the resort's gates.'

'You live there alone?'

'No, sir, with my in-laws. They work at the resort too. This weekend, they are away, though, for a wedding in Bareilly. They would have liked to meet you.'

'And I, them,' KK murmured. His busy hands paused a moment. 'And does your husband work here as well?'

'Oh no, sir, he works in Indore. He's a driver for a big company.'

'Indore. Isn't that far?'

'Yes, sir, overnight train. But he comes home every couple of months.'

KK laid out another carrot, started chopping it with a flourish. 'Life is such a struggle when you are starting out, isn't it?' he said, remembering his own youth. 'I'm glad your husband is able to come home to spend some time with his family every once in a while.'

8

The fish was a streak of silver in sun-shocked water, a burst of brilliance as it snapped at the lure and seized it greedily. It felt the stab of pain as the point of the hook dug into the soft tissue of its mouth, and the tug of the barb holding it prisoner, sensing the hook plunge deeper and deeper into its flesh. Had it known any better, it would have died right then from the shock of betrayal.

But it was a young fish, strong and unreasonably proud. It tried to pull away. It tugged and lashed and tossed about, fought against the strong current, against the pain, against its captor; it fought downstream and upstream, fought for its life, fought to get away. But it was caught, inexorably, its fate sealed.

The angler was an expert one. This was not his first catch; it would not be his last. And the jungle brought out something primal, something feral in him. He gave the fish its head, letting it fight, letting it thrash about and writhe and tire itself out, admiring, all the while, its tenacity, its spirit, even as he reeled it in slowly, skilfully. He could feel the force of its entire weight, its fierce life twisting and pushing and protesting in his hands; it was the biggest turn-on ever. He held onto it, savouring its struggle; it would be a beauty when he finally brought it in.

He felt the pressure at the end of the line give a little; he straightened his neck a fraction, adjusted its weight. Slowly, he started moving backwards, turning the handle on his rod, bringing it closer and closer. Summoning some last reserve of savage determination, it fought him in the sun-dappled shallows, churning mud, froth, anger, steam; the splashing grew more violent and agitated and then, inevitably, spluttered out. The water grew calm once more.

Dev sighed and wiped the sweat from his face. It was over, their tango, their waltz, their dance of death. He had subdued his quarry; he felt sublime.

The helpers sprang forward as he reeled in the rest of the line, as the shimmering fish emerged, spent and glassy-eyed, from the muddy shallows. It took two of the helpers to take its weight, hoist it up. It shone like a jewel in the blazing sun.

Three kilometres upstream, at the Treetop Restaurant in the Jungle Book Resort, Chef Purushottam Prasad leaned back on a slatted recliner and propped his feet up on the wooden railing that wrapped around the deck. Below him, the river shimmered and flowed gently through the afternoon, torched with sunlight. Above his head, a gnat buzzed lazily, flirting with the light fixture.

He thought he noticed something move in the distance; he raised his binoculars and trained them on the wide, shallow rock in the river. It was a gharial, sunning itself. He watched it for a long moment, then he let the binoculars fall and reached for his mug of chilled beer.

'Making yourself useful, I see,' an amused voice drawled behind him.

He turned his head to see KK walking towards him.

'Just studying the terrain,' he said. 'There's a croc on the rock at two o'clock.'

He held out the binoculars, smiling at his own joke.

KK observed the gharial for a long moment, then put down the binoculars. 'This is the life,' he sighed.

'When you're up here, absolutely. I'd hate to be out there like your poor contestants, though.'

'They're young; they can rough it out.'

He glanced up as the door to the restaurant swung open and a server stepped out with a large tray in his hands. 'Ready for lunch, sir?'

'Yes, thank you,' KK smiled. 'What's this?' he asked, as the server set the tray down on the nearby table. On the tray was a plate of round, puffy pooris and red chutney that accompanied the vegetable stew, gosht korma and raita.

'Ragi shakarkandi pooris and chilli garlic chutney,' the server said. 'Chef's compliments, sir.'

'Really?' KK said. 'Well, please give the chef our compliments.'

'I'll let them know, sir.'

'Them?' Chef Prasad said. 'I thought the chef was a Gopal Bhargava?'

'Yes, sir. Chanda Ma'am is his assistant.'

Chef Prasad took a bite of the still puffy poori as the server left. 'Mmm...' he murmured.

Moments later a slim girl walked in through the swinging door wiping her hands on her apron. 'Everything to your liking, I hope?' she said.

'Ms Chanda,' KK said, rising gallantly to his feet. 'Let me introduce you to Chef Prasad of Kemaal's Culinary Institute.'

'Ms Chanda Singh?' Chef Prasad said, reading the nametag. 'So these pooris are your creation? They're brilliant.'

'They really are quite unique,' KK said. 'So crisp – what exactly did you put in them?

'Careful,' Chef Prasad warned Chanda. 'Better safeguard your recipe; we're all poachers here!'

'It would be an honour for me if KK Sir accepts my recipe,' Chanda said.

Spread out through the thickly wooded forest on the other side of the river, with the sun obscured behind the dense foliage, the ground covered with dried branches and leaves, the contestants were in the final section of the assigned area for the challenge. The air around them was still, the trees rustled from time to time with the movements of their denizens; the dead leaves on the ground crackled beneath their footsteps.

'Look. Over there.'

Shaq froze at the whispered words and turned his head in the direction that Vicky had indicated. At first, he saw nothing besides the dark earth and the tangled debris of dried grasses and broken branches that littered it. Then, as Vicky pointed, his gaze settled on an area not five feet away, where the faintest trace of a small shape, no larger than a hand, was barely discernible; so well camouflaged that had Vicky not pointed it out, he would have walked right over it. Shaq motioned for Vicky to stay still; he himself advanced with measured steps, softly, noiselessly. He held his breath and drew closer to the bird, a partridge, until he was just a step away. Then he stopped and slowly lowered himself to the ground.

Vicky felt his heart beat faster as he watched Shaq crouch, motionless, apparently holding his breath.

Then, slowly, very slowly, Shaq lifted his left arm from the ground. On his wrist, Vicky could make out the barely visible, squirming worm. Inch by inch, Shaq extended his arm towards the frozen bird. Several seconds passed. Then finally, hesitantly, the muddy spot on the ground came to life. An eye opened, a body inched forward, the head turning left and right in small, quick movements, the beak quivering. One step; two. Shaq's right hand shot out and grasped it. A quick flick of the wrist, one sharp twist of the neck; there was barely a squawk before it was silenced forever. A couple of other birds nearby lifted off in a flutter of wings, a cloud of dust, and flew away.

Vicky released his breath and stepped forward. Shaq looked up briefly and then went back to the task of securing the lifeless bird.

'Nice trick,' Vicky said, crouching down beside him. 'Where did you learn to do that?'

'Catch or kill?'

'Both are useful skills.' Vicky held a hand out for the bird. 'Well, I know what I'm cooking for dinner.'

'And what is that?' Shaq said, retaining his hold.

'The bird.'

'I caught it.'

'And I found it.'

'And I killed it.'

'And I let you.'

They stared each other down for a long moment.

'Makes us accomplices, then,' Shaq smiled.

'Partners in crime,' Vicky agreed.

Chef Prasad, settled in his slatted recliner after a bigger, more delicious lunch than he'd had in a long time, put his feet back up on the wooden railing, took a sip of his post-lunch chai and waved his hand out across the horizon. 'They should be getting done now, don't you think?' he asked.

KK looked at his watch. It was 2.45 p.m. 'Soon enough,' he said.

'Who do you think will win?'

'The best chef, of course.'

Chef Prasad snorted and glanced sideways at KK. 'Oh come now, KK. Don't be coy.'

KK sat back in his recliner and raised his cup of chai to his lips. He gave the question serious consideration. 'They each have their strengths and weaknesses, I suppose,' he said. 'Not to mention audience appeal.'

'Oh yes, let's not forget the audience appeal,' Puru said, a smile hovering about his lips. 'I wonder where Sharon and Dev would be if it weren't for that?'

'Certainly not here as part of the show at this stage.'

'They've been good for your ratings, I'll bet!'

'Heaven-sent.'

'Think you'll lose them any time soon?'

'Probably not in this episode,' KK said. 'This one is more about survival, and they're both survivors.'

'As is that boy, Shaq,' Puru agreed. 'Were those real knives he was juggling in those promos?'

'He knows how to take a risk,' KK said.

'He has heart, that's for sure.'

'Just not enough talent.'

'No? I thought he had a chance to win this thing.'

'He's a skilled technician, I'll grant you that,' KK said. 'And an experienced, efficient worker. I see him as a reliable sous-chef, an able right-hand man. But *Hot Chef*?' He shook his head dismissively. '*Hot Chef* is about talent and vision – someone unique, who brings something new to the table.'

'Like Leena?'

'Leena?' KK sighed, and shook his head. 'She's a good cook and she's been getting better with each episode, but there's something missing still. She's too much of a copycat. And an amateur one at that.'

'What about Pallavi? I heard she's Cordon Bleu-trained?'

'She's good, very good. Trained, focussed, intelligent, talented. I'd say she has a strong chance of winning. If only she learned how to get the audience to like her.' KK took a sip of his chai. 'You can be the world's best chef, but if your attitude makes the milk go sour then what's the point?'

'Which leaves us with Vicky...' Puru said.

'He's going to win.'

Chef Prasad glanced up, surprised. It was unlike KK to say something so definitive.

'That boy is exceptional,' KK enthused. 'He's got good ideas, good instincts and he's not afraid to take risks. Reminds me a bit of myself when I was his age.'

'I thought he came across as spoilt and insolent,' Chef Prasad said with a frown.

'He's a maverick,' KK smiled with affectionate pride. 'He's going to take the culinary world by storm.'

9

Night had fallen, swift and sudden, in the jungle. The dense vegetation and tall grasses that stretched for hundreds of thousands of acres resonated with nature's ritual sounds and silences – the shrieks, the calls, the chirps and rustles; the soft splashes around drinking holes, as herds quenched their thirst and refreshed themselves, followed by the unnerving stillness as their predators stole up through the shadows and silenced them.

The moon was a couple of nights past its peak, a diminished circle low in the sky, but still burning bright; the stars were out in scintillating abandon. Below, at the Jungle Book Resort, the Treetop Restaurant was ablaze with light. Dozens of lanterns – hovering, flickering, dancing dots of light in tiny wrought-iron cases – hung low from the beams and rafters of the enormous roof; still more nestled amidst the white linens on the tabletops; others floated above the wooden parapet that encircled the large terrace. They twinkled and sparkled against the dramatic backdrop of the night, enhancing the mood of elation that had settled upon the guests in the aftermath of the day's shoot.

What a shoot it had been!

Not one mishap, not one misstep. Just a pitch-perfect, symphonic performance, with everyone, from the crew to the cameramen to the entire cast of the show, at the very top of their game. The contestants, especially, had outdone themselves. They had entered the jungle tense with fear; they had emerged from it dirty and creased, their faces lined with fatigue, yet aglow with the triumph of achievement, their arms heavy with spoils: mushrooms, berries, nuts, herbs, quail eggs and quail, and fish – such fresh, abundant, glorious fish!

And it had all been captured on camera in perfect light and loving detail, along with some exquisite footage of birds flying, snakes slithering, monkeys chattering and a National Geographic-worthy, fourteen-second uninterrupted video of a herd of nilgai sprinting amidst the stumps and trunks and branches of trees, hooves flying, tails up, their shadowy backs undulating in perfect tandem as they thundered like storm clouds through the hot, sweltering jungle.

Jimmy, standing at the bar with a glass of bubbly in hand, described it once again for the benefit of his audience.

'There were at least twenty of them, maybe more,' Jimmy enthused, 'just powering their way through the forest!'

Shetty, the cameraman who'd taken the shot, took a long swig of his beer and shook his head in lingering disbelief. 'It was unbelievable… like a gift from God…'

'And you grabbed it with both hands,' Jimmy said, throwing a loving arm around his shoulders. 'Man, I could watch that footage all night long. Just something about those big animals flying by on their long, spindly legs…'

'It was magical,' Ruby sighed happily. 'And that other shot, too, of that owl in the tree, just sitting there, glaring into the camera… Gave me goosebumps, I swear!'

'What gave *me* goosebumps was watching Dev Nair catch that mahaseer,' Mansi breathed.

'Like sex on toast,' Jimmy agreed. 'Especially that long shot of him against the backdrop of the river, his muscles flexed as he pulled the fish in; his ass…'

'Easy, Casanova,' Ruby said, wagging a finger. 'No hitting on the cast!'

'The guy's good for the camera, I have to say,' Shetty grinned. 'All sweaty biceps and rugged silhouette… Should get him some serious audience votes from the ladies. '

'He did such a good job cooking that fish too,' Mansi gushed.

'It was good,' KK agreed, turning in his seat to join the discussion. 'He surprised me. And Pallavi, too. I thought her mushrooms in garlic and herbs was her best showing so far.'

'And what about Shaq?' Chef Prasad added. 'Those quail eggs were perfectly done. And they're not easy to do right. And Sharon did a fine job with that bhekti and mustard, too, I thought. Simple, hearty, authentic.'

'They all seemed to have raised their game a notch this time round, na?' Ruby beamed.

'I was disappointed with Vicky's quail cream curry, whatever you might say,' Chef Prasad murmured.

'Insipid. Isn't that what you told him?' Mansi chuckled. 'Not that he cared very much for your opinion.'

It's a new-age dish, sir, Vicky had shot back cheekily in response to Chef Prasad's criticism. *I didn't expect you to get it.*

'The boy is plain disrespectful,' Puru scowled. 'He needs taking down a peg or two.'

'Vicky's all right,' KK maintained. 'If anyone was disrespectful tonight, it was Leena.'

'I was surprised she chose to make Malabari fish curry,' Mansi said. 'Isn't that Mala's signature dish?'

'It was,' KK said.

'I thought she pulled it off...' Puru said.

'No, she totally ruined it,' KK countered, an angry glitter in his eyes. 'And, what's worse, she was trying to be oversmart, suggesting she had *improved* upon the dish.'

And he had cut her down to size. To smithereens. She had gone white, been close to tears. As she should, KK thought with bitter satisfaction.

'I thought you were a bit harsh on her,' Puru insisted. 'It tasted fine to me.'

'It was a desecration.'

'But I thought you wanted her to take more risks?'

'Not with Mala's legacy,' KK bit off.

'I'd hate it if she gets voted off the show because of this one episode,' Ruby mused, playing worriedly with the rudraksh on her finger. 'She *is* one of our strongest, most popular contestants.'

'There's no room at the top for errors.'

'Be a darling and cut her some slack in the next episode, all the same,' Ruby suggested. 'Speaking of the next episode...' She turned to Jimmy with a questioning look.

'Don't look at me, darling,' Jimmy said, holding up both hands in a defensive gesture. 'Right now, I'm just glad *this* challenge is over!'

'You know what *I'm* glad about,' Ruby confided. 'That it's over and nothing untoward happened. No short circuits, no set collapse, no poisoning, no one falling into the river and being eaten up by a crocodile.'

'Silly girl!' KK said with an amused look. He raised his glass playfully. 'Here's to no one being eaten by a crocodile!' he said.

A movement on the path directly below the restaurant caught his eye as he tilted his head back. He squinted into the darkness, trying to identify the two silhouettes walking up the path: Vijendra, tall, lanky, with his long, unhurried stride, was easily recognizable, but the woman next to him, lithe and graceful, was a mystery. There was a dancer's fluidity in the way she moved, a fighter's confidence in the way her feet touched the ground. KK had a feeling that he had seen her somewhere before. He watched, brows knitted, as they stepped into a pool of light cast by a lantern. The woman lifted her head and he felt a shock of recognition shoot through him.

'What's the matter, KK?' Ruby asked. 'You look like you've seen a ghost!' She turned to follow his gaze. 'Oh my God, is that SP Marwah?'

'She's *here*?' Jimmy said.

'SP Marwah?' Mansi asked, turning to KK with a puzzled look.

'The Superintendent of Police, Shimla.'

'Shimla?' Chef Prasad said. 'Isn't that where Mala – ?'

'It is,' KK said. 'SP Marwah was the investigating officer.'

'So why is she *here*?'

'That, dear Puru, is an excellent question.'

Over on the south side of the resort, a bonfire burned gaily in the clearing between the two villas. The six contestants sat in a loose semicircle around the fire, chatting, resting, clinking bottles of beer, with Barkha and Binod keeping them company. The mood was festive for once; the insecurities and rivalries that were their constant companion seemed to have faded into the background or, at least, were temporarily suspended. The day had been too taxing, the triumphs and upsets at the end of it too momentous to leave room for anything but a mellow, cheerful truce.

Even Barkha and Binod, whether owing to the lushness of the surroundings, the brightness of the stars, or the simple fact of having spent most of the day free of the contestants' gnat-like presence, appeared to have been lulled into an uncharacteristic spell of goodwill; they watched with lazy indulgence as Shaq stoked the fire higher and higher, as Dev launched into a lusty rendition of 'Mehbooba' and Sharon got up and started gyrating in the middle of the small circle.

Leena leaned her head on Vicky's shoulder and watched as Sharon took a swig from her beer bottle and swayed her hips with exaggerated abandon. Vicky, grinning, put two fingers to his mouth and emitted a low, sharp whistle.

'Really?' Leena frowned.

'She's an original,' Vicky grinned.

'I'm glad *someone's* enjoying himself.'

'Aren't you?'

'No, how could I?'

Leena blinked back tears as she remembered the tasting, the look on KK's face. His eyes had flashed; his face had hardened; he had spat out the spoonful of curry he had placed in his mouth. *Spat* it out.

'I'm finished,' she said, her voice trembling. 'KK hates me!'

'He's just a bitter old man,' Vicky soothed, putting an arm around her shoulders.

'Yes, but he's a judge. The most important judge.'

'So make it up to him in the next challenge.'

'But what if there isn't a next challenge? What if this is the end of the road for me?'

'Then find a way to stay.'

'But how? The challenge is over, the judging is done. What can I possibly do?'

'Well...' Vicky said, appearing to give the matter some serious thought, 'you could always push Pallavi into the river. Or serve Sharon to the tigers...'

'Vicky, be serious.'

'Or just knife KK in his sleep.'

'Will you stop?' Leena raised her head and turned angry eyes on him. 'Please. Just stop.'

Vicky wiped the tiny tear that escaped her eye. 'Don't cry, Leena Ballerina,' he said, his voice as soft as a caress. He flicked her bangs gently. 'There are any number of things you could do to win this thing,' he whispered, his gaze holding hers. 'You just have to be resourceful enough to do them.'

10

Rags, called upon by his father to perform for the VIP guests at the Treetop Restaurant and mindful of his duties as assistant manager and host, had made a special effort for the evening, although left to himself he'd have preferred to join the contestants around their bonfire on the south side. He had showered and shaved and put on a buttoned-down black shirt under an elegant black suit; his black Oxfords, newly polished, gleamed in the night. He stepped out onto the open-air deck with a winsome smile and took his seat on a barstool with a poise that belied his age.

He played a few airy chords on his guitar; his voice, surprisingly soulful, filled the air. The audience stopped talking and drew close to listen.

'He's not so bad, is he,' Vijendra murmured with a father's quiet pride. 'If only he brought the same enthusiasm to his studies.'

Niki, who stood beside him, leaning against the wooden railing overlooking the river, smiled. 'He's very talented. You must be so proud of him.'

'He's a good boy,' Vijendra said, gratified. 'But he has a lot to learn.' He frowned as his mobile phone began to ring. 'Ah, excuse me, I have to take this call.' He moved quietly towards the stairway and put the instrument to his ear.

Niki leaned back against the wooden railing, enjoying the simple melody, the strumming of the guitar.

'He's good,' an amused voice spoke up at her elbow. 'He could be on *Indian Idol*. Or even *Hot Chef*.'

Niki turned to see KK, who'd walked over to join her. '*Hot Chef*?' she asked.

'Jimmy's already asked him to audition for the next season.' KK's teeth glinted in the moonlight as he smiled. He held out the glass he'd brought. 'Some wine, Ms Marwah?'

'Thanks, I'm fine.' Niki raised her glass of nimbu pani to her lips and took a sip. 'I thought one needed to know how to cook to be on *Hot Chef*.'

'It doesn't take much to learn how to cook,' KK said. 'Someone or the other cooks three meals a day in every household. Most of them do an excellent job, too.' He smiled again in the darkness. 'No, cooking is the easy part. Winning is the challenge.'

'Quite the challenge. Can't be easy when you're up against such a talented group of contestants.'

'You think the contestants are talented?'

'Don't you?'

He nodded, slowly contemplating the amber liquid in his glass. 'I suppose they're each talented in their own way. Just not as much when it comes to cooking.' He glanced at Niki, a bemused smile on his face. 'This year's focus seems to have shifted more to the "Hot" part of *Hot Chef*.'

'Does that bother you?'

'Oh no! Our ratings are phenomenal. We could never have achieved such ratings with a plain cooking show. You have to think of the customers, no matter what business you're in. When it's a restaurant, you give them a culinary experience. When it's a TV show, you *entertain* them.'

Niki regarded him over the rim of her glass. 'Is that the recipe for your success?' she asked.

He smiled and Niki got the feeling that he had been asked this question many times before; that the answer she was about to get was an answer that had been given many times before. 'The recipe for my success, Ms Marwah, is *me*. I started out forty years ago with nothing but my grandfather's blessings and a ten-rupee note in my pocket. But I had a vision. And all through the many days and years and decades, I have never let go of it, not for a single instant.'

'And may I ask what that vision was?'

'*This*, of course.' He waved his hand at the bar, the night sky, the glittering lights, but Niki knew he was referring to more, much more. 'My recipes and my cookbooks and my restaurant and *Hot Chef* and the Culinary Institute and Kemaal's... All of it.'

'And yet something tells me you're just getting started.'

'I'll drink to that.' KK smiled and raised his glass to his lips; he took a sip and joined in the applause as Rags's song drew to a close.

Niki indicated the empty table at the far end of the restaurant near the steps as Rags warmed up for his next number. 'Shall we sit, Mr Kapoor?'

'Dare I refuse?'

KK set his glass down on the tabletop and pulled out a chair. He waited for Niki to be seated, then sat down in the chair across from her. He crossed his arms over his chest and looked her squarely in the eye. 'Ruby told me I wasn't supposed to ask, but I'll ask anyway,' he said, speaking softly as Rags started on his next number. 'What brings you here, Ms Marwah?'

'I'm taking another look at the Mala Joseph case.'

'Is this about that packet of Celphos in the pantry?'

'Amongst other things.'

'I appreciate your concern.' KK leaned forward, his expression serious. 'So what do you suggest we do? Replace the pantry manager? Put a guard outside the pantry? Install CCTV cameras?'

'I think you should take every step you can to enhance security for your show,' Niki said. 'But coming back to Mala... You mentioned, when we met in Shimla, that you were considering collaborating with her on a north-south fusion chain.'

Even through the semi-darkness, Niki caught the momentary frown that flickered across KK's brow and the slight hesitation before he answered. 'It was at a very preliminary stage, like I said earlier,' he finally murmured.

'But Mala was busy finalizing recipes for the venture. In fact, she had almost finalized them right before the incident in Shimla, hadn't she?'

'What makes you think that?'

'Her emails to you.'

'You went through her emails…' he said, his displeasure obvious. 'Well, then you know. She was developing recipes, yes.'

'So why did you hide that from us?'

KK took a sharp breath. 'I didn't *hide* anything,' he said, making a visible effort to rein in his annoyance. 'I wasn't hiding anything, Ms Marwah,' he repeated in a much calmer voice. 'I just don't like to talk about my projects before they become a reality. Call me superstitious or call me cautious. Either way, these are confidential business matters; surely I'm entitled to keep them that way?'

'Not when your testimony might have a bearing in a police investigation.'

'Forgive me, but I don't see what bearing my discussions with Mala about a joint venture could have had on her death. The two are completely different things.'

'Perhaps. But I'd still like you to explain the last email she sent you. The one where she mentioned that something had come up, which was why there would be a delay in the final recipes. She said she'd tell you why when she saw you.'

'Did she?'

'She did.'

KK put a hand to his forehead; he rubbed his temple with one finger, frowning. 'It's been a while,' he said. 'So much has happened since then… I can't quite remember.'

'Try,' Niki advised. 'It's important. Why was there a delay in her sending in the final recipes?'

'I honestly cannot say, Ms Marwah. We never got a chance to talk about it.'

'So you have no idea what the reason could have been?'

'None. But I didn't get the sense that there was any crisis or anything. I'd imagine it was just a small glitch that needed fixing. I wouldn't read anything more into it.'

Niki regarded him silently for a moment. 'So tell me,' she said, 'what happens to the recipes now?'

'I'll make sure Mala's work doesn't go waste.'

'So you'll use them…' Niki said. 'In the north-south fusion chain?'

'If it works out.'

'And will you be collaborating with Mala's husband now?'

'No. Why should I?'

'Well, since they're recipes that Mala developed – '

'That Mala and *I* developed,' KK corrected. 'We worked on them together. And now that she's no more, they're mine to do with as *I* please.'

He saw Niki's brows draw together.

'Ms Marwah,' he said, 'if there's one thing I've learned in the past forty years, it's that there is no room for sentimentality in business. You can be successful or you can be sentimental. You can't be both.' He smoothed an imaginary crease on the top of the spotless table, then looked out over the dark, glittering surface of the river.

'I grew up poor,' he said softly. 'Very poor. I saw my grandfather run his tiny dhaba day after day after day, daybreak to midnight, seven days a week, and he barely managed to make ends meet. He was sixty-five when he died; he'd lost all his teeth; he was nearly blind; he looked like he was a hundred. The poverty, the misery, the debt – they crushed him. So after he died, I vowed I wouldn't let that happen to me. I moved to Delhi; I started Kemaal's. What my grandfather used to charge fifty rupees for, I priced at five hundred. And you know what? Suddenly, everyone started taking notice. Suddenly, those same kebabs that the rickshaw-wallas in Lucknow used to haggle over were in demand by MPs, film stars, cricketers, foreigners... People started standing in line to get a table at my restaurant. They started making reservations weeks, months in advance. That's when I realized that the only way to succeed in this world is if you stake your claim, brashly, unashamedly. You don't do anyone any favours. You make people pay you your due.'

'An interesting philosophy.'

'It's a dog-eat-dog world.'

And who are the people who have paid for your *success*, Niki wondered. She pushed back her chair, rose slowly to her feet. 'Thanks for your time, Mr Kapoor,' she said. 'Let me know if you recall what Mala was referring to when she said the recipes would be delayed.'

'I certainly will.'

The bar at the other end of the restaurant was busy, the bartenders bustling about behind the large wooden counter as they mixed, poured, shook, stirred. Rags announced he was taking a short break and headed out amidst hearty applause and multiple conversations started up amongst the *Hot Chef* crew as they stood about chatting, glasses and plates of appetizers in hand.

Niki wove her way through the revellers and towards the lone figure seated on a barstool in the shadows. 'Mind if I join you?' she asked, slipping into the empty seat beside him.

Rajat Tripathi looked up with clouded eyes. 'SP Marwah,' he said, and his voice was more than a little slurred. 'Sorry, I haven't had a chance to say hello.'

'That's quite all right.' Niki glanced at the glass in his hands, noticed the way his fingers shook as he lifted it to his lips. 'Nice party,' she observed.

'You think so?' He tossed off the drink in his glass and signalled to the bartender for a refill. 'Perhaps I'm just not in a party mood tonight.'

'You could have fooled me.'

He blinked confusedly a moment, then followed Niki's gaze to the glass in his hands. 'Oh, this,' he said, laughing shakily. 'This is just empty solace.' He took a long sip from the new glass the waiter set before him. A little bit of the liquid sloshed over onto his hand; he dabbed at the spill with a napkin.

'Perhaps you've had enough solace for one night?'

'Oh, I'm just getting started,' Rajat said with a bitter laugh. 'It's not against the law, is it?'

'No, but why drink when it's just empty solace?'

'What else is there to do in this godforsaken place?' He swirled the whisky in his glass. 'They have S.D. Burman on the gramophone and a nineteen-year-old playing the Beatles on an acoustic guitar. We could be in the previous century. Or the one before. But tell me, Ms Marwah, what brings *you* to this wilderness? The tigers or the crocs?'

'I'm tying up some loose ends around Mala's death.'

'Loose ends? What loose ends are there?'

'A few,' Niki said. 'For instance, we never did discover where the cyanide came from.'

Rajat contemplated the countertop in front of him, rubbing absently at the wet spot. 'What does it matter where it came from?' he said finally. 'What matters is why she took it.'

'Why did she?'

'You're asking *me*?'

'Maybe, if you have the answer.'

Various emotions flitted across his face as he stared silently into his near empty glass.

'We went over the camera footage from the Gaiety,' Niki said softly. 'Especially, the last few minutes of the tasting.'

Rajat looked at her, his face aglow in the soft yellow lights that decorated the bar. 'What did you see?' he whispered.

'The very last image before the cameras went blank was of you.'

'Me?'

'You passed right by the judges' table.'

'I suppose I must have. So?'

'So you had plenty of opportunity to slip something into Mala's drink or onto her plate of food.'

'Slip something?' His hand trembled as he closed it around his glass. 'But why would I?' he asked, his voice hoarse.

'You said you and Mala were close. Could it be that you were too close? Were you having an affair?'

'An affair? *Me and Mala*…!' Rajat closed his eyes and let out a long sigh that was equal parts disbelief and pain, reverence and despair. 'Me and Mala…' he repeated, and this time there was only pain in the ragged breath he drew. He picked up his glass and drained it, then set it down very carefully before pivoting in his stool to face Niki.

'Do you know, Ms Marwah, that until two weeks ago I'd been off alcohol for six whole months?'

Niki regarded him silently, impassively.

'I was a drunk.' He looked at Niki and smiled a humourless smile. 'Big secret, huh? But it *was* a secret six months ago. I was the cool, hip party boy, living large, drinking heavily, shooting some of the more fancy stuff too. I had my pick of girls; my coterie of hangers-on. It was a damned crazy life.' He closed his eyes, shook his head. 'Whisky, gin, vodka, rum… I was drinking every day; sometimes, all of them on the same day. But I was careful. I made sure to not drink too much in public, to always arrive at work sober. I hid it well. No one seemed to notice anything. Except Mala.'

'She knew?'

'Right away,' Rajat said, his lips twisted. 'She saw right through me. Took me aside during rehearsals, and this was when she was a nobody contestant in Season One and I was the heartthrob host, and told me that since I obviously had no use for my liver would I consider donating it to this crash victim she knew? She even had a damn picture and a pamphlet that she waved under my nose.' He laughed a ragged laugh and shook his head. 'I still remember that day. This mousy little contestant comes up to very-important me and calmly tells me that since I'm such a worthless piece of shit, my liver would be better off inside some driver named Badri Prasad who has a wife, three kids and stage three liver cancer even though he has never touched a drop of alcohol all his life.'

'So you stopped drinking.'

'What else could I do?'

'And you fell in love with her.'

He swivelled back to face the bar as Rags stepped back up to the microphone and started up a soulful rendition of 'People Are Strange'.

'Were you having an affair with her?' Niki asked.

'I loved her.' The words, softly spoken, were heavy with sorrow. 'She was my friend, my saviour,' he whispered. 'How could I even dream of anything as sordid as an affair with her?'

The evening's celebrations at the Treetop Restaurant continued into the night as the moon rose higher and higher in the sky. The *Hot Chef* crew, enjoying the rare treat of a day's work well done and a day of rest ahead, partied on, loath to depart. Rags performed his last song to a standing ovation. The dinner buffet was served and removed, the dessert plates cleared, the candles on the tables carefully extinguished, before, sated and sleepy, the guests finally started to turn in. As the hands of the clock approached midnight, only a few of them remained, lingering over their coffee and chai, watching, as the last of the lanterns sputtered in their filigree covers.

Niki, sitting far out on the deck overlooking the water, sipped on her cup of post-dinner chai and looked out over the parapet at the brilliant panorama that was the late night jungle sky. The moon was a brilliant jewel high above, the trees a shadowy silhouette in the distance, the river a gurgling, glittering sheet. The air was quiet, punctuated now and then by the distant hoot of an owl, the sudden howling of monkeys.

Niki took another sip of her chai and sighed as she watched Orion's belt shine bright and bold. She wondered if somewhere across the miles that separated them, Ram could see Orion too...

'Lovely, isn't it?'

Niki glanced at Ruby, who'd walked up with a steaming glass of chai to stand behind her.

'Breathtaking,' she agreed.

Ruby pulled up a chair and sat down beside her. 'You've probably had a very long day...'

'This view kind of makes up for it.'

'I really appreciate your coming out here, SP Marwah.' Ruby sat forward, clasped Niki warmly by the shoulder. 'I've been carrying on normally, but underneath this calm exterior, I have to tell you, I'm very spooked.'

'Boo!'

Ruby jumped and then turned her head to glare at Rajat who was standing behind her, laughing softly.

'Rajat,' she said. 'Sit down, babe. And stop sneaking up on people.'

'Then stop whispering in such an enticing manner, babe.'

Rajat dragged over another chair and sat down beside her. He seemed to have revived somewhat, Niki noticed; he'd brought with him a large cup of black coffee. 'So what were you two beautiful ladies whispering about?' he asked.

'Oh, we were just admiring the jungle,' Ruby said. 'Isn't it lovely?'

'Not really.'

Ruby reached out and patted his hand. 'I miss Mala, too, babe… Think she's up there somewhere?' she asked, glancing up at the stars.

'Perhaps,' a quiet voice spoke up behind her.

Niki turned her head to see KK standing by the wooden parapet, a few feet away. 'Mala was a beautiful person,' he said. 'Brighter than anything up there.'

Niki watched him without comment as he walked over to join their group. He had disappeared after their last conversation; she had not seen him since. She wondered where he had been, what he'd been up to.

'I wish she could be here,' Ruby murmured.

'I wish she'd not been so hasty,' KK sighed. 'I wish she'd come to us with her problems, whatever they were…'

'I can't think what problems she might have had,' Ruby said. 'She was beautiful, smart, successful; she had a husband who adored her and friends who loved her and a fan following of millions…'

'Maybe that was the problem,' KK said. 'Maybe it was all just too much for her. There were just too many expectations placed on her. Not everyone is cut out for this kind of life.'

'You're probably right,' Ruby sighed. 'She probably hated it.'

'I should have known there was something going on with her on Saturday night,' Rajat spoke up suddenly.

'You mean, when she didn't join us for our post-rehearsal dinner?' Ruby asked. 'I thought she was unwell.'

'So did I.'

'She *was* unwell,' Niki said.

'What was wrong with her?' Rajat asked, sitting forward, frowning. 'Did you find out? Was it something serious?'

'Was it a tumour?' Ruby asked. 'Cancer...?'

'No,' Niki said. 'It was morning sickness.'

She heard the sharp intake of breath from the man who sat on her left; saw the man who stood leaning against the parapet on her right grow still.

'You mean...!' Ruby gasped.

'She was pregnant,' Niki said.

Out on the south side of the resort, in the clearing between the two villas, Vicky, Leena and Shaq sat in comfortable silence, watching the flames die down. In front of them, the river rippled on its way downstream; behind it, the gentlest of breezes teased the leaves on the trees. Leena, almost asleep on Vicky's shoulder, stirred as a distant clanging ruptured the quiet spell of the night.

'And it's midnight,' Vicky murmured above her head.

'Time to go inside,' Shaq said, feeding one last twig into the dying fire.

'I don't want to go inside,' Leena sighed. 'I'd rather stay out here.'

'With those two jokers?'

Leena followed Vicky's amused gaze to where Dev and Binod lay snoring side by side on the hammock, one curled up like a baby, the other with his mouth wide open.

'Like two little lambs,' Shaq grinned.

'Sleeping with the contestant manager,' Vicky tsked. 'That could do some serious damage to dear Dev if it went viral. Maybe even get him booted off the show.' He got up, dusting off his pants.

'Where are you going?' Leena asked.

'To see if they're alive.'

'They're alive,' Shaq said. 'Corpses don't snore.'

Vicky walked up to the hammock. 'How hard do you think it would be to roll them both into the river?' he asked, rubbing his chin speculatively.

'Vicky, no!' Leena giggled.

'Too much work,' Shaq said.

'Pity.' Vicky reached for some ashes from the periphery of the fire and let the tiny powder drift down into Binod's open mouth. 'Swaha,' he said.

Binod frowned as the ashes tickled his nose. His mouth moved and made sucking sounds as he swallowed. Then his lips parted again on a sigh.

'You're going to get yourself disqualified!' Leena hissed.

'Anything to help you win, sweetheart.'

'And what about me?' Shaq complained.

'I could get you disqualified, too,' Vicky offered.

'You're mental,' Leena said.

'No,' Vicky said. 'I'm just in love. With you.'

Leena felt her breath stop, her cheeks burn. She got up, dusted off the seat of her pants more vigorously than she needed to. 'Now I know you really *are* out of your mind,' she said.

'I'm *not* out of my mind,' Vicky said. 'Watch this.' He crouched down beside the sleeping duo and lifted the lighter that lay on the ground beneath the hammock. He clicked it once and a small flame shot out.

'What are you doing?' Shaq asked, as Vicky brought the lighter up to his mouth.

'Watch and learn.'

Leena watched, her face white, as he put the lighter inside his mouth, filling his cheeks with the gas. Then he pulled it out, lit the flame once more, inches from his face.

'Vicky!' Leena gasped. 'No!'

Vicky stared at the flame, unheeding, letting it burn a moment in the night. Then, like a conjurer performing a magic trick, he exhaled the gas through his pursed lips straight into the flame. A giant fireball, the size of a cannon, shot up into the night.

'Vicky!'

'Oh-oh-oh, I'm on fire,' Vicky sang and his soft voice filled the night air.

The silence at the Treetop Restaurant following Niki's revelation stretched on for what felt like an eternity.

'Pregnant? Are you sure?' Ruby finally hissed out. She glanced at Rajat who sat with his head in his hands, at KK who stood frozen.

'It was in the autopsy report,' Niki said. 'She was ten weeks along.'

'And she never breathed a word!' Rajat lifted his head, his face was contorted, his voice confused, angry.

'Poor, poor girl!' Ruby murmured. 'Pregnant…!'

'And the whole time I thought she was mad at me or something,' Rajat bit out.

'Why would she be mad at you, babe?' Ruby asked, puzzled.

'Because I was in love with her!' He got up from his chair with controlled fury. 'I was crazy about her and I told her that if she quit the show, I'd start drinking again and… Oh damn, damn, damn! What an idiot I've been!' He picked up his cup of coffee and flung it hard against the wooden railing.

Ruby shrieked and jumped away, as a shower of coffee and shards of ceramic sprayed them all.

'Hey, take it easy,' Niki said. She reached across and pushed Rajat back down in his chair. 'It's okay,' she said, patting his heaving shoulders. 'It's okay.'

'No, it's not!' he sobbed. 'It's all messed up, don't you see? Mala's dead! Why is she dead? She was pregnant! She must have been overjoyed! She loved kids! She was always talking about how she wanted to have at least four! So why did she kill herself? It doesn't make any sense!'

'No, it doesn't.'

Niki turned to look at KK, who'd spoken so softly that for a moment, she thought she'd imagined it. Her gaze travelled from the dull look in his eyes to the dark, wet spot above his left brow.

'Mr Kapoor? I think you're bleeding,' she said.

'I'm sorry?'

'You're bleeding,' Niki repeated, pointing to the cut.

He lifted a hand to the spot above his brow. 'I guess I am… Excuse me,' he said and, without a backward glance, shuffled slowly away.

11

The night was finally quiet in the Jungle Book Resort. The lights were out; the fires had died down; a lone guard dozed at his post outside the main resort gates; the other stared sleepily into the night. Past the boundaries of the resort, in their secret places out amongst the trees, the nocturnal animals were busy hunting, guarding, stalking, feeding. Nearer the resort, the river was a sheet of molten glass, shimmering softly under the moonlit sky.

Inside the boys' villa on the south side, the air was still and silent, except for the soft sounds of breathing coming from behind the closed doors of the various rooms.

Vicky, lying in bed in the room that looked out onto the clearing and, across it, to the girls' villa, listened for another minute, then turned on his side and threw off his blanket. His long legs snaked out; his feet found the floor. He sat up, watching the shadows flicker across the curtains on the window.

Above his head, the fluorescent hands on the clock confirmed the time: it was just past two. Almost an hour since they'd finally come inside, dragging a protesting and near comatose Binod and an equally dead Dev behind them. Almost an hour of lying awake.

Vicky eased himself off his bed. He walked barefoot to the window and drew aside the curtains. In the clearing between the two villas, the last embers from the bonfire glowed orange.

Vicky watched them, mesmerized. Fire, he thought. What a wonderful thing it was! It created and consumed; it cleansed and purified; it was the force and source of all life…

He felt an old, familiar impulse grip him. His breathing quickened; his heart beat faster. No, he shouldn't, he told himself.

And yet, it was impossible to resist, he knew.

Silently, as if pulled by a force greater than his better instincts, he pushed his feet into his shoes, opened the door of his room and tiptoed across the hall. With a silent click, he opened the front door and stepped outside. He let the door close shut behind him, then very quietly picked his way towards the dying fire.

12

It was the smell that alerted Niki.

It was a sharp, acrid smell, of smoke, ashes, burning wood, coming through the wire mesh of her open cottage window. She was out of her bed in a couple of seconds, swinging open the door of her cottage in the third. Two hundred metres down, past the treetops, she saw a black plume of smoke rising up into the sky.

She reached for the resort phone. 'Vijendra?' she said, as soon as she heard the sleepy voice at the other end. 'Call the fire brigade. There's a fire on the north side.'

She pulled on her jeans and jacket. Within moments, she was rushing down the path in the direction of the blaze.

'It appears to be coming from one of the VIP cottages,' Vijendra said, running up to join her, his anxious gaze fixed on the glowing plume in the distance. 'There's a cluster of five at that end, numbers eleven to sixteen.'

'Sound the alarm, start vacating the premises,' Niki directed. 'I'll head to the fire and secure a perimeter around it. Make sure no one gets near it.'

'But what if someone is already inside?'

'Let's hope there isn't,' Niki said, breaking into a sprint.

The smoke was rolling, thick and black, down the path towards her. Behind it, one of the cottages had turned into a blazing inferno, she saw. Angry flames kicked and danced out the windows, pushed through the door, shot branches up through the roof. Niki covered her face with her muffler, ducked low and charged down the path, narrowing her eyes against the sharp sting of the smoke. She felt the metal plate in the stone pillar that flanked the cottage; it was blazing hot and burnt her fingers. *Cottage 13*, she read, before a fresh burst of smoke obscured it again.

Unlucky number thirteen, she thought, even though, unlike Ruby, she did not believe in superstition. Just this once, she hoped against hope that no one had been foolhardy enough to pick it.

Two hundred metres away, the Jungle Book reception lounge had become a scene of frenetic activity. The dozen or so staff members who lived on the premises had been roused by Vijendra; they now gathered round him, wide-eyed, grim-faced.

'There's a fire in the north sector,' he told the men. 'Cottages eleven to sixteen. I've called 101. The fire truck is on its way from Khajuraho; ambulances too. Meanwhile, I need a team of two to head there with me, with extinguishers, sand buckets, helmets, emergency lights. I need another team to start cutting a fire line isolating that sector from the rest of the resort. Get as many of the local workers as you can to come out with their axes and saws. And Raghu, I want you to go with Jaspal to each of the cottages and start evacuating the guests.'

'All the guests?' Raghu asked.

'Lets start with the guests in cottages eleven to sixteen,' Vijendra said. 'And then move back to seventeen to twenty-two. Also, alert the guests in twenty-three to twenty-eight to be on standby to vacate, if necessary.'

He pulled out a handful of walkie-talkies, handing them out to the staff. 'Let's keep in touch as we go along. Alert me in case of any questions or problems.' He reached for a helmet and strode to the door. 'Let's get going,' he said, 'we have no time to lose.'

Mansi Malhotra stood dazed and confused in the doorway of Cottage 16. She'd woken, sleepy-eyed and hung-over, to the sound of frantic pounding on her door; she had opened it to find Raghu standing at her doorstep wearing a scarf around his nose.

'Miss, sorry to disturb. Are you okay?' he asked.

'Ye-es?'

'Your name?'

'Mansi Malhotra. What's going on?' Her eyes grew wide as she noticed the smoke and haze past the open cottage door and her nostrils registered the ash and soot in the air.

'Cottage 16, Mansi Malhotra, check!' Raghu called into his walkie-talkie. He turned back to Mansi. 'Ma'am, step outside and follow the signs to the reception lounge. Right away, please.'

'But my things?'

'Leave them. The fire engine is on its way. Right now, our first priority is to make sure you are safe.'

Mansi stepped into the cold night air and shivered, as much from fear as from the cold. The fire was an eerie orange glow to her left; above it, dark clouds of smoke were hurtling into the sky. She coughed, wrapped her shawl tight about her face and headed down the path indicated by Raghu, who was already sprinting towards the next cottage.

Less than 50 metres away, Niki crouched just inside the gate to Cottage 13, shielding her eyes against the smoke and heat, unable to go any further. Before her, the cottage was ablaze, flames engulfing and consuming it, wood, body and soul. As she watched, the fiery roof crumpled like a sheet of paper and disintegrated into the middle with a whooshing sound, sending up a giant shower of sparks and debris and erupting in a loud roar.

Niki ducked her head as the blankets of smoke billowed up and a long branch of fire shot up into the sky. She felt the heat crawl up her back and burn the nape of her neck. She shielded herself as best she could from the sting of the sparks, ran back several paces to a row of bushes and ducked behind the scant cover they provided.

She held her breath as long as she could, waiting for the waves of smoke to disperse. Her chest hurt from the acrid air, she wiped her streaming eyes and forced them open. Her gaze followed the path of the flames, the ones that danced straight and intent, the others that flirted wildly in unpredictable trajectories and still others that shot out sudden, deadly tentacles. The night air was still, she noted, but it wouldn't take much more than a gentle breeze to start fanning the fire out to the treetops nearby and the cottage to the left. She looked back as she heard the shout of men behind her and saw Vijendra leading a group of them. She dearly hoped the fire engine was on its way.

Ruby Talwar stood, wide-eyed, panicking, in the doorway of Cottage 15, her bare toes curled against the cold, a hand clasped over her mouth, as Raghu ran up the short path to her.

'Ruby Ma'am? Are you okay?'

'Yes, I'm fine.'

'Anyone else inside?'

'No.'

Raghu nodded and spoke quickly into his walkie-talkie. 'Cottage 15, check. Please,' he said, taking Ruby by the arm. 'Come with me.'

'But the fire – '

'Is dangerously close.'

'I know.' Ruby's eyes were bright with alarm. 'But isn't that – isn't that coming out of that *cottage*?'

'Ma'am, let's go – '

'But you have to tell me what's going on! These are my people! Is – was anyone in the cottage?'

'It's too early to say, ma'am.'

'But do you know which cottage it is?'

'We think it's Cottage 13, ma'am.'

'*Oh God!*' Ruby moaned, covering her face.

In the distance, a high-pitched whine became audible and slowly grew louder. A fire truck, finally, Niki thought with relief, as she, along with Vijendra and his men, worked on clearing the surrounding ground of twigs and dried leaves; a feeble attempt, she knew. She straightened a moment, listening; in her mind, she measured the minutes it would take for the truck to arrive. Five, seven minutes, tops, and if they were lucky, they'd have it under control without further damage. She looked round at the neighbouring cottages, close, too close, to the blazing inferno. Hopefully, they would have had everyone evacuated, counted and accounted for.

Raghu regarded Ruby anxiously, supporting her. 'Who was in number thirteen?' he asked.

'Rajat,' Ruby moaned.

'Rajat Tripathi! Are you sure?'

'I gave him the keys to number thirteen when we checked in,' Ruby sobbed.

Raghu reached for his walkie-talkie. 'Jimmy Zariwala in Cottage 14, check,' he heard Jaspal confirm.

'That leaves numbers eleven and twelve,' he heard Vijendra's voice say.

'And number thirteen,' he said. 'According to Miss Ruby Talwar, Rajat Tripathi had the keys to cottage number thirteen.'

There was a pause at the other end. 'Okay, I'm putting a search out for him right now,' Vijendra's voice answered.

Niki's face grew pale as she listened in on the exchange on the walkie-talkie Vijendra had handed her.

'Are you sure it was Rajat?' she asked.

'Ms Talwar says she gave him the keys,' Vijendra said.

Damn, damn, damn, damn!

Niki turned as the fire truck finally arrived behind her, its lights flashing, its siren screaming. She ran up to meet it.

The fire chief, a grizzled man in his late thirties, listened attentively, his gaze never leaving the conflagration that crackled and roared before him as, in a few, quick words, Niki apprised them of the situation.

'So he may still be in there?' he asked,

'We haven't found him anywhere else yet.'

'We'll do our best, ma'am.'

Niki stood back as he briefed his men. Within minutes, they had the equipment unloaded, the hoses unwound, the ladders raised. She watched as they advanced to form a tight, careful perimeter around the cottage, wishing there was more she could do.

She froze as the walkie-talkie in her hands came alive again.

'We've found Rajat,' she heard Raghu's voice say suddenly, miraculously. 'He was asleep on one of the chairs at the Treetop Restaurant.'

Thank God, Niki breathed.

'So he wasn't in Cottage 13?' Vijendra's voice said.

'No, Ruby was mistaken. Rajat was supposed to be in number twelve,' Raghu said.

A hollow feeling rose up in Niki's chest. 'So who was in number thirteen?' she asked.

There was a pause. Then, 'Kemaal Kapoor is the only guest on the north side still unaccounted for,' Raghu said.

The fire was a nasty one; it took several men, working non-stop for over an hour, before they finally managed to put out the last of the flames and enter the cottage. Niki watched, her face black with soot and sweat, as they climbed over the mountain of smoking debris in their fireproof boots, their faces and heads covered in protective gear. Far away, across the horizon, the jungle was still shrouded in darkness. It would be another hour, at least, before the sun broke through the darkness of the night.

Niki watched anxiously as two of the firemen sifted cautiously through the blackened, soaked rubble with their fluorescent torches and fire-retardant sticks; she caught her breath as one of them crouched down beside a long, charred object. He shone his light over it, then glanced briefly in her direction, shaking his head. Several excruciating minutes later, the fire chief finally emerged from behind the mountain of burnt debris and walked towards her. He took off his helmet and wiped the sweat-streaked grime from his face.

'Almost everything is gone,' he said. 'It's been completely burnt down. Some accelerant is almost certainly involved.'

'Accelerant?'

'Kerosene, most likely. The good news is that we found no human remains. No sign of anyone, dead or alive.'

Niki felt her chest relax as she let go of the breath she'd been holding in. A great weariness invaded her limbs; she felt dizzy with relief. She squatted down on the ground, only just realizing that she'd been on her feet, coiled like a spring, for the better part of two hours.

'So then, where the hell is he?' she asked.

The fire chief shrugged in response, then stiffened as a movement behind the flashing lights of the fire truck caught his gaze. Niki turned to see a bulky figure crouching in its shadows, a dark shawl wrapped around his head.

'Hey!' the fire chief called, sprinting towards the figure, Niki behind him. 'Hey you! What are you doing there?' He barred the path as the figure started to dart away. 'Get back, you're not supposed to be here!' he said.

'But where else am I supposed to go?'

Niki met the confused, disoriented gaze; she felt dizzy with relief as she lifted the walkie-talkie to her mouth. 'Vijendra? Everyone is accounted for,' she announced.

The phone rang out, loud and shrill, in the predawn stillness of the girls' villa on the south side of the resort. It continued to ring for a long time before Barkha staggered out of her room.

'I don't get paid enough for this,' she muttered, picking up the receiver.

Her eyes narrowed as she tried to decipher the hysterical words at the other end, as Ruby told her, in fits and starts, not to panic, everyone was safe, by some miracle, they had been delivered, the Gods were still looking out for them, everything would be okay.

'Yes, everyone's still in bed here,' Barkha yawned, looking out the darkened window of her cottage at the calm night sky. 'Considering it was just a few hours ago that everyone finally *got* into bed… Yes, sure, they'll be ecstatic to get the morning off… Wait! Does this mean we won't be getting any bed tea?'

The answer was evident in the droop of her shoulders as she put the phone down. She turned and found Leena and Pallavi, who had stumbled out of their respective beds at the sound of the ringing phone, standing at the entryway, watching her.

'That was Ruby,' she said shortly. 'There's been a fire on the north side of the resort. KK's cottage burnt down.'

Leena clapped a horrified hand to her mouth.

'He's okay,' Barkha added.

'What happened?' Pallavi asked.

'They don't know yet. Apparently, they first noticed the fire at two-thirty in the morning. SP Marwah spotted it. They've evacuated everyone on the north side.'

'SP Marwah? That Shimla Police officer?' Leena asked.

'What's she doing *here*?' Pallavi said.

'Who knows?' Barkha shrugged. 'Maybe she's psychic. Maybe she knew something like this was going to happen.'

'Okay, this is beyond suspicious,' Pallavi said. 'This is serious. This is unbelievable.'

'Maybe it was just an accident,' Leena said.

'And maybe someone's got it in for us.'

'Either way,' Barkha said, 'don't expect to be fed any time soon.'

13

The mid-morning sun burned high in the sky, flooding the veranda of the Jungle Book Resort's main reception lounge with light. SP Marwah, rested and refreshed from the ordeal of the night, crossed one slim leg over the other as she sat against the cushions on one of the cane sofas and gravely regarded the man sitting across from her.

He seemed jittery, unsettled; the cool arrogance that defined him was nowhere in sight this morning. His chin and lip were covered in unsightly gray stubble; his eyes were dull; his hand trembled as he stirred his third spoonful of sugar into his cup of chai. He didn't look like he'd got any sleep, even though they'd managed to coax him into bed in Vijendra's guest room with a thick blanket and a couple of sedatives. He didn't look like he'd get any sleep for some time to come.

Niki waited for him to raise the cup of chai to his lips. She watched him take a small sip, then another. He lowered the cup, his large hands curled around its warmth.

On the low table between them, there was an untouched plate of sandwiches and a side of boiled eggs that Gopal had managed to rustle up, along with the tea. Niki pushed the plate towards KK. 'Nothing like some food when you're feeling low,' she reminded him, as he started to shake his head.

KK sighed and, with a slight grimace that she assumed was an attempt at a smile, reached for one of the small sandwiches. He took a bite, chewing on it meditatively, his gaze travelling to the river that sparkled and glistened in the sunlight.

'Feel any better?'

KK withdrew his gaze from the river; he met Niki's eyes for an instant before looking away again. 'How – how are the others?' he asked.

'Everyone's fine.'

'The contestants?'

'They didn't even know there was a fire until it was all over.'

KK nodded, then resumed his quiet contemplation of the river. In the harsh light of the climbing day, he looked old, ill.

'So tell me about last night,' Niki invited, once he was halfway through his chai.

KK sighed deeply. 'I really don't know what I can tell you.'

'Let's start with when you returned to your cottage last night.'

KK nodded, took another sip of chai.

'What time did you get back?' Niki asked.

'Just past midnight, I think. I left the restaurant and walked straight back to my cottage. You saw me. I had this cut on my forehead,' he pointed to the dark scab above his left brow, 'so I went to the bathroom and applied some antiseptic and a bandage. Then I changed and got into bed.'

'And then?'

'I was in bed.'

'And the fire?'

'I have no idea… !'

Niki sat forward and regarded him gravely. 'According to the fire chief's assessment, some sort of accelerant was involved,' she said. 'Kerosene, in all likelihood.'

'Kerosene? You mean from one of those lamps they have all over the place?'

'Possibly. Did you notice any smell of kerosene when you got back to your cottage?'

KK shook his head.

'Did you, by any chance, keep a lantern burning in your cottage?'

'No.'

'Did you notice any kerosene lamps that were lit close to your cottage?'

Again, he shook his head.

'Also, a canister of kerosene is missing from the resort's supplies room. Do you remember seeing a canister of kerosene anywhere near your cottage?'

'I'm quite sure there was no such thing.'

'What about the fireplace?' Niki asked. 'Did you happen to leave a fire burning in the fireplace?'

'No. I didn't even light a fire.'

'What about a matchstick? Or a cigarette?'

'No!' KK said vehemently. 'In the first place, I don't smoke; and in the second, I'm very, very careful about fire safety.' He shot Niki with a sharp glance. 'I run one of the most successful chain of restaurants in the country, Ms Marwah, and I don't do it by being negligent. Whatever caused the fire, I had nothing to do with it.'

'Actually, Mr Kapoor,' Niki said, her eyebrow lifting a fraction, 'I think you had everything to do with it.'

It was hot and hazy out by the river on the south side, even though it was barely eleven in the morning. The sky held patches of occasional, fleeting cloud; the barest breeze stirred the very tips of the trees. The river was an expanse of shimmering light flowing gently along its wooded banks.

Bored, restless, Pallavi stood at the water's edge, tossing stones into the current. Her drawstring shorts were damp with perspiration and clung limply to her bottom; her thin hair was caught up in a ponytail, the frizzy tendrils clinging to the clammy skin at her temples. It must be in the thirties already, she thought, shading her eyes against the glare off the water; the sun was probably burning an angry red rash into her arms, shoulders, the nape of her neck...

Her shoulders sagged. She was so tired, so sick of it all. Of *Hot Chef* and the lawyers and the family and the jungle and the constant mishaps... She was done; done being someone else's stooge, done hanging out with a bunch of losers, done trying to fix a mess that had been created by someone else. It was time to quit. To get on a plane to New York and get a job – in advertising or fashion or even childcare (shudder) – and leave it all behind – the Bandra home, the Indian fans, the bloody, screwed-up, dangerous *Hot Chef* world…

She waded out into the water, surprised by its chill as it splashed around her ankles. She walked out farther into the water, bent to pick up a river stone, sent it sailing across the shimmering surface. It skipped like a giggling, gurgling child – once, twice, seven times – before plunging into the middle of the slow current. Pallavi watched as the tiny rings of water rippled out from it. A whiff of an earlier, carefree time floated back to her, a time when her mother had been around and her father had been sober. She lifted her head and closed her eyes a moment, savouring the heat, the memory.

'Well, well! Look what crept out from under its rock today…'

Pallavi whipped round to see Sharon standing on the riverbank, wrapped in a beach towel, a straw hat on her head and enormous goggles covering half her face. The smile that had creased Pallavi's cheeks gave way to her customary, defensive sneer. 'I thought I smelled something rotten,' she scowled. 'Did Barkha send you here? Did she say when we'd be leaving?'

'Do I look like your personal messenger?'

Sharon flung off her hat, stripped off her towel and goggles and waded out into the river in a dizzying black and white zebra-striped bikini. Pallavi's gaze swept over her with disgust. The woman was thickly, almost indecently built, her boobs virtually popping out of her bikini top as she bent to pick a stone out of the water, her bikini bottom anchored precariously on her fleshy hips. She straightened unselfconsciously and tossed the stone across the water's surface with a casual flick of her wrist. Pallavi counted five skips before it sank into the water.

'That your best shot?' Pallavi selected another elongated pebble, rubbing it with her fingers. It was soft and smooth. She tossed it expertly, its trajectory long and nearly parallel to the horizon. She watched with satisfaction as it skipped nine times.

'Nice.' Sharon lifted her arms high above her head in a lazy, feline stretch, then sat down where she had stood so that the water lapped around her bottom and thighs. She scooped up handfuls of it and poured it over her bare shoulders. 'Mmm,' she said. 'This sure does beat that prison in Mumbai. I hope we get to stay another day.'

Pallavi tossed another stone. It skipped eleven times before sinking. 'Bet you can't beat that.'

'No, I don't think I can.'

'Aren't you even going to try?'

'No.'

'You're not even going to *try*?'

Sharon fixed Pallavi with a pitying smile. 'You know what your problem is? You try too hard.'

'On the contrary, I'm not trying at all. If I were really trying, you'd see the stone skip all the way to the other side.'

'You think I'm talking about river stones?'

'Whatever,' Pallavi said, turning her back on Sharon. 'Bottom line: you forfeit; I win.'

'Hooray for you.'

Pallavi whipped round angrily. 'Don't you patronize me!'

'And I thought I was merely getting out of your way.' Sharon leaned back into the riverbed, resting her weight on her elbows, allowing the water to ripple over her belly, her arms. 'Why do you want to win so badly?' she asked, squinting up at Pallavi. 'And why the hell are you so pathetically obvious about it? You want to have it all – the biggest boobs, the sexiest pout, the nicest clothes, the highest scores, the biggest fan following, the maximum number of stone skips in the river… Why do you have to constantly prove yourself? And to whom? What makes you so insecure?'

'I don't know what the hell you're talking about.'

'I'm talking about you skipping stones like it's an Olympic sport. Is that your life's consuming passion? Skipping stones?'

'Screw you!'

'Give it a rest, darling. Save up the energy for the things that really matter.'

Sharon lowered herself farther into the water so that her shoulders were now immersed; the river was flowing round her neck and chin, the water framing her face.

'Hey,' Pallavi said. 'Are you trying to drown or what?'

'Why? Worried they might blame you?'

'No. I just don't fancy the idea of having to haul you out and give you CPR.'

Sharon turned over on her side, grinning at Pallavi through narrowed eyes. 'Now there's something I haven't heard before. Anyway, what are you standing around getting burnt for? Sit down, chill.'

Pallavi shrugged, then sat down gingerly on the bed of river pebbles. The water felt cool against her clammy skin. Sharon scooped up a handful of water and sprayed it in Pallavi's face, making her gasp.

'There, doesn't that feel heavenly?'

'This feels even more heavenly,' Pallavi said and flung a handful of water right back at her.

Sharon chuckled, then wiped the water from her face. 'Isn't this the life!' she said, sinking down once more and submerging herself fully before popping her head up again, spluttering, spitting out something that seemed alive.

Pallavi looked down at Sharon, gagging and spitting, and smiled despite herself.

Sharon wiped the water from her eyes, laughing; then propped herself on her elbows again. 'My stepfather used to drive us out to the river for picnics when I was little, you know,' she said. 'Me, my sister, my mom. That was before she went loony and he started beating us up.'

Pallavi glanced at her curiously.

'He was quite the artist,' Sharon reminisced. 'See this?' She pointed to a jagged scar on her forehead, just inside her hairline, that Pallavi had not noticed before. 'He broke a bottle there once.'

'By accident?'

'That's the way the story goes.'

Pallavi was silent.

'He was a charming son of a bitch when he was sober, I have to admit,' Sharon went on. 'And a raving lunatic when he was drunk. He'd have killed me and my sister if he hadn't killed himself first.'

Pallavi's eyed widened.

'When I was twelve,' Sharon nodded. 'Guy got stark raving drunk one evening; my mother was in rehab somewhere. He ran out of booze; then he started picking on my sister. Punched her in the face, poor baby. She was just nine...'

'So what did you do?'

'What could I do? He was bigger, stronger than the two of us together. So I ran and switched off the mains in the house and then grabbed my sister's hand and we ran and hid in the storeroom.'

'And then?' Pallavi asked, riveted.

'Oh, he stumbled around in the dark, drunk and cursing for the longest time, and then he staggered to the mains and tried to fix them.'

'And...?'

'There was a short circuit, a fire of some sort.'

Pallavi froze. 'A fire?'

'Yeah. Poor sucker; he was burnt alive,' Sharon said, her voice devoid of all emotion.

'And you and your sister?'

'We survived.'

'You think *I* set fire to the cottage?'

KK set down his cup of chai, his expression incredulous.

No, Niki thought, she didn't. Not even the best actor in the world could have pulled off the look of bewilderment and terror that had been on KK's face last night. 'I think *someone else* set fire to your cottage,' she said.

KK blinked as he tried to assimilate what Niki had just told him. 'You mean *on purpose*?' He shook his head. 'All these people here, they are *my* people.'

'And yet it was *your* cottage that was set on fire. And if you had been inside it, we would not be having this conversation today. Speaking of which, where were you when the cottage caught fire?'

'I'd stepped out.'

'In the middle of the night?'

'I couldn't sleep,' he said, pouring himself another cup of chai. 'So I just stepped out for some fresh air.'

'Despite all the signs around the resort warning guests to *not* step out at night?'

KK shrugged, his thoughts hidden behind his lowered lids as he stirred sugar into his cup.

'So where did you go?'

'Just around the resort.'

'Around the resort?'

'Yes, I was just walking along the paths…'

'And what time was that?'

'Maybe one-thirty? Two?'

'And how long were you "just walking along the paths"?'

KK shifted in his seat. 'I don't know… I didn't check the time. I didn't have my watch.'

'And when did you return to your cottage?'

'Well…when you saw me, I guess.'

'Which was at twenty past four. Which means you were gone from anywhere between one-thirty and twenty past four.'

'I suppose.'

'And you were walking the entire time?'

'I suppose,' he said again.

'Bullshit.'

KK looked up, startled, and met Niki's steely gaze.

'You were not walking around the resort, Mr Kapoor,' Niki said, 'or else you would have noticed the fire. Or the frenzy of activity around you. Or someone would have seen you, especially since several people were out searching for you. So I repeat my question and I expect a truthful answer this time: *where were you*?'

KK was silent. When he spoke, finally, his voice was barely audible. 'It's a bit of a delicate matter,' he said.

'Where were you?' Niki repeated.

'I'd gone to visit someone. Someone who lives outside the resort's gates.'

'And this person's name?'

'Do you really need it? He had absolutely nothing to do with the fire.'

'Well, then, *she* should have no problem confirming your story.'

The colour came rushing to KK's face.

'Your friend's name, Mr Kapoor?' she prompted.

'Chanda Kumari,' he said.

'The assistant chef at the resort?'

He nodded. 'I met her yesterday. She was picking vegetables from the garden. I helped her and we got talking and – it's not what you think.'

'Mr Kapoor, my only interest is in finding out who set that fire.'

'Ms Marwah, you have to believe me; nothing happened between me and Chanda.'

Niki regarded him impassively.

'When you told us about poor Mala being pregnant last night, I was so shocked! I couldn't lie still; I kept thinking about her and her baby and why she did it… After a while, I just had to get up and go somewhere, see someone, anyone… And then I remembered Chanda telling me she lived right outside the resort's gates. So I just walked over on a whim and when I saw the light on in her house, I knocked. She let me in and…we just chatted, that's all. Please believe me!'

'I believe you.'

'You…you do?'

She nodded. 'You were clearly devastated last night.'

KK swallowed; his eyes filled with tears. 'Poor Mala! She was like a – '

'Mr Kapoor, please don't say she was like a daughter to you. You know and I know she wasn't.'

His gaze faltered under Niki's cool stare; he hung his head again. 'She was my protégée,' he said after a long moment. 'I taught her everything I knew.'

And you took advantage of her, Niki thought.

'I guess somewhere along the way, our friendship changed into something deeper...'

'Did you know about the baby?'

KK shook his head.

'Was it yours?'

He was silent.

'*Could* the child have been yours?' Niki repeated.

The question hung in the air for a long moment. Then, 'I don't know,' he groaned. 'She didn't tell me!'

'What would you have done if she had told you?'

'I don't know. But she *didn't* tell me. So maybe it wasn't mine?'

'But what if it was?'

He sighed and looked up, his eyes dull. 'I would have advised her to get an abortion,' he said. 'It would have been painful; I love children. But I'm a married man; I have my wife to think about.'

'Did she know about the affair?'

'She knows me,' KK shrugged.

So Mala wasn't the first one, Niki thought.

'I don't expect you to understand,' KK said, 'but ours is a very lonely profession. And when you work long hours in close quarters with someone...it isn't always possible to control your emotions.'

'Sharda, my wife, understands this.'

'And she's okay with it?' Try as she might, Niki was unable to keep the incredulity out of her voice.

'She knows I'll never leave her,' KK said. 'We've been married for thirty-three years. She is the mother of my child.'

'And what if Mala had wanted to be the mother of your child as well? What if she'd wanted to keep the baby?'

'Then it would have been her responsibility.'

14

It had been a busy week in Shimla.

The Dussehra season had burst upon the hills in full splendour, bringing with it the usual bacchanalia of melas, thelas, traffic, chaos and, inevitably, crime. A prominent electronics goods shop on the Mall had been broken into and ransacked; a group of college girls from Delhi had lost one of their members while partying; a German businessman had been relieved of his passport, laptop and euros by an enterprising gang of pickpockets. And while the excitement was dying down in Shimla and the action had relocated farther north to the massive celebrations under way in Kullu, the backlog of paperwork that had piled up on ASP Sahay's desk was enough to pull not only him but also a highly obliging and resourceful Inspector Deepika Chauhan, bearing a thermos of Joginder's elaichi chai, to the office on a Sunday morning.

They were barely a third of their way through the files when the 'Waka Waka' ringtone of ASP Sahay's mobile burst through the silence.

He picked it up with a start, then relaxed as he saw the caller's name. 'Boss,' he said, putting his phone to his ear. 'Where have you been? I've been trying to reach you all morning! All well?'

'Yes and no. Any chance you can head to the office? And call Deepika in too?'

'We're both here, boss. Post-Dussehra clean-up. What's up?'

'Why don't you put me on speaker?'

Sahay beckoned Inspector Chauhan, who'd looked up from her files at his words.

'It turns out Mala was having an affair with KK, not Rajat,' Niki said.

'KK?' Sahay blinked. 'Boss, are you sure?'

'I have it in his own words.' Quickly, succinctly, Niki brought them up to speed on the events of the previous evening.

'A fire!' Sahay said, eyes widening. 'Boss, you sure you're okay?'

'I'm fine,' Niki said. 'But KK's not. He's had a miraculous escape. From a fire that was definitely not an accident.'

'Shall I coordinate with the local police on the investigation, ma'am?' Deepika asked.

'No, let them conduct the investigation. We have enough on our plate, as it is.'

'Boss, do you think KK set the fire himself?' Sahay asked.

'I thought about that,' Niki said, 'but his alibi checked out. Also, he's quite shaken by the incident. I don't think he's feigning it.'

'So first, Mala Joseph, now KK…' Sahay mused. 'I doubt it's a coincidence.'

'In a murder investigation, nothing ever is.'

'And it looks like whoever's behind the attacks is getting bolder and more dangerous,' Sahay said with a worried frown. 'Do you think someone else knew what was going on? Maybe KK's wife…?'

'She certainly has a motive,' Niki said. 'But she doesn't fit the profile. Besides, he's been cheating on her for years; why go ballistic now, when their daughter's about to get married?'

'And we've already ruled out Joseph… So who else would want to do them both in? Rajat?'

'He was in love with Mala,' Niki said. 'But it was one-sided.'

'Unrequited love can be an ugly thing.'

'Yes, but he worshipped Mala. She was his "saviour", he said. And his reaction to the news of Mala's pregnancy was very real. He was angry and bewildered. It was clear he had no idea.'

'So if we rule out the spouses and the unrequited love…' Deepika said.

'I'm beginning to think that this has nothing to do with the affair or the pregnancy,' Niki said.

'But boss, what other motive could there be? The joint venture?'

'You think someone is trying to prevent the joint venture? But why?'

'Beats me,' Sahay said. 'What other connection is there between Mala and KK?'

'They were both chefs,' Deepika mused.

'They were both chefs *and* judges on *Hot Chef*,' Sahay agreed. 'And all the incidents have been happening either during the show's shooting or during rehearsals.'

'And while everybody else had access to the judges at other times,' Niki said, 'the only people who had access to Mala and KK *exclusively* during rehearsals and shoots – '

'Were the contestants,' Sahay completed.

15

Leena Dixit paced back and forth on the path outside the girls' villa on the south side of the Jungle Book Resort, her thoughts in turmoil.

She felt like screaming. Why, she silently wailed. Why am I here? What kind of people am I hanging out with? What kind of person have I become?

She stopped, her gaze resting on Sharon and Pallavi who were still sitting in the water, chatting like long-lost friends. Who were they really, she wondered. Friends? Rivals? Mortal enemies?

It was a game of cat and mouse, *Hot Chef*. So confusing, so toxic. She'd been a fool to think that she could win it, fair and square. There was no way. It wasn't just about the food, the contest; it wasn't even *about* the food. It was, in fact, about everything besides food. About manipulating and scheming and knocking out your rivals before they did the same to you, no matter who loved whom.

She leaned back against the warm brick wall of the villa and sighed. That was what was troubling her, she knew. Love. She was in love with someone who was her rival, someone she knew she couldn't, shouldn't trust. Not even when he told her, under a night sky ablaze with stars, his face aglow with the fire he was breathing, that he was in love with her. Because of all the manipulators on the show, he was the most accomplished, the most unreliable.

She glanced at the blackened patch in the clearing that separated the two villas, at the remnants of the bonfire from the previous night, where Vicky had declared his love.

He'd been in a strange, dangerous mood. Not drunk, but not sober either. And she hadn't known whether to believe him or beware of him. What if it was all a ruse? That declaration of love, the camaraderie... What if the only reason he had even befriended her in the first place was because he was trying to get her bumped off the show?

Because she knew, in her heart, that he was everything she was not. He was smart and sexy; he came from a world of entitlement and affluence, where it was cool to be outrageous, to take risks. Whereas she came from a world of careful economy, where one was forever on the precipice between respectability and ruin.

All it took was one misstep.

And Vicky was more than a misstep; he was a wild, flying leap into an abyss. He was reckless and he was unpredictable; and even when he looked at her with that strange light in his eyes and flicked her hair in that caressing way, it was terrifying to think that he might be serious. And yet, it was even more terrifying to think that he might not…

Last night had been the scariest of all. He'd been in a trance-like state, with his crazy talk about setting the world on fire and dancing amidst the flames…

She stopped short and stared into the bonfire ashes again. He'd been talking about setting the world on fire. He'd been blowing clouds of fire.

And then KK's cottage had caught fire.

Shaq, playing solitaire on the coffee table in the lounge of the boys' villa, looked up as he sensed a movement outside the window. He frowned as he spotted Leena pacing outside. She had her hands clasped tightly behind her back; she appeared to be talking to herself. From time to time, her gaze went to the site of the bonfire, to Sharon and Pallavi in the water, to one specific window of the boys' villa…

Shaq glanced at Dev, snoozing on the nearby sofa, and Binod, who had his nose buried in a paperback novel. Vicky's door was still closed.

'I'll be right back,' he murmured to no one in particular and headed for the door.

He caught up with Leena as she circled the remnants of the bonfire for the hundredth time; she seemed a thousand miles away.

'Hey, Leena. Looking for something?'

She jumped at his voice, then relaxed. 'No, just killing time,' she said. 'Any idea when we'll leave?'

'They're still cleaning up on the north side,' Shaq said. 'Binod mentioned something about Ruby trying to get us on tomorrow's flight.'

'Tomorrow?' Leena wailed. 'Oh, I wish we could get out of here right now...'

'I know what you mean.'

Leena looked at Shaq, anxiety writ large in her eyes. 'What's going on, Shaq?' she whispered.

'You mean the fire? I'm sure it was an accident.'

'You are?'

'Just look around you,' he said. 'Wood and kindling; and then they go and light up the place with all those kerosene lamps. Just asking for trouble.'

'So you don't think...' Her gaze shifted past him to the boys' villa, to Vicky's window. It was closed, the curtains drawn shut, as it had been all morning.

'I don't think...?'

'Forget it; stupid thought.'

'Don't worry, it'll be fine,' he said, as he noticed her gaze slide to the bonfire again. 'We'll be out of here soon.'

'Yeah.' Leena forced a smile, feigned a casual, mocking tone. 'Meanwhile, we can watch the new bosom buddies frolicking in the river.'

Shaq followed her gaze to where Sharon and Pallavi were just getting out of the water. 'Not an entirely offensive sight, I have to say,' he smiled.

'Don't you start too...!' Leena wagged a finger at him. 'So where's Vicky?' she asked in what she hoped was a casual voice.

'Still asleep. I guess he needs to sleep off whatever cocktail of drugs he was on last night.'

'Yeah,' Leena said, her cheeks flaming once again. 'He was pretty crazy, wasn't he?'

Shaq was quiet for a moment. Then he turned to Leena with real concern in his eyes. 'Look, Leena,' he said. 'Normally, I believe in minding my own business. But you're like a sister to me...'

Leena nodded; she felt her eyes prick with tears.

'Vicky's not a bad guy,' Shaq said. 'I like him too. A lot. But he's messed up. I'm worried that he's going down. Don't let him take you down with him.'

16

Why would a contestant want to kill the judges?

Niki pondered the question as she sat in her cottage, going over the notes from her interview with KK. The man was arrogant, ruthless and a womanizer, but why would a contestant want to *kill* him for that? And why kill Mala first?

'They are all desperate to win. They'll do anything to win,' Barkha had said to her, not two weeks ago.

Which was understandable, Niki thought. But would they be willing to kill to win? And what would any of them gain by killing Mala and KK? They may want to kill each other, maybe, but why the judges?

And yet, all the previous incidents had occurred *only* on the sets. The implication was too great to ignore.

Niki opened up the document with notes from the Gaiety episode on her laptop. She went over it again. Dev Nair was the one who had failed to impress that evening; he was also the last one to present his dish to the judges. Was it possible that he had somehow poisoned Mala to avoid getting eliminated?

But why Mala?

Niki clicked on the file attachment that Deepika had emailed her just a few minutes ago, titled 'Contestant Information'; she scrolled to the page on Dev Nair. He came from a family of jewellers, she noted. Which meant he would have had easy access to the poison. And the guy had perseverance; that was clear from all the auditions he had been to in all the previous years. Could he have decided, once he got his golden chance, that there was no way he was going to let it go?

But if that were the case, Niki wondered, sitting back in her chair, why had he gone after KK last night? Of all the contestants, Dev was the one who had come out ahead in yesterday's challenge. For the first time ever. So why would he set fire to KK's cottage?

It made no sense.

Niki turned back to her laptop, scrolled back to the notes on the first contestant, Leena Dixit. KK had been displeased with Leena last night; there had been some mention of him reducing her to tears.

Niki glanced through the background information on Leena. She could have had access to the poison too, Deepika had noted in a comment; she and her father had been in and out of medical facilities and testing labs on a regular basis. And, Niki noticed, not only was Leena's father ill, but he was also heavily in debt. He was behind on the monthly rental for their flat; he had been borrowing heavily from a neighbour the past two years. In fact, the only thing that was keeping the neighbour from throwing them out of the house was Leena's status as a strong contender in *Hot Chef*.

Could Leena have been so desperate to stay on that she set fire to KK's cottage?

Perhaps, Niki thought. But that would still not explain Mala's death. Because Leena had been ahead of the game at the Gaiety. Mala had loved her Thai curry. So why would Leena poison Mala? And how?

The same went for Pallavi Aanand and Vicky Gulati. They had both been doing well throughout the contest and especially at the Gaiety. Neither of them had any incentive to poison Mala.

Which left Shaqeel Khan and Sharon Sen…

'Vicky?'

Shaq knocked on the closed door of Vicky's bedroom and called out again, louder this time. 'Hey Vicky, wake up! It's past noon!'

Binod looked up from his paperback and glanced at the clock on the wall. 'It's actually twelve-thirty,' he said.

Shaq rattled the doorknob; it was locked from inside. 'Vicky? You okay?'

Binod heaved himself off the sofa and walked up to join Shaq at the door. 'Vicky, open the door,' he called. He waited a moment, frowning, as there was no response.

'Must be in the bathroom,' Shaq said.

'I tried to wake him up when the maid came to clean, but there was no response then either,' Binod said. 'Arre, Vicky,' he growled, 'are you acting funny again? Is this some joke? Open your door right now or I'll call Barkha!'

'Barkha?' Shaq said, throwing Binod a look of utter disgust. 'What can *she* do?'

'She can have him disqualified. She can have you all disqualified.'

Dev, who'd been munching on an apple, sauntered over. 'What's wrong?' he enquired. 'Why are we getting disqualified?'

'Vicky's locked himself in his room,' Binod said.

'So now you're going to start disqualifying us for staying in our rooms?'

'No, but I will if you break the rules,' Binod threatened.

'And what rules are we breaking exactly?'

'You're not supposed to endanger yourself or any of the other contestants.'

'I'm not feeling particularly endangered,' Dev shrugged.

Shaq pressed an ear to the door. 'Vicky? It's me, Shaq. Open up.'

There was silence at the other end.

'Hey, Vicky! Come on, yaar, open up!' Dev called. 'We're beginning to get disqualified here!'

Shaq jiggled the doorknob again and waited several seconds, then turned to Binod. 'He's probably just very deeply asleep,' he said.

'I'm calling Barkha,' Binod said.

Shaqeel Khan. There was no official birth certificate to be found, Niki read, but his date of birth, going by the *Hot Chef* records, was 10 June 1985. Place of birth: Lucknow. Mother: Saira Aslam Khan; father: Javed Jehangir Khan. He had one younger sister, Sohaila, who was currently studying at Jamia Millia in Delhi.

Niki skimmed over the basic information; there appeared to be no red flags. The guy had taken his tenth and twelfth standard board exams privately; had also obtained a diploma in home science and hotel management through a correspondence course in Lucknow.

And, all the time, he had been working at various restaurants in Lucknow, Kanpur, Allahabad...

Niki frowned distractedly as her cell phone rang. It was ASP Sahay. 'Boss, I think I may have found something,' he said.

'About one of the contestants?'

'Vicky Gulati, specifically. Remember, Barkha mentioned that he got thrown out of boarding school? Well, guess why?'

'Discipline issues?'

'Arson. Apparently, Vicky set fire to the boys' hostel.'

'What?' Niki frowned. 'Was he arrested?'

'That's the thing,' Sahay said. 'There is no official record of the incident. Apparently, there was an FIR filed at the local thana, but three days later, it was withdrawn. And the whole investigation was scuttled. But Chauhan dug deeper and found one of the SIs who'd been on duty that day and got him to spill the beans. According to him, Vicky's parents paid off the school to hush it up; they even donated a new wing to the boys' hostel.'

'Refresh my memory,' Niki said, 'Vicky's parents – they're both doctors?'

'They own one of the biggest pathology labs in Lucknow.'

Which meant easy access to cyanide...

'And there's more, boss. Guess why he dropped out of medical school.'

'Arson again?'

'Suspected involvement in theft at the college laboratory.'

'Suspected?'

'They could never prove it, but there were repeated instances of chemicals reported missing from the labs.'

'And Vicky was behind it?'

'Once again, the trail fizzles out, boss. But I spoke with the dorm warden myself. He said there was something seriously wrong with the boy. That he routinely set things on fire and talked about burning the place down.'

'I'm on my way to speak to him now.'

Leena watched, her face pale, as Barkha placed her hefty bulk against the door of Vicky's room.

She had been sitting in the lounge of the girls' villa trying to decide what she'd say to Vicky when she saw him, glancing from time to time at his still-shuttered window, when Binod had come rushing in. She had followed him and Barkha back to the boys' villa and now stood watching with growing apprehension as Barkha pounded on Vicky's locked door.

'Vicky! Open the door or I'll have someone break it down.'

There was nothing but silence, the same echoing silence that had been emanating from behind the door for the past twenty minutes.

'Vicky?' Leena called out, her voice high with anxiety. 'It's Leena. Can I talk to you for a moment?'

Barkha listened for several seconds, then shook her head. 'Okay, Vicky Gulati,' she said, 'this is it. I'm calling the resort manager to break open this door. And unless you have a Nobel Prize-worthy reason for this nonsense, you're disqualified.'

'Vicky?' Leena called again, her voice trembling. 'Please…?'

Behind them, through the open door of the lounge, Pallavi and Sharon ambled in.

'What's up darlings?' Sharon asked.

'Vicky's inside and he's not opening his door,' Dev replied.

'Maybe he's doing his private business,' Sharon quipped, the arch of her brows and her suggestive glance downwards making her meaning clear. 'Why don't you all leave the poor kid alone?'

'I bet he's just lying there stoned,' Pallavi said. She walked up to the dining table and picked an apple from the fruit bowl. 'Hey, how come we didn't get a bowl of apples in the girls' villa?' she complained.

'I think he might be sick,' Leena murmured to Barkha. 'He wasn't feeling well last night…'

'Vicky? Do you need a doctor?' Barkha called out.

'He seemed his usual self to me,' Sharon reasoned. 'The guy's probably just wasted. I think we should leave him alone.'

'Yeah. I think he's just doing this for attention,' Pallavi said with a roll of her eyes.

'Vicky?' Leena called out, pressing her ear to the door. 'Shh! I think I heard something."

'Be quiet, everyone,' Shaq said.

Leena put her ear to the door again. From the other side, the faintest hint of a gurgling sound could be heard.

Shaq leaned in to listen too. Faint, indistinct sounds seemed to be coming from within. Shaq frowned, trying to decipher the slurred words. 'Vicky,' he called. 'What's wrong? Shall we call a doctor?'

'*Fuck the doctor!*'

The strangled shriek, like an animal in pain, had Leena and Shaq recoiling from the door.

'Hey, Vicky!' Binod called.

Once again, there was nothing but silence.

'Okay, that's it,' Shaq said. 'Let's break down this door.'

'Do it,' Barkha said, nodding grimly. For the first time, there was a worried frown on her forehead.

They braced themselves, Shaq, Leena, Binod and Barkha, and, at a signal from Shaq, slammed their shoulders against the door and pushed with all their might. It gave a little, but held.

'Wait,' Dev said. 'Step back, everyone.'

He took a few steps back, then stepped forward and kicked the door with all his might. It flew open with a crash.

Inside, on the bed, Vicky lay curled up in a foetal position, sucking on his thumb. From his throat emerged incoherent sounds, barely audible, of gagging and choking, as though from an injured animal.

'Oh my God, Vicky!' Leena rushed up to cradle his head. 'What's the matter? What happened?'

'His pupils are dilated,' Shaq said as he held Vicky by the shoulders and looked into his eyes. His pulse was erratic, faint. 'Something is wrong.'

'Vicky, what is it? What's wrong?' Leena murmured as she started to rub his chilled hands.

'I think he's having some kind of seizure,' Pallavi opined from the door.

'Hey, there's the lighter from last night,' Binod said, staring at the blue object on the side table by the bed. 'What's it doing in here?'

'And what the hell is all this?' Dev asked, walking over to the adjacent bathroom. On the floor by the toilet was a mess of plastic vials and a small heap of white powder.

Barkha picked up one of the plastic vials and held it to her nose. Then she frowned and looked down at Vicky, at the small film of froth collected at the corners of his mouth, the twitching limbs, the sweat-soaked bed.

'Out, everyone!' she ordered grimly. 'Binod, call an ambulance. Call Ruby. And call SP Marwah.'

17

Niki's expression was grim as she raced down the path towards the south-side villas.

A history of arson, chemicals gone missing from a medical laboratory – these were serious charges; they should have been investigated thoroughly. Not for the first time, she felt a sense of frustration at the inefficiencies and corruption within the system, within the very police force of which she was a member, that allowed crimes and criminals to go uninvestigated, unpunished. Fraud, theft, assault, murder...

But then, that's why *she* was a part of the system, she reminded herself. So that she could ensure that no one got away; at least, not on her watch.

She slowed down as she neared the two villas and came to a halt at the site of the bonfire. There was a circle of burnt branches, a thick dusting of ash, a few empty bottles still scattered around on the ground. She crouched down beside one of the bottles, then glanced up sharply as she heard the sound of running footsteps and saw Binod sprinting down the path.

'Mr Bose?' she called.

'SP Marwah!' Binod stopped in his tracks, changed direction and came running up towards her.

'What's going on?'

'It's Vicky,' Binod said, panting from the unaccustomed exertion. 'I've just called an ambulance.'

Vicky was lying on his bed staring at the ceiling, surrounded by the other contestants, when Niki raced in. 'What's wrong with him?' she asked, feeling his pulse.

'We don't know,' Barkha said. 'But we found these in the bathroom.' She held out the plastic vials. 'I suspect he may have eaten something.'

Niki looked at the vials and felt her heart sink.

'And we found this in his room too,' Binod said, indicating the lighter.

'Anyone know how it got here?' Niki asked.

The contestants looked at each other. Sharon and Pallavi shrugged; Dev shook his head. Shaq looked down at his feet. Leena, trembling, shot a quick glance at Vicky. She fingered the Ganpati pendant she wore and took a deep, resolute breath. 'He was playing with it last night,' she said.

part 3

There will be killing till the score is paid.

Homer, *The Odyssey*

1

The first snowflakes of the season blew softly past the window on the third floor of the building that housed the offices of the Superintendent of Police, Shimla. They sailed along on a gentle breeze, drifting, dancing, like little white specks of confetti, as if heralding the advent of something momentous.

Niki, in the middle of a ninety-page document on the new guidelines and protocols for VIP safety as recommended by the Centre, put down her pen and walked over to her window, pushing it open. The frigid air of the valley came rushing in and made her catch her breath. For a long moment, she stood watching the bustle on the street as the snowflakes sailed down around the tourists, getting caught in their jackets and mufflers, their hair. She resisted the impulse to lean out the window and stick her tongue out, to try and catch a tiny flake. Perhaps later, if it were still snowing, she might step out, she thought, feel the brush of the breath-like flakes against her ears and neck and face…

She turned as there was the gentlest of taps on her door and Pradeep, huddled in a tight muffler and wool coat, walked in with the morning mail. He winced as he saw her open window.

'Nice out today, na?' Niki said with a teasing smile.

'Like Kailash Parbat, ma'am.'

'Cheer up; maybe it'll only snow a foot or two.'

Pradeep smiled a cheerless smile and dumped the mail with considerable relish on her pristine desk.

Niki regarded the pile of letters, cards, envelopes and fliers and sighed. Mail – it was one of the many things to love about a Monday morning. 'Anything that might explode in my face?'

'No wedding proposals, unfortunately,' Pradeep said, permitting himself a little smile.

It was a running joke in the department, the wedding proposals his boss got on a fairly regular basis in the mail. Apparently, there were many eligible bachelors across the length and breadth of the land united in their conviction that they were the perfect match for Shimla's beautiful and single Superintendent of Police. The record had been fifteen proposals in one day – all from the same gentleman. The craziest one had been from a seventy-year-old man in Kangra, whose dead wife had apparently come to him in a dream and told him that she had been reincarnated as the SP of Shimla; could he please come and take her back home? He had sat outside the office all day and all night in his sehra and Niki had not known whether to put him in lock up or frame the proposal and put it up on her wall.

'There is an invitation, though,' Pradeep said cryptically, on his way out.

Niki walked back to her desk, rifled through the various complaints, suggestions, statements, credit-card solicitations and Christmas-package offers that made up the bulk of her mail and located the thick, magazine-sized envelope that lay at the very bottom. The words 'Hot Cheff' were splashed across the red envelope in a fiery orange. Hot Cheff? Niki tore the envelope open and gazed at the thick, glossy brochure that fell out.

The
HOT CHEFF
Grand Finale
GOA, 23 DECEMBER
IGNITE YOUR SENSES!

Niki opened the smaller, card-sized envelope that accompanied it and pulled out the gold-embossed invitation.

Dear Esteemed Guest,

    We are delighted to invite you to be a part of our distinguished panel of judges at the *Hot Cheff* Grand Finale to be held on Sunday,

23 December, at 6 p.m. at the Royal Resorts, Goa, and request the pleasure of your company from Friday, 21 December, through Sunday, 23 December, for a weekend of tributes, music and fashion, that will have as its highlight a food extravaganza to delight every taste bud and ignite all five senses.

A judge? Niki unfolded the handwritten note that accompanied the invitation.

> *Dear Ms Marwah,*
>   *I never did get an opportunity to thank you properly for all your help in Shimla as well as at the Jungle Book Resort. I don't know if I ever can. Please know that we would never have got here without you. Please accept the attached invitation on my behalf and that of the entire cast and crew of* Hot Cheff. *We will be honoured to have you as our special guest judge.*
> *Warmest regards,*
> *Ruby Talwar*
>
> *P.S. You will notice that we have changed the show's name. It appears to have calmed down the planets, touch wood!*

Niki set down the invitation and flipped idly through the brochure. It was glossy, expensive, with double-page spreads of gorgeous food and spectacular locations, of the contestants cooking, performing, celebrating, weeping, of the judges tasting, guiding, commenting, consoling. An episode-by-episode recap filled the centre pages, the number of contestants diminishing with each elimination...

Niki paused at the page that featured the Gaiety episode. A life-size black and white portrait of Mala Joseph, her lips parted in a small smile, her eyes alive with laughter, stared back at her.

Niki closed the brochure and gazed out her window.

Her thoughts drifted back, to that fateful night in the jungle, the fateful morning that had followed. To Vicky Gulati. Cocky, charismatic, contradictory Vicky Gulati, whom she'd found lying curled and catatonic on his unmade bed, his cheeks grey, his eyes dull as stones. They had rushed him to the hospital, unresponsive and uncommunicative; the doctors had poked and prodded and put him on anticonvulsants and muscle relaxants.

Ruby had tried to call his parents. It hadn't been easy. Dr Vinod Gulati, it turned out, was at a conference overseas; Dr Rajni Gulati was in the middle of seeing her patients. It had taken Ruby nearly ten minutes to convince the maid who answered the landline that it was a matter of life and death; another twenty had elapsed before Vicky's mother came on the line. She had listened with a harassed air as Ruby told her that her son was in the ICU.

'Has he been taking his medicines?' she had asked.

'Medicines?'

'He has bipolar disorder. He's supposed to be taking his Lamepril.'

'Lamepril?'

'I'll try and get there as soon as I can,' his mother had sighed.

It had taken several hours before the doctors had finally updated Vicky's condition to 'stable'. Niki had stepped into the sterile white room and found a pale, emaciated ghost of a boy lying under a white sheet on the bed, staring up at a spot on the ceiling.

'Vicky? It's SP Marwah. How are you?' she had asked.

Vicky had continued to stare, glassy-eyed, at the ceiling.

'He'll be fine,' his mother had looked up from her iPhone long enough to respond.

'How is he doing?'

'He's been off his medication for months, what do you expect?' had been the exasperated response. 'This boy has been a nuisance since the day he was born! We've given him everything,' she had continued bitterly. 'Money, care, medicine… But nothing, *nothing* matters! And now this!' She'd held up the empty vials with their traces of white powder and looked down at her son with anger and frustration. 'Do you know how many patients I had to leave hanging this afternoon to come here and deal with your nonsense?' she had cried. 'All you had to do was to keep taking your medicines. One pill a day. Why is that so difficult? When will you stop torturing us like this?'

Vicky had been rapt in his study of the ceiling.

'He can hear me. He can hear every single word,' Dr Gulati had said. 'This is just another joke to you!'

He'd been out of danger and still staring at the ceiling when Niki had returned the next morning. She'd glanced at the steady heart and pulse graphs on the monitors, the regular flow of the drip through the tubes and into the thin, bony hand, as it lay on the white sheets. The mother had been nowhere in sight.

'I wonder if I may have a word with him?' Niki had asked the young nurse who'd been on duty. The nurse had left the room and Vicky had continued to browse the pattern of the whitewashed ceiling overhead.

'I'm surprised you didn't flush the Lamepril down the toilet,' Niki had said, her words breaking the long silence.

Vicky's gaze had shifted from its contemplation of the ceiling to a point just above her shoulder.

'Remember, no evidence, no crime?'

This time, his gaze had shifted to meet hers. 'I didn't commit any crime,' he'd said, his voice a dull, flat whisper.

'I know.'

'So you're not here to arrest me?'

'Why would I arrest you?'

'Mom said you were going to throw me in jail.'

'Should I?'

He had gazed into her eyes for an interminable minute and then slowly, his face pale and weary, he'd shaken his head.

'Then let's talk.' Niki had pulled up the empty chair and taken a seat; she had sat back and regarded him gravely. 'There is a lot of speculation going on you know; about your condition and how you hid it from everyone; about the fire in KK's cottage, about how the two may be connected. You may or may not be in a lot of trouble. But I'd like to hear your side of the story first.'

He had studied her a quiet moment, then gazed back up at the ceiling. 'It started when I was six or seven, I suppose,' he said, his voice low. 'That's when I knew something was wrong with me, when the beatings started in right earnest.'

She had leaned forward in her chair and listened with a growing frown as, dispassionately, he'd told her about the childhood mood swings, the uncontrollable tantrums, the frequent beatings, the bitter punishments and finally, at the age of nine, the diagnosis.

Bipolar disorder, Paresh Uncle, a leading Lucknow psychiatrist and close family friend, had told his parents after a particularly nasty episode, in which Vicky had swung a cricket bat at his Dad's car and his Dad had swung it right back at his leg.

'They were horrified, Mom and Dad,' Vicky said. 'He might as well have told them I was a mutant alien from another planet. They walked around, shell-shocked, for days afterwards, wondering how it was possible for two super-perfect geniuses like them to have produced such a freak of nature like me.

'They put me on a cocktail of medicines after that. It worked, I suppose. I stopped acting out, I started doing well at school and they were relieved. They pretended that I was fine, that they were fine, but I could see how they were ashamed of me; they avoided me. Like I was something diseased and contagious and if they came within five paces of me, they might catch it too...'

He'd turned his head towards Niki with a twisted smile that did little to disguise the hurt. 'Hilarious, huh? Two medical college gold medallists – and they were mortified by my existence. You'd think as doctors, they'd understand that bipolar disorder is just a chemical imbalance in the brain, not a curse upon their family!

'After a while, I just gave up. What was the point of trying to make them love me? Of trying to make anyone love me? I stopped playing with my friends. I stopped going out of the house. I sat in front of the TV all day, eating; I crossed seventy kilos before I turned ten. And then, the summer I turned twelve, Mom and Dad flew to London for a holiday without me. They took my cousin along, but they didn't take me. They left me home with the servants, because they thought I would be "calmer" that way.'

The ghost of a smile had flitted across his worn face.

'The afternoon they left, I started collecting eggs,' he'd said. 'I collected a whole bucket of them and set them out in the sun. And then the day they came back, I turned on all the fans in the house and lobbed the eggs, one by one, at the fans.

'The looks on their faces when they got back! Mom ran out of the house screeching like a madwoman and Dad chased me round the colony with his belt. And then, once the hysteria died down and the house had been fumigated, they told me it would be best for everyone if I went to boarding school.'

'And was it?' Niki asked.

He'd grinned momentarily, that lopsided, rakish Vicky Gulati grin. 'I had the time of my life there,' he said. 'The priests, the rules, the discipline…it was a dream come true. Oh,' he said, as he noticed Niki's puzzled frown, 'they didn't tell you? I also have ODD. Oppositional Defiance Disorder. It means that the minute someone tells me I can't do something, I just have to do it. I am programmed to break rules.'

Niki nodded gravely. It was starting to make sense – Barkha's exasperation, his own erratic behaviour… 'Is that why you set fire to the boys' hostel at your school?' she asked.

A faraway look had come into his eyes. 'I've always been fascinated by fire,' he'd said. 'I love how it burns, how it dances; what it can do… I've spent a lot of time playing with it; I've set many things on fire – newspapers, leaves, pencils, erasers, cotton balls, sacks of jute, strips of cloth, bags of crackers, sticks of camphor… I even tossed my Mom's gold jewellery into a bonfire once to see if it was real.' He smiled wanly as Niki's brows shot up. 'I know, dumb thing to do, but it seemed like a good idea at the time. But that fire in the hostel?' He shook his head emphatically. 'It was an accident, I swear. I was just trying to cook up a midnight treat for my friend's birthday, but the canister of oil slipped from my hands and fell straight into the fire. My God, the blaze! I was lucky I just escaped with this.' He'd shown her a long patch of burnt skin that snaked up his arm and across his shoulder. 'The "fathers" and "brothers" went ballistic, though. They thought I'd been out to kill everyone. As if. Why would I want to do that? They were my friends. They were the only friends I'd ever had.'

'So you were sent back home.'

'You can imagine my parents' delight!'

'They must have been happy when you topped the CBSE exams.'

'Worst mistake of my life,' Vicky had sighed.

'Why do you say that?'

'Because it got me into medical college. And what an unmitigated disaster that was! Imagine it, Ms Marwah. Imagine spending day after day in rooms just like this one – with the tubes and monitors and steel beds of doom, the cold hallways outside with the sounds of suffering and the smell of disinfectant everywhere…

'I couldn't handle it,' he'd said. 'Three months and I knew I had to do something or I'd lose my mind.'

'Is that why you started stealing from the labs?'

'It was just a silly prank,' he'd sighed. 'I never did anything with the salts and chemicals I took, you know. Just drained them down the sink.'

'And so you were asked to leave.'

'I was sent home again. And the parents were livid. But this time they had a plan. They told me I was over eighteen; I could go wherever I wanted to, do whatever the hell I pleased, just as long as it did not involve them. So I went to Mumbai and became a bum.

'It was a good trip,' he said, his voice softening. 'I loved Mumbai. I started playing guitar at my friend's restaurant; I waited tables and helped out in the kitchen; I started experimenting with dishes and flavours, papaya and garam masala, stewed apples and fresh ground cinnamon, buttered corn and mangoes…'

There had been a reverence in his voice that had reminded Niki of Ram; of how he always said that there was something about working with food that put one in touch with one's inner God. Food had transformed Ram, given him purpose and direction…

'So the restaurant was therapeutic?' she'd asked Vicky.

'It gave me my life back,' he'd nodded. 'I made friends again; I lost weight; I was happy as a buffalo in the mud, messing around with curries and saalans and spice rubs and marinades… I knew I was finally where I had always wanted to be. And I knew I wanted to share it with people; I wanted my own restaurant.'

'And so you auditioned for *Hot Chef*...'

'And these past few months on *Hot Chef* have been the best days of my life.'

'So how did you land up here in this hospital room?'

He had gone silent; a shadow had crossed his face. 'I don't know,' he said finally, his voice filled with sadness. 'I guess I should have kept taking my meds...'

'So why didn't you?'

'I thought I didn't need them.' His shoulders had lifted a fraction as he lay on the bed. 'I thought I was cured. Pretty stupid, huh?' He had looked at Niki, his eyes burning into hers, pleading for her to understand. 'Imagine being on mood medication all your life, Ms Marwah. Imagine needing a pill to feel like a human being. Day after day after day. Imagine the tyranny of that tiny white pill. I control you, it says. You can't survive without me. Take me or else...!'

Oppositional defiance disorder, Niki had thought sadly.

'I just wanted to live like a normal person,' Vicky had sighed. 'And so I stopped taking those stupid pills. And it was great. I wasn't a zombie any more. I could actually feel things – curiosity, excitement, exhilaration, love... And then Mala died.'

Niki had gazed at him, trying to read him as he lay there in the hospital bed. 'Mala?' she'd asked.

'She was such an amazing person, you know. I must have met her just a handful of times, but each time I did, I just felt this positive vibe coming off her. Like she was a well of happiness. And she was this crazy talented cook to boot, this winner of *Hot Chef*; she was someone who had everything. You looked at her and thought, "Hey, *this* is who I want to be."

'And then one fine day, she goes and kills herself.' He shook his head. 'I couldn't believe it. I lay in my bed for hours, thinking, why did she do it? Why Mala? And if Mala didn't think her life was worth living, then whose life was worth living anyway?'

Niki had looked into his eyes and seen nothing but sincere bewilderment in them.

'And that's when it began,' he'd said.

'You felt your symptoms return?'

He nodded sadly. 'I didn't recognize them right away; it had been so long. I felt alternately angry and exuberant; I couldn't understand why...'

'They found a lighter in your room,' Niki said. 'Someone spotted you going outside at two in the morning, around the same time that KK's cottage caught fire.'

He'd looked at her, his eyes dull, anguished. 'I did go outside,' he said. 'I went to the bonfire; it had almost burnt down. It was the saddest, most desolate sight ever – that dark pile of ashes, the black smoke rising into the night sky. It was like a glimpse of hell. So I tried to light it up again, the fire, but it was done. It didn't want to be revived. And that filled me with despair. Such despair...

'I sat there for the longest time, staring at this blackened, burnt mess, thinking about Mala and my parents and *Hot Chef*, about how nothing ever changed, nothing ever mattered...

'And then, somehow, I managed to drag myself back to my room. And I took out all the medicines and powders I had and crushed them; then I scooped up fistfuls and stuffed them down my throat...

'I'm quite sure I didn't set fire to KK's cottage,' he said sadly, meeting Niki's gaze. 'Why would I? But you should arrest me all the same, I suppose. Keep me out of trouble.'

And Niki had known then, that whoever had set fire to KK's cottage, it wasn't Vicky. 'Not today,' she'd said, getting to her feet. 'You have a lot to deal with in the coming days and weeks. It won't be easy, but I'm sure you'll make it.'

'But why? What's the point?'

'The point is that Mala didn't kill herself.'

He'd turned startled eyes on her.

'You mean – ?'

'I mean that Mala wanted to live. She thought her life was worth living. And I'm sure she'd feel the same way about yours.'

She'd squeezed his shoulder and wished him luck, before quietly leaving his hospital room.

She'd flown back to Shimla that afternoon, her heart heavy. Someone had killed Mala, had then tried to kill KK; but it was not Vicky. And while there was not a clue left unexplored, no piece of evidence she and her team had not examined, they had failed to find anything, any single trail that led to any one suspect.

She'd told herself on the way back that some cases were like that – tragic, unsolvable. Sometimes, no matter how hard one tries to prevent it, people did get away with murder.

At least, for a while.

And so she had come back to Shimla and put it behind her; she had immersed herself in her work, hoping, waiting for another opportunity.

And now it was here, staring her in the face. *Hot Cheff*. The Grand Finale. Goa, 23 December.

2

The Royal Resorts, the latest five-star hotel to make a splash on Goa's beautiful southern beaches, was a staggering property, boasting a nine-hole golf course, an award-winning ayurvedic spa, tennis, basketball and volleyball courts, a multilevel swimming pool, in-room whirlpool bathtubs, world-class dining facilities and a children's play area, wading pool and petting zoo.

The extravagant vision of a deep-pocketed, Dubai-based billionaire investor, it was equipped and embellished with every conceivable luxury, staffed with top-class employees, advertised globally and promoted lavishly; and in the seven short months since its opening, it had already become the preferred playground of the rich and famous.

The hotel had had the satisfaction, after the inaugural splash and the subsequent rave reviews, of seeing every single one of its 233 rooms and suites fill up for the Christmas week by June; and it was a major coup and act of foresight on the part of *Hot Cheff* and its executive producer, Ruby Talwar, to have snagged every single room and suite for the entire weekend preceding it.

She sat now on a podium in the marble and gold-trimmed banquet hall, with its twenty-foot-high ceiling, facing dozens of reporters and cameras for a pre-lunch briefing, as an army of unseen staff bustled about the property, erecting props, posters, banners and backdrops.

'It's the event of the year,' Ruby announced, radiant in a red silk batik designer dress, paired with a chunky orange necklace, and matching Jimmy Choos. The room was packed, she noted with satisfaction. Dailies, weeklies, fortnightlies and monthlies, local, national and foreign, English, Hindi, vernacular, radio, internet websites and TV channels – all the crews were there. They'd been pampered, courted, entertained and seduced all weekend long. The show had pulled out all the stops for the Grand Finale, and it had paid off. Practically every single invitee had agreed to attend. Every single one, besides the SP of Shimla. But then, Ms Marwah had her reasons, as Ruby well knew.

She glanced at Rajat, seated to her left on the dais, dashing in his new look of stubble and statement glasses. He was a natural, Ruby thought with silent admiration, as he kicked off the press conference with a dazzling build-up to the Grand Finale and the treats in store. He was articulate, charming, enthusiastic – the perfect host, especially now that he had cleaned up and turned sober again.

If there was one good thing that had come out of that awful night in the jungle, Ruby reflected, it was that. Somehow, something that SP Marwah had said to him had clicked.

She raked her freshly manicured fingers with their multiple gemstones through her newly highlighted hair and turned to listen as a young woman from one of the prime-time TV networks asked the first question.

'All season long, you've had the contestants cooking in the unlikeliest of places, facing the most bizarre challenges,' the woman said. 'So what amazing feats can we expect from the Grand Finale?'

'I'll take that question, darling,' Jimmy said, leaning into his mike.

Seated beside Rajat, he was in his sartorial and creative element this weekend, Ruby thought with a silent smile. His white linen shirt, worn over orange denim jeans, was embellished with hand-embroidered *Hot Cheff* logos. 'We're in Go-aaahh,' he told the reporter, playing with the mike, clearly enjoying himself. 'Land of parties, beaches, parties on beaches! So think two mind-blowing concept restaurants on the beach, each designed by the two finalists, each serving their own special signature dishes...'

'But where *are* these restaurants?' the journalist asked.

'They're being put up as we speak!'

'But the finale is scheduled for 6.30 this evening!'

'Yes!'

Ruby smiled and took the mike from Jimmy. 'When you're working with an insane genius like Jimmy, you learn to expect the unexpected,' she told the young reporter. 'The restaurants are being constructed on a secluded section of the Royal Resorts beach; we've had architects, interior designers and decorators working round the clock. The restaurants will open at 6.30 p.m. sharp this evening. Each will seat fifty guests at a time; each will meet the highest standards of international dining.'

'What kind of restaurants will they be?'

'Like nothing you've ever seen,' KK, seated to Ruby's right, promised.

He was dressed simply in a white kurta and pyjama, yet everyone else on the podium paled beside him, Ruby knew. As restaurateur, celebrity chef and star judge, he had commanded the media's respect and attention since the beginning of the show, but following the fire in the jungle he had captured imaginations in a way she had not thought was possible. Vivid footage of the burning cottage, captured on Raghu's smart phone and played non-stop on the news channels in the days that followed, interspersed with footage from the show of KK cooking, running, guiding, leading, had created an image of him as a cool daredevil; of someone who might not court danger, but who knew exactly how to handle it. Overnight, KK's real-life adventure had eclipsed the contestants' fabricated ones; the show's ratings had climbed even higher and KK, above all, had emerged the true hero.

Shrewd businessman and showman that he was, Ruby thought dryly, he had milked it for all he could, spinning the incident in his favour at every opportunity, in every interview, substituting myth for reality, until all that remained was the impression that had it not been for KK none of them would be alive. It was as if the near brush with death had reaffirmed his faith in his own immortality and consequence; he had become even more grandiloquent, more condescending, even more puffed up with his own importance than ever before. Ruby gritted her teeth as he spoke into the mike, expounded on his own virtues, alongside those of the contestants.

'Every great chef has a dream,' he said. 'A dream to create his own establishment. I had that dream and I've been fortunate enough to realize it. Kemaal's, as you all know, where it has been my humble endeavour, my life's work, to create the world's finest kebabs. Tonight, our two finalists will also have a chance to share their dreams. Tonight, all of India will get a glimpse of their talents. Tonight, India will decide whose dreams deserve to be realized!'

An array of flashlights exploded across the hall and Ruby had no doubt she'd be hearing the sound byte playing several times over through the next few days.

'Sir, how will *India* decide?' a husky voice asked from somewhere in the back.

Ruby craned her neck and noticed the attractive young journalist in a pink Lucknawi salwar kameez who had asked the question.

'There will be a hundred diners at these restaurants tonight,' KK said, beaming. 'Representing the voice of India.'

'Can you say that again, sir?'

'You heard right, my dear,' KK said. 'Instead of our regular panel of three judges, there will be *one hundred* judges tonight. We have invited, as our esteemed guests and judges, prominent people from all over the country, from the world of food, arts, media, cinema, literature, sports, politics, government... Tonight, India's best and brightest will pick India's *future* best and brightest.'

'But how will the contestants manage to cook for a hundred people?' another journalist piped up.

'This is *Hot Cheff*,' KK said haughtily. 'I can't imagine how they *can't* cook for a hundred people. At Kemaal's, we regularly serve five times as many in one evening.'

'The finalists will have the full support of the Royal Resorts kitchen staff,' Ruby added. 'As well as of the four contestants who have been eliminated in the last episodes.'

'You mean – '

Ruby nodded, smiling widely as the camera flashes went off in her face. 'Tonight, once again, you will see the *Hot Cheff* Top Six in action!'

3

Leena Dixit shielded her eyes against the glare of the sun and gazed out across the isolated expanse of sand at the north end of the Royal Resorts property. This small stretch of sand, with the afternoon breeze stirring the leaves on the coconut trees, the sun high above the water, the seagulls scrapping noisily for titbits – it was hers. Her beach, her territory, her restaurant.

A gluttonous orgy of the senses! The cook-off of the year! The clash of the Titans!

It was an understatement to say that the pressure was on. The *Hot Cheff* promotional machinery had worked itself into a fevered frenzy over the past couple of weeks, with magazine and newspaper spreads, cross-network TV appearances, mall events, hoardings, banners, posters – all with the two finalists' images blown up, touched up and splashed across every conceivable media outlet.

A mega battle of epic proportions, they promised; a Mahayuddh, a mela, a spectacle to be watched live by millions, as one contestant devoured the other. Or so it seemed.

Leena took a deep breath. She'd made it all this way and she could make it past the finish line too. The rest was just noise. She fingered the Ganpati pendant that lay warm against her skin and looked out as the crew went about setting up her masterpiece, as they brought into existence her guilty pleasure, her secret dream.

Chatpatty.

That's what she had named her restaurant. The Chatpatty Beach Bazaar, where everyone could eat their fill, till their eyes shone with delight and streamed with tears. A loud, bustling mela, with balloonwallas and pony rides and Bollywood hits blaring from loudspeakers; with chana jor garam, ragda patties, bhelpuri and pani puri; sev puri, batata vada, pao bhaji; gola, nariyal pani, ganne ka juice and tufts of pink candyfloss on sticks.

But with her own special twist. Flavours, from all around the world, from saffron to sumac, wasabi to ghost chilli powder, juniper berries and kaffir lime leaves, black truffle salt and grains of paradise – she had experimented with them all, incorporating them in subtle, playful, unusual ways in the timeless patties, pakoras, bhaji and bhel. The results, surprising in some cases, sublime in others, were bold, innovative, provocative. Whatever the verdict after tonight, no one would be able to accuse her of lacking in imagination or daring.

She watched as the design team wheeled out the brightly painted carts, with their enormous griddles for the patties and brass handis for the ragda, and wound streamers and balloons and garlands of fresh flowers round the tents and bamboo poles that covered the seating area; as a chaiwalla set up enormous pots to brew thick, sweet tea; as gajrawallas and champiwallas and paanwallas set up shop on the beachfront outside.

Yes, she was going for Chowpatty – timeless, kitschy and completely refreshed for the new century, but still noisy, still smelly, still sensational. She was taking a huge risk, but it was the finale and it was all or nothing now. And if the judges didn't like it…

Well, they *would* like it, she thought grimly. They'd have no choice.

Fifty metres down the sand, farther north, Pallavi Aanand was putting the finishing touches to her vision, her restaurant: La Palla Vié.

India was ready, she had decided, for authentic French food – simple, elegant, classic, exquisite. And who better to introduce *la cuisine française* in all its timeless glory to the Indian palate than Pallavi Aanand, trained in Le Cordon Bleu, Paris?

She was playing on her own turf, finally. And she knew that this time Leena would not stand a chance. A rank amateur pitted against a classically trained pro; it was going to be laughably easy. Still, this was the final challenge. She was just one step away from winning and she was not going to take any chances.

She had chosen her menu carefully; it was going to be both distinctive and decadent, from the Dom Perignon apéritif to the VSOP digestif – and everything in between. It was going to be a symphony of flavours playing on the palate, on the scale matched only by Beethoven's Ninth.

She inspected her main entrée, the Helix Burgundy snails, imported from France, especially procured, along with two dozen snail plates, snail tongs and tiny, two-pronged snail forks, to be served with chewy, oven-fresh mini baguettes. Escargots à la Bourguignonne, the way they were meant to be. She was going to prepare and serve them in the classic style, the meat simmered in red wine and mirepoix, shallots and thyme and stuffed back into their tiny shells with a special sauce of red chillies, garlic, brandy and parsley butter, the contrast of flavours so startling, it was guaranteed to floor anyone adventurous enough to try them. And for the squeamish ones she was serving an elegant roasted squash and potato bisque in buttermilk and heavy cream, topped with a sublime medley of freshly chopped chives, parsley, thyme, rosemary, tarragon and marjoram.

This would be followed by the *plat principal* and pièce de résistance: a precise rendering of Julia Child's ratatouille, rescued from its 'wholesomeness' by the substitution of fresh coriander in place of parsley and a dash of tamarind-lemon-white pepper paste that sparkled on the palate. The only thing that could potentially overshadow it, she felt, would be the silky dark chocolate mousse with whipped cream and juliennes of candied orange that would follow it, along with a plate of ripe, creamy Camembert, flown in from Normandy.

Attention to detail – that's what she'd been trained in; that's what it all came down to. Cooking was as much art as craft and the key to achieving the perfect product, as any skilled craftsman knew, was precision, precision, precision. She straightened a fork on Table 7 that lay slightly off-centre and removed a flower arrangement on Table 3 that contained a wilted bloom. She held a wine stem up to the light and pointed out a thumb smudge, asking for it to be replaced.

This was the finale, dammit, and La Palla Vié was going to serve up perfection tonight.

The multilevel award-winning swimming pool at the Royal Resorts, the centrepiece of the ambitious, sprawling, picture-perfect property, had been designed in the shape of the resort's logo – a giant 'R' that sat tucked between the ten-storey resort building and the exclusive strip of sand that undulated out to the cool waters of the sea. In the middle of the shimmering blue letter, there was a tiny island bar, buzzing with cameras and mikes and excitement, as the four *Hot Cheff* celebrity contestants who had been eliminated in the previous rounds answered questions for a prime-time exclusive.

'So we hear you've been signed on by YRF?' a young journo asked Dev, as he sat relaxed and handsome in his 'Ignite Your Senses' promotional orange tee-shirt and scuffed blue jeans.

'Yes, the film goes into production in February,' he grinned, his face reflecting real pleasure. 'I play the role of a heartless Casanova.'

'Does this mean we'll be seeing more of you on screen next year?'

'You can count on it,' Dev promised.

'He'll be all the rage,' Sharon, seated beside him, raved. She crossed her bare legs and her tiny white shorts, already dangerously high, rode farther up her thighs.

The journalist turned to her with a wry smile. 'And you too, I'm sure,' she said. 'But what is this we hear about you and a certain hot Spaniard…?'

Sharon smiled coquettishly. 'Let's just say I've been working on perfecting my Spanish the past few weeks…' she crooned.

'And what about your art?'

'Taking it international, darling, as you can see!'

'Sharing her talents with the world,' Shaq, seated next to her, quipped.

'Charmingly put,' the journalist said. 'And what about you, Shaq? What are your plans?'

'Plans are for later,' Shaq said with a smile. 'For now, I'm just grateful for the love and support of my fans and so happy to be here with my friends again.'

'Everyone was shocked when you were eliminated in the last episode,' the journalist said. 'How did it feel to come so close and then walk away?'

'Life's like that,' Shaq shrugged. 'You just have to keep trying, keep moving on.'

'So no hard feelings?'

'None whatsoever. I wish both Leena and Pallavi all the best tonight; they are both gifted cooks. It was an honour to compete beside them.'

'Shaqeel Khan, always the gentleman,' the journalist smiled, 'and Vicky Gulati, we haven't seen you since the "Jungle Mein Mangal" episode! Where have you been?'

'Just trying to stay out of trouble,' Vicky said with a saucy grin.

'The wild child, Vicky Gulati, staying out of trouble?' the journalist joked. 'Now that's got to be tough!'

'You have no idea,' Vicky drawled.

4

A couple of kilometres down the western shoreline, away from the razzmatazz that was the Royal Resorts, ASP Shankar Sahay sat back in the shade offered by the thatched roof of an unassuming beach shack, his toes nestled in the cool sand, a chilled glass in his hands. In front of him, a wide swathe of beach, wind-tufted, gravel-studded, stretched away to greet the glittering, shifting waters of the Arabian Sea.

He took a sip from his drink and sank farther down in his folding chair. 'This is the life!' he murmured, as a server came by to replace his depleted plate of tiger prawns with a fresh one. 'Bring me another,' he said, indicating his glass of club soda. 'And another nimbu pani for the lady.'

The 'lady', cool and comfortable in a white cotton top and brown cotton pants, looked up momentarily from her laptop. 'With some mint, please,' she added with a smile.

'My, my, someone's really living it up!' Sahay teased. 'Now if we could only find a way to lose that laptop.'

'Sure,' Niki said. 'We could go back and have our meeting at the lodge?'

'God forbid!' Sahay shuddered. 'Did I tell you there was a frog in my bathroom last night?'

'No, you only told me about the lizard on the ceiling.'

Sahay sighed, drank down the rest of his soda and pulled off his dark glasses. 'Remind me again, boss, why I'm spending three valuable days of my paid leave in a musty old government guest house populated with miscellaneous green reptiles?'

'Because you want to help me catch a killer.'

'About that, boss. I've been having this rethink – '

He paused mid-sentence as he caught sight of a tall, skinny woman, dazzling in a red batik dress, orange espadrilles and orange-framed sunglasses, an enormous tote bag on her bony shoulder, trotting down the narrow path towards them.

'Ms Marwah! And ASP Sahay! How *are* you?'

She kissed them roundly on both cheeks, as if they were long-lost friends, then sank down into the empty chair beside them. 'Sorry, I'm a bit late – so hard to get away – oh, this place is *sweet*! Tiny and quaint and so, so quiet!'

'Nothing like the Royal Resorts, that's for sure. I hear they have a beach bar in the middle of the swimming pool?' Sahay asked, unable to keep the envy out of his voice.

'With sixty varieties of beer,' Ruby confirmed. 'So you're both staying at the Beach View Lodge? Sounds cosy!'

'Oh, it is,' Sahay said. 'Lovely view of the beach, once you use one of these,' he indicated the binoculars on the table beside him, 'and the wildlife comes right inside your room.'

'ASP Sahay encountered a frog in the bathroom,' Niki explained.

'Lovely! Frogs are supposed to be very lucky!'

'I tried to flush mine down the toilet,' Sahay said.

'Don't worry,' Ruby said with an encouraging smile. 'Maybe another one will appear tonight.'

'I live in hope.'

Ruby smiled mischievously. 'You know, don't you, that I still have rooms for you at the Royal?'

'Do they come with free bar access?'

'Thank you, but we're very comfortable at the Beach View Lodge,' Niki said firmly.

'Yes, the Beach View Lodge,' Sahay agreed. 'They even have running water and electricity. Imagine!'

'Not to mention clean sheets and wifi,' Niki smiled.

'We're positively spoilt, aren't we?' Sahay took a resigned sip of his soda and hailed the waiter. 'Something for you to drink?' he asked Ruby. 'The boss forbids beer, but the club soda's rather good. Chilled, too.'

'Thanks, a cup of tea would be nice,' Ruby said. 'All those exotic cocktails...'

She placed the order and watched the waiter leave, then turned to Niki with a grave look. 'So, they're all here, just like you asked,' she said. 'Every single person who was at the Gaiety and the Jungle Book Resort.'

'Good,' Niki nodded. She knew it wouldn't have been an easy task to pull off, getting everyone to come, especially the other contestants, now that they were no longer under any contractual obligation.

'And I've brought you a copy of the master plan for the event, including all the venues, the schedules, the guest lists, the vendors.'

Ruby pulled out several slim folders from her tote bag, each in orange and red. 'And here's the resort map...' She rolled a large map out on the table. 'This is the entire layout of the Royal,' she said, pointing. 'Main entrance, lobby, lounge, shops, business centre, coffee shop, café. The spa, fitness centre, billiards room, children's play area and four restaurants are all on the second floor; the guest rooms are on floors three through ten. The contestants are on the eighth floor, the judges and other key members of the executive team on the ninth. We've placed security guards on each floor, by the elevators and the fire exits, as well as at the front gates, the lobby, the pool and at each of the finale venues.'

Ruby ran a finger over the long strip of beige that ran north to south behind the hotel and its lawns. 'This is where the two finalists are setting up their restaurants,' she said, pointing out a secluded stretch at the north end of the map. 'It's at the far end of the property, away from the main building and shielded by this large outcrop of rocks. We will have heavy security all around it, as well as all along the path leading up to it from the resort building.'

'And the audience?'

'The general public will come from the parking lots here –' Ruby pointed to an area adjoining the beach. 'They'll go straight through to the beach, bypassing the main resort building and reception lounge. We're keeping that area free for the red carpet, the press and the VIP guests and judges.'

'And how many people are you expecting?'

'The show is sold out,' Ruby said. 'Which means we'll have about two thousand people on the beach; we'll start allowing them in by five. We've hired a private security company to man the resort gates and parking lots; they'll be checking each individual and vehicle as they enter.'

She sat back and gazed at Niki, the anxiety clear in her eyes. 'We've vetted all the invitees, we've inspected the venues, we have our own teams supervising the kitchens and stores and we've got one of the best private security companies in the country managing the show. We've taken all the precautionary steps as you advised, Ms Marwah. But once filming gets under way...'

She looked up as the server came back with a tray of tea; she thanked him and poured herself a cup. 'I'm wondering if we should go through with it, given the risk...' She shook the contents of a sugar sachet into her cup and added a dash of milk. 'I mean, what if, despite all the measures, something untoward happens?' She took a sip of her tea and spat it out instantly.

'What is it?' Niki frowned.

Ruby snatched up a napkin. 'Salt,' she said, her mouth pursed in distaste. She took a sip of water and rinsed her mouth.

'Hey,' Sahay said, stopping the waiter as he hurried by with another order. 'How come there's salt in the sugar bowl?'

'Oh! Sorry, sir,' the waiter said. 'So sorry, madam. I'll get you some fresh tea right away!'

'My fault, I suppose,' Ruby said, sighing, as he sped away again. 'I must be going crazy. Imagine confusing salt and sugar!'

Niki picked up the fragments of the sachet Ruby had discarded. The paper was white, but thinner and smaller than the others in the bowl. 'Good God!' she said. 'So that's how it happened. It must have been in one of the sachets in the sugar bowl!'

Sahay frowned as he followed her gaze to the tea tray on the table. 'You mean – '

'That night at the Gaiety, someone must have slipped a sachet of cyanide into the sugar bowl on the judges table!'

'And Mala put it in her coffee during the break?' Sahay frowned.

'But Mala never took sugar in her coffee,' Ruby said.

'No, she didn't, but she had just eaten some foul-tasting chicken,' Niki said. 'And she reached for some sugar to take away the foul taste.'

'Except, it wasn't sugar; it was cyanide.'

'But boss,' Sahay said, frowning, 'wouldn't the killer have known that Mala never took sugar?'

'Yes,' Niki nodded. 'And he or she would have also known that *KK* always took *three* sachets.'

'You mean – '

'It was KK! He was the intended victim all along.'

Back at the Royal Resorts, KK sat out on the spacious balcony of his ninth-floor luxury suite, a glass of chilled beer on the table beside him, enjoying the view.

It was a glorious day out – blue skies, wispy clouds, golden sands below and the brilliant sea beyond, aglow with the colours of the late afternoon sun. He took a sip of his beer, glancing out across the horizon with a contented sigh. His gaze shifted to the pool below. The beach bar was quiet at this hour, but the shallow pool at the far end was alive with the shrieks and cries of a group of youngsters frolicking noisily with a bright red ball. He watched their antics with a smile, then turned his attention to the swimmers in the lap lanes as they cut through the water from end to end, the fluid, graceful motion of their arms slicing through the water with speed and ease.

He sighed wistfully. He wished he could swim like that. Wished he could swim, play golf, polo, tennis and all those other wonderful upper-class sports; he wished he could avail of the fancy amenities that the resort provided, that all those around him so easily enjoyed. Rajat, Ruby, Jimmy, even Puru – they were all from the class of the self-assured élite, with their upper-class upbringing, their English-medium education, their easy banter about ancient history and British novels and American politics. And while he had earned their grudging respect, he knew he was still not a part of their world.

No, he was a self-made man of humble origins, who had learned everything he knew about the world not in any classroom or on a field trip or vacation abroad, but in the gullies of Chowk and Ghantaghar and Nizamuddin, behind sizzling tavas and baking tandoors.

And now here he was, perched high above the world and, even at sixty-two, still soaring. So what if he didn't know how to swim? There was a lot, a precious lot he did know.

He looked back down at the iPad on his lap and the email his lawyers had sent him that very morning. The property in Laad Bazaar near the Charminar that he had had his eye on for the past several months was finally available. The owner, a Mohammed Aslam Beg, had met with an unfortunate accident the previous week and his widow was anxious to accept Mr Kapoor's offer if it was still available.

Absolutely, KK typed with his slow, deliberate fingers. *In fact*, he added as an afterthought, *please offer her my condolences and advance 10 per cent cash right away to take care of the funeral expenses.*

He hit 'Send' and sat back with a sigh. Poor woman, he thought. To be widowed at such a young age. And now to have to sell her husband's ancestral business, which the belligerent young man, now deceased, had claimed had been there since the days of the Qutb Shahis.

'I will never sell this as long as I am alive!' he had told KK's agents angrily, before throwing them out of his crumbling dhaba.

But KK had persevered. 'Give him time to reconsider,' he had told the agent.

Time was a powerful tool; time took care of everything. Patience and persistence – KK, who'd built a restaurant empire from scratch, knew the value of both. And he'd known that he'd get that property – eventually.

He said a silent prayer for the young man and wished that it could have been different. If only he'd had the sense to accept KK's offer six months ago, he'd have had enough money to move into a nice flat in the upcoming gated suburbs and would have, this very minute, been playing with his children, instead of getting crushed under the wheels of some nameless truck driven by a drunk. And now, as was the case every day, all across the country, there was no justice, no recourse to redress, no finding either truck or driver... The folly of youth, KK thought, shaking his head again. Clinging to the past and false pride, while the world and time ground relentlessly on.

But it was a fine property. Steps, mere steps away from the 400-year-old world-famous monument. Visited by lakhs of tourists every year and, until now, not one decent place in the vicinity where they could eat. Well, that would change. He would have Kemaal's Charminar up and running in less than six months. Air conditioning, elegant interiors, a choice upscale menu upstairs; a brisk, fast-turning, fast-food menu downstairs. He'd invite the governor, the CM, the tourism minister, the Sunrisers for the inaugural week. It would pay for itself several times over before the next year was out.

Now if only that wretched dhaba near Haji Ali in Mumbai would become available, he thought wistfully. It was an unbelievable site; practically every one of those 10,000 daily visitors passed by it on their way. And all it served was overpriced, tasteless fare, the meat purchased from the cheapest vendors, the spices old and stale. If only there were a Kemaal's there instead, the worshippers would have a real place to eat, a place in keeping with the sanctity of the shrine, where food was worshipped, not just sold.

But the dhaba owner was a lazy, worthless lout, lacking in both culinary skill and business acumen. He would never realize that the offer from Kemaal's was the best he was ever going to get. Not without a little persuasion…

Thank you for closing out the Hyderabad property, he emailed his agent. *What is the status of the Haji Ali property? I am very keen to close as soon as possible.* He looked up, contemplating the vast panorama before him. *Whatever it takes*, he added.

Out at the beachside shack a couple of kilometres away, Niki paced to and fro in the sand, kicking herself. She should have seen it sooner, the reason why Mala's death had seemed so baffling, why Mala had seemed such an unlikely candidate for either suicide or murder; it was because she had been neither. She had just been unlucky.

'You mean Mala's death was an accident?' Ruby asked in a horrified whisper.

'Mala's and her baby's,' Niki corrected.

'So it was never about her…' Sahay said, his voice tinged with sadness.

'But that's – that's just unconscionable,' Ruby murmured.

Niki nodded. 'It is. And it goes to show just how determined, how ruthless our killer is.

'The cyanide was meant for KK,' Niki said. 'Someone's been trying to kill him all along.'

'But boss, why?'

Up on the balcony of the ninth floor of Royal Resorts, KK sat back and closed his laptop. Ten Kemaal's before next summer. Now *that* would be something! Chowk and Hazratganj in Lucknow, Nizamuddin in Delhi and Park Street in Kolkata, M.G. Road in Bengaluru, the Taj in Agra, Johri Bazaar in Jaipur, the Charminar in Hyderabad and, if all went well, Haji Ali in Mumbai. Soon, there would be a Kemaal's at every site of history, pilgrimage and tourism across the length and breadth of the country. And then onwards, to Dubai, Singapore,

London, Paris, Rome. Before the decade was out, there would be a KK's at every site worth visiting in the world…

It was a grandiose dream, but KK knew he had what it took to make it real.

He glanced at his watch. Almost four-thirty, he saw. Which meant he had plenty of time before he had to go downstairs and start greeting the guests for the finale. There would be politicians, cine stars, cricketers and society bigwigs… It would be useful to renew old acquaintances, make some new ones. Should he wear his white silk sherwani for the finale or the black suit with the red silk tie? Mala used to like him in white. Sweet, lovely Mala, he thought with a pang, remembering her shy smiles, her bronze skin.

He looked down as his phone, resting on the coffee table beside him, buzzed with a text message.

'Kemaal sir, do you have a few minutes to take some questions?' he read. 'I'd be grateful, Nikhat.'

Nikhat. That young journalist in the pink salwar kameez from the press conference this morning. She'd been lovely as a rose, with her fair skin and pink cheeks, her long, dark hair tied back in a ponytail. She had tried to have a word with him afterwards, but had got elbowed out by another, more determined young lady in a business suit and sharp heels. He had noticed her even then, the hesitant manner in which she had handed him her business card, the tentative smile that had revealed that she too did not belong in this world of luxury and elegance; that she too did not, perhaps, know how to swim.

'Certainly,' KK typed back. 'Come to my room. Nine-zero-one.'

'I can think of many reasons why someone would want to kill KK.'

Ruby looked out across the ocean at the tide that was starting to come, the waves inching farther and farther up the shore. She turned to ASP Sahay. 'He's powerful, calculating, ruthless. And he makes no apologies for it.'

It was a trait all too familiar amongst the rich and the successful, Niki knew. The self-made man; the many favours forgotten and toes trod upon on the way up. Such people made enemies, not friends. And they had an uncanny ability to keep moving on. Mala's death, Vicky's illness, even the fire in his own cottage – nothing had fazed him.

'He's been on the warpath ever since we got back from Panna,' Ruby said in a troubled voice. 'He's fought with the network, he's fired his agent and he's moved ahead on the Kemaal's Malabar venture. I've heard he's even pushing to open a couple of new Kemaal's in the next few months.'

'But none of those sound like a motive for murder,' Sahay said.

'And yet someone has had him in his or her sights all along,' Niki said.

'I'm worried,' Ruby said, playing with the pukhraj on her finger. 'Maybe we're taking too big a chance? Maybe we should cancel the finale?'

Niki shook her head. 'It's taking a risk, I know,' she said. 'But cancelling would be an even greater risk. The finale is our last chance to catch the killer. We may never have another. We have to close this.'

'But what about KK?'

'We'll do our best to protect him. Alert him,' Niki said. 'Tell him that there is a credible threat to his life, that there is a need for extreme caution. Post a dedicated guard outside his hotel room and make sure he eats nothing, goes nowhere without a bodyguard.'

'He's not going to like it,' Ruby sighed.

'He's going to like being dead even less,' Sahay said.

In the bathroom of the ninth-floor luxury suite at Royal Resorts, KK was whistling softly. He tucked his pale blue shirt into the waistband of his black pants, fastened his black leather belt and noted with satisfaction that he had moved in one whole notch on the belt. Another month on the new diet and he'd be giving all these Rajat types a run for their money... He was applying a final dab of cologne when his phone rang.

He frowned down at it as it lay by the vanity in the bathroom. It was Ruby, he saw.

He let it ring. A moment later, it popped with a text message.

'KK, I need to talk to you urgently. Call me back.'

Another minor niggling adjustment, no doubt, he thought in exasperation. Like 'KK, can you please approve the streamers for the lobby decorations?' Or, God forbid, 'KK, we can't find the salt shakers!' They really were an incompetent, bumbling lot, Ruby and her so-called team of experts! He thought of getting a new team on board for the next season, an international team. In fact, maybe they would take the whole show international. International contestants, locations... He should start exploring some of the foreign networks that had sent out feelers.

He heard a soft knock on the door and smiled in the mirror. Miss Nikhat. He rinsed his mouth with mouthwash, patted down his hair with a drop of gel and walked up to open the door.

'He's not answering his phone,' Ruby said, hanging up. She turned to the officers with a worried frown. 'I know he was in his room, knocking off some emails when I left...'

'Try the front desk,' Niki suggested.

Ruby rang the hotel. 'This is Ruby Talwar,' she said. 'From *Hot Cheff*. Can someone check if Mr Kemaal Kapoor is in his room? Thank you.' She collected her things and rose from her chair. 'I'd better be off,' she said. 'I'll go and see if I can catch him myself.'

Sahay watched her go, her dress swishing about her long, bony legs as she sped down the path with a preoccupied, worried air.

'This changes the whole picture, boss,' he said.

'It does,' Niki agreed. 'It means that we now have one distinct target instead of a vague, diffused threat. It means we can focus on KK and not worry too much about the others.'

'So what's the plan now?'

'The same as it was before. Except that we tweak it somewhat. We'll let the security company cover the finale venue, as planned, and we'll focus our own efforts around KK. We'll keep a close watch on him, make sure he's covered at all times, but not overtly so. We want to catch the killer in the act, not scare him or her away.'

'Do you really think the killer will try something with such heavy security all over the place, boss?'

'We have a very determined killer, ASP Sahay. This person will find a way.'

Sahay glanced at his watch. It was 4.45 p.m. 'We don't have a lot of time,' he said.

'I know,' Niki said. 'Let's run through these quickly,' she indicated the maps, plans, schedules and lists that Ruby had left them with, 'and then let's get going.'

'Shall I alert the Goa Police?'

Niki hesitated. 'Tell them to be on standby for now, just in case we need backup. Also, get hold of that tea-coffee guy, Abbas. Grill him; find out if any of the contestants took a special interest in his tea tray that evening at the Gaiety; if any of them was hovering around. Ask him specifically about the sugar sachets – where he got them from, where they were kept.'

'I'll get right on it.'

'Meanwhile, I'll head back to the lodge, have Deepika look into KK and send me what she can,' Niki said. She saw Sahay's look of surprise. 'I know, we have all the notes and information on him already; we've been through it all several times. But I need her to dig up some more information. Dig further into his past.' She looked out across the sand. The sun hung low over the ocean, descending quickly towards a darkening mass of clouds that had gathered low over the water's surface to receive it. In a few minutes, it would be enveloped.

'This is not about *Hot Chef*, ASP Sahay,' Niki said. 'This is about vengeance. About something terrible that KK has done, someone whom he has crossed in the past, who has been nursing a grudge against him. I need to find out what that grudge is, who that person is before it's too late.'

5

Nikhat Yasmin Malik was younger, quieter than she'd first appeared, KK observed, despite the kohl in her eyes, the pink lip gloss she'd applied to her lips. She sat, nervous and hesitant, on the edge of the sofa in his suite; her fingers played with the tiny sequins that sparkled in her pink dupatta, her eyes kept darting to the closed door.

'Thank you for taking the time to speak with me,' she said in a small, shy voice, as her fingers smoothed the edge of her pink kameez over her knees. 'You must be very busy.' She smiled tentatively and picked up her notebook and pencil from the table.

'I am,' KK smiled. 'But for you, I can spare a few minutes. I always like to encourage youngsters. What magazine did you say you were from?'

'It's an online blog, actually, called *Bibi*. We provide insightful news and views about things women care about.'

'A blog?'

'Yes. We're affiliated with the bestselling Dubai-based magazine, *Gulf Views*. It is circulated in eleven countries and is the third-largest English-language magazine in the Middle East. Our multimedia content reaches over one million readers worldwide.'

It was a well-rehearsed marketing speech, ardently delivered; it made KK smile. Youngsters; they were so zealous, so committed. 'Third-largest English magazine in the Middle East,' he said, sounding suitably impressed. 'Are you happy there?'

'Oh yes. They're very good employers,' Nikhat said with a smile, smoothing a runaway tendril of hair and tucking it behind a small ear. 'I am very fortunate.'

'I'm sure they feel the same way. So are you from Dubai?'

'Well, sir – ' She started at the loud knock on the door.

'Excuse me,' KK said. He walked up to the door, opened it a fraction and scowled at the security guard outside.

'Yes, what is it?'

'Sir, are you all right?'

'Of course I'm all right. What's going on?'

'We were asked to check if you are all right, sir,' the guard said.

'This is what we're paying lakhs and lakhs for?'

'Sir, Miss Ruby – '

'Tell Miss Ruby that I'm busy and that I'll call her when I'm ready, okay? And don't you dare disturb me again.' He pushed the door shut and walked back to the sofa. 'These producers, I tell you!' he complained. 'Can't find the noses on their faces without running to me for help.'

Nikhat twisted the pencil nervously between her fingers. 'Sir, maybe I should leave; I really didn't mean to disturb – '

'No, it's all right.'

'But sir – '

'Relax,' KK repeated kindly, but firmly. 'And call me KK, please.'

'Sir, but – '

'I insist.'

'KK, then,' she said with a shy smile.

'Much better.' KK smoothed a cushion and then sat down on the sofa beside her. 'So you were telling me about Dubai?'

'Actually, sir, KK, I'm Delhi-based.'

'Lovely. Have you eaten at Kemaal's in Nizamuddin yet?'

'No, but I've eaten at Kemaal's in Hazratganj.' She smiled as his brows rose. 'Actually, I grew up in Lucknow.'

'Lucknow?' KK leaned forward, patting her knee with his large paw. 'Well, well, what a coincidence! That makes us humshahar. I grew up in Lucknow too!'

'Yes, I know.' She looked down at her notebook and smiled shyly. 'You grew up in Chowk, right?'

'I see you've done your homework, my dear.'

'I've always been a big fan.' She glanced up at him; in her eyes was unmistakable adulation. 'It had always been my dream to meet you,' she murmured.

At the Beach View Lodge, SP Marwah sat in her room, pencil between her teeth, a worried frown on her face. She had just finished briefing Inspector Chauhan; she had asked her to run a search on KK's childhood, his early years, his business transactions and partners, his employees, his climb to success. 'I want to look at everything we can find out about him, from the day he was born to the last cup of tea he consumed,' she had said. It was a lot of material to run through in very little time, Niki knew.

'I'll send it right away, ma'am,' had been the unflappable response.

Someone had been targeting KK, Niki thought, as she waited, curtains drawn, laptop connected, mind racing. Someone who had had access to the cyanide and the Celphos and the set and his cottage in the jungle. Someone with a very compelling motive…

Who?

'KK?'

Ruby rapped on the door of Suite 901 with her knuckles; she glanced at her watch again. It was ticking past five. The audience would have started streaming onto the north side of beach; the guest judges would start to arrive in the lobby downstairs in less than an hour, and she still had a million things to do.

'KK!' She called again, banging on his door. 'Is he in there?' she asked the guard who stood outside.

'Yes, ma'am, I just spoke – ' He broke off as the door flew open.

'What the hell…?' KK stood in the doorway, with the door half-open, a deep scowl on his face.

'Oh thank God!' Ruby said. 'Are you okay?'

'Of course I'm okay! Why wouldn't I be okay?'

'Well,' Ruby hesitated. 'The thing is, I've been speaking to SP Marwah – '

The scowl on KK's face deepened. 'Ruby, I told you I did not want that woman coming near our show again.'

'But KK, she thinks there might be another attack tonight!'

'How the hell does she know that? And doesn't she have anything better to do? No tourists in Shimla this year?'

'Actually, she's right here in Goa.'

'What!'

'For the finale, KK. I invited her. And,' she said, cutting him short as he started to explode, 'she's quite certain you're the target.'

'Nonsense!'

'It's not nonsense, KK. Mala's dead, remember? That fire in the jungle – it happened.'

'Yes, but nothing has happened since. And whatever the police might say, its clear to me that Mala committed suicide and the fire was caused by someone's negligence.'

'But KK – '

'And anyway, aren't you supposed to be busy supervising last-minute preparations for the finale? Considering you're the executive producer of the show?'

'Yes. Which is why I can't stay here with you. But I'm posting Satpal outside your door.' She indicated the security guard. 'Promise me you'll stay in your room till I call you.'

KK shook his head and looked at his watch. 'I'll see you down in the lobby at six,' he said. 'And you'd better not disturb me,' he glowered at Satpal.

'But KK – '

But KK had already slammed the door shut.

Ruby sighed and turned to the security guard. 'Stand right here and call me when he heads out. And make sure no one goes in.'

'That was Ruby, executive producer of *Hot Cheff*,' KK said with a roll of his eyes as he returned to the sofa and the young girl seated there, her hands in her lap, her legs primly crossed.

'Running around like a headless chicken.' Nikhat glanced at her watch. 'Perhaps I should leave now?' she asked.

'Already?'

'You'll need to get ready for the finale.'

'Yes, I will. Care to help me?'

'Help?'

'For some reason, I can't quite decide what to wear. My white sherwani or my black suit…'

'I'm sure you'll be very handsome in either,' she said.

'You are?' KK stood up, walked over to the closed door of his room. 'Why don't you help me choose, all the same?' he invited, pushing the door open.

At the Beach View Lodge, Niki sat in her room skimming through the fact sheets on the six contestants. She had been so sure that one of the contestants had killed Mala… She flipped through the photographs, the several comments she had made in the margins and the notes, the questions she had jotted down.…

Had one of them been targeting KK?

She placed her pencil between her teeth and leaned back in her chair, lacing her fingers behind her head. Someone had targeted KK in the second episode with the short circuit, the set collapse in the fourth, the rat poison in the rehearsal, the Celphos in the back kitchen, the cyanide at the Gaiety, and the fire in the jungle…

Someone had targeted KK again and again and again. On set, on location and always when the contestants were present – *only* when the contestants were present.

And that someone had failed and failed and failed. How would that have felt? How would it have felt to see Mala and not KK collapse at the Gaiety? Would the killer have been upset, dismayed, distraught? Or would he or she have just shrugged it off and gone on to plan the next move?

An image of Leena, flustered and nervous, came to mind. She had been white as a sheet when they questioned her, Niki remembered. Nervous, and looking as if she had something to hide. Could she be the one…?

But why?

What was her link to KK?

She looked at her watch. Five-thirty. And still no word from Deepika. She called her again. 'Any luck, Inspector Chauhan?'

'I'm sorry, but the network is down in the office, ma'am.' The frustration was clear in the inspector's voice, even though she tried to hide it. 'I've called maintenance to resolve the issue; I'll call you as soon as they have it up and running again.'

'Do that,' Niki said and hung up.

Damn. They were running out of time. And she needed to be on her way to Royal Resorts. She rose reluctantly from the desk, turned to her suitcase and flipped the top open.

6

The action was starting to heat up at Royal Resorts.

The lanes leading up to the resort's main gates bustled with incoming cars; the parking lots were starting to fill up. Around the massive arched gateway that had been erected for the finale, security guards, some in uniform, some carrying flashlights, all armed with walkie-talkies, bustled about, inspecting cars and passengers and clearing them slowly, one by one. Farther in, outside the sweeping marble foyer at the main entrance, a lavish red carpet had been laid out, where TV and news crews were up and live, ready to capture the early arrivals, to comment on their choice of clothes, hairstyles, accessories, escorts. Scores of security guards in suits and equipped with earpieces stood ranged amongst them, braced for action.

Inside, the hotel's magnificent lobby had been transformed into a spectacular, pulsing movie set, breathtaking in its splendour and over-the-top opulence. The Italian marble floor was covered in a carpet of red roses and orange blooms; the ceiling above was lined with tens of thousands of orange and red helium-filled balloons. The walls were draped with hoarding-sized posters and banners of the show. The gigantic podium that had been installed at the back was draped in red satin and flanked by 10-foot-high orange and red decals that fluttered in an artificial breeze, simulating hot flames leaping up into the air.

Behind the podium, a red vinyl screen hid the hi-tech sound system on which sound technicians played around with volume, bass, amps, mikes. A small army of bartenders in tuxedos and bowties set out glasses, trays, ice and napkins on the mahogany-topped bar to the left of the lobby, while from the swing doors that led to the kitchen, a non-stop stream of servers poured in and out, setting up tray after tray of bite-sized appetizers.

At the top of the marble stairs leading up to the front entrance, Ruby Talwar stood braced and ready against the gigantic *Hot Cheff* backdrop, dazzling in a shimmering red strapless dress with matching red sequinned stilettos and dangling chandelier earrings.

'Darling!' she trilled, hugging and air-kissing Ashika De, as the latter tottered up the steps towards her in a show-stopping green cocktail dress, 'I loved your movie! Loved it, loved it, loved it! Thanks for coming! You look unbelievable! God, how long it's been!'

'Oh, how I've missed you all!' Ashika responded with a radiant smile. She wrapped a slender arm around Ruby as she posed for the cameras that were flashing all around. Then, as Ruby ushered her into the lobby towards Jimmy, who was deep in conversation with a Bollywood producer, and Rajat who was shaking hands with one of the Mumbai Indians batsmen, Ashika asked in a lowered voice, 'I heard about the fire in the jungle! How is KK? Where is he?'

'Oh, he should be here any minute,' Ruby beamed, without missing a beat. 'He'll be sooo excited to see you!' She plucked a wine glass off the tray a server held out and pressed it into Ashika's hand. 'Enjoy!' she beamed, before hurrying out to the steps to greet the next arrival.

'Maaaansi!' she squealed, as she spotted the fashion designer alighting from a silver Toyota in a flowing red-orange chiffon shift. 'You came in the show's colours! And that handbag – oh my God!!!' She air-kissed the designer and the flashlights went off, yet again, capturing Mansi Malhotra in all her new-age designer glory. 'Is that really cobra skin?'

'Looks authentic, no? It's faux cobra skin. I'm readying my animal-print line for the next season,' Mansi beamed. 'Inspired by the "Jungle Mein Mangal" episode.'

'No way! That's just fantastic! Hey Bhavna,' she called out, grabbing the nearest journalist by the wrist. 'You have to, *have* to cover this!'

She introduced the two women, then spotted yet another VIP just pulling in. 'Oh, Mr Nanda!' She ran down the steps as he emerged onto the red carpet. 'Thank you sooo much for coming, sir! Let me show you to the lobby…'

Her voice, welcoming, excited, energetic, tireless, rang out in the evening air, as she ushered the guests in. Each time, with each new arrival, her expert gaze swept round the lobby, finding Rajat, Jimmy, some of the younger assistants… They were all there. Everyone, except KK, who'd promised he'd be down at six. Which was now. *So where was he?*

She motioned for an assistant producer to take her place at the top of the steps, hurried into the lobby and the nearest ladies' bathroom. She ducked inside a stall and, with shaking hands, fished out her mobile.

Pick up, pick up, pick up...

KK heard his mobile ring as it sat on the bathroom counter. Once, twice, three times...

He strained to pull his hands apart as it continued to ring, but they were bound together behind his back. The thick, wet dupatta cut into the flesh of his wrists; a flash of pain shot through his elbows. He let out a soft moan and relaxed his clenched buttocks. The phone stopped ringing.

He felt the bile rise inside him, felt the urge to throw up; he held in the waves of nausea with a huge effort. There was no hope, no escape. This was the end; this was how they would find him, half-naked, face down, in a hotel bathtub, in a pool of his own making, his belly slathered with his own urine, his face pressed against the sputum-encrusted drain, his neck, with the noose around it, suspended from the steel spout inches above.

He felt fresh tears prick his eyes, felt them slide down his cheeks. He had lost track of how long he'd been lying in the cold blackness of the unlit bathroom, in the chilled silence of the locked, deserted room. It could have been minutes or hours or even days ago that it had happened, that an afternoon of pleasure had morphed into an unspeakable nightmare.

And the worst part was that he feared it was still far from over.

Nikhat Yasmin Malik. What a sly little snake she'd turned out to be, with her large almond eyes and shy, sweet smile! How she had led him on, with her fake adulation and her wide-eyed innocence, her small, young breasts straining as she'd leaned forward over her notepad. He'd been pleasantly surprised when she'd followed him to his room, delighted when she'd freed her hair from its tight ponytail, letting it fall, thick and lustrous, round her shoulders. He'd hardly believed his luck when she'd picked up his red necktie from the bed and draped it suggestively round her neck. Then, unbelievably, with a soft giggle and a whispered half-promise, she'd disappeared into the adjoining bathroom.

And he'd followed her, his whole being focussed on the unmistakable message in those smoky, kohl-lined eyes, the promised pleasures of her tight, young body.

She'd laughed as he unbuttoned his shirt; she had helped him unbuckle his belt. Then, with her lips pursed in a teasing smile, she had taken the red tie and wrapped it across his hungry eyes. He had felt his heart pound as she nudged the shirt off him, as she took off her dupatta and trailed it down his chest before tying it playfully around his wrists. Crazed with desire, he had followed her to the bathtub, complying, as with firm, caressing fingers, she had coaxed him in. She had sat astride him, her slender legs wrapped around his bare back; she had leaned forward and her breasts had brushed against his bare skin. For a moment, he'd thought he would explode with lust. The very next moment, he'd felt his head yanked abruptly back, his belt slapped around his neck and buckled to the spout. He'd blubbered and screamed into the wet towel she wrapped around his mouth, as the cold, tight dupatta dug into his wrists. He'd thrashed around like a beached whale as she stepped out of the bathtub.

'Don't worry, this isn't over yet,' he thought he'd heard her say, ominously, as she closed the bathroom door on her way out.

At the guest room in the Beach View Lodge, SP Marwah pulled on a pair of skinny black pants and a black tee-shirt, adding a black blazer to the ensemble. In the back of the waistband of her pants, she tucked in her slim pistol. Not exactly the Goa beach look, she thought with a grimace, but she couldn't afford to take any chances...

She strode over to the nightstand and checked her phone; there were still no new messages from Deepika. She glanced at her watch. Five minutes past six. Damn.

She slipped her phone in her pocket, smoothed her blazer over the bulge of the pistol at her waist and stepped into a pair of black ballet flats. Then, on impulse, she stepped back to the small desk in the corner and pulled open her laptop again.

There was a new email from Deepika.

She clicked on the attachment titled 'KK early life' and quickly scanned the memo.

Kemaal Kapoor, age 62. Born 1950 in Lucknow, she read. Matriculation 1967. Grew up in Lucknow, worked in his family restaurant.

But where in Lucknow? Which family restaurant?

A kebab shop in Chowk, Old Lucknow. That, apparently, was all the information they had.

She clicked on the second attachment labelled 'Kemaal's'.

It was a collection of articles that had been published at the time of Kemaal's' silver jubilee in 2000. 'Kemaal's, the jewel of Nizamuddin, turns silver,' the headline in the first one read, above a picture of KK shaking hands with the then chief minister of Delhi. In attendance were other dignitaries, celebrities, smiling staff.

Niki skimmed through the article. It painted an inspiring picture of KK's journey; the vision, the steely resolve, the modest beginnings in a narrow gully with six tables and borrowed money. Another article, this one headlined, 'Kemaal's, 25 years!' chronicled the long hours and backbreaking work of the early days, the challenges of rising prices, space constraints and cheaper competitors, the unwavering commitment to quality and excellence in the face of it all. The list of VIPs who'd dined at Kemaal's over the years, covered in a third article, was a veritable who's who of politics, sports and cinema; the praise heaped upon the establishment in article after article that followed was lavish. The man sure knew how to promote himself, Niki thought. 'Self-made man from humble origins,' she read, over and over, as she skimmed through them. 'Best kebabs in the world,' was another constant refrain. 'Family fled from Lahore during Partition,' one of the shorter ones mentioned.

Niki frowned. KK's family fled from Lahore? She didn't recollect him mentioning that before. Where in Pakistan did they originally come from? And why did they flee to Lucknow, such a long way away?

They must have opened the kebab shop in Chowk shortly after Partition, she surmised. Had they owned a restaurant in Lahore as well? They must have; KK had mentioned his grandfather's kebabs as being the best in the world, the Lucknow rickshaw-wallas who had enjoyed them…

So the kebab shop must have been around in the 1950s, Niki calculated. So where in Chowk had it been? What was it called? And why was there no mention of it anywhere?

She clicked on the third attachment Deepika had sent, this one labelled 'Kemaal's chain of restaurants'.

According to the information it contained, there were eight Kemaal's – in Delhi, Agra, Jaipur and Bangalore, as well as two in Kolkata and two in Lucknow. Of the two Lucknow restaurants, the one in Hazratganj had been established in 1987, the one in Chowk in 1989.

A Kemaal's in Chowk in 1989… So what happened to the grandfather's dhaba?

Niki frowned. There was something here that didn't add up.

She opened up her internet browser and typed 'Kemaal Kapoor, Lucknow, Chowk, dhaba' into the search window. She got routed back to the Kemaal's website and the Kemaal's in Chowk, opened in 1989.

'Lucknow, Chowk, historic, famous kebabs,' she typed again in the search window.

This time, it threw up links to several eating establishments and an article in a blog called *Lucknow's Heritage*, titled 'Iqbal's – the oldest kebab establishment in living memory'.

Everyone has heard of the 100-year-old Tundey ke Kebab, which now has branches in Aminabad, Saharaganj and other cities. But very few people are aware of Iqbal's, a little-known dhaba established in 1912 by 22-year-old Iqbal Khan. Hugely popular in its day, serving what those who can recall it describe as the most delectable, melt-in-your mouth kebabs, Iqbal's would have been celebrating its own centenary this year, had it not tragically burnt down in 1976.

Tragic, indeed, but nothing to do with KK, Niki figured. What a marvellous place for kebaabs Chowk must have been in its heyday. With Tundey ke Kebaab, Iqbal's, the one belonging to KK's grandfather…

The author of the blog appeared to be quite the aficionado. Perhaps he might know?

Niki scrolled down to the bottom of the page. 'Lovely, informative article,' she typed in the comments section of the blog. 'Would you have any information about another famous kebab shop in Chowk in the 1950s belonging to a Hindu family from Lahore?'

7

At the Chatpatty Beach Bazaar at the northernmost tip of the Royal Resorts property, the music was blaring, the jugglers juggling, the golawalla dispensing his wares, the magicians keeping the audience in splits as they made eggs disappear from men's pockets and reappear in women's purses.

Leena, ready at the entrance pandal, watched as the audience grew thicker, livelier and noisier outside her beachfront restaurant. Just fifteen more minutes before they cut the ribbon at the front entrance, before Jimmy broke the coconut at Ganpati's feet, before Rajat grabbed the mike and ushered in the first of her guests, the first fifty judges, the who's who of the country, to take their places in the moulded red plastic chairs.

Her gaze flew back to the chairs. They seemed gawky and unsightly in the fading light, their aluminium legs poking out like prosthetics from their dusty, rounded bottoms as they stood about the sand in loose groupings, looking rickety, garish, cheap, cheap, cheap!

Leena stared at them, horrified. It was as though she were seeing them, noticing their cheapness, for the first time. And the aluminium tables, the canvas tents, the flying streamers... Good God, the whole place was a disaster! Like something out of a raddi shop; it was a joke, a monstrosity, an insult to the audience's intelligence! Here she was, minutes away from the cameras and the limelight and millions of viewers, exposed as the proprietor of the ugliest, shabbiest, cheapest restaurant in the world!

While just next door, mere steps away, Pallavi Aanand, slim, smart, beautiful, educated at the best cooking institute in the world, was about to serve world-class fare that she had been *trained* to cook, had spent more money learning how to prepare than Leena had seen in her entire life.

Leena felt faint; she felt she might throw up. She couldn't go through with it. Maybe there was still time, maybe she could go find Jimmy and tell him she couldn't do it, that there was no point, that the judges were free to head straight over to La Palla Vié...

She felt a tap on her shoulder.

'Tired, Leena Ballerina?' a soft voice asked.

She turned slowly. A familiar hand reached out and flicked her bangs; a gentle smile met her gaze.

'Vicky!' she gasped.

'In the flesh and here to help you win.'

'Jimmy just announced we'd be helping you tonight,' Dev, standing a few paces away, seconded. He held up two pristine aprons and chefs hats, printed with the Hot Cheff logo and 'Team Chatpatty' emblazoned across them. 'Your wish is our command,' he declared, with a mock-serious hand to his heart.

Leena looked from him to Vicky, her eyes filling with tears. *I'm sorry. So, so sorry...*

Vicky smiled, put a finger to his lips. 'Come on,' he said, 'there's no time to lose. Let's go!'

'Where?'

'To set the world on fire, where else?'

Ten...nine...eight minutes to go... Pallavi stood silent, watching the clock in her spotless kitchen, while outside, the lights blazed, the cameras focussed, the crowds clamoured. Seven minutes to go...

In two more minutes, she would call in her kitchen staff, her wait staff, Sharon and Shaq who, she'd been told, would be assisting her. She would put the finishing touches to the amuse-bouche: a spoonful of homemade strawberry sorbet in coconut milk, served on spotless white ceramic soup spoons and finished with a sprig of mint. Strawberry and coconut – the perfect marriage of West and East, a tingling preview of the flavours in store...

Pallavi felt a sense of deep calm come over her as she stood alone in her kitchen. All her cares and troubles – the lawsuits, the family dramas, the ugliness – slipped away from her. She was above it all. She was magic. She was ready…

Five minutes to go, she saw. She raised her head, turned on the bright overhead lights and walked out into the restaurant where her staff was waiting. Everyone but one.

Well, whatever. She clapped her hands, beckoned them all forward. 'Show time, everyone!' she announced.

8

Up on the ninth floor of Royal Resorts, just outside the door of Suite 901, Satpal, the security guard, listened, frowning, into his walkie-talkie. For some reason, the lift on the ninth floor was stalled.

'Could someone check what's going on?' the supervisor's voice said.

Satpal glanced at the 'Do Not Disturb' sign on KK's door, then down the hallway at the closed elevator doors.

'There is an emergency in the lift on the ninth floor,' the supervisor's voice rang out from the walkie-talkie again. 'Can the nearest guard respond immediately?'

'Sir.'

Satpal raced to the elevator bank at the end of the hallway. The light on the call button for Floor No. 9 indicated that the lift was on his floor, but the door was closed. He pressed the button, put his ear to the door and listened. He thought he heard a hollow sound, the faint cries of a woman, muffled banging.

'Hello?' he called.

A voice started speaking rapidly, frantically, from inside the lift.

'Don't worry, I'll get you.'

Satpal braced himself against the elevator frame, pulled at the jammed door. At the other end of the hallway, as he grunted and pulled, a shadowy figure slipped out from the stairwell, stepped silently to Suite 901, fitted a card key in the slot and quietly pushed open the door.

KK, lying cold and miserable in the bathtub, froze as the door of the bathroom swung open.

'Help!' he cried into his gag, but no sound came out. He tried to twist his head, to see who had come to rescue him, but the belt around his neck dug into his skin and bit into him, inflicting a fresh burst of pain.

'Sorry it took me so long to get here,' a voice said.

It was a familiar voice, a pleasant one. KK felt tears of gratitude prick his eyes.

'I had a few things to attend to... You know how it is on the show.' KK felt hands – cool, firm – on his shoulders. 'Oh, you're cold!' the voice clucked.

The fingers shifted to the knot at the back of his head. KK felt a slackening as they tugged at the silk tie, the blinding brightness of light as it finally fell away. Another moment and he was no longer attached to the faucet. He sagged into the tub; his shoulders convulsed with the relief of release.

'I – I – ' He tried to get the words of gratitude out, but the belt was still tight around his neck.

Smooth hands assisted him, turned him over slowly.

'Thank you,' KK whispered, his voice hoarse.

'You're very welcome,' his saviour smiled.

At the Beach View Lodge, Niki sat, dressed and ready, chewing furiously on her pencil. Why was there no mention, no record of KK's grandfather's dhaba, she wondered? When there was so much about his life that KK had showcased, even exaggerated for public consumption, why had this critical part been left in shadow?

'My grandfather made the best kebabs in the world,' KK had said to her that night in the jungle, but he had kept this aspect of his past well concealed. Why? Was he ashamed of the poverty and struggles of his childhood? Or was there another, more sinister reason?

She sat gazing at her laptop, willing the blogger to respond, though she knew it was unlikely that he would get back to her so quickly. She waited another minute, watching the seconds hand on her watch tick slowly by; she was about to turn off her laptop when the screen lit up.

'No idea about the Hindu kebab shop in the 1950s,' the blogger had written back. 'It's possible there was one, but its existence would have been short-lived.'

Niki frowned. So had the dhaba even existed, she wondered. Or had KK manufactured his past for public consumption, concocting a story to fit the narrative? She took the pencil from between her teeth and, on a whim, typed another query.

'Would you have any information about the origins of Kemaal's in Chowk?'

This time, she had a reply within seconds.

'Call it an interesting coincidence, but the current Kemaal's in Chowk stands at the site of the erstwhile Iqbal's.'

Niki felt her blood freeze. There was no such thing as a coincidence, she knew; at least, not where crime and KK were concerned.

'Tell me more about Iqbal's,' she typed. 'Who was the owner? How did it burn down?'

'The owner of Iqbal's at the time of the fire was Jamshed Iqbal Khan, grandson of the original Mian Iqbal Jehangir Khan,' Niki read, moments later. 'Apparently, the fire was started by a kerosene spill. Jamshed Khan died in the fire and was survived by his son, Javed.'

'And what became of Javed?' Niki wrote back.

'Javed worked as a waiter at a nearby sweet shop for several years after the fire,' was the prompt reply. 'He committed suicide in March 1989 by consuming a bottle of rat poison.'

Kerosene spill. Rat poison. Niki felt chilled. 'Did he leave behind any survivors?' she typed.

'A wife and two children,' was the response. 'The wife committed suicide in 1991 by jumping into the Gomti River. The son, ten years old at that time, started working in a dhaba to support himself and his seven-year-old sister.'

'And would you know the son's name?' Niki typed.

She was trembling, she discovered, as she waited for the reply. It seemed to take forever. Then, finally, it appeared. Three chilling words.

'Shaqeel Javed Khan.'

9

Up in his luxury suite, KK was discovering that his nightmare was far from over; in fact, it was just beginning. His liberator, instead of untying the noose round his neck and the ropes round his ankles and wrists, had merely pulled him out of the bathtub, propelled him into the bedroom and pushed him roughly down on the bed. And now he was standing, smiling down at him, a maniacal expression on his face.

'Shaqeel, son, untie me, quickly. We're late! The finale must have started...'

Shaq's smile deepened. 'Don't worry, Ruby's already announced that you're down with an upset stomach and resting in your room. They've pulled someone else in as a judge in your place; a local MLA, I believe...'

'What? But I don't have an upset stomach! Has she gone mad? I have to talk to her. Untie me this instant!'

'Why? What's the hurry?'

'You've gone mad. You've all gone mad.' KK struggled against the bonds, but they were too tight. He looked at his captor again, realization dawning in his eyes.

'So *you're* behind this! You and that bitch – Nikhat Yasmin Malik!'

Shaq's eyes narrowed to tiny, glittering slits. 'Careful, that's my sister, Sohaila, you're talking about,' he said.

'Your sister? You have plotted this all along! But why? What do you want?' KK tugged ineffectually at the dupatta binding his wrists and blinked at Shaq in frustration. 'A reward? Ransom? Money?'

'I don't want your money.'

'You're doing this because you got voted off in the last episode, aren't you? Don't worry; I'll bring you back next season and make you the winner. An even bigger winner. There'll be much more prize money.'

'I *told* you I don't want your money.'

'Then what? What do you want? Just name it and I will make sure you get it.'

'Whatever I want?'

'Whatever you want.'

'Then give me Iqbal's. Give me what should have been mine.'

KK blinked rapidly. 'I don't know what you're talking about,' he said.

'I think you know exactly what I'm talking about, Kemaal *Chacha*. I'm talking about Iqbal's in Chowk, which would have been celebrating its hundredth anniversary if it hadn't "mysteriously" burnt down in September 1976.'

'You must be mistaken. I don't know any – '

'No? You don't remember your "grandfather", Jamshed Iqbal Khan? The man who took you in from the street, who gave you a home and a family, whose wife fed you with her own hands and treated you like her son?'

'Shaqeel, I swear I don't – '

He cried out as a hand slapped him hard across the cheek. It stung like a flame on his skin; he felt tears start in his eyes.

'Look at you!' Shaq said, his eyes hard as stones. 'Weeping like a woman. At least be man enough to acknowledge the person who called you his son.'

He reached in his pocket, pulled out an old black-and-white photograph. He glanced down at it, his eyes softening momentarily. Then he held it out in front of KK's face. In it was a wizened, greyed man, old before his years; next to him, his demure wife in her modest hijab staring solemnly into the camera.

Beside the couple, two young men stood arm in arm. One of them was tall and lanky, with a brooding air about him; the other, shorter, rounder, beaming wide, was unmistakably KK.

'Yes,' KK said, his voice a hoarse whisper. 'Yes, I remember. It's just the shock of this nightmare – my mind had gone blank – but that's Abba and Ammi, and Javed, my brother.'

Outside Suite 901, in the silent hallway, Satpal, stood at his post, vigilant, alert. The hallway was quiet; there was no movement, no sound, nothing to distract him. He kept his gaze focussed on the door of the room; his thoughts drifted to the girl he'd rescued from the stalled elevator. She'd been such a child, he thought with a lingering smile; she'd been so happy to see him, so effusive in her thanks.

'Aaj toh, bhaiyyaji, I would have died in there,' she'd gasped as he finally forced the door open.

'Madamji, aise thodi marne dete?' he'd responded gallantly.

'Nahi, bhaiyyaji, aap toh God ho!' she had insisted. 'What a nightmare… Brand new five-star hotel and the lift doesn't work!' She had turned back to look at the lift and shuddered. 'I don't think I'll ever be able to get into a lift again.'

'You were looking for someone on the ninth floor?' he'd asked.

'No, tenth. Don't worry, I'll just take the stairs.'

And she had hurried off to the stairwell, running past him, her feet flying as though she couldn't wait to get away.

Silly girl, he thought again as he remembered her slim silhouette, her tremulous voice. Thanking him like he was some kind of hero, when it had been so simple opening that stuck door.

Still, it felt good to be a hero every now and then.

Inside Suite 901, past the sofa and the sitting area, behind the closed bedroom door, KK watched as the clock on the chest of drawers ticked on.

Outside, on the beach, the show was on, he knew. The cameras were rolling, the judges seated in their respective restaurants, the crowds milling about, watching with bated breath. Ruby, Rajat, Jimmy, the whole show, the whole culinary world was there, laughing, drinking, having the time of their lives as all of India looked on. Surely someone would think to check on him?

And that wretched SP Shimla, harbinger of doom – where was she? Surely she should have realized that something was wrong?

He glanced at Shaq who was busy rummaging through the drawers in the nightstand on the far side of the bed. Less than six feet separated him from his captor, but his hands and feet were bound; there was no way he could free himself.

The boy was insane, he thought. He had known that the first time he'd met him at that audition in Mumbai, when he'd been so quiet, so unmoved by all that was going on around him. Where the other contestants had been palpably nervous, pacing, sweating, smiling too much, trying too hard, Shaq had sat calm and composed in his chair, giving nothing away, making no attempts at friendship or flattery. He had waited patiently till his name was called; and then he had strolled up to the workstation and turned out a perfect nihari. So perfect, that Mala and Jimmy and Rajat and Ruby had been speechless after the first taste; so sublime, that they'd included him on the show, overriding all of KK's qualms.

And he had had qualms about Shaq, even back then. Perhaps it was a sixth sense that had warned him, an inner voice that had murmured that there was something amiss? Too serious, too stiff, not telegenic enough, had been some of the objections he'd voiced, but everyone, including him, had been bowled over by that nihari. It had made him sit up; it had stirred long-forgotten memories. And now KK knew why. It was the same nihari that Ammi used to make on those cold winter evenings…

Abba and Ammi. They had taken him in when his own father had abandoned him; they had included him in their lives. They had become his true family. If only Javed had included him as well…

Damn Javed, KK thought, tears of self-pity filling his eyes. He had begrudged KK the love that Abba and Ammi had bestowed so freely on him; he had resented his presence; he had complained bitterly when KK had started helping out at Iqbal's. Even though Javed himself had had no interest in the business, had only ever been scornful and ashamed of the dhaba. No, Javed had thought himself destined for higher, greater things; he had considered himself to be above it all.

Naturally, Abba had started relying on KK, teaching him the craft, the art of the kebaab, even joking that KK would be the heir to his cooking empire, whenever he had one...

Was success a crime? Was it his fault that he'd succeeded where Abba had failed? Was it his fault that that tinderbox of a rundown dhaba had gone up in flames, taking its poor, wretched owner with it?

Evidently, the young man who came back to stand over him thought so. 'You're nothing but a common thief,' he spat at KK. 'You took what belonged to my family.'

'I stole nothing,' KK said, once again.

'And what about the Kama Kebab recipe you so proudly go around telling the world you inherited from your great-grandfather?'

'Abba taught it to me.'

'You said it was passed down the generations of *your* family.'

'But Abba *was* my family! I loved him like a son would his father.'

'And that's why you never looked back? Not once, while his ancestral business was crumbling?'

'Abba was a proud man. I knew he would be insulted if I tried to help him.'

'He was in the restaurant the night of the fire,' Shaq said. 'He was all alone that night. He'd just gone there to borrow some money from the till; to pay for his medicines. He was in the kitchen, cleaning up a kerosene spill, when it caught fire. He had no chance; he was burnt alive.'

'I know,' KK said, his eyes wet with tears. 'I had a narrow escape myself in the jungle...'

'Unfortunately. I should have checked that you were inside before I set that cottage on fire.'

KK's face drained of colour. 'You mean – it was you? *You* set fire to my cottage?'

'But it didn't work, did it?' Shaq sighed. 'I have to hand it to you – you really are a lucky bastard.'

'But why? Why did you try to kill me?'

'To even the score, why else? To have you suffer as my grandfather would have suffered.'

KK's mouth fell open. For the first time ever, he felt fear, cold, black fear, rise inside him. The boy – the man standing before him was not just crazy; he was also in dead earnest. 'But I didn't set that fire!' he croaked, trying desperately to make Shaq see reason. 'It wasn't my fault!'

'Just like my Abba's death wasn't your fault?'

'You mean Javed? It wasn't! Poor Javed, I don't know why – '

'Yes, "poor Javed"... Robbed and killed by the man who called himself his brother.'

'Shaq, son, I don't know who has been poisoning your ears! Javed *was* my brother! I tried to help him, but he slammed the door in my face. He was the one who was too proud, too foolish – '

'So it was Abba's fault that he and his family had to scrounge and suffer for ten whole years, while you were busy opening restaurant after restaurant, using the gifts and skills *his* father had taught you?'

'But Javed was never interested in the restaurant business! He always wanted to study, to become a lawyer...'

'But after his father's death, he couldn't, could he? He had no choice but to work day and night, washing dishes, sweeping floors, trying to feed his family. And he came to you for help.'

'And I offered it to him!'

'You offered him a job in *your* restaurant.'

'I told him I would make him a manager, even though he had no experience or aptitude,' KK said. 'But he flung the offer in my face.'

'All he wanted was to reopen his father's restaurant, to restore Iqbal's,' Shaq said. 'But you told him that was out of the question.'

'Because it was! Javed had no idea how to cook, let alone run a restaurant.'

Shaq shook his head, his eyes hardening with hatred. 'All he wanted was his dignity back,' he bit out. 'But you gave him death instead.'

'Shaqeel, beta, please, I beg of you! I had nothing to do with your father's death!'

'So convincing, Kemaal Chacha,' Shaq said softly. His attention shifted; his gaze appeared to become rapt in contemplation of a spot on KK's face. He flicked a drop of moisture off KK's cheek with the tip of his finger, held it up in front of his face. 'How many years I have waited for this moment, waited to see these tears,' he murmured. 'But it's not your tears I want...'

'Shaqeel, listen to me, I swear upon my wife, my daughter, I am innocent!'

'Innocent? Then explain how Abba died just three days after meeting you? Just three days after you told him to give you Iqbal's and he told you to go to hell?' Shaq leaned forward to stare at KK, his eyes filled with a lifetime of rage. 'Abba was in good health that evening,' he said. 'I saw him leave for his night shift at the sweet shop. He kissed me goodbye and promised to bring me a new kite the next morning. He said we would fly it together. Do you know why he said that? Because it was my birthday the next morning.'

KK swallowed the bile that rose in his mouth.

'But he didn't come back the following morning,' Shaq continued. 'I waited and waited. I didn't even go to school. And then I went to the sweet shop to see what was holding him up...'

His voice slowed as he remembered. 'There was a small crowd that had gathered outside that sweet shop,' he said. 'They wept when they saw me; they clasped me to their chests. They told me they'd found my father in the kitchen with the bottle of rat poison. That he was dead and there was nothing left to do.'

His eyes focussed with renewed hatred on KK. 'Tell me, why would Abba consume rat poison when he'd promised to bring me a new kite for my birthday?'

'I don't know!'

'They said he committed suicide. But I know and you know that my father was not the kind of man to commit suicide. Not ever and especially not on my birthday.'

'Son, he was upset – '

'*You* planted that poison,' Shaq said, almost as if he hadn't heard KK. '*You* did it so that you could swallow up his land.'

'No, never! It broke my heart when I heard the news. I wept for him.'

'And six months later, you opened a Kemaal's in the exact spot where Iqbal's used to be.'

'To honour his last wish!'

'You think my father's last wish was for Kemaal's to replace Iqbal's?'

'His last wish was to revive Abba's legacy,' KK said. 'And that's what I did. Iqbal's or Kemaal's – what's in a name?'

'Everything, evidently,' Shaq said bitterly. 'Considering you wiped out the one and supplanted it with the other.'

'Shaqeel, please! You can't blame me for your father's death. There is no reason, no proof – '

'You're right, Kemaal *Chacha*,' Shaq said, nodding slowly. 'There is no *proof*. You left no trace. And now, neither will I.'

He reached into the pocket of his sweatshirt and drew out a six-inch folding knife.

KK felt himself grow numb.

'I wasted a lot of time looking for proof, you know,' Shaq said, testing the edge of the knife on his thumb. 'So many fruitless weeks, months of going back to that sweet shop, looking for something that would explain Abba's death; of pleading with people to come forward if they'd seen anything, knew anything. But no one did. They were all silent; they had all been bought or coerced into silence. And they advised me to be silent too. So you know what I did?

'I followed their advice. So I was patient. I bided my time, waiting for the right opportunity, waiting for the day when I would come face to face with the man who had destroyed my family, when I would confront him… Patience – isn't that what you always preach?

'That day at the auditions… I thought you'd recognize me from my name, my appearance. Everyone tells me I look just like my father… But you didn't notice, did you? Javed Khan and his family were dead to you; you probably never even spared a thought for them, for your "brother", never stopped to think if he had a wife or children. You probably never even knew of my existence!

'But I was aware of yours. And I knew that day at the auditions that whatever else happened, I was not going to leave *Hot Chef* without making you pay. Without making you suffer, the way my father and grandfather suffered…'

KK tried and failed to swallow. His throat was dry, constricted, his neck muscles paralysed with fear. His gaze followed the knife as it dangled carelessly in Shaq's hands, as he waved it closer and closer in his face.

'You're a snake,' Shaq said, peering into KK's eyes. 'Cold-blooded and overfed. A snake that sheds its skin and slithers away, each time you try to kill it. A snake that refuses to die.'

KK's mouth moved without producing any sound. 'You – you mean –'

'Yes,' Shaq said. 'I've been trying to kill you for a long time now. I almost got you too, that time when I set fire to the sets...'

'The short circuit?' KK forced out. 'You...?'

'Unfortunately, the fuse caught fire a few minutes too soon... And did you really have to go to the bathroom at that exact instant that I'd pushed over the steel scaffolding in the fourth episode?

'You've been lucky, so lucky...' He parked a foot on the bed beside KK, shook his head. 'You dodged the rat poison I had planted in the baking soda; you evaded the Celphos; and you even escaped the cyanide!'

KK's eyes widened. 'That cyanide...!'

Shaq nodded. 'Pure, unadulterated, personally procured from the lesser-known gullies of Chowk, you know. Do you know how much effort it took to steam those sugar pouches open, empty them and refill them with the cyanide?'

'You're mad, completely mad.'

'I'd thought there was no way you'd escape that,' Shaq continued wistfully. 'No one else had sugar with their tea. Not Mala, not Ashika. If only things had gone according to plan... Poor Mala,' he murmured. 'She didn't deserve to die.'

'You killed her, you madman!'

'No, Kemaal Chacha, *you* killed her. She died because *you* were sitting beside her. That cyanide was meant for *you*. If I could have jumped across the stage and stopped her hand when she picked up that sachet of cyanide, I would have. But her muqaddar was not with her. And when someone's muqaddar deserts them, there's nothing anyone can do.'

He sighed deeply and straightened. 'But the time for remembrance and mourning is over,' he said. 'Now it's time for justice.'

'No!' KK cried as Shaqueel raised his knife. 'You can't get away with this! They'll know you did it!'

'Actually, they won't,' Shaq said with a little smile. 'Because *I* won't do anything. *You* will.'

He yanked KK up from the bed and twisted him round. In one smooth motion, he drew the knife's edge across the dupatta that bound his wrists. The next moment, KK found his hands were free and the knife was a hair's breadth from his neck.

'Okay, Kemaal Chacha,' Shaq said. 'Time to go.' He shoved KK into the chair by the writing desk in the corner, where he had laid out the resort's fine letter paper and pen. 'Go ahead,' he said, 'write.'

KK blinked down at the paper. 'What do you want me to write?'

'The truth. Confess your sins. Tell the world about Iqbal's. Tell everyone that your Kama Kebabs are actually Iqbal's kebabs. That you stole that recipe from my grandfather, Jamshed Iqbal Khan.'

'I didn't steal – '

'You did,' Shaq said through gritted teeth, pressing his knife against the clammy surface of KK's neck. 'You stole the recipe; you stole our land; you stole our future – '

'But son!'

'Write,' Shaq snarled. 'I, Kemaal Kapoor, confess that I am a fraud and a thief and a murderer...'

10

The Goa Police Jeep raced up to the deserted red carpet outside the main entrance to the Royal Resorts front lobby, its lights flashing. Niki jumped out of the Jeep before it came to a halt; she raced up the marble steps into the reception lounge. It was empty, now that the action had shifted to the finale that was under way at the far end of the resort. Shankar Sahay, jumping out of the Jeep behind his boss, collared the security guard who stood gaping at the main entrance. 'Police!' he barked. 'We're looking for Shaqeel Khan.'

'Sir, everyone is at the north end of the beach, sir,' the guard said, flustered.

Niki took his walkie-talkie and raised it to her mouth. 'This is SP Marwah of the Shimla Police,' she said, speaking clearly, urgently, into the device. 'I'm looking for Shaqeel Khan. He should be at the finale venue, La Palla Vié. Can someone report his whereabouts?'

She waited a tense few moments.

'Shaqeel Khan is not at La Palla Vié,' the Head of Security's voice at the other end came back on to report.

'Then where the hell is he?' she demanded.

'Ma'am, we're searching for him now.'

'Find him. Search the beachfront, the paths, the resort, his room. He has to be here somewhere. Exercise extreme caution; he may be armed; he is most definitely dangerous. I want to know as soon as you find him.'

'Yes, ma'am.'

'And get a couple of extra people on KK.'

'Ma'am?'

'Kemaal Kapoor,' Niki said, 'the creator and lead judge of the show. I want a couple of extra security guards following him at all times. Tell him not to go anywhere, eat anything, unless it's been cleared.'

'But ma'am, Mr Kapoor is not at the finale.'

'What?'

'We were told he has a stomach upset. He should be in his room.'

Niki spun round on her heel. 'What room is that?' she asked.

'Nine-zero-one, ma'am.'

'This is my full and final confession,' Shaq dictated, as KK continued to write at the desk inside the bedroom in Suite 901, the tears flowing down his cheeks.

'I have concluded, after examining all my sins, that the only way to pay for them is with my life. That is the only way that my soul will be at peace and I will be granted access to God's eternal abode. I therefore declare that I, Kemaal Kapoor, in full possession of my mental faculties and of my own free will, am now ending my life to atone for my past sins. No one, other than myself, is to be held accountable for my actions. I beg forgiveness from Abba and Ammi, Javed and his late widow, Mumtaz Begum, all of whom suffered on my account and perished at my hands. I hope and pray that my suicide will bring their children some solace and that they will find it in their hearts to forgive me.'

'Will I?' Shaq wondered aloud. 'Perhaps. We'll see…'

KK put the pen down, his face as white as the sheet he had written on.

'Mumtaz Begum?' he asked. 'Your mother?'

'She took her own life a year and a half after Abba's death,' Shaq said quietly. 'Most people think she jumped into the Gomti. But she didn't. She jumped off the roof of a building. It was exactly nine storeys high.'

He frowned as he heard a knock on the door. His knife edged closer to KK's neck.

'Mr Kapoor?' The doorknob rattled. 'Mr Kapoor? It's SP Marwah.'

KK stiffened with disbelief. His heart leapt. Finally!

The very next instant, he felt a hand, clamp vice-like across his mouth, pressing into the bones of his face, his cheeks; he felt the cold steel blade of Shaq's knife press into the overheated skin at his neck. He felt tears of pain blind his vision.

'Are you all right?' he heard the SP's voice ask.

Shaq abruptly jerked KK's head back and glared down at him. He nodded in the direction of the door. The knife pressed into the folds of KK's neck, stinging. KK felt something wet trickle down his neck.

'Yes, yes, I'm fine,' KK croaked.

'Open the door, please.'

KK, his head pulled all the way back, his neck burning, his eyes widened in terror, felt lightheaded. It would be so easy to just call out, to cry for help. They would break down the door and come rushing in…and find his body thrashing in agony, his neck split open and squirting blood all over the spotless marble floor.

'Mr Kapoor?'

Shaq held KK's gaze. *Tell her, ten minutes,* he mouthed. *And I might let you go.*

There was no way he would let him go, KK knew. Not now. But an extra ten minutes... Who knew what might happen in an extra ten minutes?

'I-I'm in the bathroom,' he called. 'Stomach upset. Can you give me ten minutes?'

KK felt the pressure of the knife against his skin ease, as the voice outside the door fell silent. He straightened his head and saw Shaq holding the letter he'd written. *Sign your name*, the young man mimed.

KK blinked back tears and put his signature to the confession.

Now get up, Shaq directed, using gestures to indicate what he wanted. *Walk*.

Shaq led him to the door to the balcony, soundlessly pushed it open. Above their heads, the first stars were twinkling in the evening sky.

11

Niki felt a draught of air through the narrow slit at the bottom of the door as she waited outside Suite 901. She frowned, pressed her ear close to the door.

'Listen,' she said to ASP Sahay.

Sahay listened for a moment. 'Sounds like music,' he said.

'It's the same music that's playing outside. He must have opened a door or a window.' Niki knocked on the door again. 'Mr Kapoor?' she called. She waited, her brow furrowed, then turned to the security guard who was hovering behind them. 'How long have you been here on duty?' she asked.

'Almost two hours, ma'am.'

'And when did you last see Mr Kapoor?'

'Ma'am, Ruby Ma'am had come at a quarter past five. Mr KK opened the door and they talked for a few minutes.'

'And after that?'

'Ruby Ma'am left and KK Sir went back inside his room.'

'And you've been here ever since?'

'Yes, ma'am. Ruby Ma'am told me to make sure no one went inside and to call her if KK Sir stepped out. But he never did.'

'And you've been here the entire time?'

The guard looked uncomfortable. 'Yes, ma'am, except half an hour ago, when I went to the lift.' He pointed to the elevator at the far end of the corridor. 'A girl was stuck inside.'

'What girl?'

'The journalist who had been in KK Sir's room when Ruby Ma'am came. She left shortly after Ruby Ma'am left.'

'And she was stuck in the lift?'

'Yes, ma'am.'

The line of Niki's mouth grew grim. 'And you let her out?'

'Yes, ma'am.' Satpal noticed the look that passed between the officers. 'I shouldn't have?' he asked, confused.

'Where did she go?' Sahay asked.

'She took the steps down, sir,' the guard said helplessly.

'I'll put a search out, boss,' Sahay said. He pulled out his walkie-talkie and had Satpal describe the girl. 'Find her; she should be in the resort somewhere,' he said into the speaker. He listened a moment, then nodded and hung up. 'They're alerting all personnel,' he said. 'And they're still combing the area for Shaq.'

'They won't find him,' Niki said, gazing at the closed door of the room. 'He's in there.'

On the other side of the door, across the room, the large balcony was filled with the sounds of the revelry and excitement below. The lights of the other rooms winked in the gathering darkness and shimmered in the depths of the R-shaped pool. The bar on the centre island wore a festive look, with coloured lights festooned around it and tiki lamps glowing softly all around. In the distance, a hundred metres or so up the private strip of beach on the north side, the sky was aglow with spotlights, floodlights and the flashes from multiple cameras.

Shaq, his knife still at KK's neck, pulled up the low, round table that stood on the balcony; it still bore the stains of the few drops of beer

KK had spilled on it earlier. Shaq pushed it against the balcony railing with his foot.

'Get up,' he ordered KK.

'Shaq, no, I beg of you!' KK sobbed, his voice breaking.

On the other side of the suite, outside the door, Shankar frowned as he contemplated what Niki had just told him. 'You're sure he's in there, boss?'

Niki nodded grimly. Shaq was in there, and he had KK hostage. He had got to him before she could. And now they were outside, on the balcony. Or not...

'Is there another key to the door?' Niki asked the guard.

'Oh! Yes, I have it right here, ma'am!'

Satpal pulled out a card key and fitted it in the door; the light turned green. Niki pushed the door open. It swung back an inch, but held as it encountered the resistance of a sturdy steel security latch.

'Mr Kapoor?' Niki called, putting an eye to the inch-wide clearance. 'Are you there?'

Strains of music from the finale came floating out to her and, above it, the faint sound of a chair scraping the floor.

Niki stepped back from the door and considered her options. They could break the door down or shoot the lock off; but it would be messy and alarm the killer. And it would take several seconds. Several seconds, in which Shaq could do anything. Including kill his hostage. They couldn't take that chance.

She put her head to the gap between the door and the frame. 'Mr Kapoor, I'll wait for you downstairs in the lobby, okay?' she called out. 'Meet me there as soon as you're done.'

She took several noisy steps away from the door and down the corridor, then paused. *Stay here*, she gestured to Sahay and the guard. *I'm going to try and enter from the room above*, she mouthed.

Sahay nodded. He pulled out his gun and cocked it, positioning its muzzle in the sliver of open space between the door and the frame.

The security guard pressed a card key into Niki's hand. 'This is a master key,' he whispered. 'It should work for one-double zero-one as well.'

Niki raced down the hallway and up the short flight of steps in the stairwell, emerging on the floor above. She read off the room numbers as she ran: 1004, 1003, 1002… She stopped outside 1001, fitted the key in the slot, pushed open the door and raced straight through the room and out onto the balcony.

Below her, she heard the indistinct sound of a man blubbering helplessly. Then a sharp voice hissed, 'You are wasting my time! Get up. Get up right now!'

'Shaqeel, please – '

'Get up at once… or shall I start chopping your fingers off – one at a time.'

So he had a knife, Niki concluded. Probably a big one, pressed close to KK's skin, his neck, most likely. She tried to picture the two of them, KK standing directly below her, Shaq behind him, but towards his right. He was right-handed, she recalled.

'Okay, now jump,' the voice below her said.

'Please, no!' KK sobbed.

Niki did a quick calculation. It was a sheer drop down, approximately 10 feet to the balcony below. She would have to lower herself down over the metal railings of the upper balcony, hang suspended over the lower one, her feet and legs clearly visible to the killer, while she herself could not see him. And then, somehow, she would have to contort her body and angle herself into the lower balcony, feet first. Go in blind, lose precious seconds finding a foothold, then jump. Enough time for Shaq to kill her and KK ten times over.

Unless…

'Shankar,' she whispered into the mouthpiece of her walkie-talkie.

Sahay, gun cocked, body taut and nerves wound tight in readiness, stiffened at the whispered words in his earpiece.

'Boss?'

'They're on the balcony. We need to distract him. *Now.*'

Sahay's mind raced. *What made Shaq tick*, he wondered. *What would distract him?*

'Shaqeel, son, think of my family, my wife, my daughter!' KK sobbed on the balcony. His knees threatened to buckle as they pressed up against the edge of the railing; his feet felt as if they could no longer carry his weight.

'Why should I think of your family?' Shaq snarled, 'when you didn't think of mine?'

'Think of *your* family, then. Your sister!'

Shaq's sister... Niki remembered. *Of course!*

'Shankar,' she spoke softly into her mouthpiece. 'Tell him we have his accomplice. His sister, Sohaila.'

'She's young; she has her whole life ahead of her...' KK's voice pleaded 10 feet below.

'Shut up!' Shaq bit out below her. 'I know how to take care of her.'

'Shaqeel!'

Shaq froze as the voice rang out from behind the door of the hotel room.

'It's ASP Sahay,' the voice called. 'I know you're in there. I know you're angry. But we have a young lady in custody. She says she's your sister.'

A shadow crossed Shaq's face. KK trembled as he felt him clench his hand tighter around the knife. Ten feet above his head, Niki held her breath.

'Open the door and we can talk here; or we can take Sohaila down to the police station and grill her there,' Sahay said.

'No, wait!' Shaq's voice, strangled, anguished, rang out in the night. 'Sohaila is innocent!' he screamed in the direction of the door. 'Let her go! I'm the one you want!'

'Then open the door.'

'Aah! I will, once I've finished my business here.'

His voice had hardened, Niki realized, stiffening. It was the voice of someone who knew the game was over, who didn't care any more...

She took a deep breath, swung one leg over the balcony railing and pulled herself over to the other side. Her toes, encased in soft black leather, encountered a two-inch width of stone parapet, which she used to balance herself. Holding on tight to the railing, she lowered herself farther down.

'Shaq?' she head Sahay call out from beyond the room door. 'Don't do it! Don't stain your hands with blood.'

'It's too late for that,' Shaq called back.

'No, it's not!' Sahay said sharply. 'Not for Sohaila.'

Shaq hesitated.

'If you let KK go, we can make sure Sohaila stays out of it. Otherwise, she will be tried as your accomplice. An accessory to murder. Do you know how much time in jail that translates into? Have you any idea what happens to young women in prison?'

'You can't do that!' Shaq screamed. 'She's just a young girl!'

'Why don't you open the door so we can talk about it?'

'This is a trick. I know it!'

'How can it be a trick? You have the door locked. You have KK. All I ask is that you hear me out. It can't hurt to talk...?'

Shaq hesitated. Then, 'Stay here!' he growled at KK.

Niki, her heart pounding, listened to his receding footsteps as he walked back into the room. She took a deep breath, pushed off the parapet with all her might and let go. A half-second later, she was swinging into the ninth-floor balcony, landing on the firm floor below with a soft thud.

A few steps to her right, KK let out a loud gasp. Shaq wheeled around. 'What the – ?'

'Game over,' Niki said, shielding KK as she thrust him behind her, her gun cocked and ready. 'Drop your weapon, Shaqeel Khan; you're under arrest.'

Shaq's eyes burned into Niki's. 'You're protecting a snake,' he said.

'Drop your weapon, I said,' Niki said, her finger on the trigger, her gaze fixed on the knife.

Shaq closed his eyes. His hand lifted to his neck.

The bullet grazed his arm just as his knife slashed across his throat. The next instant, he had slumped to the ground.

Out across the darkened sands, on the northernmost strip of the Royal Resorts exclusive, secluded beachfront, black-jacketed waiters removed the remains of the snails from the exquisitely laid tables at La Palla Vié, while a medley of fireworks at the Chatpatty Beach Bazaar showered orange and red flares into the blue-black, shimmering ocean.

12

The quietly luxurious guest room on the eighth floor of the Royal Resorts was flooded with flowers. Vases, baskets, bouquets and assortments of blooms in every conceivable hue sat on every available surface, even spilling out onto the balcony. They trailed a dizzy pattern across the floor; they infused the room with their fragrance and filled its occupant with inexpressible joy.

'CONGRATULATIONS, HOT CHEFF!' the red and orange banner strung across the door outside read.

Inside, Leena Dixit sat cross-legged and wide-eyed on her bed, hugging her arms around her, gazing out her window to where the sky was growing lighter, the night starting to fade.

A night that from the first poori – personally stuffed by her with raisins, nuts, spices and chutney and dipped in wasabi-laced red-hot paani – to the final paan, filled with a medley of mouth fresheners, coconut shavings, dark, flaky chocolate and a dollop of fresh, whipped cream, had been preordained to please. She had been wired; she had been flying from workstation to workstation, from thela to khomcha to gola stand to stall, tasting, finishing, garnishing, dressing, serving, serving, serving… And the guests had kept coming back for more. And more. And more. And she had felt herself grow taller and fuller, filled with happiness, such happiness as she had never known, would probably never recapture again.

For those three unforgettable hours last night, she had felt sheer happiness course through her.

And then it had ended, as quickly as it had begun.

And miracle of miracles… *She had won.*

And her life, as Jimmy and Rajat and Ruby and all the others had told her as they'd stood beaming, hugging, crying and celebrating under an endless shower of red-orange confetti, the cameras flashing, the firecrackers exploding all around, had changed forever.

Had it really been mere hours or was it several lifetimes that had gone by? Had she died of happiness or was it all just a dream?

She dug her nails deep into her arms, wincing as their sharp edges pricked her skin. She glanced down at the broken tracks her nails had carved into her skin and rubbed them, bemused.

So this is how it feels to win, she thought. One was still blood and bones, flesh and skin, with a steady heartbeat and breath within; except that each beat, each breath was now magnified, distilled, tingling with a quiet, steady joy.

She exhaled into the fragrance-filled room, uncrossed her legs, cramped from sitting still for so long, and padded slowly over to her window.

The sky was turning blue, the tide coming in, she saw the waves breaking higher and higher on the sand, scattering the flocks of birds that flew and alighted, dispersed and regrouped, all the way along the shore. She stood a moment watching their antics, her gaze travelling past them, past the lone jogger labouring in the distance, to an invisible point to the north, where the Chatpatty Beach Bazaar was still standing, she knew, momentarily silent, momentarily in solitude, waiting just a little bit longer for its assured place in the sun.

Soon, the housekeeping staff would slip the morning's papers under her door, her name, along with that of her restaurant, would be plastered all over.

She fingered her Ganpati pendant as she stood drinking in the new day. What a long journey it had been, she thought. What a toll it had taken. How she had changed…

Winning, that's all she had thought about all this while. It had been the air she breathed, the food she ate, her sustenance, her faith, her purpose. And yet, now that she had won, mingled in with the euphoria was a deep sense of loss.

Hot Cheff was over. And she was going to miss it. Miss its madness, its fervour, its missteps, its flawed, wretched, precious people, who had somehow become her colleagues, friends, family...

She was glad that Dev and Sharon had found happy landings, so happy for Pallavi who was going straight on to Los Angeles now, buoyed by the rave reviews, all set to participate in *Hot Cheff America*.

They were going to be all right, she knew.

Unlike Shaq...

They'd said there had been an accident last night, that Shaq had somehow cut himself, that he'd been rushed to the hospital. KK too. He'd withdrawn from the show rather abruptly and would be flying back to his home in New Delhi without making any public appearances. She wondered what had happened. There had been some whispers about SP Marwah and ASP Sahay of Shimla Police being in town and about a police investigation that was under way.

She sighed. There were many questions on her mind, many anxieties encroaching on the joy that had kept her awake all night, but the one that was uppermost had to do with Vicky.

How was he doing, she wondered. He was back on his medication, he had told her in the few minutes they'd had before the finale had begun; he was back in Mumbai, working at his friend's restaurant again. It was packed every evening, he had grinned, now that he was a mini-celebrity. His friend had hiked up the prices, put in fancy furniture; he'd talked about a partnership, a joint venture sometime in the future.

How would things be between them now that it was over and she was a winner? Dare she hope that there might be a future for them together?

She rested her head against the windowpane, felt the morning breeze lift her hair.

Below, a wave came in all the way up the beach, scattering a flock of white terns pecking at the sand. They flew off with a noisy flapping of wings amidst the spray, then circling back, alighted at another point farther down the shore. Past them, the lone jogger, returning from his run, lifted his head to meet her gaze.

He waved out, smiling his lopsided, radiant smile.

Vicky...

Leena, her breath catching, leaned out her window and waved back.

13

The weather in the Shimla valley had turned glacial in the last days of the year.

The afternoons had been frigid and grey, the nights arctic; but nothing could discourage the intrepid hordes that descended upon the city by the thousands for a week of festivities, frolic and what they hoped would be lifelong memories of fun in the snow. The Christmas weekend had seen a record number of vacationers, the Mall chock-a-block with shoppers, the Ridge decked out in every shade of winter, with a Christmas tree and a Santa in every corner and impromptu groups of off-key carollers outside every window.

The madness had abated just slightly in the week that followed. The highway had remained clogged with cars, the hotels fully occupied. The pedestrian-only streets had continued to ring with endless footfalls; the restaurants buzzed; the Lift made ceaseless trips up and down the mountainside; and the five city police stations worked round the clock to keep things from spinning out of control.

With just one more day to go before the annual party in the hills wound down, with the entire city wired and ready for the frenzy of its final hours, the Superintendent of Police, who'd been working tirelessly since it all began, allowed herself a moment to sit back, sip a cup of chai and sigh.

What a week it had been, she reflected. And what a year!

It had been marked by big accomplishments; a few disappointments, too. The Women Constables Training Centre had finally been given the green light by the Centre; the Tribal Community Policing Proposal had not. She had added a dozen young faces to the five police stations under her jurisdiction; she had lost seven seasoned ones. A handful of missing persons had been found; others remained untraced. The number of casualties for the year was down; the number of road accidents was up.

Shaq and KK were alive.

One was in prison and would, most likely, remain there. The other was under investigation for fraud and discrepancies in his various real-estate and business dealings, including possible involvement in the incident at Iqbal's in Lucknow all those years ago.

The death of Javed Jamshed Khan would be investigated again. His daughter, Sohaila, was in custody; she'd probably be released after serving a light sentence.

Mala was dead.

Revenge, Niki reflected, as she sipped her chai and gazed out her window at the pitch dark outside. What a dark, destructive force it was. Justice was blind, it was true; but revenge was without conscience. It destroyed everything and everyone in its path, the guilty and the innocent alike.

Well, at least it was over. The case, heartbreaking as it had been, was finally closed. And those who had been affected the most could begin the long process of healing. Vicky and Rajat and poor, wretched Joseph, who'd called to thank her and tell her that he was moving to Dubai to try and start his life afresh.

Niki sighed, putting down her cup. Life. It was finite, fleeting, unpredictable… So what was she doing spending hers in an icy-cold third-floor office, miles away from her family, her friends, Ram?

She glanced down at the memo on her desk, left for her by Deepika on her way out. It was the security detail for the following day – the master plan for dealing with the annual New Year's Eve revelry.

One more day, one more night; and then it would be over, Niki consoled herself. The tourists would head home, the valley would fall silent, a new year would begin.

She'd do things a bit differently next year. She'd make more time for the people in her life, more time for herself. Maybe kick off the year with a nice, long vacation. Europe, Italy, Florence… She'd put in her application for her two weeks of gazetted leave right away, she thought, warming to the idea. The Chief should have no problem;

nothing ever happened in January. January was the quietest month of the year. She'd fly out and surprise Ram, whisk him away; they could go skiing in the Alps…

She opened her laptop, clicked on a travel website and started looking up flights and fares. She jumped as the phone rang.

'Marwah,' the crisp, no-nonsense voice said at the other end of the line. 'I'm not bothering you, I hope?'

'Not at all, sir,' Niki said.

'All set for tomorrow?'

'Absolutely, sir.'

'Good, good. I like the additional checkpoints you've placed, leading up to the Mall; that should help take some of the load off.'

'I expect so, sir. Sir…' She hesitated. Should she bring up her vacation? 'Um, sir, I was wondering if next month – '

'About next month. I have some good news and some bad news,' the Chief said abruptly, cutting her off.

'Sir?'

'Good news first. I'm recommending you for a President's medal for meritorious service in recognition of your exemplary response to the terror threat at the Gaiety.'

Niki swallowed. 'Thank you, sir. I – I'm speechless.'

'The bad news is that I have just signed off on your transfer orders. You're moving to Delhi.'

'*Delhi*, sir?'

'As special Police Liaison Officer to the Ministry of Home Affairs.'

'The task force on National Women's Security Force, sir?' Niki asked, blinking back confusion. But they had already sent her a curt note turning down her candidacy…

'No, that's on the back burner,' DGP Kapoor said. 'They have to rethink everything, start from the ground up. With the tragic events of the past couple of weeks, the capital, the whole country is shaken up.'

The Nirbhaya case. Of course, Niki thought. The brave young girl had not survived; she had been cremated in the capital just the previous day.

'They need to move swiftly on a series of policy measures, Marwah, and they need people like you driving the change. You'll be joining effective the first of January.'

'The first, sir?' Niki gulped.

'First of January,' the Chief confirmed. 'In two days.'

'Sir.'

'It's a big responsibility, Marwah.'

'I'll do my best, sir.'

'It's not easy letting you go,' he continued and she thought she heard him sigh. 'But they need you down there and they need you right away. So go home, pack your bags, get out first thing in the morning. I'll have Kumar take over Shimla. Bhargava can handle Crime and Sahay can take independent charge of Manali, if you think he's ready?'

Niki swallowed the sudden lump in her throat. 'Oh, he's ready, sir,' she said.

'Good. So we're all set. Any questions?'

'No, sir.'

'You were going to say something? You were wondering if next month…?'

'It's nothing, sir.'

'Are you sure?'

'Sure, sir.'

'All right, then. Goodnight. And good luck. It's been a pleasure working with you, Marwah.'

'Likewise, sir.'

'I expect I'll see you the next time I'm in Delhi.'

'I'll look forward to it, sir.'

Niki put down the phone. She looked out the window; her chest hurt with the tumult of emotions within. Tomorrow would be her last day as SP Shimla, she thought.

Slowly, reverentially, she poured out the last of Joginder's extra-special elaichi chai and lifted her cup in the direction of the valley, *her* valley, outside. Tomorrow, she'd be gone. And the next day, a new year, a new chapter would begin.

Acknowledgements

Many thanks to:

All my readers, for believing in Niki.

My dear friend Gayatri Yadav of Star India, for her love and assistance.

My dear friends Juhi, Bhavna and Namita, for an unforgettable weekend in Goa (frogs and pheni included).

The charismatic, hunky Rajiv Lakshman of MTV *Roadies* and *Master Chef India*, for some invaluable gyan and a delightful look into the world of reality TV.

The dynamic, talented Chef Ajay Chopra of the Westin Mumbai Garden City, for an unforgettable meal and some very hot and spicy tidbits.

Srikanth Malladi, Vaibhav Modi, Tanya Bami, for all their help and insights.

Manish Agrawal, Anurag Kumar and Suman Nalwa of the Indian Police.

My fabulous editor and friend Poulomi Chatterjee, for always managing to find the 'engine' of the story and pushing it fearlessly into fifth gear.

Thomas Abraham, for being the ultimate collaborator and enabler.

Sohini Bhattacharya, for her infectious energy and enthusiasm.

Friends and family, for patiently putting up with my 'kindly excuse, I'm a writer only' behaviour.

Mom and Dad, for their infinite support and unconditional indulgence.

And Raima, Neel and Vivek…for being my sensational partners in crime.

DROP DEAD

Swati Kaushal

'I'm the Superintendent of Police, Shimla... And, with all due respect, sir, who the hell are you?'

When a body mysteriously appears at the bottom of the otherwise serene hills of Sonargam in peak tourist season, Superintendent of Police, Shimla, Niki Marwah, and her crack team of investigators must act quickly to find out how Rak Mehta, the hotshot President & CEO of a super-successful publishing company, landed there.

As they scour the grounds of the luxurious Lotus Resort, where Indigo's employees have checked in for their annual conference, the police team uncovers bitter rivalries, secret grudges and vicious lies – not to mention the victim's own sordid past that has made him more enemies than friends.

Lipstick stains, condoms, a notebook full of rambling code; bribery, mind games, broken promises – everything points to murder. And, with the list of suspects growing, it will take all of Niki's ingenuity and skill to catch the killer before Sonargam's idyllic landscape is disrupted once again...

'Kaushal's writing is crisp and refreshing...what she does well is master the popular fiction category' – *Verve*

'Filled with the drama of a good, gripping thriller' – *The Hindu*

'The perfect holiday read' – *Mail Today*

For further details and information, please visit
www.hachetteindia.com